The Angels of Opi

Peter D. Cimini

The Angels of Opi

ARPress
ILLUMINATING IDEAS.
EMPOWERING VOICES

ARPress
45 Dan Road Suite 5
Canton MA 02021
Hotline: 1(888) 821 0229
Fax: 1(508) 545 7580

Ordering Information:
Quantity sales. Special discounts are available on quantity purchases by corporations, associations, and others. For details, contact the publisher at the address above.

Printed in the United States of America.

ISBN 13:   Paperback   979-8-89330-819-8
            eBook   979-8-89330-820-4

Library of Congress Control Number: 2024902561

TABLE OF CONTENTS

In this novel, the author describes an existing midevil Italian mountain town, formed in an unknown century, by the out cropping of rocks from a mountain(s) in the Appeniene mountain range. The tall rock structure located in a rural area of Europe, centuries before the area became the Sate of Italy.

The quote below comes from novelist Padgett Powell, in her debut novel Ediso, 1984, which was nominated for The American Book Award.

"Fiction is taking strange truths and making them less strange lies."

ACKNOWLEDGMENTS

I am deeply grateful to my daughter, Cara Adair, a linguistic specialist, for the assistance she provided by editing and formatting this novel. She teaches English as a Second Language, at Swansea University in the United Kingdom.

A good deal of information relating to the dates and events of the German occupation of Italy was obtained from the book titled The Germans, the Allies, the Partisans, and the Pope, by Robert Katz.

To my granddaughter Isabella who solved the many computer problems I experienced in writing this novel. Without her computer knowledge, this book may never have been born.

PREFACE

In the Italian province of L'Aquila, in the region of Abruzzo, lies the medieval town of Opi, considered to be one of a few geological curiosities, due to its location close to the Apennine Mountain range. It was developed on rock outcroppings and sits on the high, flat stones now known as the village of Opi. The Opici tribe were the first settlers of this rock formation in 200 B.C. when they settled on the flat surface formed by the outcropping of rocks from the Apennine Mountains. The Opici tribe built a narrow dirt road which ended at a lush green valley of grass, for grazing their sheep.

Today the medieval town of Opi is in a vast national park in the Abruzzo region of Italy (Parco Nazionale d'Abruzzo). The national park has a landscape of high mountain peaks, rivers, lakes, and forests, and covers 74,000 acres in the upper Sangro valley. The central point of the park is the village of Pescasseroli, and the starting point for the climb to the top of Monte Marsicano (2242m). A dense forest of beech, pine and maple trees is situated at the end of the green grass. This valley and forest are the natural habitat of the Marsican brown bear, wolves, wild boars, and Chamois, an agile, goat-like antelope that climbs mountains.

CHAPTER 1

Leopoldo Ciarletta emigrated to America in 1900, with his wife and two boys Peter and Daniel. Leopoldo worked for the Knickerbocker ice company in New York City, delivering ice blocks in lower Manhattan for customers who kept their food in ice boxes. After two years working for the Knickerbocker Ice Company. Leopoldo decided to purchase a horse and wagon to deliver ice and coal to his Knickerbocker customers, who were in Lower Manhattan. He then removed both of his sons from school to assist him in his new business venture; they were in the fourth and fifth grades. Leopoldo and his two sons worked hard during the first six months of his new business. His customers were spreading the word to other customers that Leopoldo and Sons Ice and Coal Delivery was charging ten cents less than the Knickerbocker Ice Company. It took a few months, but Leopoldo's delivery company was beginning to make a profit from their deliveries. However, Leopoldo's wife Francesca was not happy; they were living in a tenement apartment in lower Manhattan, with a bathroom at the end of their floor.

She told her husband Leopoldo, and her children, Daniel, and Peter, that she was giving up on this country, with its foul-smelling apartment, dirty sidewalks, and neighbors that hate Italians. She told her husband and children that lower Manhattan does not have a single blade of grass growing, and that she cannot see a snowcovered mountain to rest her soul. She sailed back to

Italy and returned to her hometown in 1912. Leopoldo, Danny and Pete continued their hard work, expanding the business that their father created. Eventually, Leopoldo determined that his two sons were now old enough and strong enough to manage the ice and coal routes themselves. He informed them that he must leave them and return to his wife in Italy, knowing that his two sons would prosper in America.

In 1921, Pete and Danny met two sisters, Kate and Susan Russo, at a Saturday night dance sponsored by the Mary Immaculate Church, in the Parkchester section of the Bronx. The two men dated the two sisters for nine months, often going on dates together. Both men were pleased that Suzy and Kate had introduced them to a new social crowd. Their weekends had been spent with groups of friends from their Bronx neighborhood and writing letters to their parents. But now Suzy and Kate took them to parties and dances with new friends. They now spent their weekends socializing with a new group of women and men. Daniel and Pete could not wait for Friday night to roll around with the Russo girls and their friends. In March 1922, Daniel surprised his brother Pete by announcing his engagement to Kate Russo. Daniel married Kate in April 1922. Pete and Susan married in October 1922.

In 1924 Pete and Suzy invited Daniel and Kate to their apartment in the western part of the Bronx to discuss a house that Pete and Suzy had seen in a semirural part of the Bronx that was available to rent. Suzy and Pete liked the area that was walking distance to water, and on the other side of the water was the Whitestone Bridge, going to Queens, New York, and LaGuardia Airfield.

Suzy told Kate that the house had two master bedrooms, on the second floor, a bedroom for Suzy's two girls, and an attic bedroom for Suzy's son Daniel. Kate had learned that she would never be able to have children, so Kate and Daniel loved the idea of living in a house with Suzy's three children.

They also loved the idea that both couples could live together splitting the monthly rent.

Kate and Daniel were anxiously wanting to see a house, described by Suzy, which would be able to accommodate both couples. After Daniel and Pete examined the structure of the house, both couples agreed that living together was a wonderful idea. Pete called the owner of the house, and the deal was made.

CHAPTER 2

One day in 1925, the doorbell rang at 533 Beach Avenue in the Bronx. Suzy Ciarletta opened the door, and saw it was the mailman. He handed her the letters for today, and then said, "I have a telegram today that you must sign for. Use this pen and write your full name on the line below." After signing the telegram, Suzy thanked him. Before leaving the mailman said, "It's from Italy, I hope it's not bad news." Before closing the front door Suzy noticed that her son Daniel was playing stick ball on the street. She called her daughter Barbara, who was home from her elementary school at the Holy Cross Church to go outside where the boys were playing and tell her brother Daniel to come in the house when he sees Poppa getting home from work. Francis was not home from her high school in Manhattan, but she would be home by four thirty. When Francis arrived home, she noticed a strange looking envelope on top of the mail bundle. She asked her mother, "what is that strange envelope on top of the mail"? Suzy told her it was a telegram for her father, and "I hope he comes home soon, because I'm dying to find out what the telegram says." It was unusual to receive a telegram from Italy in 1925. The Ciarletta children and their mother were curious about the message in the telegram for their father.

The suspense was becoming unbearable for Suzy. She went to the mail bundle a third time, picked up the telegram envelope, examined it to see if there was a way for her to open the telegram without her husband noticing it had been opened. She finally said to herself, as she was placing the telegram back on the bundle of letters, "Suzy, control yourself, your idea is foolish and wrong and you can wait, along with the children, until Pete is home."

Her girls were also curious about the funny looking telegram envelope. A telegram from a foreign country was an unusual, rare treat. Pete arrived home to his excited family; Suzy immediately handed the telegram to her husband Pete. He read it once and repeated the message to his family. Pete, *your father has had a heart attack and believes he may die before ever seeing his only male grandson. He is home from the hospital but expects you to travel to Italy, with Donato. Aunt Alessandra.*

Pete embraced Suzy and his three children, kissing each child on the forehead. Pete told his wife that he would go up the stairs to clean up before dinner. And then yelled down. "Don't forget to show the telegram to Danny when he comes home from work. When Danny arrived home from his job at the A&P grocery store, on Westchester Avenue, he was given the telegram from Italy. He was surprised to learn that his thirteen-year-old nephew was wanted by his father to travel to Italy. Kate was the last to arrive from her work as a door-to-door salesperson for women's undergarments. She read the telegram, and told Suzy, we must go to Holy Cross Church on Saturday, and ask Father Justin to have a novena for Leopoldo, Pete, and Daniel.

Pete came down the stairs for supper with his family. When he saw his brother Danny, they both embraced, Danny held the embrace for a long moment, then broke the embrace, and both men took their place at the dinner table. When dinner was over Pete went to the kitchen, as Suzy and Kate were washing the dinner dishes. Pete said, "Suzy, I appreciate that you have not complained about the cost of our trip to Italy."

"Pete, I understand that you must honor our father's wishes." Suzy said. He thanked her and kissed his wife on the cheek. "I will be in the living room with Danny to discuss my trip to Italy. Danny was talking to Pete when Suzy entered the living room. Danny said, "Pete when you arrive at the home of Poppa, tell our mother Francesa how much we have missed her after all these years."

"That's right Danny, this was a tough period in our lives. We were so sad that our Mama hated America and returned to Italy."

Danny said "I can remember the last thing she said before getting on the boat – *'My children, you may not understand why I must leave you both, but I can no longer live the rest of my life in this place called lower Manhattan, which does not have a single blade of grass growing and no snowcapped mountain to calm my soul; but most of all, I refuse to live among Americans, that hate me for being Italian'.*

Danny added, "tell Mama we don't hate her for leaving us, and that we will always love her." Pete agreed with his brother, "I will make sure I tell her we still love her."

Pete then said, "Suzy, what do you want to say?" and Danny asked if Pete and Suzy wished him to leave.

Suzy said, "No, you may have something to add." Suzy then continued, "you know that your boat will be landing in Naples."

Pete responded "Yes, I saw that on our tickets. What's so important about Naples." Pete gave Suzy a strange sarcastic, almost comical look, and said, "What's going on in that head of yours? When you get like this, you're up to something."

Suzy simply said, "Pete...Naples...the Presepe nativity set, it will make my long dream come true." Suzy then looked up to the ceiling and said "Oh, dear God, how you work in such strange ways." Suzy lowered her head and said, "Naples has always had a special religious meaning for me." One of Suzy's great joys during Christmas was to display her three American Christmas nativity sets to impress upon her children the true meaning of this glorious holiday.

Suzy continued, "I read in a magazine an article about the Italian Presepe Christmas nativity scenes that could only be purchased in Naples. I have fallen in love with the Presepe figures made by the artist Matteo Prencipe and produced by the Gramendola Company."

Neapolitan people have a strong tradition of using Presepe nativity settings and figures during their Christmas celebration. The Neapolitan Presepe tradition consisted of placing the infant Jesus within the context of their everyday life in Naples, and using figures dressed in Neapolitan Renaissance clothing. These figures can only be obtained by visiting Via San Gregario, a narrow cobblestone street crowded on both sides with workshops that exhibit every grade of Presepe paraphernalia, made and hawked year-round.

Suzy informed her husband that they would leave the west side of Manhattan in two days and land in the City of Naples. Giggling like a schoolgirl, she asked her husband, "Pete do you know what that means...my dream of owning a real Neapolitan Presepe nativity that looks like Naples!"

Pete interrupted his wife before she could finish her sentence, "Suzy, c'mon, now don't start that. I am not at all happy about having to go shopping in Naples, for Nativity figures, and how am I going to bring this home to America?"

"Pete, why would you refuse to do this for me? If it's money, I'll save it from my weekly food budget."

"Suzy it's not about money, it's about finding this street, Via San Gregario in Naples." Suzy was now crying, and through her tears saying to her husband, "you are not acting like the man I married."

"OK, stop crying, I will find the street in Naples that sells your Presepe Nativity figures. Write down the name of the figures you want, and the name of the street where they are sold".

The following day Pete and his son Daniel would begin their journey to Italy.

CHAPTER 3

In 1943 Suzy had inquired about the Pan Am flight that usually left from Port Jefferson, Long Island, but because of the war years, they no longer flew to Europe. The only way to get to Europe was by converted troop ships. During the trip, men slept in one large room, and women had a separate room. Pete was very upset with the food on his trip to Italy. Meals were not served at a table; people lined up at a long serving counter, taking a tray for their plates, a water glass, and forks, knives, and spoons. Behind the long table were strange looking men using long handle forks and spoons to place food on each passenger's plate. The passengers then proceeded to one of the many tables to eat their food. Pete and Daniel spent most of their time on the boat deck, on long wood chairs, enjoying the clean air and sun, while they enjoyed the calm sea. They also enjoyed strolling on the deck. One day their ship passed the Rock of Gibraltar. Daniel was shocked to see funny looking monkeys roaming up and down a large rock that was in the water. Pete told his son, "I once read in a magazine called Smithsonian the story about these monkeys. They are called Macaques.

Pete and his son were not far from Italy. They had repacked their luggage and would soon be docking in Naples, they were anxiously ready to disembark from the boat. Daniel said to his father, "look at that big statue in the park."

Pete said to his son, "you will see many statues in Italy like the one in the park. We do not have statues like that, and especially the Bronx which does not have parks or statues. OK Daniel, the line seems to be moving to the dock. Pick up your luggage, and we will soon disembark from the boat and go to Naples. I expect that your Aunt Leonita will take us to my father and mother's house."

When they left the boat. Pete told his son "Aunt Leonita was given a current picture of myself, as an adult, she has never seen me in person."

Father and son had been waiting for about five minutes. Pete was, now getting nervous, 'what if she does not recognize me, she has never seen me as an adult.' Suddenly, Pete saw a woman running toward him and "Pete, Pete." He was now standing next to his Aunt Leonita, hugging, and kissing her. When she was finished, Pete introduced his son Daniel to his Aunt Leonita, they were soon following Aunt Leonita to her car.

CHAPTER 4

Zia Alessandrina, and her husband Ruffino, along with their two children were the first to arrive for dinner in Italy at Leopoldo's house. Soon thereafter, Zia Pia, her husband Rudolfo, and their six children arrived. Last to arrive was Zia Leonida, her husband Iseo, and their five children. Like the Ciarletta family in America, Daniel's Italian family was friendly, affectionate, and loud. There was the same need to make physical contact, and during the general conversation they continued the physical expressions of hugging and kissing while laughing with each other. Daniel went through a series of cheek pinching, hugs, and kisses, as each aunt and uncle told him how handsome he was.

During the introduction process, Daniel was thinking, *I'm thirteen, and they're still pinching my cheeks?*

Watching his aunts, uncles, and cousins interacting, Daniel couldn't help but notice how dramatically they expressed simple emotions. Although Daniel did not understand the words being used by Zio Ruffino, as he conversed with him and Zio Iseo, he knew from his dramatic body language that Zio Ruffino felt strongly about whatever it was he was saying.

Pete and Leopoldo came down the stairs, with Pete on his left side holding Leopoldo around the waist, while Leopoldo used the 'bastone' (walking cane) in his right hand. He was still dressed in his formal white shirt, tie, vest, and beret. His pants were neatly pressed, and along with his vest, he was now wearing a cardigan sweater.

The family was ready for their meal. The adults were standing around the long wooden table in the first room as one entered the Ciarletta house. Nonno Leopoldo took his customary place at the head of the table and removed his beret, exposing a full head of white hair. Only after Nonno was seated, and comfortable did the other adults take their seats. Nonna Francesa sat next to her husband. Daniel's aunts brought large platters of food to the main table and to the smaller table in the kitchen. The women then took their seats next to their husbands. Daniel saw that there were no empty chairs at the dinner table. Daniel remained still and quiet, and in place.

Then Nonno Leopoldo waved his unaffected arm towards the children in the room, and said in a hushed, but demanding voice, "Viene qua (Come here!)" At that command, the children stood behind their seated parents, Daniel moved quickly to his father, and stood tall.

The adults held the hand of the person on either side of them, forming a complete connection, and standing behind their fathers, the children also began holding hands. Daniel quickly clasped his hand to both children on either side of him. Both children and adults bowed their heads in silence, and Daniel followed the other children and bowed his head. Leopoldo made the sign of the cross, the adults and children disengaged their hands and followed Nonno in making the sign of the cross. All remained quiet, listening to Nonno's prayer.

Daniel understood "Grazie a Dio" (thanks be to God), but there were other unfamiliar words. Then he heard the names "Pietro" and "Donato," then other Italian words that once again he did not understand. When Nonno Leopoldo finished praying, everyone followed Nonno in making a second sign of the cross. Everyone began talking as the kids rushed to the kitchen. Daniel stood still for a moment, not sure what to do until his father motioned for him to go to the kitchen with his cousins.

After dinner, Daniel's aunts cleared the tables and washed the dishes while the men continued their brisk conversation, sipping wine, and enjoying fruits and nuts.

After dinner was completed, and the dishes and cutlery were washed and stored by the women in the kitchen, the families began to putt on their coats and hats to say good evening to other family members. Leopoldo and Francesca had finished their meal and the room turned into a disorderly and noisy gaggle of family members, hugging, kissing, and shaking hands, some with tears of joy, and others with friendly smiles. Fifteen minutes later, Alessandrina was telling her son Ruffino to hurry, they were about to leave for home.

As Ruffino was parting from Daniel, to join his parents, he reminded him, "I will pick you up at Nonno's house tomorrow, after school, and show you around our town."

Daniel and his father were tired that night. While preparing for bed in one of the small, chilly second floor bedrooms, Daniel was curious about his grandfather's attire. "Dad, when we saw Nonno in bed, I was surprised to see him so dressed up. Do people in Italy always dress so fancy when they are about to sleep?"

Pete grinned and said, "No, I'm sure he usually wears pajamas in bed like the rest of us. Nonno is a very proud man, to him illness is a weakness. I think Nonno was trying to tell us that he was not seriously sick, even though he had a heart attack. Your grandfather is a man who likes to be in control. It's my guess he asked Nonna to dress him that way because we were coming to see him. That's your grandfather, a proud man, just as I remember him when I was your age."

Daniel's father reached into his side pocket, and gave his son a few Italian coins, and told him to use them to purchase gelato for Ruffino and himself. To be given money and encouraged to purchase ice cream was both a surprise and a treat. It was rare for the Ciarletta children to be given money to spend on treats.

CHAPTER 5

When Ruffino arrived, he embraced his American cousin, and off they went, after Nonna cautioned Ruffino to be careful. They walked all afternoon. Ruffino showed Daniel the dock area, the piazza, and the narrow, curvy cobblestone streets of his hometown. Daniel marveled at how the automobiles and noisy motor scooters were able to navigate the narrow roads at such high speeds. The vehicles seemed to be clumsy, out of place machines, alongside the donkey carts and pedestrians that mingled on the equally narrow sidewalks. Both cousins enjoyed their gelato and each other.

Ruffino invited Daniel to go with him on Saturday to see a local 'partita di calcio' (soccer game). Daniel accepted the invitation with excitement. "We'll ask Nonno and your father if it's okay for you to come with me on Saturday."

Daniel, trying to impress his cousin with his independence, said, "C'mon, Ruffino, I'm thirteen. I go to games all the time without asking permission"!

Ruffino, knowing better, said, "Yes, but with Nonno, it is best for us to ask permission." When they arrived at Nonno's house that evening, Ruffino asked Nonno and Pete if Daniel could accompany him to the Saturday calcio game.

When Pete found out how far the calcio field was from Nonno's house, he casually said to Ruffino, "I'll come along, just to be on the safe side. If you two went alone and Daniel got lost, he doesn't know enough Italian to ask for directions to get back to Nono's home."

Daniel was furious when he heard his father's response. "Dad, how could I get lost? And s'pose I did! I'm old enough to take care of myself! I can find my way home by taking the same road I took to go to the field. I'm not a baby. You don't need to come"!

Pete felt as though he was being challenged by his youngest son in front of his parents, and he responded defensively. "Daniel, I've heard just about enough from you today. What's gotten into you? You know I don't allow you to talk back like that."

Although Daniel felt he was being treated unfairly, he realized challenging his father as he had in front of Nonno and Nonna was a tactical mistake, and he apologized to his father. Subdued, and now speaking very politely, he said, "I know you're worried about me because I can't speak Italian, but how would it look if I was the only kid at the game with his father tagging along? The other kids might think I'm a baby. If I can't go alone with Ruffino, I'll just stay home. It's no big deal."

Nonna broke the sudden tension in the room, assuring her son that the boys often went to the Saturday calcio games alone, and that it would be safe. Nonno interrupted his wife and spoke to Pete quietly and in Italian. After a few minutes of discussion between Nonno and his son, Pete turned to Daniel and said, "I have decided to let you go to the calcio field alone with Ruffino. I want you to understand that I will not tolerate another disrespectful word out of your mouth while we are on this trip. Is that understood, young man?" Daniel dropped his head repentantly, "Yes, Dad, I understand."

That Saturday afternoon, when Ruffino and Daniel left the house for the calcio field, Ruffino told Daniel, "Nonno told your father that he was being too worried about you, and that no one in Castellammare di Stabia would hurt two young boys. Nonno also told your father that he should trust you more, because you would not grow up well if you were to always be restricted." It was then that Daniel realized his father, who could be very stubborn at times like this, was easily influenced by his father.

Ruffino and Daniel walked to the calico game asking questions about each other's lives. Ruffino wanted to know about America, and Daniel was curious to know what it was like living through a war. Daniel had been in Italy seven days, and in that short period of time the two cousins had become good friends. Perhaps it was because they were so interested in each other's backgrounds, perhaps it was a family thing, or maybe it was because the two cousins were so different. Ruffino was a very serious and studious boy, while Daniel had little interest in his schoolwork.

During their walk, the conversation seemed to change. Ruffino was no longer talking about America. He seemed sad and uncertain as he talked about his schooling. He was sure his parents would not be able to afford his advanced studies, and without an opportunity to attend a university he would have to become a tailor like his father. Ruffino loved science and wished one day he could become a scientist. Daniel tried to be encouraging. "I'll betcha your school can find a university that would give you a scholarship. With your grades that should be easy." Ruffino did not understand the word scholarship, so Daniel explained. Then he began comparing himself to Ruffino. "Look at the difference between us. You're six months older than me and look how much more you know."

Daniel continued trying to get Ruffino to smile. "Ruffino, you talk about things I haven't even thought of. I've known you only seven days, and I've learned a lot just by listening to you. You're such a smart kid. I wish I was as smart as you.

Ruffino smiled for the first time and said, "Grazie." Daniel then used the English word mature. Ruffino didn't know this English word, and Daniel found it difficult to translate its meaning. However, Ruffino generally understood what he was trying to say.

As the two boys walked along, Ruffino responded to Donato's questions about the Italian government and explained how difficult it was to live in a country experiencing such political chaos and disorder. "Before the war, Mussolini and his Black Shirts took over Italy. The people hated the Black Shirts and the Fascista military. The young men were mad because they had to serve a year in the army. Then Mussolini became ipnotizzato by Hitler." Ruffino was unable to translate the word ipnotizzare into English.

Daniel could see Ruffino's frustration, so he encouraged him to go on. "Zio Rudolfo has been to school and knows many things. When we get home, I'll ask him about this word he'll be able to explain it in English."

Ruffino explained in more detail the actions of Benito Mussolini. "He was to blame for Italy's entrance into a war the people never wanted. All I've known is poverty, and politicians who are thieves, fear of the Fascista, and then the mean Nazis. And now the politicians have told the people that they must adjust to another change, our country has become something called a republic."

Daniel, once again feeling embarrassed by his lack of knowledge, asked, "Is a republic a bad thing?"

"Oh, I don't know. Some say a republic is what we need; others think, no good. Zio Rudolfo is very happy that Italy has become a republic. He has read a book by a man named Machiavelli. This book says if a country is to be good, it must collect money so it can have police and an army, not to fight others, but to protect people and make sure there is justice for everyone. Zio Rudolfo told me the book says this can only happen if we have a republic, but my father thinks that a republic will only help the big cities, and the people in the small towns like Castellammare di Stabia will be left behind. People choose the leaders, and if the leaders don't do good things, the people are allowed to choose others who will. He told me if the leaders of police and army act like the 'black shirts' then in a republic, the people can reject leaders like Mussolini, and put in another who will stop the men from doing bad things to the people. Zio Rudolfo really believes what this person Machiavelli has written in his book, Discorsi Sopra la Prima Deca di Tito Livio (Discourses on the Decade of Titus Livy)."

Daniel, still confused, had grown up in a democracy all his life. He had never given much thought to elections in America, and asked a second question, "If the Fascists were so bad to the people, why didn't your King kick them out?"

Ruffino was not sure of the answer to this question and responded. "When we get home after the calcio game, we'll visit with Zio Rudolfo, and I'll ask him." Ruffino told Daniel that Zio Rudolfo was a smart, well-read man. "Even when I was younger, I noticed how everyone in town showed him respect because of his knowledge. I want to go to school and learn many things, and then the people in town will respect me like they do Zio Rudolfo."

The boys arrived at the calcio field as the game was about to begin. After the game, while on their way back to Nonno's house, they stopped to speak with Zio Rudolfo. Ruffino asked him about translating the word ipnotizzare into English. Zio Rudolfo went into a long explanation in Italian. He seemed to be giving Ruffino more information than just the translation of one Italian word into English. When Zio Rudolfo finished, he seemed visibly pleased at the boy's question. Ruffino then told Daniel that the word ipnotizzare meant hypnotized, he was trying to tell Daniel that Hitler had hypnotized Mussolini.

Zio Rudolfo interrupted Ruffino and once again had an unusually long discussion with Ruffino in Italian. When Zio Rodolfo finished, Ruffino turned to Donato and began to translate what Zio Rudolfo had said.

"Nono Leopoldo, your grandfather, returned to Castellammare di Stabia after he lived in America for nineteen years. The Italian men who immigrated to America, and returned to their home in Italy, were revered as Padrone, considered the smartest and wealthiest man in the town."

CHAPTER 6

Daniel then reminded Ruffino to ask Zio Rudolfo about his question regarding the King. Ruffino spoke to Zio Rudolfo in Italian about Daniel's question. Zio Rudolfo said kings don't belong in a republic, Zio Rudolfo motioned for the boys to sit next to him, he seemed eager to explain and pleased that Donato was interested in such a complicated question. Because of his limited English, Zio Rudolfo began speaking to Ruffino in Italian. Ruffino listened intently. There was renewed emotion in Zio Rudolfo's voice and gestures. Zio Rudolfo stopped and motioned for Ruffino to relay his negative reaction to kings.

"Zio Rudolfo told me that the answer to your question is a good example of why Italy is needed to become a republic. When Mussolini was made prime minister by the King in 1919, the people were not happy about his leadership, but the people were not allowed to say they didn't want Mussolini. Only the political leaders could get rid of Mussolini, but they were more afraid of a communist revolution than they were of Mussolini, so he remained in power no matter what his black shirts did."

Ruffino looked to Zio Rudolfo for the remainder of the answer, "Once he was in office, Mussolini kept the people happy by making work for them. The King didn't know that Mussolini was only doing this to make himself more powerful than the King, but soon Mussolini joined Hitler, thinking that together they'd win the war in Europe. If Italy had been a democracy, as you are in America, the people would have been able to vote Mussolini out of office, because a democracy has laws that let the people remove their leaders."

When Ruffino was finished, Zio Rudolfo arose from his chair, gave Daniel a robust hug, and said in his limited English, "Daniel, I'm pleased you think such interesting thoughts."

On the day before they were to return to America, Ruffino suggested that Daniel meet him at his school at around one in the afternoon. He wanted to introduce his American cousin to his teacher and classmates. Ruffino's teacher gave him permission to make up his homework assignment for that day, so the two cousins could spend their last afternoon together. Daniel told his father the exciting news that he had been invited to Ruffino's school.

Pete looked at Daniel and in a voice that was firm said, "Walking to Ruffino's school alone is out of the question. I'll take you to the school, and then you can come back with Ruffino when school is over, but you're not going to his school alone." Daniel assured his father he would not get lost. "Ruffino already took me to his school, I would know the way to walk because I did it before. Daniel protested, "Dad, I'm not gonna get lost. You don't need to take me. I'm thirteen."

"Yes, I know you're a thirteen-year-old boy who doesn't speak Italian. If you go to Ruffino's school, it will be with me, not by yourself." Daniel remembered the error he had made during their last disagreement on the topic of getting lost, so he spoke respectfully to his father about his objections. "Dad, I know you're worried, and don't want anything to happen to me, and that's what a father should do, but a thirteen-year-old boy brought to school by his father? Do you know how embarrassing that would be for me?"

Pete, not angry whit his son responded, "Embarrassed? I'll tell you what would be embarrassing. Your father running around Castellammare di Stabia trying to find you after you've gotten yourself lost!"

Daniel's Nonno understood some English from his years in America, so it was not surprising that he understood the disagreement taking place between his son and grandson. Leopoldo interrupted and started to talk in Italian to his son Pete. Daniel didn't understand what they were saying, but it was obvious they were disagreeing, and Daniel was the center of their conversation.

At the end of Pete's discussion with his father, he turned to his son with a somewhat conflicted look on his face. "Ok, you can go to Ruffino's school alone, but only under this condition. If you get lost, stop anyone you see on the street or go into any store and tell them you're the grandson of Leopoldo Ciarletta. Everyone knows your Nonno and where he lives. Anyone you speak with will make sure you get home safely."

Daniel thanked his father very politely and then turned to Nonno and gave him a hug. That evening, Pete and his son were preparing to sleep in the small upstairs bedroom. Daniel had washed, and changed into his pajamas, about to get into bed. Pete asked his son to sit on the bed, "I have something to say to you." Pete took both of his son's hands in his, and Daniel noticed the serious expression on his father's face. "It's important for you to know why I changed my mind about you going to Ruffino's school alone. Nonno told me you are no longer my little boy, you're soon to become a man. Nonno reminded me that he had left me and your Uncle Danny alone in America when we were about your age. Then Nonno added that he was confident in Uncle Danny and me, and put us in charge of the ice business, even though we were about your age. He gave us this responsibility, knowing it would make his two sons become men. He is afraid you will never become a man if I keep protecting you. Maybe he's right. I think of you as my baby because you're my youngest child, and maybe I do protect you too much. Your Nonno is right about one thing, you're becoming a man all right."

Pete then immediately changed his mood and said, "But you must promise me you'll be careful and follow the road that Ruffino showed you. Promise me; I mean it. I'm very serious about you going off on your own, and if you get lost, stop the first person you see and say, "Portami a casa di Leopoldo Ciarletta" (Take me to the house of Leopoldo Ciarletta). I have written this phrase on a piece of paper, and I want you to take it with you, in case you accidently get separated from Ruffino."

"I will, Dad. I promise I'll be very careful." In a spontaneous sudden move, Daniel jumped up from his bed and gave his father a loving, strong hug. With his head resting on his father's shoulder, Daniel whispered, "Thanks, Dad. I love you." Pete said nothing, and his eyes became moist as he simply returned to his son's embrace. Pete then took his son's face in his big, fleshy, warm hands, as he so often did, kissed him on his forehead, and said, "I don't know what I would do if anything happened to you. So, make sure you are careful.

The next morning, Daniel felt energized now that he was going to be on his own for an adventurous afternoon. He kept busy, hoping the morning would pass quickly. The Italian family had their usual pranzo meal at noon. The meal ended with Nonno sipping his digestive aid, Fernet Branca, while the others were sharing fruit. Daniel was anxious to get on his way, but knew he had to stay at the table until Nonno finished his small drink. When Nonno finished, and after Daniel helped clean the table, he kissed Nonno, and Nonna, and his father goodbye. After he had kissed his father and started to leave, Pete grabbed his arm and said, "Remember what I told you. Do you have the paper I gave you last night?"

Daniel said, "Yes." He removed the statement from his pants pocket and showed it to his father. "Remember to be careful," said an anxious Pete. Still holding his sons' hand Pete added. "If you do get lost, show the first person you see the Italian phrase on the paper, and they will make sure you get home safely."

"I promise I'll be careful." Daniel turned and tried to get out of the house as fast as he could for fear his father might change his mind. He moved down the narrow stone sidewalk and then continued to walk straight until he got to a wider street. He knew to turn left, and then proceed three blocks to the overhead archway that connected two homes. At the archway, he made the second right, now on a street ascending to higher ground. Daniel knew that Ruffino's school would be on the opposite sidewalk. Daniel was thrilled to be on his own after so many weeks. It made him feel like an adult, mature like Ruffino, who did this every day.

He knew to cross the narrow street ahead on his right. He crossed the street at the proper intersection, to be on the same side as the school. One more block and he would be there. A few yards ahead he saw a man smoking a cigarette as he was leaning against an open door. As Daniel passed, the man nodded and said, "Buona iurnata, ragazzo (Good afternoon, young man)." Daniel smiled and continued toward the school.

As he entered the building, a woman seated behind a counter smiled as though she was expecting him. She got up from her chair and said, "Avanzarsi" (come forward). Daniel followed her down a narrow hallway to where Ruffino was waiting in front of an open door. The woman acknowledged Daniel with a bow and said, "Statte buono, ragazzo (Goodbye, young man)."

Ruffino introduced his cousin to his teacher, Professore Saltarelli, and then to his classmates as his cousin from America, New York City. The students, both boys and girls, were sitting at their wooden desks. Ruffino went to his seat, and the teacher, speaking in English, explained to the class that the rest of the day would be spent asking Daniel questions about America. Professor Saltarelli reminded the youngsters that this time would be part of their English lesson, and they were required to ask their questions only in English.

Daniel was nervous, standing in front of the class, having to answer questions. A boy in the middle of the class stood and asked, "Is every person in America rich and do they live in big houses?" After an hour and ten minutes, the clanging handheld dismissal bell could be heard clearly throughout the school. As the two cousins left the classroom, Daniel asked, "Why didn't you tell me they would ask me questions?"

Ruffino explained it was not his idea. The teacher had suggested it during the morning. "I didn't think you would mind," said Ruffino.

"I didn't mind, it was great, but I was nervous, afraid I would not know what to say."

Ruffino and Daniel enjoyed their last afternoon together. Daniel mentioned to Ruffino that when he returned to America, he was going to study hard and be a better student, "Like you. Ruffino." Ruffino than gave Daniel a modest smile and told him he was glad Daniel had come to Italy, and that he was pleased they had become such good friends. Ruffino reminded Daniel that he was serious about one day visiting New York City. He also reminded Daniel about his promise regarding schoolwork. Then, as two adolescent boys usually do when they leave, they shook hands and were about to part when they both spontaneously hugged each other. Everyone was up early the next morning. Daniel and his father were packed and ready to start their journey back to America.

There was a farewell meal at Nonno's house the night before Pete and Daniel were to leave. After dinner, Pete was given directions to Via San Gregorio in the old part of Naples, where Pete could purchase the Presepe nativity set for Suzy. He then suggested a restaurant, by the name of Port 'Alba Restaurant, where pizza was first served in 1860 which was in walking distance from Via San Gregorio. Having pizza from that restaurant would be a special treat for Daniel. He would be able to tell all his friends that he had lunch in the Italian restaurant that invented pizza." Pete liked the idea. He wanted his son to taste what he called, 'real pizza, the way it should be made, unlike American pizza which is full of gravy, cheese, and meat.'

Nonna Francesca gave a box to her son Pete and said this is for your trip on the boat back to America. It is not much but you will enjoy what I prepared, salami, olives, biscotti, a full caciocavallo cheese, and the final item, a bottle of Zio Ruffino's homemade wine.

As Pete was fitting the food box into his suitcase, he reminded his mother not to make lunch. He had promised to treat Daniel to pizza while they were in Naples. "The boy can't leave Naples without tasting "real pizza."

The sun was just beginning to rise as Nonno Leopoldo came down the narrow steps alone. Pete tried to climb the steps to assist his father, who had now stopped on one of the steps above his son and spoke. "Go to the table and start your breakfast. I can get down my own stairs, now go." Pete, knowing it was useless to argue, slowly moved back toward the table.

Nonno slowly continued his descent, holding the banister rail, with his bastone (cane) swinging from his right arm by its crook. When he arrived safely on the stone floor, he ordered Daniel to get his sweater. This was Daniel's official task each morning, to retrieve Nonno's cardigan sweater. Daniel retrieved Nonno's sweater from a small closet in the living room and held it open as Nonno placed his arms in the sweater. A smiling, proud Nonno, wrapped his arm around his grandson's shoulder as they both proceeded to the table for their espresso and roll.

After breakfast, Pete and Daniel said their sad farewell, hugging and kissing everyone several times. Nonna was concerned that her son had not taken enough food for the trip. Pete kissed his mother and assured her they had plenty of food. The hugging and kissing continued, and soon Pete became nervous that this would continue, for another twenty minutes he was anxious to get on the road to get his wife's Presepe figures.

Pete said, "I'm sorry to break this up but we must get going to catch our bus." Pete and Daniel walked on the narrow cobblestone streets with their suitcases and bags, until they arrived at the bus stop. The bus arrived almost immediately, Pete and Daniel struggled getting on the bus with their luggage. The bus driver was concerned about the time it was taking for his new passengers to store their luggage and take their seats. Eventually the bus door closed, and Pete and Daniel were on their way out of Naples and then on to America.

CHAPTER 7

Pete was already beginning to complain, mumbling under his breath about the extra Presepe packages he would have to carry to the boat dock. They arrived at the Piazza San Domenico Maggiore a few minutes after nine. Pete referred to his directions, and then, with bags in hand, the pair began walking west on the Via Benedetto Croce, looking for the San Gregorio Armeno church opposite a big red building. At this intersection they would find Via San Gregorio, the narrow cobblestone street where the vendors of Neapolitan Presepe figures had their stores and workshops. Pete, already annoyed about having to do this task for his wife, was not pleased about having to walk with his son in this noisy, dirty, rundown neighborhood. As they proceeded toward the church, Pete whispered to his son, "Daniel, stay close to me. I don't like the looks of some of these people."

Daniel was nervous about his father's concerns and asked, "Do you think those people are Gypsies, like the person we saw on the bus going to Nonno's house?"

Pete, in no mood for questions, responded to his son in an uncharacteristic manner, "No questions now. Just move along and make sure you stay close." Pete put his arm around his son's shoulders as he picked up his pace. Daniel chose not to protest his father's angry expression. The San Gregorio Armeno church was the home of Benedictine nuns, living in a convent attached to the church and presiding over its various daily functions. The cloistered nuns, provided a quiet haven in a rowdy neighborhood, known for its noisy vendors, stores, and street traffic. Zio Rudolfo had suggested that if they had time, they might enjoy a visit to the church, which was noted for its Baroque interior and contained many frescoes by the Italian artist Luca Giordano. Pete had put that suggestion out of his mind while in Castellammare di Stabia, and now the appearance of the neighborhood did nothing to encourage Pete to follow Zio Rudolfo's suggestion.

Via San Gregorio was a narrow cobblestone street lined with stores and workshops that sold Presepe figures. At the store entrances, various men were hawking the Presepe nativity figures. Pete found a store that sold Gramendola figures made by Matteo Prencipe. He picked out the specific figures Suzy had listed and a Neapolitan pastoral setting, which included miniature houses that rose up as though they were built on a hill. The Renaissance figures would be displayed in and around the pastoral setting. The vendor carefully wrapped the delicate, intricately made figures in paper and then in small boxes. He placed the boxes in the Neapolitan setting, which was now too large for a box. He then heavily wrapped the entire pastoral setting in layered paper and taped it. The package was much too bulky to carry with their suitcases and other bags. A frustrated looking Pete spoke with the vendor for a few moments, and the vendor went to the rear of the store. Thankfully, he reappeared quickly with pieces of rope, and arranged the rope, so that it became a holder with two large loops for the large package. The vendor helped Pete slip his arm into one of the loops, and then he shifted the package so Pete could slip his other arm through the opposite loop. Finally, the package rested on Pete's back, like a backpack.

Although they had plenty of time before boarding their boat, Daniel's father was reluctant to depend on the casual Italian bus schedules to get them to the dock on time. He asked the vendor if it was likely they could find a taxi at the Port`Alba Restaurant for their pizza lunch, which they would have at the boat dock. The vendor assured Pete that taxis were available at the restaurant, and if they did not immediately see a taxi, there were many people with cars and even donkey carts who would be happy to take them to the dock for a nominal fee.

Daniel and his annoyed father left the store and walked to the corner where the red building and church were located. Sensing his father's mood, Daniel did not bother to ask if he wanted to stop at the church, as his uncle had suggested. They made a left at the red building and began walking to the restaurant. Pete asked his son to reach into his side pocket and take out the directions. Pete was relieved when he realized the restaurant was only two short blocks away. Pete reminded Daniel to walk in front of him because his vision was limited by the package on his back. Daniel, feeling more comfortable, said, "C'mon Dad, I'm thirteen! Don't be so worried if I'm not exactly next to you each second!" Pete stopped walking, turned, and glared at his son. Daniel knew it was time to end the argument. "Okay, okay, I'll walk next to you."

His father growled, "No, you won't! You'll walk in front of me." Daniel nodded, knowing the discussion was over. As he walked in front of his father, Daniel was intrigued by this section of Naples, which was the older part of the city. As they walked, Daniel found it interesting that a beautiful Romanesque Cathedral was standing gracefully next to run-down shops, old brick warehouses, and stone homes, with faded painted surfaces and missing stucco, all these different buildings were situated atop multiple layered ancient Greek and Roman streets.

The two Americans found it difficult moving on the crowded narrow sidewalks, irritated by the constant harsh noise of the motor scooters as they zipped past small cars and slowly moving donkey carts on the congested roadway. Daniel's attention was suddenly drawn away from the noise and sights when he heard his father say, "I see the Port`Alba Restaurant sign." They pushed forward, picking up their walking pace. Pete suddenly stopped and put his luggage down, immediately realizing they were blocking the narrow sidewalk as irritated people passed them.

"When they arrived near the restaurant, Pete said, "Let's move our bags to the wall of the building next to the restaurant and let the crowd pass freely."

CHAPTER 8

Next to the entrance of the restaurant was a narrow counter with a glass opening onto the street and a sign that read 'take-away.' Pete was silent for a few moments as he looked at the moving cars. Although the traffic was heavy, the cars and scooters were moving rapidly, but not quickly enough for Pete. He stood silent for a few moments, looking at the take-away sign and then shifting his gaze at the speeding traffic, considering whether to have lunch at a table in the restaurant or order their pizza as take-away. He thought *coming to this restaurant wasn't a good decision. Had I known the traffic was going to be this heavy, I would have waited at Via San Gregorio for a taxi. The cars at this spot are moving without delay here, but what happens if we run into heavy or stopped traffic before we reach the boat? Well, we're here now. Instead of eating our pizza in the restaurant, I will order a pizza at the take-away window. We can eat it at the dock, but I won't be able to carry the pizza box flat with all these bags and this damn nuisance tied to my back. Okay, I know what we'll do!*

Pete told Daniel to pick up his bags and walk in front of him. They moved to the curb, in front of the take-away window. Pete told Daniel, "Here's what we're gonna do - you stay here and keep an eye on our luggage while I go to the window and order our food. Don't move from this spot, I'm going to be only three or four feet away from you while I'm at the window ordering the pizza, and I don't want you to move even an inch! Stand next to our bags, if you happen to see a taxi, wave for him to stop. I'll order pizza and a drink, but if a taxi should stop before our order is ready, I'll leave the order line, and after our bags are loaded, we'll have him take us to the boat dock. Only stop a taxi, I don't want to be taken to the dock by horse and cart, or a private car.

Without the bags, and only the Presepe purchase fastened to his back, Pete moved the four steps to the takeout window and ordered a large Margherita pizza and a soda for Daniel, Pete had Zio Ruffino's wine. After ordering Pete moved to his son and luggage, anxiously waiting for his order to arrive. The man at the takeout window, eventually called Pete to pick up his order. Before Pete moved to the window, he told Daniel to keep an eye out for a taxi, and wave him down. I'll be back in a minute. The unassuming Daniel said 'okay.'

As Pete approached the take-away window, the man behind the counter was handing another man his change, Pete waited a moment as the man behind the counter placed a large white box on the countertop. Pete placed five lire on top of the box. The man at the takeaway window was counting the change for Pete.

Daniel was standing at the curb next to the luggage, looking over his shoulder to see a taxi among the swerving speeding scooters and small cars rushing. A small black car stopped abruptly at the curb next to Daniel. The rear door opened, and Daniel was shocked when a man reached out and pulled him into the rear of the car. it swiftly pulled away from the curb. The back door, still open and hinged at the center of the automobile, slammed shut from the force of the car lurching forward, Daniel was so surprised that it took him a moment to get his breath. He began struggling and shouting, "Let me go! Let me get out of here! What are you doing?"

The man holding Daniel had already started to tie a rope around Daniel's hands. Daniel could see a figure in the rear window running in the middle of the street, as scooters and small cars swerved around him. He knew it was his father. Soon the figure was no longer in sight.

Although he had been intimidated by the man next to him, Daniel decided he needed to find the courage to be more aggressive. The car continued its rapid movement through the city streets, ignoring caution and road signs, while veering and zigzagging as it passed other vehicles. Soon the car was on a highway. As they sped along, Daniel could only think of how he had reacted when he was dragged into the car. *Why didn't I fight him harder while the man was pulling me into the car? Why are they doing this? Why did they choose me? What are they planning?*

Many confusing questions kept running through his mind. Then, in an instant, reality replaced his confusion. *Oh my God. I'm being kidnapped.*

For a few moments, his brain stopped functioning. When his mental process returned, the car was moving on to a highway, Daniel was frightened and unsure how best to act, he remembered how kidnapped characters were portrayed on fictional radio stories. The bad guys were sarcastic, annoyed at the kidnapped character hysteria, and they talked about using their guns! He kept telling himself that the person in the story was always rescued. He thought he was being childish, comparing his situation to fictional radio programs, perhaps the fictional characters keep from crying. In any case, his naïveté was not helpful considering his predicament.

Soon he began to discard thoughts of radio programs as the reality of his situation became real. Daniel told himself to calm down and relax, and try to determine why he was being kidnapped, and how he could get free. He had never seen any of these men with his father, *so why did they take me?* He began to find it hard to breathe. He took a few deep breaths, which seemed to help. *These men must come from Castellammare di Stabia. Like all Ruffino's* friends, they must think because I'm an American my father is rich and will pay them money to return me.

Daniel's capture was beginning to make sense. He remembered the day he had walked to Ruffino's school, and his father had said everyone in Castellammare di Stabia knew Daniel's grandfather. They're going to call Nonno and ask for money. Daniel was feeling much better now that he had figured out the motive for his kidnapping. His mind immediately skipped to his release. Dad won't let them get away with this; he'll make sure they go to jail for what they've done. The man next to Daniel was acting as though he was alone in the rear seat, paying no attention to his terrified passenger. He was a large man with thick black hair. Daniel could only see the back of the head of the driver, who had been chain-smoking cigarettes. The two men in the car talked very little. They exchanged a single word now and then, but there was no formal conversation between them. It was hard for Daniel to determine just how long they had been driving, but he guessed he had been driving in the car for about an hour. The driver entered a lane to exit the highway. It suddenly dawned on Daniel that it would be wise if he started to remember landmarks and other clues as they were driving. He wasn't quite sure how he would use this information, but it seemed like something he should have been doing. The first clue appeared immediately after the car left the highway.

Daniel saw a sign that read Abbazia di Monte Cassino. He didn't know what the sign meant, but he kept silently repeating the words on the sign so he would not forget. Soon they were traveling up a winding road, going higher and higher. We must be going into the mountains, thought Daniel. The man in the back seat continued looking straight ahead, rarely looking at his captive. Daniel decided, if he could get the driver to stop the car, he might have a chance of running away. He was becoming more aggressive. He would swing his hips away from the man next to him and use his feet to kick him in the face. If I could get a solid blow to the face with my shoes. The driver might have to stop the car to help his companion.

Daniel took a deep breath and swung his hips hard to his right while trying to lift his legs. The man reacted with unusual speed, grasping Daniel's legs, and pulling them upward, causing Daniel's upper body to roll off the seat and onto the floor between the front and rear seats. The man was infuriated, raising his voice, and shouting in Italian. While placing his feet on Daniel's legs he began to bind Daniel's ankles with a second piece of rope. Daniel was now completely immobilized; his body was wedged in the narrow space between the front and back seats. The car continued on the winding road, climbing higher and higher into the mountains. After about forty-five minutes, they came to a stop. The man in the back seat opened the locked car door on his side. He placed his hands around Daniel's ankles and dragged him across the floor of the car and had him stand on the edge of the road.

The driver of the car immediately drove the car across the road, backed up, and sped away from a horse drawn wagon. On the back of the car, Daniel could see the word Renault and the license plate number, CA 264, Daniel kept silently repeating the car's plate number, and the car's name. Daniel was forcibly dragged forward toward the wagon, at the wagon, the two men pushed Daniel into the bed of the horse wagon.

There was a person in a heavy coat and wool hat on the front seat of the wagon holding the reins of the horses. Daniel's wrists were fastened to the side of the wagon with rope. The wagon driver threw a heavy coat and two wool hats at Daniel's captor. The man put on the coat and hat, and then put the other hat on Daniel's head.

The man in the front of the horse drawn wagon slapped the reins on the horse and the wagon began moving forward. After a short time, the wagon turned right onto a winding road going into the mountains. Daniel's captor sat in the bed of the wagon across from his captive. Daniel was able to clearly observe the man for the first time. He was not very tall, but he had a stocky build. The disinterested look on his face remained, as it had in the car

Daniel yelled across to the man, "I demand that you tell me where you're taking me!" Daniel's plea was ignored as though he had never spoken. Daniel's adrenalin was still flowing, and in about fifteen minutes he noticed that Naples was much warmer than where he was now. He was glad he was wearing his heavy jacket, the one he planned to use on the deck of the troop steamer. The slow-moving wagon was now on a road that seemed to be ascending. It was a slow ride, perhaps a half hour or more. Daniel had not been concentrating on time. He was making every effort to remember all the important clues, which he knew were going to be important when he was released.

CHAPTER 9

Daniel noticed that the horse drawn wagon continued ascending the winding road. The man across from him continued to stare straight ahead, not looking at his captive. Daniel noticed a road sign with the word Opi on it. He started to repeat the word Opi—yet another clue. Just past the Opi sign the wagon moved onto a flat road but still through a thick forest on both sides of the road. The length of time that the wagon was on this road led Daniel to conclude that the forest must be awfully deep. Suddenly the wagon was in an open green pasture area, and a high mountain town began at the green pasture.

Soon the wagon was on a narrow road that was steeply ascending. When the wagon reached a cobble stone road, Daniel could see white stone houses with red roofs on both sides of this high flat surface; Daniel could see a church located in the center of the highest point of the town. On the right side of this high town Daniel could see a green valley with sheep grazing. The green valley separated the town from the deep forest. On the left side of this town were large mountains, and large green bushes and many trees that acted as a buffer, separating the high town from the mountains. Danial thought it strange that he could not see any other houses, only vegetation surrounding this high town for as far as his eyes could see. Daniel thought, *ah, so this is where they're gonna hide me until Dad comes with the ransom money.*

The horse-drawn wagon quickly arrived on a flat narrow cobblestone road, with stone houses on both sides. Off in the distance, the cobblestone road led directly to a church, the wagon stopped in front of a house that had the number 25 over a blue door. Daniel reminded himself, remember the numbers over the door, *another important clue I gotta remember, number twenty-five.*

Daniel had not thought much about the time of day until he noticed it was starting to get dark. His captor removed the rope on his ankles, and holding him tightly by the arm, brought Daniel down from the bed of the wagon and moved him toward the blue door. Daniel and the man entered a dark room. Daniel's captor moved to the center of the room and pulled a string hanging from a bare light bulb fixture. He untied the rope from around Daniel's sore, irritated wrists. Then, without a word being said, he left the room. Daniel heard the door being locked.

The room was large and windowless. There was an upholstered chair close to the entrance, a bed, a hot woodstove, and a large stack of cut wood. By the bed, attached to the stone wall, was a wooden rack with pegs. There was a small rectangular table and a wooden chair in the center of the room. Daniel walked past the table toward the rear of the room. In the left corner there was a white porcelain circle on the floor with a hole in the center. Daniel had been in Italy long enough to know this was an Italian toilet. Near the toilet was a small sink. Directly over the sink was a blue metal container, flat against the wall, round in front, and a pipe leading from the top of the container into the ceiling of the room, and a faucet at the other end of the pipe over the sink.

There was a door on the back wall. Daniel approached the door, suspecting it would also be locked. Surprisingly, it was not. He opened the door slowly but stayed behind it for fear that someone might be on the other side. The door opened into a large room that housed two horses in stalls, a few sheep, two pigs, a goat and mule. At the far end of the room there were black iron bars covering the entire opening and embedded in a half concrete and stone wall. The black iron bars were embedded into the concrete ceiling. These bars looked like the hand railings on the front steps of some houses in the Bronx. In the center of the stone wall was an opening that seemed to be the way the animals would enter and exit this area. The hinged door was made from the same iron bars. The door was at least seven feet tall, extending to the edge of the concrete ceiling. It was secured with a heavy metal lock that Daniel unsuccessfully tried to force open. Discouraged, he returned to the warm room, removed his coat and hat, and sat in the upholstered chair, imagining what might happen next.

Unbeknownst to Daniel, his captor, Vincenzo Sgammotta, lived above the room where Daniel had been placed. After washing, Vincenzo entered the dining room, where a table was being prepared for a meal. He asked his wife, "Gelsomina, have you prepared food for the boy?"

"Yes, Vincenzo, his plate is ready. He's probably hungry by now, go bring him his meal before we have our evening meal."

When Vincenzo saw the amount of food on the boy's plate, he said, "Gelsi, this is too much food for the boy. He won't be able to finish all this."

"Vincenzo, it's his first night, and he probably didn't have lunch. Besides, he must be tired and confused about why he's been brought here. He'll need a good meal to make him feel better. Now go and bring the young boy his plate."

Vincenzo took the plate and a metal cup half-filled with red wine out the back door and down one flight of stairs. He unlocked the gate leading to the animal stable, proceeded to the inside door, and entered the room. He looked around the room, glanced at Daniel, and placed the plate and cup on the rectangular table, and spoke. "Mangia,"

Daniel understood the word, but angrily protested, "I want to see my father! The police will put you in jail! I'm Americano." Without responding, the man turned and left the room the same way he had entered. Daniel was not hungry, even though he had not eaten since breakfast. With a nauseated stomach, his head reeling, Daniel spoke out loud, as though he was talking to someone in the room. "I don't need this jerk's food. My dad will have the cops here soon enough to arrest this guy. I wouldn't be surprised if I was outta here before morning. My dad will find me even before this guy can contact him for the ransom money."

Daniel returned to the upholstered chair and sat in front of the warm woodburning stove. Some of the tension and frustration Daniel had been feeling since being dragged into the car slowly began seeping from his body. He knew he needed to write down the clues he had been silently repeating in his mind so he wouldn't forget. He didn't know how this information could be used, but it seemed like an important thing to do. Daniel looked for a pencil and paper, but the room was bare except for the furniture. He returned to the upholstered chair, concerned he'd forgotten the information.

As time passed, the room was getting chilly, Daniel placed some cut logs in the belly of the stove. Noticing the charred wood, Daniel had an idea. Using the metal poker, he took a piece of the burnt wood out of the fire and let it cool. Looking around the room, he decided the best place to write the information was on a stone wall. He moved the bed that was against the far stone wall, and using the burnt piece of wood like charcoal, he wrote the information on the lower part of the wall. Then moved the bed back against the stone wall, so his captor would not see his writing. He felt as though he had accomplished something important, and he was proud of himself for finding a clever way to record the clues.

He returned to his chair, his head still whirling. His stomach was still queasy, and he had no desire to eat. *I won't touch this guy's food. That'll show him that I'm angry.* He put a few more logs into the stove and lay down on the bed, which was like the bed in Nonno's house.

CHAPTER 10

Once Pete had lost sight of the car, he gave up the chase. He immediately ran back to the restaurant and began screaming, "Police! Get me the police! Somebody took my son!" An older man behind the bar said, "Abbastanza" (enough)! I will get the police. Sit and calm yourself." The man began dialing before Pete could respond. Pete was too agitated to sit and stood next to the man who was calling. When the man had finished, he ordered one of his waiters to go to the street and bring in the man's luggage from the street. Then he said, "Please, Signore, come with me to a quiet place where you can talk to the police when they arrive."

Pete, who was now in a daze, was led to a back room where the man poured him a whiskey. "Drink and become calm." The manager of the restaurant was more concerned about the man's hysteria, which might worry his customers. The whiskey had little effect, Pete continued pacing at the open door of the room, waiting for the police to arrive.

A police officer was soon escorted to the rear room by the manager. Pete hurriedly explained what had happened. After writing down Pete's statement, the officer escorted Pete and his luggage to the police car. They drove to the main police station, Pete was informed that an immediate trace would begin on the license plate car number, CA 264. A sergeant took a detailed statement from the distraught American. When he was finished, the officer said, "We'll have the information on the owner of the vehicle late this evening. I would suggest that you return tomorrow morning for the details."

"Tomorrow morning?" repeated Pete. "How long does it take to trace a license plate? I'm not leaving until I have the information on the car, and you better have it before tomorrow morning."

Although the sergeant was annoyed with the rude American, he tried to be diplomatic. "Mr. Ciarletta, I can see you're very upset over the loss of your son, but you must try to understand we have other cases we are working on, and we must follow certain procedures. This will take time. We'll have information for you as soon as you arrive in the morning."

Pete refused to accept the sergeant's answer. "Procedures! Who the hell knows what will happen to my son by tomorrow morning? I want information now, and if you can't give it to me, then I want to see your boss!"

The desk sergeant asked Pete to sit while he went to get the captain. In a few minutes, a tall man with a thin closely trimmed mustache entered the front office desk area. He was dressed in a fancy dark blue uniform with golden laced shoulder epaulets, shiny brass buttons, and a peaked hat with a silver bar fastened to its front. He greeted Pete and asked him to come with him to his office.

Once in the office, he offered Pete a seat directly in front of his desk. "I am Captain, Sollazzo, Mr. Ciarletta, I agree that time is important in kidnapping cases. I will do everything in my power to speed this investigation along. If you return this evening after six, I guarantee we will have the most up-to-date information on the license plate number you gave us." Pete thanked the captain and said, "I'll be here at six." The two men shook hands, and as Pete left the police station, he meekly thanked the sergeant at the desk for his assistance.

When Pete returned to the police station that evening, the desk sergeant told Pete the license plate number he had given the officer earlier in the day had been reported stolen two years ago. Pete was shaken by this news. "What are you going to do now?" he asked. The policemen told Pete that Captain Sollazzo wished to see him first thing in the morning. "Tomorrow! Are you people crazy? Tomorrow will be too late!"

"Mr. Ciarletta, the captain is no longer on duty, but he has rearranged his schedule to meet with you first thing in the morning." This answer was not good enough for the distraught father. "Tell me where the captain lives. I want to go to his house. I need to speak with him."

The desk sergeant refused to divulge that information and insisted that Pete return in the morning as requested. Pete left the station frantic, seething at the fact that he could do nothing until morning; even though he understood, he knew he had taken the matter as far as he could for now. It was going to be a long, restless night in a hotel while he waited for the morning meeting.

He arrived early the next morning and informed the officer at the desk who he was and why he had come. "Oh, yes, Mr. Ciarletta. Captain Sollazzo is waiting for you. Let me take you to his office."

When Pete entered the captain's office, he immediately said, "How will you find my son? What do you intend to do?"

The captain was sitting behind a large desk, and he offered Pete a seat. "Mr. Ciarletta, I know you are suffering, but I feel I must be candid with you. Your son was most probably taken by gypsies, and I'm sorry to tell you that gypsies don't usually request a ransom for the return of a person who, like your son, is unknown. In situations like this, they often sell their captive to the highest bidder."

Pete glared at the captain. "Sell my son? Are you telling me there is no way to get him back?" Captain Sollazzo moved from behind his desk and sat next to Pete, and said "No, no, Mr. Ciarletta, I am not saying that at all. I might be able to find you a contact that has, shall I say, the ability to speak directly about your son with the Gypsy King of Naples. Every action of the gypsies in Naples goes through him, he will know about your son, and you will be able to negotiate with him."

Pete understood the captain's meaning. "I am willing to show my gratitude if you could find this person for me."

Captain Sollazzo said, "I will make a few calls to ensure that the gypsies will take no action until they speak with you." He told Pete to return to his office the next morning. "In the meantime, for your own sake, don't agonize over this dreadful situation, my call will stop any quick arrangements by the Gypsies; and I'm sure that by tomorrow morning I will be able to help you."

Pete agreed and asked Captain Sollazzo if he could provide a phone so he could make a collect call to his family in America. As he was being led to a private room, Pete asked the captain if he knew where the nearest Western Union office was located. "Yes, I will write the address for you as you are making your call to America.

As the captain was obtaining an outside line, Pete gave Captain Sollazzo his American phone number. Captain Sallazzo dialed and spoke with an operator, requesting a collect call to America, New York City: TY3-5259. After a few moments Captain Sollazzo handed the receiver to Pete. "Your call to America has been accepted." Captain Sollazzo wrote out the address of the nearest Westen Union office slid it across the table to Pete as he had the phone to his ear. Captain Sallazzo left the room, closing the door behind him.

"Hello, Suzy?" The first words out of Suzy's mouth were, "Pete, why are you calling, has your father died?" Pete dreaded the next moment, "Suzy, I have some terrible news. Daniel has been kidnapped by gypsies."

Suzy, screamed, "Oh, my God," as she fell into the chair next to the phone and began pulling at her hair. "Damn you, Pete! How could you have let this happen?"

Pete quickly shouted back over the phone, "Suzy, stop! Listen to me! Get a hold of yourself. I need you to do something important."

Dazed by the shocking news, a disturbed Suzy said, "You need me to do something? Damn you, Pete, you better do something, and get Daniel back."

"Suzy, I know you're upset. How do you think I feel? Now please, I need you to calm down!"

Suzy took a deep breath and said, "Tell me what you need."

"Call my brothers and tell them I need two thousand dollars by tomorrow. Wire the money to me through Western Union. Do you have a pencil?"

Suzy was ready. "Yes, give me the address." Pete spoke slowly, "Send the money to me in care of the Western Union Office, Via Pisanetti, Naples, Italy. Now repeat the address back to me." Suzy repeated the Western Union address in a low, agonizing voice. "Suzy, I must have two thousand dollars in my hands by noon tomorrow, Italian time, not American time. Do you understand?"

"But, Pete, suppose…." Pete interrupted his wife with anger in his voice, "Suzy, listen carefully, and no 'buts.' This must be done. I must have two thousand dollars tomorrow by noon, Italian time. Is that clear?" A resigned Suzy answered, "I understand."

Pete continued with more instructions, "When Danny comes home tonight, tell him to contact the caporegime (street captain or soldier designation) of the Fordham Road Sicilian crime family. He will know how to reach this man."

Suzy gasped, "Pete, why are you doing this?"

Pete responded, "Suzy, this is not the time for a discussion. Do you want to see Daniel again?" Without waiting for a response, he continued, "I know what this means, but we have no choice. The caporegime will be able to arrange a meeting with the Don of the Fordham Road family. Danny must secure a loan for the ransom money we will need to get Daniel back." There was shocked silence at the other end of the phone. Pete pleaded, "Suzy, get a hold of yourself. I need you to be strong. Don't go to pieces on me now."

With a tone of resignation in her voice Suzy said, "Okay, Pete, you're right, I understand."

Pete repeated his orders, understanding that she was still in shock from the horrific news. "I know this isn't easy for you, but when you hang up the phone, I need to know you can deliver for me. Can you do what I ask?"

Holding back tears, Suzy said, "Yes Pete, I'm okay now. Everything will get done." Pete repeated his orders one more time so there would be no mistake. "Suzy, are you sure you understand what you have to do?"

Suzy replied, "Yes, Pete, I know what you need. Just get Daniel back."

Pete was reassured by his wife's words. "As soon as I find out the amount of the ransom, I will call you. I expect this will take two, maybe three days."

Pete knew his plan was contrary to everything they believed and honored, but there was no other way to get his child back. "Suzy, if I thought there was any other way, I wouldn't be asking Danny to get involved with the Fordham Road family, but it's the only way to get our son back."

Suzy, now somewhat calmer, repeated, "Okay, Pete, I understand. Don't worry we'll do what needs to be done at our end."

CHAPTER 11

The following afternoon, Pete met with Captain Sollazzo. He handed the captain an envelope containing five hundred American dollars. The captain looked pleased. He reached into his upper right-hand drawer and gave Pete a piece of paper with the name Janui Kwiek, and a phone number written on it. The captain explained, "First call Gypsy Kwiek; he is expecting your call. He has my guarantee that you plan them no harm. Then explain how you are ready to cooperate. Please understand, Mr. Ciarletta, you must be willing to show your appreciation to both Gypsy Kwiek and the King of the Gypsies, Mr. Django Mahai, as you have shown your appreciation to me. You can be sure both men will appreciate your generosity."

"I understand what needs to be done," said Pete. As he started to leave the office, he hesitated and turned to the captain. "Captain Sollazzo, please don't get me wrong. You've been very helpful and I'm grateful. It's just that, well, I don't understand. Why are gypsies allowed to kidnap children?"

The captain rose from his desk and joined Pete in the middle of the room and placed a reassuring hand on Pete's right arm. "Mr. Ciarletta, you have been very generous toward me regarding this matter. I would ask you to take a seat once again. Since you have shown me the proper respect, I feel obligated to share with you some gypsy customs and behaviors that I believe will be useful to you during your negotiations with Django Mahai, the Gypsy King. Your meeting will be more effective if you have some understanding of their rituals. To begin with you should know that Gypsies are the direct descendants of Adam and Eve's oldest son Cain, who killed his brother Abel. For this reason, they are destined to roam the earth in their caravans. They don't believe in toiling for a living, nor do they work the land. They prefer to take care of their modest needs by stealing and begging from gadje, the name they give to non-gypsy people they neither understand nor like. Now in answer to your original question, we arrest a Gypsy and put him in jail knowing there are ten others to take his place. They are a race of people who choose to live outside of normal society."

Pete tried to hide the look of skepticism on his face, as he listened to the captain's explanation regarding the behaviors of Rom Gypsies. Pete was not particularly interested in hearing about gypsy culture but choose not to challenge the Italian police captain.

Captain Sollazzo began by saying, "Gypsies who pass through Naples are usually from the Rom tribe and adhere strictly to tribal allegiance. Rom Gypsies live the life of a nomad; they are wanderers who travel throughout Europe and many other countries around the world. As a race of people, they enjoy living in constant motion, like tree branches in a windstorm, like flowing water. These vagabonds are known as Kumpania. However, Django Mahai and members of his clan have made a place for themselves in Naples and have built a structure of protection for other gypsy tribes through their network of crime in Southern Italy, and in this way, they owe their loyalty and safety to Django Mahai. The Gypsy King of Naples has gained his power along with strict allegiance to the Kalderash Gypsy nations that travel constantly, at times covering entire continents. It is therefore important for you to understand that you will be dealing with a powerful man, who will have you killed if the mood strikes him.

Pete interrupted the captain. "Should I go to the meeting armed with a gun?" Captain Sollazzo quickly said, "Oh no, Mr. Ciarletta, please trust my judgment in this matter. Arriving armed would be counterproductive. You will be thoroughly searched before you are even brought to Django, and they would form an immediate distrust of your intentions if they found you were armed for your meeting with Django.

Now that I have told you how irrational and violent they can be, let me tell you how best to act during this meeting. If you are polite, courteous, and not arrogant in your manner, they will be peaceful and willing to deal with you, knowing they can obtain more lira from a father than from a stranger. Equally important, do not crouch in fear of them, as they despise weakness in any form. Mr. Ciarletta, I know this must sound confusing, but dealing with Gypsies is often difficult. On the one hand I am telling you not to be forceful, but on the other hand don't tremble as you present your proposal to Django. Your meeting will be a difficult balance, but I strongly suggest you try to walk this fine line when meeting Django."

Captain Sollazzo summarized the Gypsy culture with an expression of fatalistic acceptance. "They are a race of strangers who have lived among our people for centuries. Gypsies choose to hide from the people they call Gadjes,' you must think of Gypsies as people who do not trust progress. They live only in the present moment of their time and are happy to be—how shall I say—a footnote to history. They will have no compassion for you or your son. The only bond that matters is their family unit, and when I say family unit, I am not referring to what you and I think of as our family. Their family unit consists of all Kalderash Gypsies around the world. This is hard for me to tell a father, but your son is a Gadje, a pawn, used by them to gather lira. However, one point that may work to your advantage. The Kalderash Gypsie family controls this area of Italy. They must gain Django's approval for any transaction; he is both judge and jury. This means time is on your side, they will be unable to secure approval from Django, to sell your son in one day. I suggest you contact Kweik this morning."

Pete was a bit suspect regarding the power Captain Sollazzo insinuated Django Mahai held, but decided not to debate anything the captain was saying.

"As if reading Pete's mind, the captain continued, "You may be wondering how Django Mahai can maintain such control over such a large area. Gypsies communicate through a web of contacts known only to them. This secret network is so sacred they are willing to give their lives, rather than reveal contacts. Maintaining this secrecy over time has been accomplished by not recording their history. Transactions and decisions are completed only by word of mouth. For this reason, Gyspies have no mystical or legendry heroes, no documentation of their individual bravery or their origin."

Pete remained patient, wondering, *I don't care about Gypsy history? Tell me what I need to know of this man called Django.*

Captain Sollazzo continued. "The Rom Gypsies follow a strict allegiance to their tribal family unit. They may live among us, but they refuse to socialize with the Italian people of Italy. They have no religious allegiance to a heavenly God, their religion is based on superstition and irrational beliefs, such as influential ghostly ancestors. Gypsy religion is in the form of ancestral worship, based on ancestry.

Pete's frustration with Captain Sollazzo's harangue of Gypsy practices and history could no longer be held in. "Captain Sollazzo, please forgive my interrupting your interesting comments about Gypsies. I know it will be very helpful when I meet with their King, but there is something else I need to know. Will the King of the Gypsies understand Italian or English?"

"That's a good question, Mr. Ciarletta. Django Mahai's language is Romani, which is a derivative of Sanscrit. However, they will never use Romani in front of 'outsiders.' They consider this their secret language, another weapon to be used against Gadje. Gypsies have a saying, Tshatshimo Romano, which means, the truth is expressed only in Romani. In answer to your direct question however, Django will understand the Italian language, and uses that exclusively for his business affairs."

Pete felt that he had enough information to aid him when meeting with the King of the Gypsies but was curious how Captain Sollazzo knew so much about Gypsy culture and history if they are so secretive. "Captain Sollazzo, I am fascinated by your deep knowledge of Gypsies. How were you able learn so much about them?"

"It is true that Gypsy behavior is different than that of any other group of people. My Uncle Giorgio Frassineti fell in love and married a Gypsy fortune teller, a woman with the Gypsy name of Yojo. As a child, I would ask Yojo to tell me stories about her background. You may find it interesting to know that when she decided to marry my Uncle Giorgio, she was not only excommunicated from her Gypsy family tribe, but also feared for her life. Uncle Giorgio provided a security detail for an extended period."

Pete exhaled deeply. "Thank you, Captain Sollozzo, for the time you have granted me. I know you are a busy man, and I don't wish to take more of your time. I will call Mr. Kwiek immediately and hope to meet Mr. Mahai as soon as possible."

Although Pete had listened carefully to the long-drawn-out talk about Gypsies, he was conflicted about the usefulness of the information for his meeting with Django Mahai. Pete warmly shook Captain Sollazzo's hand and left his office.

CHAPTER 12

Daniel's father was searched for weapons, before being escorted into the building to meet the King of the Gypsies. The room was dimly lit, and a man was sitting at a small table under a naked light bulb hanging from a wire. The man was wearing a brightly colored, grease-stained suit with a striped shirt and a fedora that was equally stained. He motioned to Pete to sit in the chair opposite him. The Gypsy, Janui Kwiek, stood against the closed entrance door. Two other men stood at a side entrance.

Django Mahai, the King of the Gypsies, spoke first. "So Gadje, you paid for my time. What is it that you want from Django?"

Pete was very careful not to irritate Django Mahai. "Sir, Captain Sollazzo will be able to vouch for my honesty in this matter. I wish to cause no trouble for you or your people. All I want is my son—and I am willing to pay for his safe return."

Django Mahai looked at Pete with a blank facial expression, and then speaking Italian with a strange accent said, "Gadje, do you think you'd be brought to me if we thought, for one moment, you would bring harm to me or my people?"

Thinking he had said the wrong thing, Pete began to apologize. He assured the Gypsy leader he meant no insult, but Django quickly interrupted him. "Gadje, I have no time for your groveling. If you've lost a child, it's not my people who have taken him. You can be sure of this, because we would be most pleased to exchange your child for your lira."

Pete went numb, but recovered quickly enough to stammer, "Then other Gypsy people have my son. Please tell me of other Gypsies who might have him. I promise no harm to anyone. All I want is the safe return of my son."

Django's smile radiated confidence. "Gadje, if you were one of us, you would know better than to ask such a foolish question. Nothing happens in southern Italy that I don't order or know of." Django's posture eased and a smooth, sympathetic look took over his piercing eyes. "Mister, believe me when I say, whoever took your child, it was no Gypsy."

Django Mahai stood up and told his aide, Janui Kwiek, "Take this Gadje back to his pickup location. We have no further use of him."

Janui Kwiek grabbed the elbow of the stunned and shaken father, but Pete broke away from him and moved toward Django Mahai, continuing to plead for information. Django Mahai turned quickly, showing a long switchblade knife. The two men at the side door moved quickly to either side of the Gypsy king. Pete immediately stopped his advance. "Come forward if you want to feel my blade, Gadje," said Django. "If not, then leave as I have said. Now take him away."

Janui Kwiek and the two other men were having a great deal of difficulty dragging the powerful American toward the door. Losing all sense of submissiveness, Pete pulled his arm from Janui Kwiek and punched him. Then he slammed his free arm against the hand of the other man, sending his knife sliding across the stone floor. Having freed himself, he kicked the third man in the groin and quickly moved toward Django Mahai, screaming, "You dirty bastard! You have my son. Give him to me!"

Django was unprepared for the suddenly crazed Gadje. Pete's lightning attack enabled him to get both hands around Django Mahai's neck. Django was able to remove a knife from his belt scabbard and thrust the sharp blade into Pete's upper left arm. A startled Django managed to firmly hold onto his knife, which was now embedded in the arm of Daniel's father.

Although seriously cut, Pete continued to hold Django's neck, while screaming, "You're going to bring me to my son. I won't leave without him. Do you hear me? I want my child, now!"

The three other Gypsies recovered and pulled Pete away from Django. With Django still holding the knife handle and Pete being pulled away from Django, the blade slid out of Pete's arm, slashing more bloody tissue and skin. Pete screamed as the sharp metal ruptured more skin, causing excruciating pain. He went limp for a few moments, but then quickly recovered by ferociously kicking his legs, trying to free himself while being dragged backward. Janui Kwiek had his left arm around Pete's neck and his knife poised above Pete's chest. He asked the Gypsy King, "Shall I end this Gadje's life with my knife in his heart?

"No!" said Django. "I thought this Gadje was another slobbering coward, but he surprised me with his courage. He is a fearless one. Let him live for now, but do not let this man's courage blind you. He may be a warrior, but he is a Gadje warrior, and is still our enemy, so do not bandage his wound. If he is truly as brave as he appears, he will survive. Out of respect for his courage, let him die on his own terms. Gypsies do not needlessly kill warriors. Either way, he is no longer a threat to us. Take him away and return him as I have said, dump him away from here and come back quickly so we may return to our home."

Pete stopped struggling when the tip of a sharp knife broke the skin on his back. "One more sound, Gadje, and this knife will cut you—this time into your chest," said Janui Kwiek.

The Gypsies dragged Pete to the car and thrust him into the rear seat between two men, who were each holding exposed knife blades. They handed Pete a rag and told him to hold it over his wound because they did not want his blood on their clothes or on their car's upholstery.

Pete Ciarletta finally knew his battle was over, and as the car moved swiftly through this dirty run-down area, all he could think was, what am I to do now?

The car came to a stop, Pete was dragged from the rear seat, and left in the middle of the road, as the car sped off. Pete dragged himself to the brick wall of a deserted building and sat against a wall. He made a tourniquet for his upper arm, using his pants belt. The bleeding quickly stopped. He stood, placed his coat over his shoulders, and moved to an intersection, with cars speeding in all four directions. He struggled to the center of the intersection, not paying attention to car horns or near brushes with cars suddenly swerving and braking. He placed himself under the intersection stoplight and waved his good arm at the cars that had stopped for the red light. After a short period, he was welcomed into a small car, and asked the driver to drop him off in an area where he could summon a taxi. He was able to find his way back to Castellammare de Stabia by two in the morning. Pete banged on the door of his parents' bedroom, awakening them.

Francesca, upon seeing the wound, immediately got dressed and went to fetch a local man to stitch Pete's wound. Meanwhile Leopoldo covered Pete with as many blankets as he could find to keep him warm. He poured a large glass of whisky for his son and began to clean the wound with his one usable hand.

CHAPTER 13

After his cut was stitched, cleaned, and bandaged, Pete explained the series of events that had taken place over the past several days. Totally exhausted, he allowed the alcohol to dull his pain and quickly went to sleep. He slept through the day and into the early evening. Upon waking he was given a hearty meal and rested the remainder of the evening. By sun-up, a wounded Pete told his father what had happened.

The next day, they went together to see Captain Sollozzo and explained what had happened.

"You were very fortunate to have had your life spared by the Gypsies, I can assure you that if Django was not willing to make a deal for your son, you can be sure the Gypsies did not kidnap him. We will now have to make your son's case a priority. I assume you will be remaining in Italy for the near future?" Pete indicated that he would be staying with his parents in Castellammare di Stabia. Captain Sollozzo then instructed Pete to leave his contact information with the sergeant at the front desk. "We will need to be able to speak with you frequently, and perhaps even call you to come to the station."

Pete thanked the captain and asked him to recommend the best private detective agency in Naples. The following day, he met with the head of the detective agency. A fee was negotiated for a two-month period. Pete called

Suzy, explained the events of the meeting with the King of the Gypsies, leaving out the fact that he had been wounded. After a series of questions from Suzy, she inquired what was being done to find her son. Pete was about to finish the phone call with directions for his wife, he remembered one other thing. "Suzy, make sure that Danny delays his arrangements for the ransom loan, and immediately wire me four hundred dollars which I will need to pay the detective agency fee."

CHAPTER 14

Daniel noticed his captor had brought a metal cup of what looked like coffee and a roll on a plate. His captor now lowered his voice and spoke more slowly, as though that might help Daniel understand what he was saying. He kept pointing to the plate still holding the food from last evening. Daniel surmised that his captor was upset at something to do with the uneaten food. He used the word bottino, which Daniel thought meant bad food.

Daniel wondered if the man was angry because he had not eaten the food, or whether he was upset because the food had spoiled. The man picked up the dinner plate and cup, and once again began speaking in Italian and pointing at the plate with the roll. Daniel understood he was being told to eat what he had been given this morning. Daniel's appetite was now stronger than his desire to be defiant, and he gladly ate the roll and drank the espresso. Having been in Italy for three weeks, Daniel was becoming accustomed to espresso. It did not seem as bitter as it had the first time, he tried it at Nonno's house.

Daniel remained alone in the room for the rest of the morning. He was pleased that he had correctly memorized the road signs, the information about the car, and the word Opi. The morning went by slowly. He appreciated the warmth provided by the wood-burning stove. Daniel was surprised that the man didn't return for what became a full day alone in his room.

That evening, his captor again brought food and left it while ignoring Daniel. The following morning Daniel decided that resistance was not helping. If I stop yelling at him and try making myself understood, he might tell me why he has taken me and when he is going to release me.

Daniel knew a few Italian words and gestures, and he hoped that the man might know some English words. Maybe I could make him tell me why I was brought to Opi, and then hopefully the man will tell me when my father was coming to take me home to the Bronx.

Vincenzo spoke of the problem caused by the language barrier during dinner with his wife and two daughters. "It's hard to tell someone what you want them to do without the use of words. I correct the boy or yell at him in the only language I know, but we do not understand each other. What else can I do?"

Gelsomina, Vincenzo's wife, tried to reassure her husband. "Like many other things, it will take time," she said. Vincenzo was not consoled by her words. He continued as though his wife had not spoken. "This business of a foreign language was not given enough thought during our planning. I must find a way to make it clear to the boy, without using words, that I am the one in control. I don't like to be this way, but he must learn to fear me if this is going to work.

I know that in time, he will learn escape is useless, but until he learns our language, I'm forced to treat him as I would a new horse, accepting a saddle. I must be strict and firm, and never smile. I don't like to be feared, but if he has no fear, he will continue to challenge me. I see no other way. Perhaps when he learns Italian, this problem will pass." The following morning, Daniel's captor came to his room for breakfast and motioned Daniel to get out of bed. After throwing Daniel's work clothes on the bed, he left the room. When Daniel tried getting out of bed, he could hardly move. Every part of his body was stiff and aching. When he finished his coffee and roll, he began dressing, his sore muscles and limbs moved awkwardly, as he bent his throbbing joints and muscles, putting on the cloths Vincenzo left on the bed. Soon both captor and victim were in the wagon returning to the valley.

CHAPTER 15

The farmer caught up to Daniel, yelled a command to the horse, and pulled on the reins. Daniel's immediate thought, *here we go again, he's gonna start yelling in Italian and I'll have no idea what the jerk is saying.* Much to Daniel's surprise, the man talked calmly and even had what seemed to be a little grin on his lips.

The farmer talked to the boy, even though he knew the boy did not understand a word he was saying. He proceeded to reposition Daniel's hands and made him understand by his demonstration how he had to lean forward so the plow blade would penetrate the soil. He positioned Daniel's elbows away from his body, pushed his shoulders forward, and started the horse moving forward. Daniel was still quite clumsy but soon the plow was digging into the dirt layer of the soil and moving smoothly. The plowing was going quite well by mid-morning, and a large area of dirt and manure had been tilled. Daniel worked the land that had previously been planted, and the man plowed the pasture area, which had been covered with grass. When the church bells rang, their work stopped, and both farmer and captive went to the rest area to eat as they had the day before.

Daniel decided it was time to run, and he positioned himself next to a few rocks. He could easily hide a rock in his hand next to his leg when he stood up. Daniel would wait until after they had eaten when his captor would be more relaxed, probably smoking a cigar as he had done the day before. Daniel finished his midday meal, and then sat upright with his arms clasped around his knees. The farmer began to smoke his cigar. Daniel sat looking at the mountains, becoming more nervous with every passing minute. He kept telling himself to relax and not to rush. He would just move slowly and act as casually as possible. He was concerned he might not knock his captor out with a single blow, so he reminded himself to hit the man hard. Then Daniel had a horrible thought. *What if I hit him so hard that I kill him? Daniel had never considered this possibility.* He whispered to himself, Oh God, please don't let me kill this guy. The thought made him very uneasy. After a brief period, he told himself, the longer I wait, the worse it's gonna get. It's now or never.

Daniel casually scooped the rock into his right hand, remained still for a few moments, and then stood up a few feet from his captor with the rock pressed against his leg, hidden from view. Daniel pretended to stretch and bend as though he were stiff, still looking at the mountains and trying to be as casual as possible. His legs felt as though they were trembling, but when he looked down, they did not seem to be moving. He told himself to be calm, but it didn't help. *I must do it now*, thought Daniel. He was sure his captor would never expect such a brazen move after his crying scene in the car.

Continuing to look at the mountains while his captor sat against a tree, Daniel slowly inched closer to the man as he continued his pretend limbering. He dared not move too close for fear his captor would become suspicious. Daniel hesitated a moment, he had never felt as nervous as he now was. This is it, he thought. Do it now. His plan was to lunge toward the man the moment he was able to see him out of the corner of his eyes. He made his slow turning move. He saw the legs of his captor out of the corner of his eye and lunged forward with the rock in his hand above his head. The farmer, who was now up on one knee, was not surprised to see his young captive coming toward him. As Daniel's hand lunged toward the man's head, the farmer's powerful hand grasped the lower part of Daniel's arm and twisted it. The rock fell to the ground. The farmer pushed Daniel to the ground, yelling incoherently in Italian. Daniel, expecting his captor to retaliate by hitting him, tried immediately to get to his feet to defend himself. By the time Daniel got up on one knee, the man was pressing down on Daniel's shoulders. Daniel did not have the strength to rise from his knee, experiencing for the first time the strength of the farmer. The man did not physically strike Daniel, he only spoke quickly in Italian and appeared to be quite agitated.

The man soon calmed down and Daniel did as well. His captor moved away, attempting to locate his cigar. With cigar in hand, he moved to the side of one of the shacks, farther away from his captive so Daniel would be unable to reach him a second time, being tethered to the anchored rope. As Vincenzo drew some smoke from his cigar, he stopped mumbling. Daniel tried to remain confident after the escape attempt by quietly repeating to himself, "Don't lose hope. There will be other chances to run. He can't hold me forever."

That afternoon, the farmer and the boy continued plowing the previously planted field as well as the grassy pasture area. The freshly plowed soil was now at least eight to ten times the size of the smaller planted area. At the end of the day Vincenzo and Daniel arrived at the cobble stone road and Vincenzo escorted Daniel to his room. Before locking the black animal gate, he took a piece of paper from his pocket and read English words, *tomorrow morning no work in the valley, after food we will work in the valley.* Daniel stayed warm and rested.

Vincenzo used the morning to discuss Daniel with six other farm managers who also had young foreign men captive. Do the boys make numerous attempts to escape from our town? Yes, they do. Do the boys speak Italian? No, they don't. I'm afraid that we should have talked about these things during our planning and found the best way to learn how to correct these annoying problems, we never considered how best handle things, we all thought we would face these problems by treating our boys with kindness. Let's spend the rest of the morning discussing ways to smooth our relationships and solve these problems.

CHAPTER 16

The farm managers all agreed to begin to deal with these problems. They spent the next three hours sharing new ideas to make their life easier between them and their young helpers. The farm managers now had new ideas that might help their relations with the seven captives. Each Opi farmer returned to their homes ready for something new with their helpers. In the afternoon, Daniel and Vincenzo began raking the soil and breaking clumps of plowed soil and raking the surface area. Daniel no longer expected his father any time soon. Daniel was mentally preparing himself to escape the first time the situation presented itself. Daniel was confident, because of the nature of his work while in the valley. There were times when he would not be bound. Perhaps, escaping was not going to be as difficult as he had expected when he first arrived in Opi.

As Daniel thought about his next escape attempt, he decided it should be from the road out of the farms and or maybe to the forest. It all depended on where Vincenzo was working when he was unrestrained. He reminded himself, *I must remain alert when in the valley, and notice when Vincenzo is far enough away from me so I can have a good head start to either area.*

The church bells rang at midday and Vincenzo stopped working. Daniel expected to be brought to the stake and shackled as before, but instead

Vincenzo moved Daniel to the bed of the wagon and did not secure him to the wagon. As Daniel was having a bite to eat his eyes were directed to the mountain range on one side of the town. Daniel was now able to admire the beautiful scenery that surrounds this high rock structure, with a town at the top. I'm gonna try my best to escape from this scenic area, depending on when I am not bound to a piece of farm equipment. As it turned out, this was the afternoon that Daniel had been bound to some piece of farm equipment; but tonight, rather than taking Daniel to his room in the lower part of the house. where he was being held, Vincenzo guided Daniel up the rear stairs to the second floor. They entered a room like Daniel's grandparents dining room, and in addition to Daniel and his captor, there were three women, two women preparing food, one older than the other, and a third women placing dishes and utensils on a table.

The older woman, with a warm, gracious smile, moved toward Daniel. She touched his arm and said, while patting her chest, "Sono (I am) Gelsomina Sgammotta." Still holding the boy's arm, she moved him a step toward his captor. Holding out her hand toward the farmer, she said, "Questo è (this is) Vincenzo Sgammotta. Vincenzo's scowl remained. Gelsomina turned to Daniel so that he was now facing the two young girls. Gelsomina pointed to one of the girls and said, "Questa è Maria Antonia Sgammotta." Then she introduced the other girl, "Questa è Angelina Sgammotta." Maria Antonia smiled warmly; Angelina's face showed no emotion. She continued examining Daniel with cold eyes as she placed the last glass on the table.

Gelsomina was a short, thin woman with an attractive, round face that appeared worn by the fatigue of hard physical labor. She looked older than Vincenzo, Daniel assumed she was Vincenzo's wife. Her voice had a sad quality, even though she seemed happy. She wore a simple black dress that went to her ankles. Her brown hair was combed back into an intricate, round bun.

Maria Antonia was an attractive, personable teenage girl. Her facial features were like her father's. She had the same color skin except her skin was smooth and appealing. Her thin nose made her look stately, and her long light brown hair was tied back. Her build was like Gelsomina's, short and thin.

Angelina looked older than Maria Antonia, she was tall and hefty, and did not look like either Gelsomina or Vincenzo. She had an elongated face and long, brown hair that cascaded over her shoulders and down her back. She was an attractive woman, but looked more cautious and guarded than Maria Antonia, who Daniel assumed was her sister.

After this brief introduction, Gelsomina took Daniel by the arm and brought him to a room past the dining area, which had a sink, toilet, and what looked like a metal washing tub that was built so a person had to sit in it rather than stretch out. Gelsomina gestured for Daniel to wash at the sink and then closed the door. *This must be Vincenzo's family,* thought Daniel. I wonder why he brought me to his home.

After washing and drying himself with a thin towel, he returned to the dining room. The two girls, Maria Antonia, and Angelina were carrying food to the table. Gelsomina was seated at the dinner table and motioned for Daniel to sit next to her. Vincenzo was nowhere to be seen, and for a moment Daniel thought about running for the door, hoping it would be open. He heard someone coming down a flight of stairs. It must be Vincenzo. Daniel quickly decided against a run for the door and followed Gelsomina's invitation. After everyone was seated, Vincenzo made the sign of the cross and said a brief prayer. Platters of food were first passed to Vincenzo, who filled his plate and passed the platters by way of the girls to Gelsomina, who, after taking her food, passed the platters to the younger girls and finally to Daniel.

The food was delicious. A brisk conversation took place throughout the meal. The kidnapped boy did not understand what was being said, nor did the family attempt to include him in their conversation. Eating in this room and the friendly reaction of the women was unexpected but pleasant. Except for the lack of verbal interaction, they seemed to be treating Daniel like a guest rather than a hostage. Daniel wondered. *What if the women don't know Vincenzo kidnapped me? Maybe this guy told them he hired me to help him, and they think he's letting me live downstairs.*

The meal ended with a delicious dessert, and the women began clearing the table. Vincenzo took Daniel to a small sitting room with a sofa and two upholstered chairs. As he made his way to the sofa and began to smoke a cigar, he motioned for Daniel to sit in one of the chairs. They sat silently for more than an hour. Daniel no longer heard the rattle of dishes and pots coming from the kitchen. The house was quiet. He could not imagine why he was spending the evening in Vincenzo's house just one day after he had tried to escape. *It's as though I'm being rewarded for something. It just doesn't make sense, but maybe, being in his house, might be his way of preventing me from escaping.*

With his mind no longer focused on escaping, he was now anticipating seeing his dad come through the door to take him home. Looking out the window from his chair, he could see the position of the sun in the sky was still early evening. Gelsomina arrived at the entrance to the sitting room with neatly folded clothes over her arm. She gestured to Daniel to come to her and took him to the bathroom where he had washed before lunch. She handed him a large thin towel, and pointed toward the round, deep, metal tub that was now filled with water. She made gestures indicating she wanted him to use the tub for bathing. She smiled at him, gently tapped his arm, and left the room. Daniel heard the door lock. He put his hand in the tub of water, it was warm. Not having had the opportunity to shower or bathe since being brought to Opi, Daniel gladly took off his clothes and stepped into the metal tub.

Now he was positive he was going to be released. As he washed, he relished this time in the water, thinking of his family and friends, and how good it would be to see them once again. Much soapy warm water was still in the tub. He stayed in the warm tub bathing, relaxing, and listening for more activity beyond the door. Daniel came out of the bathroom clean and with different clothes on and Vincenzo led Daniel outside and down the front steps. Daniel pleaded with Vincenzo, "Father, Father."

Vincenzo again did not bother to respond. Daniel looked up and down the cobblestone street, but he was nowhere to be seen. Vincenzo brought Daniel to the lower room, unlocked the blue wooden door, and pushed Daniel into the room, locking the door behind him. Daniel did not know what to make of this day, and told himself, *No I'm not gonna let this bother me, dad will be here, look I have these nice clothes, I'm clean, why else would they do this for me, if it didn't mean Dad is coming. He'll be here soon; just be patient.*

CHAPTER 17

In the early evening, the door of the animal stable opened, and Daniel's spirits jumped. He moved toward the door, yelling, "Dad, Dad!" But it was only Vincenzo with a light meal. Daniel asked him once again, "Father mio? Father mio?" Vincenzo, now completely frustrated, looked up at the ceiling and said, "Statte zitte, nu parle semp'a papa." (Please stop asking about your father) Vincenzo slammed the plates on the table, gave Daniel an irritated look, and again said, "No Papa!" He turned and left the room.

Daniel's spirits sank lower and lower with each passing minute. Where was his father, why had he not come and taken him away from this place? What was the purpose of this afternoon? Daniel sat in front of the wood-burning stove, stubbornly anticipating the unlocking of the front door and his father's arrival. Eventually, he fell asleep with moist, sad eyes.

The following morning, the opening of the back door of the basement awakened Daniel from his sleep. He jumped up from the bed, still hoping to see his father. Again, it was only Vincenzo with a roll and espresso. He placed the food on the table and left the room without saying a word. While eating his breakfast, Daniel thought only of his dad coming for him. Why else would Vincenzo's wife have given me the clean clothes if my father was not coming this morning? Daniel rinsed his face with cold water, tucked his shirt into his trousers, and waited, still confident that his father would be here any minute.

Suddenly he heard the front door being unlocked. He jumped up and yelled, "Dad, Dad, I'm here!" But again, it was only Vincenzo. He was not dressed in his work clothes, but rather had on a clean white shirt, neat pants, and a jacket. He motioned for Daniel to get his jacket and come with him. Daniel grabbed his jacket from the wall rack and moved quickly to the door, still expecting to see his father. Vincenzo held Daniel's arm tightly and closed the door behind him. Daniel's father was nowhere to be seen—only Gelsomina, Maria Antonia, and Angelina standing by the door on the narrow sidewalk. Daniel resisted, as he was being moved in the direction of the church. The Sgammotta family acted as though he was a confused little boy, ignoring his insistent demands to move down the road away from the church and out of town. Vincenzo continued to forcibly move Daniel forward. Although he was angry and frustrated, Daniel eventually stopped resisting. He was about to cry, but he somehow held back his tears.

A dejected, Daniel was walking next to Vincenzo. Gelsomina and the girls were happily greeting others as the family proceeded towards the church. Daniel started yelling, "parla inglese?" (Do you speak English?) The people continued walking, paying no attention to Daniel or his question. He pleaded, "aiuto mio! (help me!)" To everyone that passed him, but not no one responded to his plea for help. Surprisingly, Vincenzo made no attempt to muzzle his captive, nor did he seem to care that Daniel was trying to communicate with others.

The family stopped on the church's front steps, where many people were gathered. Daniel once again tried to get their attention, but no one acknowledged his pleas or even looked at him. Daniel and the women were led into the church by Vincenzo and sat in a pew, while Vincenzo remained in the doorway of the church. Daniel looked around to see if there were any other doors he might be able to reach before Vincenzo could stop him, but there was only the main entrance and another small side door, which was located between Daniel and Vincenzo.

CHAPTER 18

Daniel noticed people in the back of the church standing in line waiting to go to confession.: *He would pretend he was going to confession, and when he got into the confessional, he would tell the priest he had been kidnapped. Priests are educated, Daniel reasoned. Let's hope this priest speaks English. If so, I will tell him he had been kidnapped, and the priest would help him. Even if he only knows a few words of English, I'll bet I can make him understand me.* His only fear was that Vincenzo might prevent him from going to the confessional box.

Daniel motioned to Gelsomina, indicating he wanted to go to confession. She understood, and under the watchful eye of Vincenzo, he moved to the confessional line. Vincenzo made no move to stop him, which made Daniel suspect that the priest did not speak English. He decided to stay in line, hoping he could somehow get the priest to understand he had been kidnapped. Finally, it was his turn. He entered the small cubicle and knelt. Soon a small panel slid open, and the priest blessed him.

Daniel whispered, "I am an Americano. Father, do you speak English?" The priest replied, "Yes, my son."

Thank God, thought Daniel. He whispered again to the priest, "A man from this town kidnapped me I need your help. Call the police; have them come and arrest him. His name is Vincenzo Sgammotta, you probably know him." There was a moment of silence. "Father, do you understand what I'm saying?"

Father Mascia answered, "Yes, my son, I understand everything you have said."

Daniel's heart was now pounding with excitement. "Father, be careful. He's standing at the entrance to the church. I'll be sitting with his family by the side door."

The priest answered after a pause "My son, there are things that might be very difficult for you to understand this day. You must trust me when I say that in time you will take a great deal of pride in the loving assistance you will impart to the people of Opi."

Oh no! He doesn't understand what I am saying. "No, Father, please, try to understand, I really am being held as a captured person. Daniel repeated himself, this time more slowly and deliberately. "I am an Americano, and I have been taken from my papa. I'm what you call a hostage. Uh..., you know, taken against my will, do you understand? Father, please, try to understand. I'm a prisoner and you are the only one who can help me. You gotta bring the police so I can go home! You must understand."

"I assure you, my son, I understand what you are saying," replied the priest matter-of-factly. I speak English well. It is you who must understand, your presence in Opi was destined. Fear not my son, God will bless you all your life for your presence in our humble town."

"Do not be concerned, you are a welcomed member of the Sgammotta family. We will talk often while you are here," said the priest.

"You will someday come to love your new home. Do you wish to confess your sins?"

Daniel persisted, "Father, how can I make you understand? I was taken from my father about nine days ago. I am a prisoner in house number 25."

Daniel was struck silent. Eventually the priest covered the screen with the sliding panel. Daniel continued to plead, "Father, Father," but he could hear the priest already blessing the person on the other side of the confessional. Daniel knelt there for what seemed like forever, paralyzed in the barren cubicle, until another person moved the outer curtain and gestured for him to leave.

The confessional booth was in the back of the church under the choir loft, to the left of the front entrance. Daniel moved in a daze past Vincenzo and down the center aisle with wooden pews on either side. He climbed over two people and sat next to Gelsomina. He stared at the raised stone altar, which had burning candles at each end. The top of the altar was covered by a starched white cloth. Behind the priest was a raised platform, on this platform was the shiny, metal tabernacle that held the paper-thin wafers that would be consecrated and distributed during Mass. Behind the tabernacle was a large wooden cross with the figure of Jesus nailed to it. There were two statues on either side of the altar: a statue of San Giovanni Battista and one of Mary, the mother of Jesus.

Daniel remained seated in his trance-like state for a long period, trying to understand what had just happened in the confessional. Nothing makes any sense since I've been brought to this hell hole. Daniel's thoughts were interrupted by the ringing of bells, he looked up and saw the priest he had spoken to in the confessional box enter the church. He was dressed in a green, sleeveless chasuble, holding a chalice, which was covered by a square white top. He was hopelessly confused. Could it be the whole town is part of a plot to keep me captive? That can't be! Why would other people be involved with this bully Vincenzo?

About twenty minutes later, the ringing of bells jarred him out of his mental haze. It was then that Daniel noticed the statue of the Blessed Mother to the right of the altar. Suddenly he remembered, during these past nine days, I have completely forgotten about prayer. How disappointed Mary and God must be in me, for forgetting to pray. Daniel began a simple prayer, *"God and Mary, please forgive me for forgetting to pray, but I've never been this scared in my life.* During the remainder of the Mass Daniel prayed to Mary to help him in this, the greatest crisis of his young life. Daniel had learned his special devotion to the Blessed Mother from the example of his mother and his Aunt Kate. When the Mass concluded, he followed Gelsomina and her daughters out of the church. Many people stood on the steps, engaging in conversation in the bright morning sun. He was standing near Vincenzo and his family, who seemed to be more interested in conversing with others than in watching him.

Daniel noticed that the houses surrounding the church were not attached. To his left he noticed a narrow alley between two houses, at the end of the alley was a low stone wall. Beyond the wall was freedom. If he was able to reach the stone wall, he could easily jump over it and run down the mountain and out of the town. Daniel slowly moved a half-step away from Vincenzo in the direction of the alley and stopped. Vincenzo didn't seem to notice. Daniel slowly started to inch his way in the direction of the alley. He stopped again, now pretending he was looking at the church and its bell tower. He was trying to see how far he could separate himself from Vincenzo without alerting him. Vincenzo was still engrossed in conversation, and Daniel had successfully moved about three feet from his captor. The beginning of the alley was approximately twenty yards away. Daniel felt he could easily reach the stone wall, and vault over it, before Vincenzo could stop him. The element of surprise was on his side.

After a few seconds, Daniel decided to do it. He took a deep breath and bolted for the alley, running as fast as he could. Almost immediately, he was at the entrance to the alley, with the open hill only yards away. His heart was pounding and his adrenalin flowing. *This is it; I am going to make it.* At the low stone wall, at the end of the alley, he hesitated, as he placed both hands on the top of the low wall and began his leap over the stone barrier. With one leg in the air, he saw the area beyond the stone wall was a sheer, straight drop hundreds of feet to the ground. He halted his forward momentum by dragging his back leg while maintaining a tight grip on the top of the wall.

Now able to straddle the stone wall, one leg in the alley, and the other on the mountain side of the wall, Daniel boosted himself backwards onto the flat gravel alley. The back of the two houses on either side of the alley were built only feet from the retaining wall. Sitting with his back against the low stone wall, Daniel began to catch his breath, thankful he was able to maintain his grip on the top of the wall, preventing a fall that would have surely ended his life. As he was inspecting the cuts and bruises on one leg and both hands, he was interrupted by an angry Vincenzo, who was lifting his captive with his arms. Vincenzo began forcing Daniel to look out over the wall, turning his head to the left and then to the right, so he could see the vertical face of the precipice. Continuing the tight grip of his captive, Vincenzo pushed him back up the alley between the houses.

Daniel was upset at yet another missed opportunity to escape, and he jerked his arm out of Vincenzo's hand and shouted, "Stop pushing me!" Vincenzo was unable to understand Daniel's words, but he clearly comprehended the meaning of his emotions. He glared at Daniel, grasped his arm once again, and somewhat more gently led him out of the alley. The people on the church steps were now looking at Daniel. He mused gloomily, well whadd'ya you know; now they decide to look at me.

Vincenzo moved Daniel past the front of the church and continued to the other side of the road, walking into an alley between two houses. This side of the town had a dirt road on the edge of the precipice with a high mesh wire fence. Vincenzo once again made Daniel look right and then left. This side was also a sheer drop. Vincenzo, still talking rapidly in Italian, marched Daniel out of the alley, and began walking Daniel down the main cobblestone road, past the house where he had been keeping Daniel captive. They arrived at the point in the cobblestone road where it bent sharply to the right, gradually descending the dirt road to the pasture and farm area.

At this bend in the road, Daniel saw two older men in a small two-seated, horse-drawn wagon. Directly behind them was the dirt road into the valley. Daniel had seen men sitting in a wagon on the three days Vincenzo had taken him to the pasture area but had thought nothing of it. Vincenzo, still talking in Italian, pointed to the men in the wagon and then back at Daniel, and then he pointed to the dirt road leading to the pasture. As Vincenzo was talking, the two men in the wagon raised their rifles and placed the butt handle of their weapons on their thighs. Daniel quickly grasped the meaning of Vincenzo's gestures. The two men were stationed on the road was to ensure that Daniel could not escape from the only road leading out of town. Vincenzo marched Daniel back toward the beginning of the town, stopped in front of the blue door with number 25 over it. He pushed Daniel into the lower room and locked the door.

Daniel sat in front of the wood stove, angry with Vincenzo, Opi, the people, and the priest. He reviewed in his mind how the priest had responded to him in the confessional. He spoke English, and I asked him twice if he understood what I was saying. He said, "Yes, my son, I have told you I speak English." With a confused frown on his face, Daniel thought, *if he understood English, why did he refuse to help me?*

Daniel thought about the other things the priest had said. People will appreciate my charity, I'll feel proud. Your kidnapping was destined? God will bless you all your life. You'll come to love Opi? What's wrong with that priest? Nothing makes any sense. From the way he talked, you'd think he knew I was a prisoner. It sounded like Vincenzo said something to him about kidnapping me. Daniel then spoke out loud, as though to firmly disagree with his own conclusion, "But that's crazy. Why would the guy kidnap me and then tell the town priest? That's just too weird."

CHAPTER 19

In 1937 a young devout man by the name of Giordania Mascia was ordained a Catholic priest after his studies at San Giovanni Evangelista the seaside palatial seminary in Giuilianova Italy. The building and the carefully tended grounds had been deeded to the Italian Catholic Church by a wealthy Italian citizen in 1901. Giordania Mascia entered the seminary in Giuilianova at sixteen years of age, he was ordained eight years later, and assigned to his first parish in the town of Opi. The twenty-four-year-old priest replaced Father Giancarlo Fabrizio who recently passed away at the age of seventy-eight, after serving as the religious leader of Opi for thirty-one years.

Initially, the young priest, due to his age, had a great deal of difficulty being accepted as a religious leader. The older Father Fabrizio's long service to the Opi people remained a ghostly presence that Father Mascia found difficult to tear down. The young Father Mascia refused to become discouraged at the cool reception he received from his parishioners. He accepted his challenge by visiting each family in Opi, learning their history, values, and expectations. He was careful to perform his priestly duties with compassion, understanding and in a devout pious manner. Unlike Father Fabrizio, Father Mascia was a physically active young man, who believed in becoming involved in the activities of his people. He worked with the men caring for their sheep. He made it a point to be present when baby animals were born so he could assist and then bless the new animal. He was especially attentive to Opi women, comforting them during child labor, leaving the room during the actual birth, understanding of the mother's need for privacy, and then blessing each new boy or girl. Soon after the birth, he would baptize each child with water, and then place a newly made, plain white, miniature, garment, over the head of the newborn child. This baptismal garment symbolizing the purity of each child, became a treasured gift for parents.

He quickly learned to be attentive to the difficulties of the aged and afflicted. In two short years he had endeared himself to the people of Opi, and at the young age of twenty-seven he became a respected religious leader.

During his time in Opi he declined opportunities to attend retreats with his fellow priests, choosing to remain in Opi, unwilling to leave the people without a cleric to lead Mass, hear confessions and attend to the needs of his people. He chooses to ignore his personal and spiritual growth. Then during World War II, he felt it was his duty to protect civilians caught in the middle of conflict. Father Mascia felt it was more important to protect his flock, than take advantage of the opportunities for him to grow as a person and a priest. By the end of World War II Father Mascia had become so isolated that he lost sight of the meaning of the priestly vows he had taken. He now believed that God had placed him in the mountain town of Opi to protect and sustain the people of this village.

Pete stayed in Castellammare di Stabia with his parents for five weeks, traveling to Naples twice weekly to receive updates from both the police and the private detective agency. He also had his bandage changed twice and eventually the stitches were removed by the same man who had put them in. Meanwhile, Nonno was so distraught by the news of his grandson's disappearance that he suffered a relapse and was ordered back to the hospital.

During their hospital visits, the conversation was always the same. "Pietro, it is my fault that Donato is missing. If I had not been selfish in wanting to see him, he would be safe at home in America." Neither Pete nor his mother Francesca was able to console Leopoldo.

Francesca and her daughters arranged a nine-week novena to Saint Jude, the patron saint of hopeless causes, with the pastor of their church. Each Tuesday evening for nine weeks the church was filled with women in black dresses. Father Michele (Michel) Petronio led the women in special prayers for the safe return of Donato Ciarletta. Donoto's cousins were concerned and confused about Daniel's disappearance. Ruffino was the most affected by the tragic occurrence. He and his cousins were told to say special prayers each night before going to bed for the safe return of their cousin.

At the end of the fourth week, with no promising leads, Captain Sollazzo suggested that it might be helpful to file a missing person's report in the City of Rome, just to make sure everything possible had been done. Pete agreed, and the following day he traveled to Rome and filed the report with the Roma police department.

He returned to Castellammare di Stabia, booked passage home to America, and said a second goodbye to his family in Italy. Pete designated Zio Rodolfo to be his contact person with the Naples and Roma police and the private detective agency. Pete knew it would be an insult to offer money to Rodolfo for his services, so he simply expressed his undying gratitude.

CHAPTER 20

When Pete entered the front door of his Beach Avenue home, his crying wife greeted him by pounding her fists on his chest screaming, "How could you let this happen? What kind of father are you? You're supposed to protect your children." Pete stood motionless until Suzy stopped her flailing, and then he held her until she stopped crying. Barbara, Frances, and Uncle Danny and Aunt Kate each took turns embracing Pete with warmth and sympathy. Kate held Pete's arm and said, "Pete, don't mind Suzy. She didn't mean what she said. She's been frantic since she got the news. We haven't left her side since you called. She has taken Daniel's disappearance very hard, and even Father Lewis couldn't help her."

Danny embraced his brother a second time and said, "My God, Pete, you look terrible, but it'll be okay now that you're home with us. Everyone knows how much you care for your children; this is no time to be blaming yourself." It was obvious by simply looking at Pete that he had been badly shaken by the disappearance of his son. He would repeat the same mantra-like theme to anyone who would listen. "I'm responsible. I was so careful to watch him during the trip. I was only a few feet from him when he was taken. I don't know how this could have happened." Like Susy, nothing and no could comfort him.

Lunch time arrived for Daniel on this confusing Sunday morning, attempting to understand. the confessional dialogue with the Opi priest. He began to suspect that ransom money may not be the reason for his kidnapping. As Danny thought about the events of this Sunday morning, he became more confused, *if I have not been kidnapped for ransom money, why am I here?* Daniel could only conclude that the morning events, meant the entire town knew he had been kidnapped, and approved of Vincenzo illegal actions, even the priest.

Daniel was also forced to reassess his ability to escape. It's impossible to escape from this town. My only option is to try an escape from the valley area. He would wait for his first chance to run to the forest at the end of the valley. Daniel reassured himself that Vincenzo would not be able to catch him. He would be forced to travel in the forest for quite a while. He would have to stay off the one road leading to and from Opi. He would become too visible walking alone on the road. Once in the forest Daniel planned on running to his right, finding an opening in the trees and hoping he could find a different road or another town that was large enough to have a police department. Daniel was now convinced of what had seemed implausible earlier: Vincenzo had captured him to work on his farm. Still, the strangest part was that other people in the town knew what Vincenzo had done, and their refusal to help meant they condoned his actions.

Later that afternoon, without consciously understanding his own thought process, he began to wonder if he had been too hard on himself regarding what he initially considered cowardly behavior when he was first captured. Sitting in front of the wood stove he began to think about what had happened to him. *I was just standing on the sidewalk and my father was a few feet away. Who would have thought someone would drive up in a car, pull me in, and speed away? Why am I blaming myself? I had followed my father's directions, and here I am, in this stupid town, being a farmer's helper.*

As he considered the past nine or ten days in Opi, alone and frightened, he thought, *I never imagined I'd become someone's prisoner. It's no wonder I got scared. I was just so surprised! Maybe being surprised is different than being a coward.*

Comfortable in front of the warm wood-burning stove, his reasoning process began to evolve from hopelessness to self-assurance. *If I am going to be successful in an escape attempt, I need to plan better and be brave. I'm a strong kid. I play lots of sports, I'm fast, that big Italian man will never be able to catch me, once I have a good head start to the forest.*

He was beginning to gain more confidence in his ability to escape. *Once I reach the police there'll contact my parents in America, and I know my dad will come and get me.* He seemed to be thinking more clearly. For the first time since being captured, he now was able to understand that his past actions were more theatrical than real. It was as though the only script he had to follow came from movies and mystery radio dramas. With this tiny glimpse of new understanding, he thought, *I was so sure my dad would somehow know I was being held in this stupid little town in the middle of nowhere, and he would blast his way into Opi, beat up Vincenzo, and take me back to Castellamare di Stabia. Oh boy, how dumb was that! Sure, that's how it's done in the movies and on the radio. O how I wish this was a movie—but this is no movie, this is for real.*

He then began to consider his "brilliant" detective work. *I was so proud of myself because I could remember the signs and the name of the car and, just like in the movies, I found a clever way to write the information on the wall. How could I have been so stupid?* His next thought would have been funny, except for the seriousness of his situation. *And that first night in this town, not eating the man's food, thinking I was getting back at Vincenzo by not eating his food. What was I thinking?*

He then thought back to the events of that first day in the valley. *I had convinced myself that I would not try to escape because my dad was going to come and get me, when really, I was scared and not sure what to do. I was more scared about what would happen if I did try to escape than about getting out of this place.*

Becoming more agitated, Daniel began to pace back and forth, talking out loud in the empty room, "Y'know, maybe I'm not such a creepy little kid. I guess when you don't know what's happening it can really give you the jitters. How many guys my age get kidnapped? Yeah, so what if I'm scared? Maybe that's Ok too. Maybe the way I've been acting since I've been here has not been so dumb. Maybe I had to experience all this to begin to understand it better."

Daniel was feeling more optimistic, as he paraded around the room with a new bounce in his step. In the past two hours of mental focus, Daniel had managed to become more accepting of his actions since being brought to Opi. He did not completely understand why his experiences suddenly became so clear. He thought, *perhaps it was the new routine over the past two days, being in Vincenzo's house, eating with the family, his wife being kind, a new set of decent clothes, and enjoying a hot bath. Or maybe it had to do with almost falling to my death over the stone wall.* Something had happened to spur this new positive attitude, and Daniel was grateful for whatever it was.

One thing that was now clear to Daniel: The entire town was conspiring to hold him prisoner. Once again, Daniel began talking out loud to the empty room, as though that would make the situation disappear. "But why would a family kidnap a kid just to work on their farm? Stealing a person to work seems so mean. People used to do this hundreds of years ago, but not today. If they had planned to use me to get money from my father, that I could understand, but kidnapping. becoming a slave? I didn't think that still happened. How can people in 1947 think they can get away with something like this, I mean even if this is a foreign country? Vincenzo and his family don't seem "wacko," but what they're doing is really crazy."

His afternoon of filtering information was surprisingly satisfying. It made him feel more mature. The exact number of days since his capture was no longer that important. He had been in Opi long enough to know that somebody should be able to tell him why he had been taken, and when he was going to be released.

This confusing day was now over. He placed a few logs in the wood-burning stove and adjusted the damper so the fire would burn slowly through the night. He slipped into bed under the covers, ready to sleep, but he lay there for over an hour tossing and turning, his mind churning with many questions. *Is it enough to just feel better? I feel great now, I hope I'm mature enough to have the courage to run to the forest. These new feelings… are they real or am I just fooling. myself, thinking that I'm more mature? I don't know, am I going nuts?* He sat up in bed and pushed the blankets down around his hips. He angrily spoke out loud, although there was no one there to listen, "Stop it. You're thinking crazy! What's with these stupid thoughts? Don't you feel good? Don't you feel like you've learned something today? Okay, so maybe you won't be Superman tomorrow, but you'll get stronger each day, and you watch, one of these days you'll escape!" He laid back and covered himself once again.

Daniel wished his parents and even Ruffino were with him. He would feel proud explaining to them that he had learned. His mother, who was always encouraging him to do better in school, would be especially proud of him. He was pleased that he had learned something new, by himself and without anyone's help. Yesterday, he had been depending on his father to come to Opi, to rescue him, and beat up Vincenzo, but now things seemed different, he couldn't identify what, but he felt different. It was as though he was no longer a child. Something was different. He seemed to understand that at least one aspect of his life had suddenly changed. He mumbled to himself, from now on it's all on my shoulders, I can't depend on the other people, the priest, my father, or anyone. No, it's just me. With these satisfying thoughts, the late hour, the warm stove, Daniel pulled the blankets up to his shoulders and soon he was sleeping.

CHAPTER 21

The next morning, Vincenzo brought Daniel his usual breakfast, along with the clean clothes he had been wearing when he was brought to Opi, and the work clothes he used last week. All had been washed. Vincenzo motioned for Daniel to dress in clean work clothes. Daniel had decided he would run to the woods at the base of this green valley, the first time he was unrestrained. When he dressed, he put on the shoes he had worn when he was kidnapped. He would be able to run faster in his shoes than in the rubber boots. He hoped Vincenzo wouldn't notice and make him change.

Shortly after Daniel had dressed, Vincenzo entered the room. He directed Daniel past the animals and motioned him to get into the rear of the wagon. Vincenzo took the reins and began to move the wagon without securing Daniel to the railing. Could Vincenzo have forgotten to tie me to the wagon? He might not have to escape to the forest if he remained unrestrained. Daniel decided to wait until the wagon arrived at the place where the town's descending road met the dirt valley road. Like last week, he was sitting in the back of the wagon with his feet dangling over the end. Now that he was not bound to the side of the wagon, he could simply slide off the wagon without Vincenzo noticing, hide in the brush until Vincenzo was down the road, and then run on the road away from the valley. Daniel's excitement level began to rise.

After passing the men stationed on the cobblestone road in the town, the wagon made a sharp right and began descending the dirt road to the valley. Daniel turned his head to determine the best place to slide quietly from the wagon and run. That's when he noticed two men with rifles in a horse-drawn wagon at the spot where the dirt road met the valley. Now he understood why he had not been tied to the wagon. The momentary excitement passed, and he resigned himself to his original plan. No problem, he said to himself. *I'll run to the forest the first chance I get.*

Vincenzo didn't make him change from his shoes to work boots. Daniel now felt excited. He thought *he'd never be able to catch me.*

When the wagon arrived at the plowed area, Vincenzo parked the wagon beside three wooden shacks next to the land they had worked on the previous week. He motioned Daniel into the smallest of the three buildings, which contained large baskets. He directed Daniel to carry one basket out of the wooden shack. Vincenzo followed Daniel carrying a basket. The containers were filled with dried, wrinkled green beans. The containers were marked piselli (peas). Vincenzo attached one of the horses to the farm device with the wooden handles and the metal blade.

Daniel was standing about ten feet from Vincenzo, unconstrained, he made his move. He began running as fast as he could toward the forest area at the base of the mountain. He was moving fast in his shoes, not bothering to look over his shoulder to see how close behind Vincenzo was. He just kept running. He must have run the length of a football field, yet he was still a good distance away from the forest and his freedom. Suddenly he heard the galloping of a horse behind him. *He's on a horse, I never thought of that.* Daniel continued running, as fast as he could. Suddenly, he felt something on his arms that was sharp and biting, bringing his arms against the sides of his body, forcing him to trip, fall, and tumble along the ground before coming to a stop. Although bruised and sore, arms and legs from the tripping, tumbling and then dragged a short distance. Daniel rose to his feet, looked up, and saw Vincenzo on a horse. He was holding a pole that had a wire loop attached at its end. The thin wire loop was now wrapped around Daniel's chest, as Vincenzo, still on the horse, forced a discouraged and hurting Daniel back to the shacks. When they arrived Vincenzo dismounted, still holding the wire attachment, he began rambling in Italian as he was removing the wire loop still around Daniel's arms and chest. Vincenzo continued his rambling as he moved his captive toward the horse-drawn farm device with wooden handles and a metal blade. Vincenzo bound Daniel's wrists tightly to the two handles. Vincenzo then snapped the reins on the back of the horse, and the animal began to move. As the horse moved the metal blade of the farm device, which made a narrow straight-line trench in the soil. Vincenzo, walking behind Daniel, dropped dried piselli in the newly made furrow. At their midday break, Vincenzo stayed alongside Daniel to avoid another escape attempt. They continued planting seeds for the rest of the day.

As the sun was getting low on the horizon, they stopped working and headed back to town. Vincenzo stopped the wagon at the bend in the dirt road leading to the village, where two men sat in a wagon holding rifles. He again spoke to Daniel in Italian, while pointing and gesturing to the two men. Vincenzo was able to make Daniel understand that these men were in place to prevent another escape attempts. When the wagon reached the cobblestone road in the mountain town, Daniel saw two other men in a small wagon in the center of the road. They were obviously stopping me from running down the narrow road, which ended at the green valley. Daniel suddenly realized *the men in the wagon with rifles are stopping me from escaping from the town.* Daniel was now aware that the town of Opi was sealed tight, Vincenzo was not acting alone; the entire town was working with him. Escape was not going to be as easy as Daniel had originally thought.

That evening, sitting in his room, Daniel reviewed his situation. Ransom would have been his best chance for release, but that no longer appeared to be an option. Escape from the town was impossible. His only way out of Opi would have to be from the valley farm area, when working with Vincenzo. He had to remain alert each time he was in the valley, his escape depended on being ready at the opportune moment. Daniel reminded himself of his new self-confidence. If these people think they can hold me here until all the crops are grown, they're mistaken. I'll find a way out, and when I do, my dad and I will bring the police back here to put this creep in jail.

CHAPTER 22

Saturday afternoons, Daniel was brought to the Sgammotta living quarters for his main meal, a rest period, and his weekly bath. And lately, Gelsomina encouraged Daniel to help her with the bread-making. On Sunday mornings after Mass, all the people of Opi spent a leisurely hour or so socializing, and Daniel was allowed to sit by himself away from Vincenzo. He was not even restricted from moving about freely. Vincenzo felt confident that Daniel understood there was no way for him to escape from the town proper. Daniel was limited in how far he could stroll, but the freedom to walk alone or sit in a specific area of the town even for this short period of time, was enjoyable.

After about six weeks of this new routine, Daniel noticed something strange about the population of Opi. There seemed to be the normal number of older men and women that might be expected to live in a town this size. There also seemed to be the normal middle-aged, and young women like Angelina and Maria Antonia. There did not seem to be many middle-aged men like Vincenzo, and even stranger, was the absence of any young men in their teens or twenties. He suspected all young men must be in the Italian army, or maybe they are away at college. Then one Sunday, he realized that there were quite a few girls his age, but he had only seen two boys his age. He concluded that boys his age are away at school, and Italian girls his age, do not have to go to school. The age make-up of the people who lived in Opi was quite peculiar. He never saw anyone use the soccer field across from the cemetery. There were no lines marked on the field and the rusty broken goals had no nets. Daniel expected that the young men and boys would return during the summer months. This was an interesting passing observation, but he had more things to worry about than the make-up of the people in his prison town. It was his plan to be far away from Opi when the boys and children came back to Opi from school.

Each Sunday after early morning Mass and socializing, Daniel and the Sgammotta family had a light breakfast in the upper apartment. He would remain in their apartment for Mass and the Sunday main meal and spent the remainder of the afternoon, alone in the upper apartment, simply relaxing. They often listened to the radio in the late afternoon. Daniel wished he could understand Italian; by now he was hungry for news from the outside world, even Italian news. He was surprised but very pleased that Vincenzo was allowing him this free, unrestricted time in their apartment, even though he was often bored due to the fact he spoke no Italian. Simply being in rooms with windows that let the sun in was in itself a pleasure. There was very little enjoyment during these months, but Sundays did offer Daniel a free day of no work, and the surprisingly pleasant family atmosphere.

Daniel decided if he was to find out why he had been brought to Opi, he was going to have to learn Italian. He figured that if he found out why he had been kidnapped, he would also find out when he would be set free. The only other person in Opi who spoke English was the priest. Daniel would often ask Father Mascia why he was being held in Opi, but the priest would only respond with general platitudes about Daniel's service to the people. Daniel began listening carefully to Vincenzo when they were working, and he made a point of repeating Italian words having to do with their farming tasks. Vincenzo seemed as interested in teaching Daniel Italian as Daniel was interested in learning. The Italian words used for communicating the farm chores came quite easily.

Daniel had tried to estimate how long he had been in Opi. It would soon be May and the air was still cool and crisp, which was usual for May in the mountains. One Saturday afternoon, Daniel was able to make Gelsomina understand that he wanted to learn Italian. Thereafter, when the dishes had been cleaned and stored, and prior to his bath he received Italian lessons in the dining room. Vincenzo was pleased at Daniel's eagerness to learn Italian. The more Italian Daniel knew the easier farm operations would be. Daniel's purpose, however, was not social or work-related, he was eager to hear about events outside of Opi from the radio, maybe even something about his incarceration, which he understood was very unlikely.

CHAPTER 23

It was time for the Ciarletta family to join Suzy's three sisters and their family on their fifth visit to the Franciscan Friars seminary grounds in Callicon, New York for a pleasant week away from New York City living. The five sisters Suzy, Kate, Margret, Grace, and Anna would bring their favorite Italian meals, which would be a special lunch for each day's visit.

She told her sisters that she was adamant in her desire to visit her son earlier this year. Pete had been dealt such a severe blow by the disappearance of his son and was brooding about the lack of information from Italy regarding Daniel. He questioned her change in plans. "Suzy, it's May. We usually go in the fall when we can pick apples." But he didn't have the energy or inclination to mount a counterargument to his wife's unusual request. He shrugged his shoulders and said, "Well if that's what you want, we'll go."

Suzy always enjoyed visiting Leopoldo, especially in the seminary's rural, tranquil setting. However, this trip was for another equally important reason: She wanted to meet with Father Benedict Dudley, the Provincial Director of the Franciscan Seminary in Callicoon. Father Dudley was an influential Franciscan priest with a powerful baritone voice and a dominating personality. He was the type of person who could draw everyone's attention simply by entering a room. He had been the pastor of the main Franciscan church at the order's headquarters on 33rd Street in New York City, Chaplain of the New York Giants professional Football team, and a very successful fundraiser for the Franciscans. Early in 1946, Father Dudley suffered a heart attack. In August 1946, he was assigned the post of Director at the Callicoon seminary in order to reduce his workload and expose him to the clean, fresh air of upstate New York. Suzy decided with her sisters and Pete's brothers to visit Leopoldo on the last Sunday in May. A caravan of seven 1930s black Buicks, Chryslers, and Chevrolets full of happy, rowdy aunts, uncles, and cousins arrived in Callicoon with their picnic feast. It was always a happy occasion not only for Leopoldo, but also for the other seminarians, and the friars.

Being Italian it was natural for the Ciarlettas and Gallos to believe the seminarians were underfed, and in a perpetual state of malnutrition, and this was their way of temporarily remedying this problem. Upon their arrival, blankets were spread on the front lawn of the seminary. Sterno cans were lit under large, aluminum, deep platters containing Suzy's lasagna verdi al forno (Baked Lasagne with a Bolognese Meat Sauce); Aunt Diane's Ravioli Verdi D'Agnello Alla Pesarese Col Sugo Di Peperoni Glalli (Green Ravioli Pesaro-Style stuffed with Lamb and Sauce with Yellow Peppers); Aunt Margaret's Gnocchi Verdi (Spinach and Ricotta Potato Gnocchi); and Aunt Gerasina's Calamari Ripieni (Stuffed Whole Squid, Braised with Onions, Tomatoes, Chili Pepper, and White Wine). Each dish was accompanied by prosciutto (spiced, smoked, cured ham), salami, cheese, crusty bread, red wine, and, finally, Aunt Kate's cream puffs and Aunt Grace's sfogliatelle desserts. The seminarians and friars waited all year for this Italian feast.

While the food was being warmed, Suzy spoke with her son in private. "Leopoldo, while I'm here, I need to speak with Father Dudley privately. I only need a few minutes of his time, but make sure you tell him it's extremely important that I see him today."

Leopoldo saw the urgency in his mother's expression and heard the deep desire in her voice. "I know he likes to stop by and greet parents whenever they visit," he told her. "So, I think he will see you, but since it is important, I'd better go to his office and check with Brother Tom, his secretary, and find out when he is available to see you. Mom, can I tell him what this is about?

Does it have anything to do with my studies here at the seminary?"

"Oh, no, my sweetheart," said Suzy. "It has nothing to do with you. I just want to talk to him about Daniel's disappearance."

Leopoldo hurried off to the main building, and when he returned to the picnic, the seminarians and friars were enjoying the food, and his young cousins were playing softball. Suzy saw Leopoldo approaching and hurried toward him.

"Father Dudley said he can see you now. I'll take you to his office." Suzy and her son walked across the open grass area to the main stone building, which was built in the style of Gothic architecture. They entered through large, elaborately carved oak doors and proceeded down a darkened hallway. The sound of their leather soles striking the stone floor echoed loudly. Leopoldo and Suzy entered the director's office. A friar typing at a small desk rose and welcomed them.

Suzy asked Brother Tom, "What are you doing here working when there is delicious food waiting for you outside? Go eat!"

Brother Tom assured her that when he finished the letter, he was typing he intended to join the picnic. He knocked on the clouded glass portion of the director's door, paused for a few moments, and then opened the door. "Go right in, Mrs. Ciarletta," he said. "Father Dudley is expecting you." As Leopoldo was leaving, Brother Tom told him, "I'll join everyone as soon as I finish this last letter. Make sure they don't eat all the lasagna, tell your family to put a portion aside, I should be there in fifteen minutes."

As Suzy entered the room, a large figure of a man in a dark brown monk's habit, with the traditional Franciscan capuche hood, attached to his garment and resting on his upper back, greeted her with a broad smile and shook her hand warmly. "Mrs. Ciarletta, I am so pleased to meet you.

Please sit down. Would you like Brother Tom to get you something cool to drink?"

"No, thank you, Father, or should I greet you as Director?" said Suzy, sitting stiffly in her chair. Father Dudley smiled, and said, "Father will be just fine. Mrs. Ciarletta, how may I be of assistance to you?"

Suzy was prepared, she had rehearsed what she was about to say numerous times. "My husband's father, who lives in Italy, became seriously ill last February. He requested my husband visit him and bring his grandson, my son Daniel. They were scheduled to land in Naples, and I asked him to buy me a Neapolitan Presepe nativity scene. I'm sure you know, the Presepe nativity can only be bought in Naples. My youngest son Daniel disappeared immediately after my husband had purchased the nativity set. I believe my son's disappearance is my punishment for being a sinful woman. Since I am the sinful one, I know God will not listen to my prayers. My only hope for my son's return is to ask you to have the friars and the seminarians pray for the safe return of my son Daniel."

Father Dudley looked lovingly at the odd expression on Suzy's face, which was a mixture. of hope and grief. "Mrs. Ciarletta, may I ask you a personal question?"

"Well, of course," said Suzy.

Father Dudley prefaced his question by saying, "Please understand, I will consider your answer to my question as though this was the sacrament of confession, which I am sure you understand binds me to silence about your response."

Suzy agreed. "I understand. Ask your question."

"Why do you believe you are a sinful woman?"

Suzy dropped her eyes, removed a tissue from her pocketbook, and held it in her hand. Raising her head and looking directly at Father Dudley, she said, "Since childhood, my mother instilled in me a special reverence and devotion to the Blessed Mother. I only prayed to the mother of Jesus, never praying to the Almighty Lord. Father, you know better than anyone, the Almighty talks to us through his divine messages. God's message to me is clear. Since I had chosen to ignore him in my prayers, and so that I would understand His displeasure, He had the disappearance of my youngest son take place immediately after the purchase of the Presepe nativity scene, which honors the birth of His son, Jesus. As you know, God has a way of making things obvious to sinners." I ignored his son in my prayers, and for that he has separated my son from me."

Suzy pressed the tissue to her nostrils and once again dropped her eyes.

"My dear, good woman, I have been a priest for twenty-eight years, and in all that time, my faith has grown for one reason and one reason only: I know that our Lord is a loving and forgiving all-merciful Father. He is not a God of vengeance who decides to punish people by taking away someone they love. Mrs. Ciarletta, you must drive this false thought from your mind."

Suzy used the tissue to wipe away her tears and then answered him in a low, trembling voice, "Father, I respect your learned views of religion, but that is not why I came to see you. I have come here today not to be consoled. I am here because I have the greatest respect for you as a powerful man of God. All I ask is that you grant my request to have your Franciscan Friars and the young men under your guidance pray for the return of my son Daniel. I beg you. Please say you will grant my request."

Father Dudley could hear the pain in her voice and realized she was not yet prepared to listen to his reasoning or to be consoled. "Mrs. Ciarletta, you have my priestly vow that I and every member of our Franciscan community here in Callicoon, will pray for the speedy and safe return of your son Daniel. I will also send out a notice this evening to our Franciscan prayer network around the world and request special prayers directly for your son."

Father Dudley assisted Suzy up from her knees and encouraged her to stay and discuss her son's disappearance.

"No, I have taken too much of your time already," she said. "You have honored me by your acceptance of my request. I will ask nothing further from you."

Father Dudley understood that the women before him was suffering great pain, and for this reason he thought it best to accept Suzy's request. He made a mental note to contact the pastor of Suzy's church alerting him of the discussion he had had with her.

CHAPTER 24

Daniel was not sure why, but he still clung to the notion that finding the reason for his captivity would somehow be useful. He had learned enough Italian from the Sgammotta family to hold brief conversations in Italian, and when he was able to make himself understood, he asked Vincenzo why he had been brought to Opi and when he would be allowed to leave.

Vincenzo's response never varied. "In time, it will all be explained." Daniel protested that his answer was not sufficient, but Vincenzo simply shrugged his shoulders and said, "This is how it will be." Daniel's continued badgering only brought silence.

He tried to get some answers from Gelsomina, but she always deferred to Vincenzo. "You must speak with Vincenzo. It's not my place to answer your questions."

Obtaining information from the two daughters during the first time they trimmed his hair and recently a short mustache. They also would know why he was held in Opi, but their answer was the same. Many Italian words, a few broken English words, and that was the end of the conversation.

One morning as Vincenzo and Daniel were proceeding to the valley for their day's work, they were greeted by many sheep, maybe a hundred or more, grazing on the grass of the valley.

"Where did the sheep come from?" asked Daniel. Again, many Italian words, but some English words, children happy and petting, he then added, feast of the patron saint of Opi, San Giovanni de Battista, soon.

On the morning of the first day of the feast, Daniel's breakfast was brought to his room while he was still sleeping. It was clear from the noise outside his door, and the fact that he had been allowed to sleep late, that preparation for the feast day had begun. He assumed he would remain in his room during the day. Around midmorning, Gelsomina entered the lower room by the front door. She told Daniel. Feast day of San Giovanni de Battista. Added the following in English, high Mass at eleven in the morning, and Daniel you come with the Sgammotta family. He quickly agreed, *saying to himself anything to get out of his dreary room.* On their way to Mass, Daniel could see the decorated houses, tables and chairs on the road, and food being prepared on the narrow sidewalks.

After high Mass, Vincenzo said to Daniel, "No work, you and me special day, so you stay outside before dusk, but you stay away from horses, entrance to the town."

Daniel didn't look he just kept walking, thinking, *well, aren't you a kind kidnapper! Oh, how I wished I were able to express sarcasm openly!*

As they continued their walk up the main road, Vincenzo explained the various events of the feast day. Daniel missed most of the Italian words but understood the gist of what Vincenzo had said. Vincenzo the spoke to Daniel with some English words. It was said awkwardly, as though he had been practicing saying the sentence for today. "Donato, I hope you accept my kindness and will not cause disturbance."

Daniel understood that Vincenzo was referring to him trying to escape. Daniel decided not to acknowledge Vincenzo, he was not about to say something in his limited Italian, which might give Vincenzo the impression he was grateful. Daniel was determined never to say grazie to his captor.

When Vincenzo finished talking with Daniel, he left to join the conversation with family and friends. No one seemed to be paying any particular attention to Daniel. It had been close to four months since Daniel had been so free of restrictions or others watching him. A tingling energy began to surge through his body as the realization of his limited freedom took hold. He stood in place a few more moments, feeling insecure. "Why do I feel so scared? Isn't this what I've been hoping for, a time when I could walk around without somebody giving me orders, and watching everywhere I go? So why am I standing here unable to move and feeling so funny?"

Three minutes passed before Daniel allowed himself to move. Then he started to walk slowly and cautiously, placing one foot in front of the other before stopping and looking to see if he was being followed. No one was paying any attention to him. He was feeling better but still moving slowly. He walked to the lower part of town and the road leading to freedom. He kept looking over his shoulder to see if someone was following him. The town was bustling with activity, and Daniel seemed to be anonymous as he strolled along the cobblestone street. He soon became more comfortable, and after about forty minutes he was feeling buoyant and happy as he moved about freely.

For the first time, he had an opportunity to closely observe the area. Looking past some shade trees growing behind homes, he could see only mountains. He crossed to the other side of Opi and looking at was left of the green valley and the small, neat cemetery. He noticed the beauty of the untrimmed edge of the deep thick forest beyond the once green valley, with the morning haze rising, and eventually disappearing against the solid stone of the snowcapped mountains on the other side of his prison town. Perhaps it was the emotion of the moment or the brief taste of freedom, but suddenly Opi seemed attractive. He smiled to himself as he walked. Eventually, he came upon the guards in their wagon at the road leading out of town. In an instant, the dark image of his reality returned, deflating his spirit once again. He stood looking at the two men in the wagon, who now moved their rifles to a ready position. Daniel thought, *I've got to find a way out of this place.*

He soon began walking more leisurely thinking that this day might present his long-awaited opportunity to escape, and he became more analytical, and more aware of his sorrowing, as he sauntered along the cobblestone street. He noticed that the people were beginning to celebrate. He thought later this afternoon, and with too much wine, someone might get careless. He intended to stay especially alert for an opportunity to run.

Daniel heard music on the main street. A small band was leading a parade of eight men carrying the statue of San Giovanni de Battista, which had been taken from the church and was now on a platform draped with a colorful silk cloth. Along the way, people were pinning lira on the garment covering the statue, as well as the platform skirt. Townspeople walked behind the statue. At various times during the parade, the band would stop playing. During these intervals, a small group of older women in long black dresses, walking directly behind the statue, recited a litany of prayers. The male leaders of the town followed the praying women. The parade continued to move slowly until, at the end of the cobblestone road, the procession turned and continued its march back to the church. The parade ended at the entrance of the church.

The statue was carried slowly up the outside stars, then into the church, and the statue returned to its pedestal.

The people spent the rest of the day eating, rejoicing, singing, dancing, and playing games. Daniel noticed a teenage boy he had not seen before. This seemed to bring the number to either five or six teenage boys, all of whom Daniel assumed were held out of school to help their fathers with the farming chores. Daniel was surprised that more teenagers were not attending this celebration. Also, the absence of young children was obvious. Daniel expected to see many more children running around and playing on such a festive day. He had, by now, also concluded that the absence of young men was due to the fact they were still serving in the Italian army, even though the war in Italy had been over for almost a year. He suspected the countries, where the war was fought, needed men to remain in the army longer than was usual.

Daniel had never been behind the church, so he decided to see what was there. He walked up the road toward the church, while looking at the various tables on the narrow sidewalk holding homemade food, crafts, colorful pots, and metal trinkets. When he reached the church, he turned around to see if Vincenzo had followed him. He was still quite surprised that he was not being restricted. He walked behind the church and saw a small stone area that extended back to a low stone wall like the stone wall at the back of the houses. He peered over the wall and saw the steep drop down the mountain. This spot looked as though it was the highest elevation point of the town.

Daniel waited until late afternoon to walk down by the bar in the area leading out of town. His hope was that by this hour the men in the wagon may have had too much wine to drink, and by now they may be sleeping. His plan was to pretend he was interested in the horses pulling their wagon. He would pretend to be examining the horses, stroking their backs, and inching his way toward the side of their cart. He was also counting on the people in the bar to also have drunk too much and be slow to react when he made a run for the dirt road leading to the pasture area.

He casually approached the two men sitting in the wagon with their rifles. He had learned the Italian word for "hello," so smiling broadly he waved at the men to see if they noticed him. As Daniel continued his slow movement toward the horses, the two men stood and shouted Italian words." The Italian words were not familiar to Daniel, but the posture of the two men, with their rifles pointed at him was clear. Daniel shrugged his shoulders, lifted his hands in anger, and turned to walk away from the town entrance and once again experiencing the anguish of failure.

CHAPTER 25

The weather continued its warming pattern. Crops were beginning to burst out of their prepared soil; strangely enough Daniel seemed to get some satisfaction from this development, but he immediately fought the emotion and quickly returned to indifference at the budding plants. Feeling sullen and angry, Daniel thought, why should I have any interest in this farm? I just want to get out of this place soon. As these feelings continued, he found himself spiraling into deep depression, beginning to lose all interest and desire for his existence in Opi. Spontaneity had left him long ago, and simple chores that used to be a comforting diversion were now drudgery. He was having difficulty sleeping. He felt hopeless and was beginning to wonder if he would ever return to America. His mental state was so clouded that he had stopped scheming about ways to escape.

The second Sunday in May began as every Sunday had for the past few months. Daniel, in his clean pressed clothes, went to early Mass with the Sgammotta family. After Mass, Vincenzo told Daniel to remain in church because Father Giordania Mascia wanted to speak with them. Father Mascia looked to be in his early thirties. He was a small, thin man with crisp, square, facial features, but his appearance was deceiving. He had the energy of three men and could lift his own weight. He was noted for his energetic stride, and he was proud to show everyone his ability to break the shells of nuts by smashing them with the fist of one hand.

As Daniel waited in one of the pews, he noticed a few other teenage boys that had remained in the church. They were the few boys Daniel had seen helping their fathers with farming in the valley. Daniel thought, oh no, don't tell me I'm gonna have to sit through a religion class with these other Opi kids. Daniel crossed his arms over his chest, threw his head back, and slouched in the pew. He was in no mood to listen to a sermon from the priest!

The priest came out of the sacristy wearing his usual flowing black garment. He asked all the boys in the church to come to the first pew. When they were seated, he said, "My purpose this morning is to explain why you seven boys were brought to Opi."

This simple, short sentence jarred Daniel from his rebellious lethargy; he was suddenly filled with new vitality. A thought that seemed too good to be true entered his mind as he and the others looked at each other, all thinking the same thought. *Is it possible I'm not alone?* Immediately there was noticeable new energy among the seven boys, they were all staring at Father Mascia, waiting for him to begin.

"When I was assigned to Opi fifteen years ago," Father Mascia began, "I studied the history of my first flock, and the unique geological formation of their town. The book I read referred to the Opici tribe that settled on this precipice, which stood like a monument overlooking the rich valley pasture area of the Sangro. Living on the mountain gave the Opici tribe a natural fortification against floods and conquerors, and the advantage of a fertile valley. They used primitive tools to remove stone and soil, constructing a single road to reach the flat mountain top. Over the years the tribe continued to remove stone and soil from the area, making a flat surface for their individual shelters.

They now had a mountain protection, and a road to the valley to tend to the needs of their grazing animals in the valley."

Father Mascia told the young hostages about the importance of sheep to the many small towns in the Abruzzo region of Italy. "Opi has for centuries depended on its large sheep herd, and its fertile valley for sheep grazing; it is the sheep that allow all the families to remain in their beloved town for centuries. Our families are responsible for the hiring of young men from Opi to act as shepherds, mule skinners, and guards who will take the sheep to Southern Italy where there is no freezing temperature and snow, which would kill all the sheep. These men must use the many "transhuman" roads that are in rural areas without buildings or towns. They know the locations of the transhuman roads, which allows them to make these winter trips south, and come back to Opi in late May, taking pride in not losing sheep during their two journeys, each year. These trained young men for centuries have allowed the people of Opi to remain in their beloved town.

Daniel was getting frustrated with this talk of sheep. He was only interested in why he had been brought to Opi. *Why is this priest talking about the history of Opi and sheep, when he said he was gonna tell us why we were brought here?*

Father Mascia continued, "The people of Opi survive on the revenue from the sale of the wool, as well as meat and cheese for their consumption."

One of the boys, speaking in English, with a British accent interrupted the priest. "Excuse me, Father, why are you telling us about sheep, when you said you were going to tell us why we were brought to this town?"

Father Mascia responded, "My son, it's important for you to know the history of Opi so you'll be able to understand the reason why you were destined to save the town and its people from losing their heritage, culture, and town. My explanation of this history will help you accept your presence in our beautiful town."

The seven youngsters were now looking at the priest with quizzical expressions. They were confused and frustrated by the priest's answers.

The priest continued as though he had never been interrupted. "But this happy, comfortable life would change forever when Italy entered World War II." As Father Mascia talked about the war, the youngsters could see and feel a change in his presentation. He no longer talked with Enthusiastic words, his voice now mournful; his posture became that of a defeated man, how strange Daniel thought. Father Mascia hesitated for a moment, and then continued his war story.

German solders with matching guns, motorcycles, and a large truck was blocking the entrance to our church, I tried to explain that their large truck had to be removed, allowing our people to attend morning Mass. Even while politely explaining the problem, I could see soldiers in a line passing boxes and placing them at the entrance to our church. I told this soldier who was acting as the leader that these boxes had to be removed. He turned to face me, with an angry expression on his face said. "Stop bothering me priest, your town is higher enough to observe the Sangro River, where the American Army will be trapped in a flowing water and easily exposed to German machine gun fire, which will kill the Americans soldiers, stopping their advance to the Italian Capitol City of Rome, by the waters of the Sangro River.

Father then returned to the topic of the sheep, and the anger of the boys once again began to rise. However, they were not yet ready to confront the pious priest. "In October, the Germans would not allow the shepherds, muleskinners, and guards to leave their work details so they could move the herd to Foggia and Frosinone for the winter. The governing council pleaded with the German commander, explaining that if the sheep didn't have grass for grazing, they would die during the winter. The German commander would not listen to reason, and in October of 1943 the people of Opi were forced to sell all but seventy-five sheep for less than their real value. The sheep that remained were kept alive by housing a few in the animal shelters of each family's homes.

Much to the continuing frustration of the oppressed boys, Father Mascia's talk now returned to the outcome of the battle of The Sangro line. He was now distracted as he explained the American forces arrived at the southern border of the Sangro River With inflatable bridges allowing them to cross the river with trucks carrying their solders and equipment to fire on the Germans when the Americans landed on the Northen shore of the river causing the Germans to retreat north. However, the leader of the German forces was so angry that he ordered a search of all the homes in Opi, finding every young able body man, labeling them as work prisoners, and ordered them to fill the German trucks for their trip to Rome. Any young man who refused to get in the truck would be shot. All the young men slowly began to jump on the German trucks, Father Mascia ignored or did not seem to notice their agitated behavior.

At that point, one of the captive boys found the courage to interrupt the priest. "Father, I don't mean to be disrespectful, but when will you tell us why we are here?"

Father asked the seven youngsters to be patient, at that moment none of the six boys challenge the priest. Father Mascia continued, seeming to be oblivious to the feelings of the hostages.

In November of 1943, The Allied forces decided to concentrate their bombing on the towns of San Angelo del Pesco and Alfredena, which were at the center of the German and Italian defensive line. We believe the prayers of the townspeople saved us from destruction. Only two bombs were dropped on Opi, one hit the side of the mountain and caused no damage and the other hit a house across the street from 25 Via Giovanni de Battista, killing four people. You can still see the empty space at this location."

Father Mascia finally commented on the boys' posture and fidgety behavior of his audience. He paused and said, "You boys seem uninterested in our history, so for now I will save further details for another time. However, that did not stop Father Mascia from completing his comments."

The priest suddenly became visibly emotional, as he described the end of the battle. "The Germans, realizing they were about to be defeated, they prepared to leave Opi on December 20, 1943, taking all the able-bodied men with them as work prisoners. Nine young men refused to leave town and were immediately lined up against a wall and killed by a firing squad. Only the old men and some of the middleaged men, who had acted as being infirmed and feeble so as not to be taken. They would remain in Opi to bury the men who were killed by the Germans. Their wives, mothers, and young children, who were in the caves, were not present to grieve for their heroic fallen sons and brothers."

Father Mascia now began to explain "Immediately after the Germans left, word was sent to the women and children in the Capracatto, Gioia De Marsi and the Parco mountains that it was safe for them to return to their homes from the caves in these mountains. When the women and children arrived, in late February of 1944, we were all saddened when we learned of the many deaths of our children due to the disease that spread among the people in the caves."

At this point, another captive boy again interrupted Father Mascia, and said, "It's beginning to sound as though we were brought here so the people of

Opi could—as you say—go on living in this town. If that's the case, why don't you just tell us the truth and forget the details, which you said you would save for another time."

Father Mascia seemed genuinely surprised by the young man's statement. "I thought you would want to know how the people tried to survive, and how we had no choice but to bring the seven of you to Opi."

One of the boys speaking English with an unusual accent, politely asked, "Well, speaking for myself, it doesn't much matter why I was captured and brought here. All that really matters is when I'm gonna to be released. I also want you to know that I am of the Muslim faith, and I wish to know if I will be allowed to pray to my God various times during the day."

CHAPTER 26

Father Mascia grimaced, shrugged his shoulders, and responded to the boy's statement. "Regarding your release that I am unable to answer at this early time. Regarding your religious practices, that decision will be made by your farming family."

"As you wish, The Governing Council of Opi planned to use the remainder of the money from the sale of the sheep herd to feed the people until the men taken by the Germans as work prisoners returned. The older men were limited in their physical ability, so only small community gardens were prepared in the spring and summer of 1944. The money from the sale of the sheep, along with gardens, fruit trees, and our grapes for wine, helped feed the families during that first year of rationing. The older people, who were unable to work in the gardens, looked after the remaining sheep, as well as our few goats, mules, and horses. They also helped with minor chores to maintain the town's various functions. The people learned to trap and kill small animals. This meat, along with a few vegetables, —and the purchasing small amounts of flour and oil— enabled the people to survive the year."

Father Mascia talked about the end of the war and the anticipation for a new beginning with the expected return of the Opi men. "November 16, 1945 was a great day—the first young man returned: Patrizio Ursitti. He came walking up Via San Giovanni de Battista. He was gaunt, dirty, with torn clothes, and he walked with a limp. But there was a bright smile on his face now that he was home. Word quickly spread that Patrizio had returned from his journey of horror was over. Everyone came out to greet him.

"Patrizio told the people about his time with the Germans. He had been quickly separated from the other young men of Opi. He confirmed that the men and boys were treated poorly and forced to do hard physical labor at the point of a rifle. There was barely enough food to sustain them, and some of the younger prisoners died in the arms of their fathers. They were forced to steal whatever clothes and rags they could find to stay warm during the winter. Taking boots off dead soldiers to replace their worn-out shoes was a common practice."

Next, Father Mascia discussed the events of the winter of 1945 in Opi. "With each passing day, hope was being replaced by the sad reality that the husbands and sons of Opi might never return. Many women would be unable to experience the final act of burying their loved ones in our beloved Opi soil."

At this point, the dark-skinned boy with the unusual speaking accent, stood and spoke once again, angrily interrupting Father Mascia. "Why do you continue to use words that have no meaning for me? You told us you would explain why we have been illegally brought to this town, and I demand to hear the reason!"

Father Mascia was clearly caught off-guard by the boy's aggressive confrontation. The other hostages were also surprised. The priest did not respond angrily as he had done earlier, but now using an apologetic tone, continued. "My son, the words I speak are meant to help you understand your needed presence in our town, which can only help you to accept your role in Opi."

Instead of calming the incarcerated youngster, the priest's statement only served to anger the boys further, he became outwardly furious at the priest's statement, and said. "It is you, and your people, who must understand, that since I am being held in your town illegally, I have no role in Opi!"

The young priest, now flustered by the boy's confrontational tone, hesitantly stated his reason for continuing. "Boys, boys, I assure you this information can only be a comfort to you."

The angry standing boy, with the unusual accent, who had identified himself, as an Egyptian boy named Omar, discontinued his confrontational tone, and sat back down with a look of resignation, realizing the priest was incapable of understanding the perspective of the seven boys.

A second boy with strong British accent, who would shortly introduce himself as George to his fellow captives, stood and asked a question. I have seen many girls and young women in this town. Instead of kidnapping us, to replace the men and boys lost to the Germans, they can replace their brothers, and help their fathers, so why are we in your town to work in the valley?

The priest gave a deep sigh and continued, "In the Italian culture, it is not considered proper for women to be assigned the type of labor needed to expand the seven farms for the people. These tasks are only allowed to be accomplished by men. Patrizio is responsible for our sheep now growing to eighty-nine. When winter arrives, he will take the animals to the southern pasture fields for another winter and return in late May. Leaving the older men of Opi to replace the pastureland in the valley, and begin spring planting, to replace the stored winter food, and prevent their families from the terrible fate of starving."

At this point in the priest's talk, it was becoming clear why these seven boys had been kidnapped, and what would be expected of them.

The priest continued to use his "history lesson" as a rationalization for the illegal detention of the seven hostages. Father Mascia, obviously still flustered at the confrontation with the dark-skinned boy, continued. "At that time, the people believed it would take ten to twelve years to increase the herd to the point where it could once again support the families of the town. However, in the fall of 1945, the governing council informed the people there was only enough money to sustain the population for one more winter, and with each passing day the people were losing hope that their men and boys had survived their labor imprisonment by the Germans.

"The governing council, now desperate for solutions, proposed the idea of adopting Italian war orphans. Adopting children would solve the problem of the town's future, as well as provide some comfort to the families who had lost children in the caves. However, this was not a practical solution. We were told by the Italian Government that the adopted teenage boys would be required by the government to attend school until they were sixteen years of age. They would, therefore, be unable to help in the expansion of the land into farms for three or four years. Then, when they became sixteen, orphans, like other children in Italy, must be free to choose their own vocation. For these reasons, this solution was not considered further."

"The council called a meeting of the entire population in early December 1943. I recall it was just prior to Christmas—to discuss their two-part plan for the continuation of the town. Vincenzo Sgammotta, who is President of the Governing Council, reminded the people that Italy was expected to become a republic through the newly adopted election process of 1946. The expected formation of the government into a republic had increased the growth and popularity of the Italian Communist Party. The council proposed that Opi be run as a model communist experiment, with men sharing in the labors to produce food for the entire community, while rejecting the atheist philosophy that was part of the world communist movement."

Father Mascia walked to the corner of the altar entrance, picked up a small wooden chair, and brought it up to the front of the pew. He sat down before continuing. The difficulty of telling the story seemed to have drained the life energy out of the thin but strong young priest. Once seated, he proceeded to describe the second part of the plan.

"The seven land-owning families recruited seven families from neighboring towns who were willing to farm Opi land as tenant farmers for the spring of 1946. Fifty percent of the food grown would be taken by the tenant farmers, and the other fifty percent would be given to the town to be communally shared by all residents in true communist fashion. The plan was implemented but the results were disastrous. The accounting of the percentage of crops going to the people of Opi could not be accurately verified. The people received far less food than they had expected and were once again on the verge of starvation. The lease to the thieving tenant farmers was not renewed for the spring of 1947."

"The despondent people demanded answers from their leaders. The governing council called an emergency meeting of the people to discuss what seemed to be a hopeless situation. Many of the people of Opi were beginning to believe that abandoning the hill town would soon become a necessity. Their culture, their homes, and their very existence would dramatically change. Many people did not know how or where they would be able to rebuild their lives."

As Father Mascia continued to explain the decision the boys had now guessed, and they were each mentally finishing his long rant.

"The council told the people what many had been thinking. The end of Opi as a town was now before them. They would meet as a council and return to the people in a few days."

Father Mascia's thin face expressed despair as he summarized the situation in a proverb. "La prima parola della guerra è pronunciata dal cannone, ma l'ultima è sempre disse dal pane (The first word of war is given by cannons, but bread always has the last word.)"

The priest sighed and looked as though the last ounce of energy had been drained from his body. He found the strength to continue, but only now with a doubtful tone in his voice. "In four days, the council returned as promised. At that time, Vincenzo stood before the gathered community and said, "Opians, my brothers and sisters, you are right to expect that your leaders will present a plan to save our way of life. We have decided to offer you the best answer to solve our problem. However, you must consider this carefully, and all must agree before we move forward, because this alternative is a distasteful one."

Father Mascia had finally arrived at the explanation of why the seven prisoners had spent the past months in Opi, by repeating what Vincenzo had said that day to the people.

Continuing Father Mascia said, "The council then asked the seven families if they would be willing to convert their seven gardens into larger farms able to feed all the people of Opi. This could be accomplished if the landowners, aided by ten of the strongest middle-aged men, some of whom are members of our governing council, will conscript seven foreign young men. Then these seven Opi men, with the help of those conscripted, would be responsible for converting our now existing seven gardens into farms. The seven Opi men willing to take on this responsibility will be paid for their service in extra sheep for their families when the herd has regained its full size. They will also receive a substantial percentage of the revenue that is earned by selling extra crops from our expanded farmland at the Saturday market in Pescasseroli."

The word conscript, a word Daniel had never heard before, was instantly defined for him. The priest continued by paraphrasing Vincenzo. "A portion of the money earned by the sale of the farm food and perhaps some craft items made by the women in Pescasseroli would provide extra income to help pay for basic town functions, and hopefully in a few years the farms would raise enough extra crops to sell wholesale to distributors."

Father Mascia conveniently failed to mention this expected earned money would result in part from the labor of the seven captives, but some form of reimbursement for the young captive's effort and toil on the farms was never a consideration of Opi's Town Council's plan.

Father Mascia's long ramble now centered on justification for what the people of Opi had agreed to; bringing to their town seven young foreign boys, who would enable the people to maintain their way of life and remain attached to their culture.

"After much debate as to the merits and moral issues of the plan, the people looked to me for guidance. Many individuals shouted out to me, 'Priest, tell us what is just in this matter. What should we do?'"

Father Mascia slowly rose from his flimsy wood chair with his head down. Then, forcing himself to stand erect with a new determination and fire in his eyes to go along with an animated body motion, he raised his voice and told the boys what he had said to the people that night.

"I knew the people were unsure and needed the proper guidance to go forward with this plan. In that moment, I knew through Divine inspiration what was right. I spoke to the people of what was in my heart. I explained that in seminary I had been taught of the suffering our people endured through the centuries by the actions of the non-believers, how they murdered God's people and stole our children to expand their power. To make my point, I told the people of Opi the true story of the capturing of the great Christian monument, the Hagia Sophia Byzantine church built in 537A.D.in Constantinople. This church was a holy monument, a landmark of medieval Christianity, which contained sacred artifacts, pieces of wood from the actual cross Christ was crucified on, the lance that pierced Christ's side, the crown of thorns, and some of Christ's own blood. I explained that Hagia Sophia was the seat of the Orthodox Patriarch, the counterpart to Roman Catholicism's Pope. In the fifteenth century, the city of Constantinople was surrounded by territories controlled by the Ottomans. After a seven-week siege, the Turks launched a final assault on Constantinople. The terrified citizens flocked to the Hagia Sophia church, expecting that its sacred walls and holy artifacts would protect them. Instead, the Ottoman Turks battered through the great wooden and bronze doors, destroying tombs, and desecrating sacred icons. Screaming wives were taken from their murdered husbands and their children chained and taken away to be sold into slavery. I told the assembled people of Opi that ever since the fifteenth century our children have been taken from us. I reminded them that we had all witnessed the taking of our children by the heathen Nazi devils."

A second boy with a British accent interrupted the priest. "I believe I know where you're heading with your conversation. I refuse to listen to a rationalization of the illegal kidnapping of us. You can talk all you want about some church in Turkey, but I choose not to listen to your justification of the criminal action of your people. The other six boy responded in unison, agreeing with the boy with the British accent.

"Well, you may all agree on this point, but I will finish what I have to say because it is proper and correct, said the priest, who then continued his comments."

"I stood before the people that evening and told them it was finally time for God's people to defend themselves, to stand up and say, 'Enough!' It is just and right for our culture and our lives to survive through the children of others, just as non-believers' have for many centuries lived and survived through our Christian children. I blessed the people and the seven men, and said, 'Go to the cities and bring to Opi our 'angels.' It is now time for Christians to serve God to avenge all those Christian children taken by non-believers. The seven families traveled to the cities, and each brought back the young, foreign males to assist in expanding the current gardens into working farms. You seven young men have become our angels, doing God's work."

Each of the boys could not help but understand the twisted logic in Father Mascia's conclusion. Father Mascia, by referring to the hostages as 'angels' was in fact allowing the people of Opi to see the captives, as saviors sent to them by God.

The priest then discussed the role of the elders of Opi. "Those Opians, unable to do physical work will act as protectors, posted on the only road out of Opi; keeping our angels safe from wolf packs and bears in the forest surrounding our mountain town, if one of you choose to stroll in the forest, which surrounds our mountain town."

Father Mascia did not have to explain how the mountain acted as a natural barrier in preventing any escape attempt from the town proper. "You have no doubt noticed when you are working in the valley that there are men stationed on the valley road in their wagons. They are stationed there to protect you and your family farmer from the dangerous animals living in the forest. In future years, after you learn to love our humble town as we do, and hopefully marry have children of your own, there will no longer be the need for your protectors."

The priest continued by referring to an essential aspect of Italian culture—the type of work considered appropriate for men and women.

"You might be asking yourselves why the women of Opi weren't expected to do farm work. My sons, it is not culturally acceptable for women to do the work of men. This would result in a devastating loss of pride for our men." Then, with a tone of finality in his voice, Father Mascia stated the reason for kidnapping seven boys.

"In August, when the Germans decided to retreat from the battle of the Sangro Line, they rounded up thirty-four of our young men and older boys, forcing them to be a labor detail, on their long march to Rome. The men and boys who would choose not to go peacefully, would face a German firing squad. Gone were the shepherds to take the sheep heard for their winter grazing in southern Italy. With no grass for grazing the sheep herd had to be sold, or they would die. The people waited through the winter months for the return of their men and boys. Sadly, only one young man returned to his family. Was it not proper justice for the families of the innocent victims of such atrocities to conscript, house, clothe, and feed a very small fraction of that number? You seven young men would, by your labor, save the lives of many."

Each captive boy clearly understood Father Mascia had sanctioned the immoral act of kidnapping seven foreign-born boys because the Germans were responsible for the death of thirty-three men and boys.

With deep sadness in his voice, the priest finally explained why the seven captives were in Opi. "A decision by the governing council of Opi was to offer seven boys a house to live in, food and clothing, and above all kindness to each of you. The hope of the people is that in time you will come to love our small town as we do. Starting today, Sundays until dusk will be a free day for you seven angels, after your normal mid-day meal. The people want to show their appreciation. But remember, if you forget to return to your homes by dusk, escorts will be there to remind you."

The young priest, finally acknowledging the frustration growing in the seven hostages asked them to be more attentive. "What I'm about to say is important for your safety and your future, so please listen to me well. The placement of the town, the forest, and the mountains form a natural barrier that prevents anyone from wandering off. Humans would be unable to survive in the forest because of the bears, wild boars, and wolves that inhabit this vast wooded area at the base of the mountain range, and if by some magic the animals did not kill you, you would be forced to roam the dense, uninhabited forest until you starved or froze to death. I ask you to look closely at the forest the next time you are in the valley. If you do, you will see only one road coming down from the mountain and through the forest, leading directly to Opi. There are no other roads leading in or out, only a circular dense forest that follows the base of the mountain range. To protect you from certain death, in the event you are foolish enough to threaten your own survival by trying to leave by the forest, each family member was given an extra horse to prevent your suicide."

"Finally, the council thought it would be wise to assign a group of our older citizens to act as 'escorts' to keep an eye on you during your free Sundays. These are men who do not have the endurance to do physical farm work."

During the priest's lengthy homily, the word kidnapping was never used. In fact, the priest's explanation of their abduction and captivity sounded as though it was an unpleasant but nevertheless justifiable act, given the hardship the war had brought to the people of Opi.

Father Mascia added one final comment, as though to convince himself of the justice of what had been done to the seven innocent boys. "Some people were reluctant to accept this survival plan until it was agreed that the families responsible for an angel would act with kindness and help their foreign angel's feel like a part of their new Opi family as quickly as possible."

Father Mascia hesitated a moment, then blessed the seven boys, and swiftly headed toward the rear sacristy. Each boy remained seated, awkwardly staring at each other, curiously uncomfortable, and wondering who would be the first to speak.

Although each hostage had often speculated on the reason they were being held against their will, hearing the actual words spoken for the first time had a dramatic almost calming impact. Father Mascia had cleverly made their abduction and captivity sound reasonable and legal. Daniel understood for the first time how people who believe they are basically good need to methodically arrange their immoral choices to pacify their conscience.

Finally, one of the boys spoke with what each boy would soon come to know as a Welsh accent. "I don't know about the rest of you lads, but I, for one, am happy to finally know why I was brought here, and it feels good to know I'm not alone."

At that comment, the others smiled for the first time since they had entered the church. The Welsh boy added, "I'm Jem Adair, and I come from Wales, England."

Another boy jumped up and shouted, "I'm from Harrogate, in Yorkshire! My name is George Buttermere."

The brief period of uncomfortable silence was now history. The boys were all standing, shaking hands with each other, and introducing themselves. In addition to Jem and George, there were Omar El-Mokhtar from El-Arish, Egypt; Paul Andrews from Sydney Australia; Jacob Houptmann from Zurich, Switzerland; Klein Wien from Linz, Austria, and Daniel Ciarletta from the Bronx, New York City.

After leaving the church, Daniel and the other boys immediately became boisterous. They had seen each other's faces around town, each believing the other was an Italian Opi teenager who was helping his father with farming chores. The seven boys were full of renewed energy for the first time in almost four months, filled with the glorious feeling of no longer being alone. The atmosphere was magical. Looking into the eyes of another person who had been experiencing and feeling the same bizarre emotions was breathtaking. They wanted to touch each other and hold on, both physically and emotionally. Each hostage had an unconscious fear that the others might disappear. If that were to happen, who would be able to understand them? Who would be there to reassure them that they were not losing their minds? Each boy had suddenly found others able to verify that his personal hell was not somehow his fault, others who were able to support and vouch for their often-confusing reality. The boys had met each other some fifteen or twenty minutes ago, yet they felt as though they were old friends. They were bound not by the familiarity gained over time, but by the similarity of their unique experience.

CHAPTER 27

It was Sunday morning. Usually, each boy would be with their Opi family preparing for the Sunday mid-day meal, but today the boys had no thought of food— which in and of itself was unique—all they wanted was each other. After leaving the church, thoroughly enjoying their freedom, and wandering about town, the first thing the seven boys discussed was how Father Mascia had used his long lecture to justify their kidnapping.

Jem was the first to comment. "The thing that got me is that he actually sounded as though he believed the line he was giving us."

Paul added, "Did you think he was ever going to stop talking about those damn sheep?

Like I could care about their lousy sheep, I hear enough about sheep from my New Zealand cousins."

As they strolled along, enjoying the brisk, sunny Sunday and each other, they eventually became more serious. They were confused, that a priest would go along with a kidnapping, and then justify the criminal act.

Omar was the first to speak about the priest's comments. "I'm disappointed in myself, and also the six of you, for not objecting and telling your holy man that he was wrong to excuse himself and his people for what they have done to us. If I had the courage to confront the holy man, I would now feel proud of myself."

At first, the boys were annoyed at Omar's statement, there was a momentary silence.

Omar made them feel uncomfortable for being so flippant about Father Mascia's talk. The seven boys had no understanding of the psychological trauma of being kidnapped and held in isolation for a period of time. The emotional and mental scars of trauma cause individuals to feel deeply threatened, and a total loss of independence. For these reasons, the teenage boys were unable to confront Father Mascia. The trauma associated with their long period of captivity would become a constant emotional burden. Fortunately, the seven boys spoke English, and after a long and gradual period, the sharing of feeling about their captivity helped to lessen, but not completely remove their burdens.

The boy by the name of Jacob broke the silence. "Uh… I… guess we did let him have his own way."

Paul, the stocky, rough-looking, handsome boy from Australia, shared a surprised feeling he had during Father Mashia's talk. "I don't know why, but when the priest yelled at us about being disrespectful in a church, he scared the hell out of me. I felt my legs and arms shaking. I was so frightened I kept my head down, so I wouldn't have to look at his face."

The other boys, who had spoken so brashly about Father Mascia after leaving the church, soon found themselves agreeing with Paul, the others were frightened during Father Mascia's talk.

The boys had no understanding of the unusual courage it would have taken to confront the priest, given the isolation and suppression they had experienced over this period of secluded isolation in Opi. Each boy was unable to fully understand the psychological implications of being quarantined as they had been without any reason or assurance when they would be released. In time they would come to understand their meekness that day in the church, but for now it was just too confusing. This was as much as they were able to comprehend at this time.

Daniel said, "Yeah, he used his little talk to cover his butt."

Klein asked Daniel, "Cover his butt? What do you mean by covering a butt?"

The other boys were also confused by Daniel's phrase.

Daniel explained that in American, butt was a slang word for ass. "Now let me see, how to explain this when a guy says, 'He was covering his butt,' he means the person is making up excuses and lying to convince the other person that he was right to do whatever it was he did."

The other boys thought the American phrase awkward, but they had their first joyous laugh when Paul suddenly started jumping around with both hands on the cheeks of his ass and yelling, "Oh look at how I'm covering my butt."

It's unimaginable how glorious it feels to laugh a hardy "belly" laugh, when one has not smiled in four months. Daniel was the most amused and he laughed so hard he was almost crying. It was one of the most intensely joyous feelings he had ever had. It was a feeling he would never forget in his lifetime.

The boys continued strolling about town, comparing experiences, and making each laugh. Each boy initially thought nothing of the fact that they were all nonItalian boys, this fact did not occur to them as odd, but later in their stay in Opi they concluded this was not a coincidence. For now, all they could feel was the excitement of being together, able to walk freely and share their loneliness. Their concentration this day took the form of appreciating the great weight that had been lifted from their mind and body. Their Italian was very sparse, but they found it interesting that they were all motivated to learn Italian for the same reason, as a means to find out why they had been kidnapped and the pleasure of hearing news about the outside world from the radio owned by each of their captors.

The remainder of the afternoon was spent walking and nervously asking each other about their backgrounds, and how their Opi families had been treating them. They were having a joyful day, teasing each other as teenage boys are inclined. They joked about their seven escorts, who walked at a distance from them, but never let the seven boys out of their sight. They strolled, talked, and laughed, with never a thought of returning to their rooms. They wanted this newfound feeling of togetherness to last forever. By late afternoon, Jem, who lived with a family in one of the detached houses by the church, said, "I'm hungry. Let's go to my family's house. I'll get my 'mam' to make us sandwiches and we can eat them on the church steps."

Daniel asked, "Would she make sandwiches for all of us?"

Jem replied with confidence, "Oh, not to worry. I can get her to do most anything I want. She loves the way I tease her." It was easy to laugh with Jem, who spoke the few Italian sentences he had learned with a strong, guttural Welsh accent, which seemed so in conflict with the flowing, rhythmic beauty of the Italian language.

They all laughed, except for the British boy named George, who inwardly cringed when he heard Jem call the wife of his Opi captor 'mam.' The word 'mam' in Wales England refers to mother, and this word brought back for George the vision of his mother who he so desperately missed.

Daniel, as early as that first day, secretly admired Jem for the way he dealt with his captivity, always with a smile and able to make jokes.

Jem told the others his name was James George Adair. In the United Kingdom, Jem is short for James. He was a 14-year-old slender boy of medium height, with blond hair and a high forehead. His thin hair came a point in the center of his forehead, and his bodily movements and overwhelming cheerful temperament made him stand out from the others. Jem had a positive, good-natured attitude, which was in keeping with his pleasant nervous energy. He gave the impression of being in constant motion. His parents had met at a youth hostel in San Francisco. His mother, Cara, was "a Yank," who came from a small town called Newington next to Hartford, the capitol city of the state of Connecticut in the United States. They started their married life in Sheffield, England. Then, with a friend, the two families bought a non-working farm in Llwydcoed, Wales, called Ty Rhos Farm. During the next five plus years of their confinement the standing joke was that in their time together the other six boys were never able to pronounce the name of the Welsh town where Jem had lived.

Jem's father was an engineer involved in building and construction. He had accepted a one-year contract for a reconstruction project in a bombed-out area in Salerno, a town on the Mediterranean, south of Naples. Jem's entire family moved to Salerno for the year. Jem and his sister attended an English-speaking religious school sponsored by the Marist Brothers, a French Catholic religious order. One April day, on his way home from school, Jem was walking alongside a series of stone row houses. As he passed an open door, a man pushed him into the house. He was kept there, gagged and tied to a chair, until late that evening when he was transferred from the room to a car and brought to Opi.

George Buttermere was quite different from Jem, except for their similar, but not identical, British accent. George was 14 years old, calm and reserved teen, tall for his age and quite slim. He had a long, thin nose to go with his long, thin face. George was verbally and physically reserved. He walked, sat, ate, and talked, all in a controlled manner. He was most concerned not to be a burden on his new friends. George was raised in Harrogate in Yorkshire, England. Harrogate was a spa town for the wealthy. George's mother and father were hotel workers. They had met while working at the St. George Hotel in Harrogate and were married within a year. He told the other boys that although he did not remember ever seeing his parents hugging or kissing "not like these Italians," he knew they loved each other and were happy together. Harrogate eventually lost its attraction as a spa town when England began to see war as inevitable. George's father was drafted into the army, and his mother continued working in Harrogate.

When the war ended, there was little opportunity for employment in the hotel industry in England, and George's parents secured permanent positions in 1947 in a hotel in Lugano, Switzerland, a lake resort town just over the Italian border. The family crossed the English Channel by ferry to France, and from Paris they went on to Rome for a one-week holiday. At the end of their week-long vacation, the Buttermere family was waiting at the Termini Train Station for their morning trip to Lugano. They had just finished a light breakfast when George visited the men's room. As he entered the toilet area, an old man sitting on a chair holding his leg pleaded, "fall hurt foot, help, help." George helped the badly limping old man out of the bathroom. The injured man directed George toward an exit door, opposite the rest room area while repeating, "my brother, my brother." There was a car parked on the street outside the exit door, with its motor running. As George and the old man moved toward the car, another man jumped out of the car and opened the front and rear doors. George and the man from the car helped the limping man into the front passenger seat. The younger man who George assumed was the man's brother, took money from his pocket and extended both arms toward a back peddling George. He suddenly pushed George into the rear passenger seat, and slammed the door shut; the injured man in the front passenger seat, reached his hand in the back, and locked the rear door. George, surprised and confused watched the younger man slide into the driver's seat, put the car into first gear and sped away from the Termini Station on their way to Opi.

Daniel, the only angel from across the Atlantic, still had some baby fat on his young 13-year-old body. Daniel was lacking in confidence in his mental ability. He had brown hair, a round face, and a pleasant smile. Daniel tended to be quiet, preferring to listen to his new friends, who he learned, even in this short period of time, were more knowledgeable than he.

Jacob Houptmann was and looked to be the oldest of the boys at age sixteen, and quite mature, but never acted superior to the other captives. Jacob was very likeable, and although the oldest he was not taller than the others. Jacob had a serious, determined face, primarily due to his piercing dark eyes.

Jacob's parents were German Jews, who left Germany in 1932 when he was sixteen months old. They resettled in Zurich, Switzerland. His father, Isaac, was a watchmaker and Jewish scholar. In the winter of 1947, Jacob's father went to Rome to study the history of Tiber Island synagogue and Jewish Ghetto. He brought Jacob with him, hoping the experience would acquaint him with his Jewish heritage. The Jews had experienced persecution in the sixteenth century when Pope Paul IV forced all Italian Jews to live within a walled enclosure, an area that is now the center of the present-day ghetto. Via del Portico d' Ottavia, the district's main street linking the ghetto with Tiber Island.

During the last two days of their stay, Jacob's father intended to finish his review of the Synagogue's historical collection. On the second day in the synagogue, Jacob was bored, and convinced his father to allow him to explore the ghetto one last time while his father completed his work. Jacob was strolling toward the ghetto along via del Portico d' Ottavia, when he passed a car that appeared to have a flat tire. A man lying on the ground by the jacked-up rear tire, called out to Jacob, in "broken" English, "hey young man, can you reach into the open trunk and hand me the lug wrench. As Jacob reached into the trunk toward the tool, he was grasped by two hands that came out of a hole in the wall separating the rear seat from the trunk. Someone dragged him into the trunk of the car. Meanwhile, the man pretending to fix tire had moved to the car trunk and slammed it shut. Jacob felt the jack being banged out from under the car, and in the next moment the car was moving, next stop, Opi.

Omar El-Mokhtar, an Egyptian, was the tallest of the boys at age fifteen. He had a broad nose and high cheekbones. His dark eyes seemed heavy, as though they were weighed down. He moved in a stoic manner and showed little joy or sadness. He always seemed to be under complete control both physically and mentally. As he had demonstrated in the church, Omar was brutally honest regarding his feelings and easily expressed his thoughts. He spoke modern Arabic and was of the Islamic faith. He proudly explained to the others that Modern Arabic is different from classical Arabic, and for this reason the Egyptian dialect varies greatly from that of other Arabic speaking nations.

El-Arish is a resort city on the Mediterranean between Sheesha and Sinai and is the Capitol of the North Sinai Governorate. El-Arish at one time, was a historic military route, now it is a restful holiday retreat on the Mediterranean, noted for the fact it is the only beach area in Egypt with palm trees. Omar had relatives in Paris, which has a large Muslim population. France allowed students the freedom to practice their religious traditions while attending school. Due to the inferior reputation of Egyptian schools Omar's parents decided he finish his schooling in France, and at the time of his capture in Italy, he was on his way to relatives in Paris. Omar chose not to reveal as much as the others about the particulars of his capture, he simply stated, "I was traveling through Rome, bound for Paris, and like you, I too was deceived by two men to enter their automobile and then taken to Opi." The boys chose to question Omar further on the details of his capture.

Paul Andrew had light pale skin, unlike the olive-colored skin of most of the people in Opi, thick, light brown, curly hair, and he was fourteen years of age. Paul was rough in manner and speech, although his Italian seemed better than the other angels. He was a handsome fourteen-year-old, in a very rough sort of way. His facial features were jagged, and some might have described them as too large, but Paul's features seemed to blend well with the shape of his body. He had a muscular torso with large upper arms and a thick, firm chest that complimented his slim waist. Paul was very friendly and outgoing. He always seemed ready and willing to accept any dare or challenge, and his Australian accent was quite distinctive to both the boys and his captors.

Paul had lived in Syndney, Australia, a port city on the eastern coast of Australia directly opposite the country of New Zealand. Paul's father was a surgeon in Sydney. At the end of the war, he was asked by the Australian government to visit Italy and train Italian doctors on the care of large body wounds, which was his specialty.

Doctor Andrews took his family to Italy for the training conference. Paul was the youngest of five children. The Andrews family was staying at a hotel in the Adriatic Sea town of Pescara, where the medical conference was being held. One day, as Paul and his siblings were sightseeing in Pescara, Paul became distracted by a street magician and eventually realized his siblings had moved on. As he walked on a broad boulevard trying to find his way back to the hotel, Paul passed two men. One was seated in a car and the other was leaning against the car's front door. He told the men he was lost and gave them the name of his hotel. They motioned for him to get in the car and told Paul they would be glad to drive him to his hotel. When he realized he was being taken out of town, he tried to stop the car, but he was quickly restrained.

Klein Wien was shy and reserved. He was good-natured and easy to talk to, and also to tease. He had wavy, light blond hair and fair skin and was fifteen years of age. Klein was very handsome, but in quite the opposite way from Paul. Klein's facial appearance was smooth and elegant, with petite and sensitive features. He had a moderate build and appeared to be on the verge of quickly growing. Klein had an interesting accent. He loved wintertime in Opi because of the snow-capped mountains surrounding the town—it reminded him of his home in the Oberösterreich region of northern Austria.

Klein had lived in the city of Linz, the capitol city of Austria. His father was head of the water department for the city of Linz and responsible for its purity. His father was an important member of the community, and his mother was a grade schoolteacher in Linz. Klein was an only child. He and his family had been on a holiday in Italy, visiting Venice, Bologna, Florence, and Siena.

In Siena, they attended Il Palio, the Siena Palio horse race, which is held in the main Piazza del Campo. Klein and his parents, among the spectators, were standing haphazardly around the dirt racetrack in the piazza that had been made especially for this event. Spectators were standing shoulder to shoulder, jumping and cheering for the various horses and jockeys. During the last lap of the race, Klein felt himself being moved by the boisterous crowd. He loudly called out to his parents, but due to the crowd noise, and the focus of his parents on the finish of the race, he was unable to get their attention. During the mass confusion, three men moved Klein toward one of the small streets leading into the piazza. Due to the excitement and movement in the crowd no one realized that the young boy was calling for assistance. His calls just blended with the cheering spectators.

Once they were on the narrow street off the main piazza, the three men rapidly pulled him a short distance and into a waiting truck that would bring him to Opi. Klein was the last of the seven "angels" brought to Opi. Daniel was the first to arrive in February; five others came during the winter or spring of 1947; and Klein arrived in July of the same year.

Klein spoke of his feelings about his parents. "Do you guys worry about your parents like I do? I can't get that day out of my mind. It was bad enough that I was taken, but my parents must feel terrible for losing sight of me."

Jem commented, "Klein, you can't think like that, or you'll really drive yourself crazy. You can't blame yourself because these Italian clowns kidnapped you. Look, it's bad enough these people kidnapped you, without giving yourself more headaches."

Paul added, "hey, Klein, what Jem is saying, you have enough trouble being a prisoner, don't add more to your plate."

Omar disagreed with the other two boys. "I agree that you should not accept responsibility for being taken. But you have reason to be concerned about the effect your disappearance is having on your parents." Omar, like Klein, had often thought about how his unexplained disappearance affected his family. Daniel said in an understated and embarrassed tone, "Klein, I'm glad you mentioned how you feel about your parents. I have to admit, I have been so wrapped up in my thoughts about being held a captive, and thinking of ways to escape that I never thought about how my mom and dad must feel about me being missing."

Jacob responded to Daniel's comment. "Hey, Dan, don't you start beating yourself up because of these Italians. The guys are right. We have more than our share of problems. Let's think of only one thing: how we're going to get out of this town. We'll have plenty of time later to feel guilty."

The boys spent the rest of the afternoon and evening on the church steps, eating their sandwiches and talking about their families and how they must be coping. Although it was difficult being held captive and consumed by their situation, Klein and Omar taught the others the need to be more sensitive regarding their family members.

As darkness approached, and the boys were about to go back to their rooms, Jem said, "Oh, wait, before you guys go. Did any of your Opi families set you up with girls from town?"

The other six boys looked at Jem in disbelief.

Jacob was the first to respond. "You've got to be kidding. Are you telling us that your family gets you dates with girls?"

"No no, this isn't dating. About two weeks ago—that's right—it was early April, on a Saturday afternoon, Caterina, the wife of the bloke I farm with, asked me if I wanted to meet a nice girl. My Italian was bad, and I figured I misunderstood her. I couldn't believe she wanted to set me up. In mostly Italian, with a few English words, and much hand movements, what does she do, she takes me out her front door, and pointing to two houses away from her home, saying 'nice girl Marisa come here, and know Jem.'

Jem flashed an impish grin and nudged Jacob with his elbow. "Now listen to this, the father comes over the next day with his daughter Marisa, and after fifteen minutes of talking Italian, and a great deal pointing, hand jesters a few words of English, I finally realize Marisa's father allow his daughter to sit with me each Sunday morning after church, and that my future farm buddy Orsolo, will sit in the room with us. How could I go wrong, sitting with a young girl, beats sitting in the same room with sour puss Orsolo? Sure enough, the next Sunday morning Marisa visits, and after arranging two chairs for me and Marisa, who by the way is not bad looking, Orsolo sits across the room reading. Marisa and I spent the next four Sunday mornings giving each other language lessons, she trying to teach me Italian, and me trying to teach her English. I guess I sound pretty funny saying Italian words with my Welsh accent, because she had a great time laughing at how my Italian words came out. It was really good to make someone finally laugh in this place. Since you guys seem so surprised at my story, I take it your families did not fix you up with a local girl?

The six others agreed that none of their families had, nor had they even hinted at such an arrangement. The boys were now interested and wanted to hear more. Jem needed very little encouragement to continue his tantalizing tale, knowing he was entertaining his fellow prisoners with slightly embellished accounts of his interaction with Marisa.

Jem started to explain how he wanted to be alone with Marisa when the escorts approached. the boys and informed them it was time to return to their homes. Before breaking up, they shook hands and agreed they would be looking forward to next Sunday.

Evenings were the most difficult time for Daniel. He would usually sit in front of his wood-burning stove, alone and lonely, thinking of his home and family in America. But tonight, his spirits were high; he had not felt this kind of joy since being brought to Opi. As he warmed himself in front of the stove, he kept thinking of Father Mascia's lecture earlier in the day. All these months wondering why he was being held in Opi, and there it was, explained in fifteen minutes. Quickly the feeling of loneliness was once again upon him, he was alone, wishing his new friends from the Bronx were with him. Their names were not Skelly, Dutch, Tiny, Mitz, Giggy, Jack, or Joe Sal, but that was okay. He would teach his new friends how to play stoop baseball, and he guessed they would teach him how to play soccer.

* * * * * *

The weather in Opi in late spring, summer and early fall was always invigorating. Sunday, during this time of year, was for strolling, socializing, and visiting each other's homes and the early afternoon was for a special meal. For the seven boys, Sundays after lunch, was for meeting at their unofficial hangout. A small stone seating area with a mini stone monument commemorating the spot where the only German World War II bomb hit Opi. During the first few months of their captivity, when residents of Opi passed the stone seating area, they were inclined to ignore the presence of the captives, looking straight ahead, pretending they were deep in conversation, and always walking with a hurried step.

Then, in late fall of 1947, approximately seven months into the boys' captivity, their routine changed when a group of young girls passed by. The hurried step was no longer evident; the girls moved slowly, smiling and giggling, and their behavior encouraged the boys to ask the girls to join them. Early on, the invitation was never accepted, although it did not prevent the girls from frequently walking up and down Via San Giovanni de Battista and passing the young captives. Ater a while, Paul and Jem refused to accept "no" to their invitation, and they pursued the girls down the road. "Oh, we are not permitted to be with you. Our fathers would not approve," said one of the girls.

Then in the late spring of 1948, the girls, presumably no longer bound by their fathers' orders, stopped and talked with the Angles. At first the boys entered the road and walked with the girls towards the church. The boys learning words in Italian, the girls' eager to learn English. Communicating became easier, and soon the girls felt free to sit with the boys in the stone area. By the end of that summer, the boys and girls were allowed to walk together for longer and longer periods of time. They were well on their way to becoming young men and women, and with the social restrictions now greatly eased, Marisa, Jem's unofficial but still guarded girlfriend, would bring female friends to visit. The escorts now had the dual role of being prison guards and chaperones. This unique supervision prevented hand holding, arms around waists, cheek kissing, and many other things on the minds of the boys, and perhaps on the minds of some of the girls. The escorts would order a girl back to her family if they noticed any physical contact that seemed even slightly provocative.

By October 1948, the seven boys were beginning their change from teenagers into young men. Jem, now fifteen years of age, remained slender and had grown to over six feet tall. His thin blond hair had darkened. Daniel, now fourteen-years old, still had teenage body fat that was beginning to change into firm muscle. He had grown in confidence and personal maturity, but he was still somewhat reticent.

Paul had just turned seventeen years of age. He was a muscular man with an outgoing, pleasant personality. George, now fourteen-years old, had changed very little in physical appearance and personality. In 1947, he was a quiet, cautious teenager, and now in the fall of 1948 he was a quiet, cautious young man. Jacob was about to turn seventeen years of age. He was the "steady rock" of the group along with Omar who was now sixteen years of age.

Klein was a handsome young teenager, almost ready to turn sixteen. When he first arrived in Opi he was a strikingly handsome figure of a young man. He had delicate, handsome facial features, and thick, golden blond hair. Klein's personality remained reserved, but his six Opi brothers had helped him grow emotionally.

Maturity was a frequent and important topic. They felt a certain strength and resolve, even though they had no way of understanding the enormous intricacy of going from childhood to manhood. They were becoming young men, and they felt normal and whole in spite of their abnormal life. They had not been defeated; in fact, they were now even more determined that someday, somehow, they would have normal lives.

As they began to mature, something also happened to the makeup of the group. They knew beyond any doubt they were as one. They had complete trust in each other. They could not lie to one another. Truth somehow had become hallowed, sacred, and they intuitively knew this bond would remain, even in freedom.

One question continually seemed to surface, although each had difficulty articulating its existence. How were they able to maintain their sanity? They used words such as madness, insaneness, saneness, mental balance, crazy, and going nuts. Omar used the phrase soundness of mind. One thing was clear: they knew they were sane, but the issue of insanity as each day in captivity continued lurked as a dark cloud somewhere in their consciousness.

One cold, windswept Sunday afternoon in the late fall of 1948, the seven captives were enjoying the warmth of the woodstove in Klein's room, when George returned to the question of his fear of eventually going crazy. "I'm frightened that if we can't escape this town soon, we will all lose our minds, and I think I'll be the first to experience what it means to go nuts. I'm afraid I won't be me anymore."

Paul, who still had a strong Australian accent, even when speaking elementary Italian, responded abruptly, forcing George to momentarily stop his negative thoughts.

"Why do you "Brits" have to look at your life as more hopeless than productive? You talk like we are doomed. Why don't you try to laugh more, and try keeping good thoughts in your head, rather than always thinking the worst?"

George, somewhat annoyed, but not sure why, said firmly, "My way of life has been taken from me, my heritage, my friends and my family, and the plans my parents had for me. I don't know about the rest of you, but I've gradually come to believe that our life on this mountaintop is an unnatural life. Six days a week, I'm surrounded by a place and people who make me uncomfortable. Thank God I have you guys on Sundays. If you think I don't smile often enough, God only knows what I'd be like if I didn't have you guys."

Omar, as he was frequently able to do, once again had come to the rescue, using as few words as possible. "George, I feel the same as you, taken from my natural life, but soon after being taken to this place I decided it was necessary for me to hold hope in my body. If not, I felt I would soon die, either by natural causes or by my own hand, and I was determined not to let that happen."

The conversation ended uncomfortably, when George said, "Yeah, you're right."

CHAPTER 28

In July 1947, Daniel had been missing for five months. Pete was furious and irritated at the lack of communication from Castellammare di Stabia over the past month, and he could wait no longer. He placed a long-distance call to his brother-inlaw to find out if there was any progress on Daniel's case. Rodolfo, hearing the anger in Pete's voice, explained that he had not heard from the police or the private detective agencies for over a month. He then assured Pete that he would visit both agencies the next day and call him in America the following evening.

"I'll expect to hear from you tomorrow, so don't let me down. "And be harsh with them, Rodolfo. Tell them I expected to have some good leads from them after all this time."

"Pete, I will do my best and will be as firm as possible with both agencies."

"I'll expect to hear from you tomorrow," Pete said in an abrupt and rude manner and hung up the phone without even saying goodbye.

The following evening, Pete waited by the phone and picked up the receiver the minute it rang. "Hello, Pete, this is Rodolfo. I have bad news. The Naples police have closed Daniel's case, and the detective agency told me that all their leads have been dead ends. Like the police, they have taken their man off Daniel's case."

Pete was infuriated by the news, and he questioned Rodolfo further, "Why wasn't I kept informed?"

"Pete, since I didn't hear from them, I thought they were still working on the case. I was surprised myself by the news,"

"Pete, it is not fair to blame me for the actions of the detective agency or the police."

Pete, although still angry, softened his tone with Rodolfo, and asked. "Is there anything that can be done to keep the police and the detective agency working on it?"

"I asked the police and the detective agency that same question," said Rodolfo. "They went over the reports with me, and I'm sorry to say they seem to have given up all hope. There's nothing more I feel I can do."

Pete was outraged with Rodolfo's defeatist attitude and slammed down the receiver. Rodolfo became the first family member that Pete would unjustly hurt, but by no means the last.

Rodolfo took a few minutes to control his anger, and then said to his wife, "Your brother speaks from across the ocean, and at no time did he even ask how his father and mother were feeling. Your father is sick over the disappearance of his grandchild, and his son does not have the manners to ask about his own father."

Pia, Daniel's aunt, was unable to respond, left the room and began to cry.

Pete, still sitting in the chair by the phone, was exasperated by Rodolfo's comments and, unable to further control his anger, he spoke out loud to the empty room. "Damn it, Rodolfo, you tell whoever has lost hope to go to hell. Well, I haven't lost hope, and I'm gonna bring my son home. You say there's nothing more that can be done. I'll show them what can be done." Pete remained seated, red-faced, and staring straight ahead for at least ten minutes. He told himself, Yeah, well I'm gonna show that jerk there's plenty more that can be done. When I bring Daniel home, he's gonna be the first to know.

That evening, Pete talked with his brother Danny. "I've decided to return to Italy and find Daniel. I need to raise money to bring him home, and I want to sell my half interest in the house. I know you don't have the cash to purchase my half, but do you think you could get a second mortgage and buy me out?"

"I'll try, Pete. Without much cash to put down, it doesn't look that great, but let me find out where I stand with the bank. Maybe they'll let me work something out. Is there any possibility of raising money through the business?"

Pete responded as though he had already considered this option. "Nah, we're working on a bank loan to make a full conversion to oil heat trucks before anyone else, we have the manpower and the customers, all we need is two more trucks, so we decided to go for a loan. With two more trucks we can capture a lot of customers. If I now added more to that loan, the whole deal would likely fall through."

The following day, during his lunch hour, Danny hurried to his bank on the corner of Westchester and Soundview Avenue. Danny received the information he was expecting. The loan officer told him he would be unable to refinance the home mortgage based on his salary and the amount he would have to put down. That evening, he gave Pete the news. "I'm sorry, Pete, but I can't afford to refinance. We'll have to sell the house."

"You have no objection to selling the house?" Questioned Pete.

Before Danny could respond, Pete said, "I hope you and Kate understand that I have to do this."

"Pete, I understand. The truth is I'd probably do the same thing if I were in your shoes."

With the expectation that he could travel to Italy and bring back his son, Pete was not yet the furious man he would soon become, Pete responded to his brother. "I feel badly for you and Kate, but this is my last chance of getting my son back."

"C'mon, Pete, no need to feel badly, sell the damn house, and take all the money, Kate and I talked this over last night and she agrees that you should take it all. Just bring Daniel back. With my salary and Kate selling her corsets we'll be ok, and you'll need some extra money for Suzy and the kids' rent. Remember, Daniel may be your flesh and blood, but he's also like a son to me and Kate."

Pete moved to Danny, and they embraced. "I love you, my brother. Only you understand.

We have been together since childhood, and we will remain together until the good Lord takes one of us."

* * * * * *

The house on Beach Avenue was sold in late August 1948, Suzy and Kate found a two-apartment family house on Bolton Avenue in Clason Point. Both women decided that living together in the same building, although in separate apartments, was the best way to maintain family life as they had known. Pete was set to travel to Italy immediately after the Labor Day holiday. Kate and Danny moved into the first-floor apartment the last week in August. Suzy, Pete, and their two daughters, Barbara and Frances, moved into the larger second-floor apartment. Frances was engaged to be married in March of 1949, and planned to live on White Plains Road a short distance from Clason Point after their marriage.

In addition to selling the house, moving, and planning for Pete's trip to Italy, the four brothers' business found itself in the middle of transitioning from coal and ice delivery to heating oil and home refrigeration, which their father, Leopoldo originally envisioned. If it had not been for the 1929 depression, the brothers had planned to purchase two oil delivery trucks, without a financial loan from the bank. The addition of two-oil delivery trucks would allow the brothers to promptly service all customers who were ready to covert to oil and refrigeration. Danny insisted that credit be extended to those customers that could not immediately transform their heating system from coal to oil. The goodwill earned by the offer of credit would encourage customers who had lost their jobs to receive our credit until they could find new work.

For many customers during this period, conversion from ice delivery to home refrigeration lagged behind the use of heating oil. It was expected that the effects of the depressed economy would result in a much slower conversion from ice to home refrigerators. These changes forced. the Ciarletta and Son's business into a period of immediate modification from coal delivery to heating oil delivery. The American economy would result in the continuation of ice delivery until people could afford home refrigerator. Financing became a new procedure for the ice and coal delivery business, until these new technologies could find ways to reduce pricing, while the economy rebounded.

The four brothers had planned for this partial restructuring of their business beginning in mid-January, 1948. They planned on selling two of their ice and coal vehicles, keeping two for the customers who still used coal and/or ice. Using some of their business saving account and a bank mortgage they planned to buy two more oil heating trucks. They would also restructure their employees; the immigrants that had been sent to America from Castellammare di Stabia as route men would no longer be responsible for a specific route. They needed the flexibility of combining all delivery routes that would need oil, as well as those customers that would still need ice and coal. This would enable the business to service all customers during this transition period. Their father's prediction and subsequent planning was now falling into place, as he had forecast.

Even though the business was busy dealing with its transition, the three brothers supported Pete's return to Italy in mid-September of 1948. The day before he was to leave, the four brothers finalized their procedures for conversion of the business. Pete began the meeting by once again thanking his brothers for understanding his need to travel to Italy and bring his son home during this busy time. Pete then proceeded to discuss the business loan, with part of his brain concerned about the business plan, and another part thinking of his trip to Italy to find his son Daniel.

Pete explained, "My brothers, I've been so busy with our families' move to the apartment from Beach Avenue and finalizing my trip to Italy that I never got around to completing the final details of our bank loan for the trucks. Al, you are the next oldest, I want you to go to the bank and get the best interest rate you can, sign the deal, and get the trucks we agreed upon.

Al smiled and said, "I'd be honored to take this burden off your shoulders Pete."

Pete then looked at Bob and Phil. "Phil, I want you to be responsible for selling the old Chevy trucks. Bob, you negotiate the wholesale contract for the heating oil, keeping in mind that we will have six trucks on the road at one time."

Phil told Pete to forget business, we all agree that you need to go to Italy and bring Daniel home.

Bob said, "Pete, don't worry about anything. We will be happy to cover everything as you have directed, from now on concentrate only on Italy and finding Daniel.

Pete ended the meeting by saying, "I'm confident you three will hold things together until I get back, and with my son at my side, things will return to normal."

* * * * * *

Once in Italy, Pete found the Italian bureaucracy impossible to overcome. He fought, bullied, pushed, and bribed until he had copies of both the Naples and Rome police reports, and the detective agency documents regarding Daniel's case. With these official papers in hand, he went to Rome, found the best detective agencies money could buy, and gave them the information he had acquired since March 1947, including a recent picture of Daniel. The detective agency planned on producing thousands of reward notices with a picture of Daniel for placement in and around Rome, Naples, Castellammare di Stabia, and Sicily. Also, a missing child advertisement in the newspapers in these cities and the Sicilian Provence. Pete hired a separate detective agency in Naples to re-open the investigation into Daniel's disappearance. He then traveled to Sicily, contacted the head of the Sicilian crime families, hiring them to inquire about his son. When that was completed, he returned to Naples and met with the head of the Camorra, the emerging Naples crime family, and hired them as well.

During this time, Pete lived with his parents in Castellammare di Stabia, sure that these new strategies would result in the return of his son. He frequently called the detectives and others involved to determine the progress being made. Leopoldo did not protest when he found out Pete had visited Sicily and also contracted with the newly organized Camorra crime family of Naples. Leopoldo was convinced that he was responsible for Pete's desperate state of mind and chose not to confront his son on these matters.

Both his parents and the rest of the family noticed how Pete had changed from the friendly, laughing, confident man they had always known, he was now a suspicious, rude, nervous, and dour man. Leopoldo, who had the most influence over his son, spoke with him. "Pietro, you have changed since Daniel disappeared. I feel as though I have lost both a grandson and a son."

Pete responded to his father's comment. "Don't ever say you have lost a grandson because I'm gonna find him."

"Pietro, I'll not scold you for the way you've just spoken because I know you're in pain. I only remind you there comes a time when you must accept the burdens you've received. There are things that even my brave son has no control over."

Pete, now visibly angry, responded. "Poppa, Daniel will be found and I'm gonna take him home with me."

Francesca approached her son and warmly embraced him, hiding the tears in her eyes as she said, "Oh, my son, what you have suffered, it is no doubt you are a changed man. Pietro, go home to your family in America. They also need your attention. Leave Daniel in the hands of the Lord. If he is still alive, then only God can bring him back to you, not the police, the fancy detectives, or those villains in Sicily."

Pete knew what he was about to say would deeply hurt his mother, but soon even this simple rational reasoning would be abandoned. His anger and hurt were about to become so intense that it would completely dominate and guide his every thought and emotion.

"Mamma, God is no longer a part of me. From childhood, I followed your example of faith and obeyed what my father taught me. I never cheated our customers, and I never turned to the Black Hand, even during those hard times in America's Great Depression. I went to church with my family, even though it was not expected of me as a man, and I have always been faithful to my wife. So how does God respond to my good deeds? He takes away my child. No, Mamma, God has chosen to turn his back on me, so I choose to turn my back on Him."

Francesca did not respond. She simply embraced her son with an understanding he was not ready to accept.

Pete remained in Italy for two months, checking his sources twice weekly and reviewing interim reports. At the end of six weeks, both detective agencies informed Pete they had found no leads and would be closing Daniel's case. Pete then visited the Camorra and received a similar report. He traveled to Sicily the next day, only to be given more bad news. Pete was now in a desperate, despondent state of mind, and broken in spirit, but he was not yet able to emotionally give his son to God, as suggested by his mother. Nonetheless, he finally agreed there was no more he could do in Italy. He followed his parents' advice and sailed back to America in December 1948, twenty-one months after Daniel's disappearance. There was a raging fire within Pete, fueled by his guilt, anger and hatred of everyone and everything that he encountered.

* * * * * *

The entire extended family visited Pete and Suzy on the first Sunday after Pete's return. Each family member entered the house uneasy, not sure how Pete would look or act. In two months, Daniel would have been missing for two years. Suzy was hurting but believed that her son would return when she was forgiven. Pete, on the other hand, was now convinced his son was dead, and his guilt was a burden that had been sucking the positive spirit from every pore in his body. As each day passed Pete seemed to be more labored and wearier than the day before. This big, strong, cheerful, kind man had changed so dramatically since Daniel was kidnapped, that it was a chore to attempt to have a conversation with him. It seemed to his immediate family that his physical body had deteriorated before their very eyes, and his personality permanently changed for the worse. His constant gloomy attitude had now turned to brooding and was slowly turning into unpredictability. To no one's surprise Pete was quiet during the meal. While having their espresso, the three brothers who were excited about sharing their good news with Pete, believing it might cheer him up; began to talk about the business arrangements they made while he was in Italy.

Al was proud of their accomplishments, and he began the progress report. "Pete, I think you'll be pleased with what we've been able to accomplish, while you have been in Italy. I got us a bank loan for the oil trucks from Chemical Bank on Gun Hill Road at the interest rate we discussed before you left. Wait until you hear the fantastic price Mack Trucks gave us on last year's models, once I told them we wanted to buy two trucks; we got an even better price. The oil deliveries have already started and the way you planned the schedule is working better than we expected."

Bob, who was impatient to explain to Pete the good news about the oil contract, interrupted. Al, "I negotiated a two-year contract with the Schildwachter Oil Wholesalers on Pugsley Creek, and the contract came in two cents lower per gallon than we expected."

Then Bob, with a big smile, placed his arm on Phil's shoulder, and while messing Phil's. neatly combed hair said, "Guess what? Our baby brother got a great price for the old Chevy trucks, a hundred and fifty dollars more than we expected on each truck." Everyone except Pete was laughing at Bob's playfulness.

The brothers suddenly realized that all their good news had not changed the expression on Pete's face. Danny could feel the chill coming from Pete and said, "Let's wait until we finish our meal before we talk business."

The brothers were disappointed but accepted their oldest brother's request. They finished their coffee, and the women began to clear the table for the "Boss and Underboss" card game.

Pete said in a somber monotone voice, "Before the game, let's go down to Danny's apartment to discuss the business changes in more detail. I have some questions."

The five brothers descended the stairs to Danny's apartment, excited about the new developments of their business.

Pete looked casually at the bank loan agreement and then looked up at Al. He hesitated a moment, and then in a soft tone, which would normally be unusual for Pete said, "After all we have been through. After all Danny and I did for you. My younger brothers now stab me in the back."

The four brothers were caught off guard by Pete's comment. Danny was about to speak, but Al interrupted. "Stab you in the back? Pete, what the hell are you talking about? For Chrissakes, when you left for Italy, you told me to sign the deal and get the trucks. I was following your orders. How can you say I stabbed you in the back? Damn it Pete, whaddya talking about?"

"You've always been this way, Al said Pete. "You'll never change. You've never pulled your weight from the first day you came from Italy. All you think about is women. If you worked like the rest of us, we might not be facing what you've presented to me today, and what hurts is that you did this behind my back while I was out of the country."

Al was furious at Pete's inaccurate, irrational comments, but he chose not to respond. He was afraid he would say something that would destroy their relationship. He sat back in his chair and lit a cigarette. Respectfully appealing to their older brother, Bob and Phil came to Al's defense. Both brothers assured Pete that they understood you had given Al the authority to finalize the loan, buy the trucks, and start servicing customers. The solidarity of the three brothers only served to make Pete more rigid, uncompromising, and provoking.

Phil asked, "Pete, what did you expect from Al?"

For the moment Pete seemed calmer when speaking to his youngest brother. "He was to present me with the interest cost of the loan, the make of the trucks, their cost and then we were to decide. How did Al know the price he paid for the trucks were the best price? And as for Bob, I expected wholesale prices from various distributors, not a negotiated contract. And the biggest insult to me was that you three started serving oil to our customers before I got back."

Phil pleaded with his brother. "Pete, all of that had been done. We had set the cost limits of the various trucks before you left. Al got the best deal on the Macks and bought the trucks for a price under what was agreed to. Bob took the best price offered on the wholesale oil from the various distributors, and I sold the old Chevys for more than we thought. Then in mid-October, the customers started calling to have their oil delivered. What else could we do, they needed oil, and we were ready to deliver, we all thought you'd be pleased that we got the ball rolling, before you got back."

Pete, now equally irritated at Phil, said, "Well, you were wrong if you thought all of that was settled."

There was a short period of silence, the three brothers looked at Danny and then each other, overwhelmed and confused.

Al broke the silence. "Pete, you're my older brother, and I don't want to be disrespectful. But I can't just sit here and let you accuse me of not working as hard as my other brothers and being the cause of our business restructuring that's.... Pete, please, I'm trying to be calm and show you the respect that comes with your position. How can you hurt me like this? We're brothers."

Danny felt it was time to mediate the situation. The words could not be taken back, but he believed the situation was resolvable if he could only find a way to penetrate the unexpected anger that seemed to have saturated Pete's entire body. "Pete, please tell us what Al did, what they each did, to make you so angry. We need to understand how you have been wronged. I want to understand what has happened. No one in this room would ever deliberately hurt you, but something has been done or said to make you feel betrayed. All we want is to understand and then make things right. I know this matter can be resolved. Did they somehow misunderstand or accidentally hurt your feelings? If you would only explain your side of it, I'm sure we can fix this. We are all Ciarlettas from the same flesh and blood."

Pete rose from the table, and without directly answering Danny's questions, spoke directly to Al. "I wish you well, but if you can't accept your faults, I want nothing further to do with you." Pete then turned to Phil and Bob. "It would seem you agree with Al, so you both are free to leave me and join Al. As for me I am now on my own, I'll take the remaining ice and coal trucks as my share of the business and continue to service the ice and coal customers, you three are now free to do whatever you like."

"Wait, Pete. It doesn't have to be this way, as brothers we can resolve your concerns. This has to be a simple misunderstanding," said Danny, who was completely bewildered by the conversation.

Pete looked at his older brother, Danny. "I told you when you left the business that you'd always be my wise brother, and I believe that with all my heart. But in this matter, I'm afraid there is no simple misunderstanding. I believe these actions have been willful and planned." Pete went over to Danny, kissed him on the cheek, and without another word went directly upstairs.

Danny followed Pete up the stairs continuing to reason with him. The three brothers silently followed Danny to the upstairs apartment.

The three brothers instructed their wives to round up the children; they would be leaving at once. The three wives were alarmed at their husband's statement. It was clear something disturbing had happened at the meeting. They immediately called the children who were playing in the street. The brothers retrieved their coats and went to the kitchen to say goodbye to Suzy and her sisters. They told the women Pete had dissolved his business partnership with his brothers. The Ciarletta wives kissed and hugged the Gallo sisters in silence. Suzy stood frozen leaning on the sink. Al left the apartment without acknowledging Pete, Bob and Phil silently shook hands with their stoic and impenetrable brother.

By the third free Sunday, the seven boys were still learning about each other. It was April, and the second week of work in the valley had begun. Vincenzo and Daniel followed the same procedures as the previous year. Daniel had become familiar with many of the tasks, which made the work easier. He had learned a few Italian words related to their work, which also made the work seem less difficult. Time passed slowly as Daniel waited enthusiastically for each Sunday to arrive.

CHAPTER 29

The month of May, although brisk and breezy in the mountains, brought with it the warmth of the bright spring sun, which helped to remove the memory of the harsh mountain winter. By the middle of May, the seven boys had become much more comfortable with each other.

The conversation had begun to move from exploring their different backgrounds to inquiring about the feelings they had experienced during the past two or three months their conversations were becoming more and more intriguing. The boys talked about those first weeks of captivity, the confusion, loneliness, and depression began to take form in words, rather than lonely thoughts.

On one bright May Sunday, Paul candidly expressed his feelings relative to his time in Opi. "For me, it was worse than being in solitary confinement in a jail. Sure, I was at times outside in the fresh air, and was kept busy, but let me tell you; I was scared and felt sad all the time. After I learned a little Italian and still couldn't get any answers from Tiziano or Rosa, I began losing hope of ever being released. Not only that but Tiziano is such a mean pain in the ass. After each of my two escape attempts, he got even meaner, yelling, pushing, and slapping me around. After my first escape attempt, I got the hell of a beating and no food for…oh I think…a day or two."

Paul then moved his conversation to a frightening thought. "I keep thinking about something scary. What if we can't find a way out of here, say in two or three more years? Is it possible that we could, you know, go crazy, lose our minds before ever being released?"

Jacob offered his opinion. "Paul, I don't think that could happen. There are people who get sent to jail for years and years. Have you ever heard of them going mad after being in a jail cell."

Klein reinforced Jacob's comment on the matter of losing their minds, "Yeah, Jacob, I'll bet you're right; a lot of people spend years in jail without going crazy.

Klein quickly changed the subject back to the possibility of escape and the others did not seem to mind. Klein was surprised to hear that Paul had tried more than once to escape. "I wish I had tried to escape. I never figured out a way to do it. I would sit in front of my stove staring at the flames. I couldn't even think clearly, and sometimes I couldn't move. Paul, I was lonely and scared. Then when I was working in the valley, I always seemed to be, the only word I can think of is numb. Is that the word when you feel you don't have enough energy to move or think?"

The other boys understood the emotions and feelings of Klein.

Jacob encouraged Klein to continue. "Well, this will seem weird, but things I saw seemed cloudy, and I thought of nothing but being home again. I can't even remember what I did in the valley during those first five or six days. Until I met you guys, the first two or three weeks were like a bad dream, a real bad dream. I kept asking myself, *Is this actually happening to me?*"

Jem chided Klein. "C'mon, mate, you gotta snap out of it. You need to try and have some laughs, give your family a hard time occasionally. If you don't, let me tell you, you're really gonna be miserable."

Jem, as was his way, quickly took over the conversation. "The second week in this lousy excuse for a town, I said to myself, I'm gonna make my time here easy. I'm gonna have as much fun as I can. Right off, I started teasing Caterina, even before I knew Italian, and I learned she loved my kidding around, but the best part was to see how mad it made Orsolo. Once I saw that, I teased her even more."

George interrupted Jem. "Yeah, Jem, but kidding comes easy to you. I couldn't be like you. I'm more like Klein. In the beginning, I was so confused and scared that it took me about a month before I even felt comfortable getting angry with Jacopo, never mind trying to escape. Then another month passed before I could even get up enough nerve, to make my first escape attempt."

Daniel was now smiling from ear to ear. "What a relief to hear you guys talk like this. When I was first captured, I was so scared and unsure of myself. I was convinced that I was a coward. Then after two failed escape attempts, I felt like a real loser. Now that I hear you guys were also afraid and couldn't escape, I feel a whole lot better."

Omar sat silently during these early discussions, unwilling to share. It was July before he was ready to discuss how he felt after being kidnapped. One Sunday, he began expressing his rage at the injustice he was forced to endure." Omar was unaware of the gradual but radical change he would soon experience in Opi.

* * * * * *

The farming season for the boys was coming to an end. It was now early October 1948. All the crops had been harvested except for root plants that grew all summer, underground. They would dig up the vegetables before the dirt became frozen, then clean, and prepare them for market.

On the first Saturday in October 1948, the farmers knew they had approximately four weeks remaining to sell their fall crop at the market in Pescasseroli. The morning sun had not yet risen, when Paul was wakened by Tiziano Vecellio, the man he farmed with. Each morning, Tiziano's loud unpleasant voice would cry out, "Rise, Paolo," It's time for us to load the wagon for market," as he pulled the covers off Paolo, exposing his warm body to the cold room. Paul learned quickly, if he hesitated, Tiziano would drag him from his bed.

Tiziano, in his late forties, was one of the men who had escaped the German work during their occupation of Opi by acting as a cripple, using a crutch pretending he did not have the proper use of one arm and leg. Tiziano's son was among the group of young men who had faced the firing squad rather than go with the Germans as work prisoners.

Soon Tiziano and his captive were on their way to the valley to load the wagon with crops. After loading, Tiziano returned Paul to his room just as the sun began to rise. Paul stoked the fire and added more logs into the belly of the stove. He undressed, returned to his warm covers, and soon fell back to sleep, knowing he had a long, free Saturday morning to sleep, stay warm, and relax.

Rosa Vecellio, Tiziano's wife, usually brought Paul breakfast on Saturday morning at around half past eight. She was deliberately quiet, trying not to wake Paul if he was still sleeping. This morning, Paul was awakened at around nine o'clock by a sweet, lyrical voice saying in broken English, "Paolo, it's time for you to get up. I have your breakfast." As Paul slowly opened his eyes, he was surprised to see Tiziano's only daughter, Theresa. He sat up quickly and said, "Theresa, what are you doing here? You're not allowed in my room alone!"

Theresa looked at Paul with her brow furrowed; lips tight, eyes narrowed and said in a slight deprecating voice, "Oh, Paolo, you're such a foolish young man. Stop telling me where I should and should not be. Now get out of bed. I have your breakfast."

Paul hesitated, knowing he was only wearing a pullover shirt and underwear. Theresa smiled and said, "Paolo, I'm a thirty-seven-year-old woman. I have seen men in their under clothing. Now stop being childish, get out of bed, and come to the table. I want to talk with you."

Theresa moved to the stove and added more logs, as Paul jumped from his bed and quickly dressed. She was waiting for him at the table.

"You better not stay here," said Paul. "What if Tiziano finds out? He'll go crazy!"

"Why are you concerned? Tiziano is at the market and won't be back till this afternoon. Besides, I want to talk with you."

Paul was aware that in Opi Pappa it was the respectful name to be used when speaking of one's father, and asked Theresa, "Why do you call Tiziano by his first name rather than Pappa?"

"A father is called Papa by his children out of respect. I have no respect for Tiziano."

As he ate his breakfast, Paul was surprised to hear Theresa talking so candidly about her father. This was very unusual for an Opi woman. "You sound like you're really mad at him."

Theresa had been smiling, lively, and happy when she entered Paul's room a few minutes earlier, but now she had a fierce scowl on her face and her warm, green eyes had turned as cold as the October chill. "He's mad! I hate the drunken, abusive pig. That's why I talk about him with such disrespect."

A sheepish smile crossed Paul's face, agreeing completely with Theresa's last comment. "Look, Theresa, I don't really care how you talk about Tiziano. It's just that I can't believe a woman from Opi would speak like that about her father. I mean I can't stand him, but you're his daughter."

The scowl on Theresa's face was now an unmistakable look of outrage. "He is the kind of man who used to think nothing of hitting his wife and daughter. Mamma had to live with that drunken pig for too many years, and like a foolish woman, I also accepted him for far too many years. Lord only knows why I waited so long before I made him stop."

"Wow, and I thought I was the only one he hit, but he hit you and Rosa? How did you get him to stop?" Theresa flipped her head to take the hair away from her eyes. "I was twenty-two the last time he hit me. When he finished, I lifted my battered face, looked Tiziano in the eye, and told him, the next time you strike me or Mamma, I'll wait for the first night you come home in your drunken stupor, and that's when I will put a knife through your heart.'" Paul smiled nervously, "You really said that to him? What did he say.?"

"You can be sure he was surprised to hear these words from his daughter."

"Do you think Tiziano thought you would really do it?"

"Oh, yes, he knew his daughter very well. Paolo, you must understand, I take no pride in threatening one of my own family. I'm sorry to say, my own flesh and blood, my father is a crudele (abusive) man." Theresa sighed, looked upward and said, "Oh yes, Paolo, Tiziano knew I meant what I said."

Paul wanted to know more of the story, "Did he ever hit you or Rosa again?"

"Is he alive and walking," Responded Theresa. "No, the coward knew he had hit us both for the last time."

Paul was surprised that Theresa used the word coward in reference to her father. "Why do you call him a coward? I've never seen him afraid."

Theresa rolled her eyes as if she was becoming frustrated with Paul's questions. "Paolo, I came to this room to speak with you about something very important to me and, I hope, also to you. That man is not part of what I have to say. So, I will answer this one last question, and then no more Tiziano. This will be the last time I speak of him today.

So, you want to know why Tiziano is a vigliacco (coward.) I call him that because only a vigliacco hits women and children who are not able to defend themselves. Only a coward uses the excuse of watching his son murdered by the Germans and get drunk. Only a cowardly, greedy man would bring to me, his only unmarried daughter, men willing to pay him to marry me. Men who pay money to marry a woman are just like him—ugly drunkards—who only want a woman who will give them pleasure by cooking and lying in bed with them. Then, when their bellies are full, and they are finished panting in their bed, they make themselves feel brave by slapping their wives. My brother was brave. He chose to die rather than be a slave to the Nazi dogs. Tiziano begged at the feet of the Germans to save his cowardly, miserable life. Paolo, your questions have spoiled my mood. I woke up this morning happy, knowing I was prepared to speak with you, but now, talking about Tiziano has made me angry. No more about this devil."

"Okay, Theresa, okay. No more Tiziano. But what if your mother is looking for you and finds you here alone with me?"

Theresa stood and walked over to the warm wood-burning stove, clasped her arms around herself as though trying to shake the chill from her body, and said, "Aha, Paolo, I hope you have not destroyed my mood."

Theresa put a few more logs in the stove and stared for a time at the red and yellow jumping flames.

Paul noticed for the first time Theresa's well-groomed hair and colorful dress, which was cut square in front and showed the skin of her upper chest and the top of her cleavage, the lower portion of the dress was even with her knees, exposing her long attractive lower legs. The women of Opi did not wear such revealing dresses, *thought Paul.*

Theresa eventually returned to Paul at the table. The scowl on her face, which had been so prominent, had vanished in the red and yellow flames, but her smile and the warmth of her green eyes had not yet returned. Theresa had facial features that matched her long legs, broad hips, thin waist, and exciting breasts. She was an appealing, long boned, mature woman.

Theresa asked Paul, "What is your age, nineteen, twenty?"

"Oh no, I turned seventeen last month."

"Seventeen, are you fooling with me. Muscular men like you with such broad arms and shoulders, I have never seen a man as big and strong that claims to be only seventeen years of age."

"Yeah, I am pretty big for my age," said Paul, feeling smug.

Theresa was now prepared to explain the reason for her visit. "Paolo, I'm a thirty-seven-year-old, unmarried woman. At my age, I don't wish to waste time with small talk, nor do I have the patience to pretend to be someone I'm not. You're very handsome and strong, and you seem like a sweet, gentle man. I'm a vital woman who has warm, passionate blood running through my veins. I want a passionate, gentle man to lie next to me in bed, and I believe you are that man."

Paul's eyes grew wide, and his sheepish grin immediately returned.

"Paolo, I can make your unfortunate life here in Opi seem like warm sunshine when you are with me, and I believe you can arouse in me passions that I've only dreamed about. Together we can make both of our dreary lives bright and happy, even if only for short periods of time."

Although Paul was only seventeen, he clearly understood what Theresa was suggesting. He had never had sexual intercourse with a girl in Australia. He had kissed girls and tried to touch their breasts, only to be rebuked.

Paul had never even seen a naked woman. Now this older, attractive woman wanted to have sex with him. He could not believe what he was hearing. Although sexually aroused, he was also nervous. Apparently, his disbelief and unsettled feelings didn't interfere with his arousal. He had no experience with women, and was uncertain about how to respond, especially to an older women like Theresa. *I'm not sure I'd know what to do,* he thought.

Theresa detected Paul's apprehension, and said, "Paolo, I know my words have taken you by surprise, and if you are doubtful about us being together, remove that thought from your mind."

Theresa slowly took Paul's hands in hers and placed the palm of his left hand on her chest above her breasts. Her green eyes had regained their warmth and they showered Paul with silent passion. She spoke slowly and in a low tone. "I will show you things you never imagined. I will teach you how our bodies can make us feel like we can touch the stars and the moon."

Still holding Paul's hand on her chest, Theresa leaned forward, forcing the fleshy part of his hand and pressed it deeply into her skin. She gently pressed her lips against his for a moment and then leaned back.

Paul's powerful, compelling urges were boiling, his penis growing erect and hard. Paul was very excited, but still restrained by the thought of Tiziano and Theresa's mother. "What if Tiziano caught us, or even your mother?" he said.

Theresa calmly replied, "As for my mother, she knows I'm here. She wants this happiness for me as much as I do, so do not be concerned. As for Tiziano, you know he is at the market every Saturday until one in the afternoon. Every Monday, he attends the meeting of the governing council, and when they finish talking business, they open their wine and stay at their meeting until late in the evening. Each Wednesday night he goes to the bar in town. He returns late and is unable to find his bed, we will often find him in a chair. Thursday morning, sleeping in a chair. There are times when he is unable to even reach the chair, and we find him sprawled on the floor. So, my dear Paolo, for now we have three times a week to relieve our tension and boredom. You can trust me when I say we will not be disturbed, and I can promise heaven for both of us three times a week. For a young man like yourself, you must admit this sounds inviting, no?"

"Yeah, but Theresa, wait a minute. What happens, you know, if you have a baby? I'm afraid Tiziano would kill me if we were not married, and I gave you a baby." "Paolo, oh my Paolo, first it was Tiziano, now you worry about what I would look like to the people of Opi if I was with child; these fears you have are about the things that have already broken my heart. This miserable town has destroyed all my hopes for a real life."

"Never mind the people; it's Tiziano that I hate.

Theresa released her hold on Paolo's hand, which was resting on her bare upper chest. She slouched in her chair, and her facial expression became sorrowful and no longer tantalizing.

"I s'pose talk of a bambino was to be expected. It's just that most Italian men who have a chance to be with a woman don't think of a bambino. They think only of what hangs from between their legs. But not my Paolo, no, he inquiries about the result of our pleasure. I can see that it's necessary to explain," said Theresa.

"In 1923, I was a twelve-year-old girl living in Opi. One day I had a pain in my stomach. I told my parents of this pain. Tiziano told me to rest, and I would be better, but when the pain stayed, he took me to Dattore Tatti. Dattore told Tiziano to go quickly to the hospital near Pescasseroli. I will never forget the long, bumpy ride in the wagon with such pain at each bump. I remember thinking; I will surely die by the time we get to the hospital. Why do I have to live in Opi, so far away from everything, with a father who tells me to rest, and not take me to a hospital the first time I felt the pain? That's why I call both Tiziano and Opi miserable. When we finally reached the hospital, the doctor said I had, oh I forget what he called the sickness, but my appendix had broken. He told my parents if I had waited longer, yes, I would have died. I did not know this thing appendix, but after the doctor removed the broken appendix, he told me the horrible news. I will always remember two words he used, gangrene and gangrenous. The doctor said that since my illness stayed in my body so long, the gangrenous material caused an infection that went to the place in a woman's body where a bambino flourishes, and even though he took the broken appendix out of my body, the infection damaged forever, the place where a baby grows. My female eggs could no longer get inside that place where the bambino matures. He then told me that I would never be able to be a mamma. How horrible, my life as a woman, over at twelve years of age. Because of Tiziano"

Since Paul's father was a doctor, he knew a little about the body and how it works. He understood the part about the appendix, but he did not realize a ruptured appendix is not treated quickly can make a woman sterile. Trying to be sympathetic, he said, "Why did you feel your life was over? So, what if you can't have children? You are still a beautiful woman."

"Paolo, you're young and not Italian, so you don't understand. There are two types of Italian men. One kind of man, a family man, willing to marry a woman who can provide him with children. This will satisfy his need to be a pappa. Then there is the other kind of man, a selfish man, who only wants a woman to give him pleasure and cook his food. This type of man does not want the responsibility of having children; he is unable to love others. He seeks only his own pleasures. This is the only kind of man who would marry a woman who can never be a mamma. Even at the young age of twelve, I knew a loving family man would never accept me as a wife. So, I decided I would rather be a lonely woman than marry a selfish man, and I was right, just look at what Tiziano has become."

Theresa continued, "We are very much the same, you and I, Paolo. We are both prisoners in this town. Can you now understand why our union together, even if only a few hours a week, can bring some joy into our lives?"

Theresa rose from her chair, took Paul's hands, and walked him slowly toward the bed. She sat him down and slowly unbuttoned his shirt. Paul couldn't take his eyes off her smiling face, as his body screamed with excitement far beyond any titillation he had ever known. Theresa slowly and deliberately removed his top shirt and then his undershirt, slowly stroking his arms and chest, and gently kissing him. She unbuckled his belt and said, "You do the rest of your clothes, and I will remove my dress."

Paul was unable to remove his eyes from Theresa, as he fumbled to remove his pants. Theresa, who was now standing before him in her plain cotton brassiere and underwear, was the most exciting sight Paul had ever seen. Her smooth olive skin, her firm breasts trying to burst from their support, her underwear, and the delicious jewel he imagined it covered, her round hips and long, thin legs had plunged Paul into a trance-like state.

She sat next to him, held his cheeks in her hands, and gave him a long, soft kiss. Theresa's full lips warmed Paul's entire body. Bending and slithering her body slowly and smoothly toward the pillow, she moved under the covers, patted the mattress with the palm of her left hand, and said, "Paolo, this spot is for you. Come next to me. I need you."

Theresa was accurate in everything she had said. Using few words, she was able to teach Paul many ways to please and sensually arouse a woman that were also quite pleasing for him. She and Paul touched the stars and the moon twice that Saturday morning.

* * * * * *

By the middle of November 1948, the farmers and their captives went through the procedure of clearing the land of dead vegetation, and then cleaned, oiled, sharpened, and stored their tools for the winter. The remainder of the month was taken up with winemaking. The last Sunday in November, Daniel was asked about the American tradition of Thanksgiving. After he had finished detailing some of the customs surrounding this unique American holiday, he was quite surprised to be taken to task, in a good-natured way, by the two British "angels" for the celebration of America's Pilgrim holiday as a separation from England. Daniel understood the purpose of the Thanksgiving holiday, but only on a superficial level. The chiding he received from the two other "angels," although cheerful and congenial, taught Daniel that Thanksgiving was not only a holiday when Americans visited with family and ate too much food, but its meaning in terms of freedom and liberty, which was a topic continually on the minds of the boys.

December brought the beginning of snow and cold weather in the mountains. It was also the time when the people of Opi prepared for their mountain weather. The activities of the "angels" during December mostly involved the splitting of wood taken from the forest for winter heating. The gathering of wood for the coming winter months was accomplished by the seven farming family men, with the aid of some of the older men to bear arms as protection from the bears, bores, and wild dangers wolves. Many mules, ten to fifteen in a set, were tied together and taken to the beech tree forest, beginning at the end of what was once grass for their sheep. There were perhaps as many as ten sets of mules tied together. Every available mule in Opi was used in this wood gathering effort. The heavily armed men were prepared to protect the wood gatherers as they loaded fallen beech wood into the canvas bags hanging from the sides of the mules. More wood was tied in bundles and rested on the blankets covering the backs of the mules. Some of the dead trees were carefully chopped down, then chopped into smaller pieces, and loaded onto the back of the mules. The wood was then brought from the forest into Opi for the seven "angels" to chop into smaller pieces for the wood-burning stoves that heated all the houses of the town. Seven days of wood collecting provided sufficient wood for each Opi family for the winter.

The boys had not completed their task of chopping all the wood that had been gathered. through early December; during this time planning for the Christmas season and its grand finale on Christmas Eve was also taking place. Traditionally young boys would walk down the main road calling out for the donation of wood for the Great Christmas Barn Fire that took place behind the church after the Christmas Midnight Mass. But since the dreadful happenings of the World War II tragedy that took the lives of so many Opi boys and young men; the gathering of wood for the barn fire event was delegated to the older men. During this time, the boys would often see some of the older men leading mules back from the outer edge of the forest loaded down with tree limbs inside bags and other wood tied to their backs. Prior to Christmas eve the wood was carefully arranged on the piazza behind the church to form a huge mountain of wood to be ignited after Mid night Mass.

The angels were told of the wonderful Christmas Eve traditional event that took place every year on the piazza behind the church. Each family was insistent that their "angels" attend this most cherished tradition. Each Opi family prepared special treats to eat along with their recipe for eggnog and wine to accompany the food. Although the traditional barn-fire was used as a joyous event to eat and drink, its main purpose was to highlight the religious significance of this most important day, the birth of Jesus. On Christmas Eve, immediately after Midnight Mass, the entire town, children included, would gather around an enormous, complicated stack of tree stumps, logs and tree limbs. The food and drink had been laid out around the stack of wood prior to Midnight Mass.

A small stable with hay spread on its floor, and three-foot high figures of the baby Jesus, and Mary and Joseph, three kings, shepherds and animals were all carefully placed around the crib of the infant Jesus. Two oil lanterns burned brightly and hung from the roof of the stable. The depiction of the birth of Jesus was placed against the back wall of the piazza. After Midnight Mass, the people took their places around the stack of wood as it was set ablaze by Vincenzo, the head of the Governing Council. The people then spent the remainder of the evening singing traditional holy Christmas carols and local peasant songs passed down by Opi people through the centuries. All the people enjoyed the singing, treats of roasted chestnuts, sweet bread, cookies, fruit, and other delicious food, washed down by eggnog or wine, and sometimes both.

Once again it was interesting that the boys had eagerly been invited to this special event, but no one from Opi made any attempt to integrate them in the festivities. They were encouraged to enjoy the prepared food and drink but were not asked to physically join the people in song or even their farming families. The angels found themselves off to one side sitting as a group watching the intriguing mountain of fire, enjoying the treats and each other, but always outsiders in the activities of the people. This was probably not a deliberate snub to the boys, but rather an unconscious statement by the people of separation between the captives and family residence of Opi. During the barn fire ritual, the seven boys apart from the town people, began to share the Christmas traditions of their various countries and families. Omar, an Islamic boy who did not celebrate this Christian event was encouraged by the other angels to talk about his God. Omar explained to the boys "The Islamic God is known as Allah and believed to be an all-powerful and allknowing creator, sustainer, and judge of the universe. Islamic people put a great emphasis on the conceptualization of Allah as Singular and Unique God and inherently one, (ahad) who is all merciful and all powerful.

When it was Daniel's turn, he focused on the traditions of his family and those of many other Italian Immigrant families living in America. On the morning of Christmas his mother and Aunt Kate would go shopping for seven different varieties of fish. When the women returned, the children helped them clean and prepare the fish for the 2:00 p.m. meal, which consisted of the seven fish varieties served in a tomato-based gravy, over linguini pasta known as (vigilia di Natale). Also, during this time preparation of the main Christmas meal would begin. The men came home from a half day of work at about 1p.m. in time to enjoy the feast.

Around four p.m. after the meal and clean up, the women prepared the seven fishes and then placed in the oven to be cooked. The seven fish was a replacement for meat for the Christmas meal. Once this was accomplished, adults and children went to bed for a nap. Everyone was up by ten-thirty or so and prepared to attend the Midnight Mass at Holy Cross Church in Clason Point. The High Mass featured beautiful choral singing. Many families had sons who served as altar boys during the High Mass.

As all the priests in the parish said a second private and traditional individual Masses at the various side alters which also use altar boys, which caused many families to get home around 2 P.M. waiting for their altar boy sons, serving at the side alters.

When the family returned to their house after the long Midnight Masses, the children busily began preparing the table as the women completed final preparations of the fish and vegetable, and macaroni dinner. The meal was ready to be served at approximately 3 a.m. After dinner everyone opened their Christmas presents, and then everyone too took a long nap before relatives arrived with presents.

Daniel explained, "That the people in Opi called their dinner a pasta meal, the Italian Americans call it their dinner a macaroni dinner. The meal was not rushed and there was a lot of laughing, eating and drinking. The kids were allowed to join their parents at meals and drink wine mixed with water."

There were all kinds of sweets, non-alcoholic drinks for the children, and alcoholic drinks for the adults. These visits to and from individual homes lasted till evening time, with no formal breakfast, lunch or dinner prepared on this day, just sweets drinks and the giving and receiving of gifts.

After the Christmas excitement the people of Opi and the angels returned to their routine of sustaining life in the cold, snowy mountain winter. February was usually the coldest month in the mountains, and most of the work that needed to be done was accomplished indoors.

On this cold January day in 1948, most of the boys had been held captive for close to a year. The young boys met at their usual gathering place, the empty, bombed plot of land on the main cobblestone road. Paul had told the other boys about his weekly encounters with Theresa. Even now, five months into the affair, the boys enviously waited to hear about his latest fun in bed with Theresa. They were living vicariously through Paul's experiences. Even Omar, who had a religious objection to the affair, listened attentively. Due to the cold, strong wind this Sunday, the boys decided to go to Jacob's room for some warmth. The seven boys were warming themselves on the floor around the wood-burning stove, and Klein was talking about his wish to get to the snow-covered mountains with a pair of skis.

Omar changed the subject by directing a statement to Paul. "Although my religious beliefs force me to disagree with your decision to be with Theresa since you are not married, I do not condemn you. If I had not met my six dear friends and never left my Islamic surroundings, I might have been more judging of your actions. I am learning a great deal from the six of you, and I am a more compassionate human being for the teaching you have been providing." Omar was the most serious and intense of the seven captives. He was approximately the same age as the others, and although the seven boys had quickly bonded, Omar initially was not as friendly as the others. However, after a few months of being together on Sundays, he gradually became more comfortable. and was very much an integral part of the angels of Opi.

Jacob continued the discussion, saying, "What I find interesting is how different we are even though we have been living the same life during this past year. Klein asked David to give some examples of what he meant.

"Well, there's one example right there. You're the one who is first to question what people are saying and the things you see. You are always interested in the differences in our cultures and our personalities." I'll give you another example," said George. "I don't understand how Dan and Jem can possibly enjoy the company of the wives in their Opi families."

Daniel was the first to respond. "I don't know about Jem, but it took me almost seven months of telling myself that I shouldn't like Gelsomina. I would lie in bed at night and think, 'How is it possible for me to enjoy working with a woman who is part of a plot to keep me a prisoner?' Then, at some point, I stopped fighting with myself and decided that if being around her made my life in Opi happier, what the hell, I'd be stupid not to use her. At some point after I was brought here, I said to myself, I'm not going to say no to any pleasure that happens to come along, even if they are pleasures that I don't understand."

George than asked, "What about you, Jem?"

"It sounds like it was a lot easier for me than it was for Dan. Orsolo is such a grouch, but Caterina was just the opposite. I enjoyed being around her. You know how I love to be a tease — well, she enjoys it. When I learned a few more Italian words, I could really make her laugh. I guess she likes to laugh, and no wonder, living with 'Mr. Sour Face.' I wouldn't be surprised if she had never laughed before I was brought here. In the beginning, when I was first brought to Opi, and I was able to make Caterina laugh, Orsolo didn't know what to make of it. Then later I could see it made him mad as hell, so that made me want to make her laugh even more."

Jem continued by picking up on the question by Jacob that started the conversation. "And how about Paul and the way he enjoys breaking Tiziano's balls every chance he gets, even when he knows he is going to get smacked around for being a ball breaker?"

"Yeah, he smacks me around a little, but Theresa is right. He's a coward."

Jacob added, "Boy, I hope he doesn't find out about you and Theresa. No telling what he would do to you."

Paul shrugged his shoulders. "The way I look at it, I have him in a corner. If he found out Theresa and I were doing it, what could he do? He can't kick me out of town. He can't kill me or break my knees. If he did, he wouldn't have anyone to help him on the farm. He brought me here. He is the one who locks me in his house. If he hadn't brought me to Opi, Theresa and I wouldn't be fooling around. Anyway, Theresa has him so scared that if she came near him with a knife, he would probably crap his pants."

Jacob continued the theme of individuality. "Omar amazes me. He is so defiant when Nicoangelo tries to take him to church." He turned to Omar and said, "You don't give an inch, no matter what he says or does. Me, I gave up long ago trying to explain my Jewish background. They just can't understand how I can believe in God and not believe that Jesus is the Son of God. More than anything, I go with them to church just to break the monotony of my daily routine."

Omar smiled broadly and said, "And I, my friend, don't understand why you are surprised by my resistance. I'm only acting as any Egyptian would if they were in a similar situation."

The seven boys were continually surprised at how differently they saw similar things so relevant to their daily lives. Being bound together by common experiences and isolated in the same environment, they assumed they would react in a similar fashion to their surroundings.

The boys offered each other a social and emotional support system, and it was a resource they learned to value. This sustenance not only helped them endure their captivity, but it also made them feel valued as human beings valued for something more than their ability to perform farm labor. Belonging to "The Angel Club of Opi," the name they gave to themselves, based on Father Mascia's comment that day in the church when he called us Opi's Angels. The name angels became their group moniker; it started out as a joke, but soon became important to the seven boys. The name angels gave them a sense of belonging to a social network that was outside of their strange, unusual existence in Opi. It was the one thing they could hold onto that seemed rational, and in turn was to become a part of our social experience in their mountain prison. The seven boys had received no formal education while in Opi. However, they were fortunate to have one day a week to be together and learn from each other. In the beginning, they didn't fully comprehend just how important Sundays would become in their lives. As the years continued to drag on, they learned to value the weekly meeting of "The Angel Club of Opi." On the last Sunday in January. The boys huddled next to the wood-burning stove in Jem's living quarters trying to warm themselves from the cold and snow.

After walking for maybe twenty minutes in the forest he bumped into a barrier. He first thought that due to its mass under the snow it was probably a huge boulder. Daniel walked to his left which was towards the end of snow-covered mass was a huge tree that had fallen and was now covered with snow. Daniel could see that the tree had been uprooted from the ground, causing a very large hole with the roots still attached to the large fallen base of the huge tree. He decided to cross the barrier by walking around the far end of this large hole of intertwined roots, with frozen dirt, still attached to the long thin roots, and snow. He was carefully choosing not to walk too close to the ridge of the circular hole fearing that the soil at the ridge might be dangerously soft. at the end of an entrance of the edge might contain loos soil which would collapse under his weight. Two steps later, the soil of the entrance collapsed down into the large hole and contained Daniel who accidentally fell into the winter bear hibernating with her three cubs now faced a Marciano bear.

He had only been able to get out of Opi, but the head start he had gained on Vincenzo would enable him to take a moment's rest. He did not know the time, but he could tell by the black night still in the sky and the quietness of the animals that Vincenzo would not detect his absence for perhaps an hour or more. By then Daniel knew he would be a good distance out of the forest and would stop at the first town he passed.

He turned and continued walking back to his tracks in the snow and sweeping the snow with the branch covering his tracks. As he moved in a backward pace his nfeet sunk deep into a soft patch of snow and dirt. He extracted his boots from the soft, muddy dirt he heard soft, muffled, weak, high-pitched barks. He immediately realized he had disturbed some animal, but from the sounds it couldn't be a big animal that would cause him trouble. So, he continued to cover the next two steps now standing on a hard surface. He could still hear the high-pitched chirping or maybe it was a barking sound, something under the hole he had stepped in in. He looked around while holding the damp, splintered, bark lined tree limb with both hands in the event he had to swing at whatever animal he had disturbed. In the pitchblack surroundings, he could only make out movements that were close to his eyes. He continued to hear the unique "babyish" sounds off to his right. He first thought it was a nest of birds, but the faint barking sounds could not be birds. He decided to ignore the animal he had disturbed, deciding that whatever it was would not be a threat. He was about to continue his trek forward in the direction of the mountain when the immature barking sound seemed to be closer. He held his stick forward, leaned over toward the ground, and peered down to identify what was at his feet. He could now see three four-footed little animals. Oh my God, bear cubs? He realized that if baby bears were in a nest-like cave, mama bears would not be far away. He immediately stood erect, intending to quickly move away, no longer concerned about sweeping the snow to disguise his footsteps. He turned and, in the pitch, black noticed a large form in front of him. Could it be a bush? After taking one step toward the hazy form, he saw a huge Marsicano bear standing over him. The mother bear was now close enough to make out the predator standing between her and her cubs. The mother bear let out a loud deep roar. Daniel found himself face to face with a bear that had the biggest eyes one could ever imagine. Both human and bear remained momentarily rigid. Daniel was afraid to move a muscle for fear of provoking an attack. He slanted his peripheral vision right and then left to see if he had time to reach a barrier. He could not make out anything in the blackness.

Realizing he was facing a brutal death, his life did not pass before his eyes, as he had so often heard. A few brief thoughts and emotions surged through him, in what felt like minutes but were seconds. The standing bear reached out with both front legs and wrapped them around her prey. The bear's front legs with her clawed paws at Daniel's waist lifted him completely off the ground and began to slowly tighten the grip on her victim. She was determined to crush this predator that had threatened her cubs.

The bear let out another roar, directly in the face of its victim. Being held three feet off the ground, in a vice-like grip by the powerful front legs of the bear, inches away from the bear's mouth, the fourteen-year-old boy was so frightened that he wet his "long john" underwear. Staring directly into the mouth of the bear, Daniel could see the slimy, long, fat, grey tongue, the saliva dripping from the pink walls of the bear's inner cheeks, the brown stained long sharp teeth, and a channel at the end of the tongue that spewed dark particles into his face. Now along with wetting his underwear, he was ready to vomit. However, gastric juices did not flow from his body as an idea suddenly entered his mind.

The disgusting ugly open mouth of the bear might have saved his life, but he had to act fast. The bear's front legs were methodically closing their grip on her victim's waist and ribs, making it more and more difficult for Daniel to breathe. Daniel raised the tree limb he was holding at his side so he could grip his feeble weapon with both hands. Waving the tree limb in front of the bear's face caused the animal to roar once again. Daniel immediately reared back as far as he could and thrust the tree limb into the mouth of the bear, forcing it deep into the bear's throat until it hit something solid. Daniel expected the bear to drop her victim so she could remove the large wood from deep in her mouth, allowing him to run toward the road as fast as he could.

It was no coincidence that an object such as a tree limb, thrust powerfully into the throat of a bear and crashing against the base of its inner skull before it stopped, would destroy, and break apart four tube like organs composed of cartilage, tissue, blood and lined by a moist pink tissue know as mucosa. The bear's Larynx, located at the back of the throat is a breathing tube containing vocal cords; blood vessels burst on two folds of mucous membrane, which caused the bear's roar to become a squeal. The Trachea, next to, and running parallel to both the Larynx and Pharynx, which are respiratory tubes connected to the voice box allowing oxygen to get to the bronchi located in the lungs. And the crushed Esophagus located directly behind the Trachea, running down to the stomach, between the heart and spine.

Much to Daniel's surprise the bear did not drop him to remove the limb. Daniel's eyes, which remained inches away from the bear's face, now noticed the once aggressive look on the bear's face turn to a look of confusion. The fourteenyear-old boy from the Bronx did not realize the physical damage he had done to the bear; nor did he understand the pain, courage, and determination a mother bear could tolerate, when faced with a challenge to her young cubs.

Daniel could feel the pressure around his rib cage and waist lessen, he found he was able to almost breathe normally, but the bear refused to be defeated. With the mother bear and its prey still inches apart, and with the animal's front legs remaining around Daniel's body, Daniel could feel the tight grip of the bear continuing to ease ever so slightly. Staring into each other's faces, the bear's front paw claws, which were dug into Daniel's waist, began ever so slightly to lose their power. The look of confusion in the bear's eyes had now turned to bewilderment. Daniel felt the severe pain above his waist as the bear front paw claws dug deep into his skin. Daniel could now feel the persistent pressure of the bear's front legs growing weaker by the moment, as its ability to take in oxygen continued to be spasmodic. Though pain stricken and weak from lack of oxygen, the bear still refused to let its prey free; Daniel found his breathing to be less strenuous, as the bear's labored oxygen intake became more difficult.

Daniel stopped struggling to conserve his breathing, and for the first time he wondered if the damage he had caused would enable him to outlast the bear. Daniel now thinks, if the bear's legs continue to lose their strength, he will have to drop me, and the minute I hit the ground I'm outta here. However, once again the fourteenyear-old boy from the Bronx had no understanding of the nature of a mother bear in a life-or-death fight to protect her cubs.

Just before the bear was about to lose a grip on her predator, she dug her sharp claws on the end of both of her paws deep into the back of her victim. Daniel let out an excruciating scream as the six sharp claws deeply penetrated his back. At the sound of the scream the bear tried to roar but was only able to produce a feeble distorted squeal. The bear was now about to fall from lack of oxygen, but through sheer strength and determination she remained standing on shaky legs, holding her prey. Moments later, with all its strength now depleted, but still refusing to let her victim free, Daniel began to slide down toward the ground with the six claws still penetrating his back. As he descended, the bear's claws were ripping through the skin, tissue and muscle on Daniel's back; the pain of this slow cutting caused Daniel to scream in tortured agony. When Daniel's feet finally hit the ground, the bear, now completely out of oxygen, fell to the floor of the forest as her sharp claws exited Daniel's back. Daniel's pain caused him to pass out a few seconds before his feet hit the ground. He fell backwards onto the snow covering the forest floor. The bear lay on its side, making a futile attempt to extract the tree limb from its throat as the last ounce of strength left her body. The Marsicano bear gave a final low squealing sound, as she looked toward her cubs, and finally died, her head landing in the soft snow, her eyes wide open gazing intently at her cubs.

Approximately a half hour after Daniel passed out in the forest, Vincenzo opened the back door to Daniel's room to deliver his coffee and roll. Not seeing Daniel dressing or in his bed, Vincenzo dropped the coffee and roll, went to the stable, saddled his horse and galloped along the back dirt road till it met the cobblestone road. As he arrived at the town entrance the two men in the wagon, who had relieved the night shift men about forty minutes ago, were alarmed to see a speeding Vincenzo coming toward them. As he pulled up his horse, he frantically told Alberto to go find another protector to aid him in his watch. He explained to Nuncio, the second protector in the wagon, "My angel has escaped. I want you to follow me in the wagon immediately."

Without waiting for confirmation Vincenzo galloped off down the road into the valley. He proceeded on the road leading to the forest with Nuncio trailing behind him in his wagon. Vincenzo followed Daniel's footprints on the road and then into the forest. When Nuncio arrived at the spot where Vincenzo entered the forest, he tied the horse and wagon to a tree and followed Vincenzo on foot with his rifle. Nuncio came to the fallen tree; saw the dead bear on its side, and Vincenzo kneeling over a prone body in the snow. Vincenzo handed Daniel's body to Nuncio and instructed him to take Daniel to Dattore Tatti immediately. Vincenzo entered Dattore Tatti's front room and continued past the white curtain.

Daniel was lying on a table on his stomach, and Dattore Tatti was cleaning the wounds on Daniel's bare back. Vincenzo was startled to see the wounds completely uncovered. Dattore Tatti told Vincenzo, "You can leave; the boy is now my responsibility."

Vincenzo gathered up a party of three other men to ride with Nuncio. The five men went back to the forest to retrieve the dead bear. It would be used for meat and the skin would be made into clothing. Vincenzo returned to Dattore Tatti two hours later to check on the patient.

Dattore Tatti explained to Vincenzo, "He is still unconscious. I have treated his deep wounds, but we will have to wait and see if the boy has the will to live." Dattore Tatti then asked Vincenzo a question, "When you found Donato, what position was he in?"

Vincenzo thought this was an unusual question, but answered, "I found him next to the bear lying on his back. I did not see the wounds till I lifted his body."

Dattore Tatti smiled. "If he does survive, it will be because of the position you found him in. His cuts were in the cold snow and that slowed the loss of blood. I believe we will know in a few days if he will survive."

Daniel did survive. The herbs used by Dattore Tatti prevented the infection from spreading. Daniel was out of his pain-induced coma that evening; and in six weeks Daniel was back working on the farm with Vincenzo. Daniel was surprised that Vincenzo made no mention of the escape attempt, nor did he discuss any disciplinary action. Daniel did notice when he was allowed back to his room that more concrete had been poured in the stable, which connected the concrete slab at the entrance to the concrete floor of the stable.

Since the split of the Ciarletta brother's business in late October 1947, Danny had made numerous efforts to repair the damage caused by Pete's unreasonable and bewildering reaction to the business restructuring plans. He decided to make one final attempt at reconciliation between Pete and his three younger brothers. In February 1949, when Danny met Al, Bob, and Phil, Daniel had been missing for over two years, twenty-seven months to be exact. After a cheerful greeting and a glass of wine, Danny explained the purpose of his visit.

"I'm here to ask if you would be willing to let Pete rejoin the business."

Al was the first to speak. "Why isn't Pete here talking for himself?

"Pete knows nothing of my visit today. Pete has no knowledge of what I am asking you, this is your oldest brother speaking."

Al continued, "Danny, Pete was wrong when he accused me of not doing my share of work. If it was anyone other than my older brother who said that about me, I don't know what I would have done. Pete hurt me deeply that day, but he's my brother and I love him. My hope is that, in time, when he comes to accept Daniel's disappearance, he'll one day approach me and tell me he was wrong and apologize for what he said. So, if you're asking me will I stand in the way by asking for an apology before agreeing, no I won't. I know he is not ready for that, but not being ready does not make a person correct in his opinion.

CHAPTER 30

With these words Danny knew the largest hurdle in unifying the brothers had been overcome. Danny arose from his chair, approached Al, hugged him firmly, and said, "Al, you're a great man and a cherished brother."

Danny turned to Bob and Phil. "Let's hear from you two."

Bob spoke first. "I've always loved and respected Pete, but when Daniel disappeared, he changed. What a burden the man has to bear, and I have nothing but sympathy for my brother. I would not stand in the way of his returning to the business. I only hope that someday he'll become the Pete we all once knew. Let me also say I'm a practical man. We could use another hand who knows our business the way Pete does. I wouldn't even mind if he came back as leader. Look, Danny, to tell you the truth, business is booming, and we've been dividing the leadership responsibilities among the three of us. I think we could use his help, and as the second oldest brother, even after what happened why not let him take his rightful place as the head of the business."

Danny reached over and squeezed Bob's hand. "You're not only a good brother but also a wise one."

Danny now looked at Phil with renewed confidence. "Well, my youngest brother, let me hear from you."

Phil responded in a similar fashion. "Danny, I remember when I came to America as a young boy. I wanted to work right away and make money, but you refused — you made me go to school and learn English. Pete would slip my money on the side during those years while I was living with Bob and Al. I'm obligated to all of you for my life in this country, but especially to Pete for his kindness. And how can I forget how Pete protected us during those dangerous days on the streets of the Bronx? I'll not object to him leading us once again. And there's another thing. I know he's too proud to ever admit it, but I think it would be good medicine for him to come back as leader. So, I say, let's make it happen."

Danny smiled broadly and tapped Phil's hand. "My baby brother doesn't forget the deeds of his older brother. Bob and Phil mentioned leadership. Al, are you willing to accept Pete's leadership?"

"Danny, if Pete's is willing to accept the fact that delivering ice, coal and sawdust are things of the past and agrees that heating oil is the future for our business, yeah, I'd gladly accept his leadership. He was a hell of a leader in the early years, and there's no reason why he can't do it now."

Al hesitated for a moment, reached for his wine, and finished what remained in his glass. Now with a deadly serious tone in his voice he said, "Bob, Phil, there is one thing you must be prepared for. If Pete comes back, and if at any time he says one word, just one word, about me not pulling my weight, then, older brother or not, I'm telling him to stick it and either he goes, or I go. That means you two will be forced to make a choice: Pete or me. I'm telling you now, I won't stand for that a second time and that's the end. They'll be not talkin', no negotiatin', no misunderstandin', and no telling me he's not the same man we once knew." One bad word about me from Pete, and I'll look at you two. And you'll have to say 'goodbye Al' or 'goodbye Pete'—

right then and there. It's gonna be as simple as that. I'll demand your answer at that moment: me or Pete."

Bob and Phil looked at each other, Bob spoke first. "Well, Phil, for me the choice is pretty easy. Pete walked out on us, so I gotta stick with Al."

Phil also agreed, but added, "God, it would be a hell of a thing telling my oldest brother I don't want him, but you're right, Bob, given the circumstances we would have no choice, I would stand with all."

Danny, understanding the risk, was not about to let anything scuttle the deal at this early stage. He was pleased with the attitude of his brothers and understood their positions.

"All right, now that I know where you guys stand," said Danny, "I'll speak to Pete and arrange a meeting. Here's what I have in mind. Give me a coupl'a weeks to talk with him about hooking back up with the business. I'll tell him I came here today and talked to the three of you about him rejoining the business, and the fact that business is booming. I'll make sure he understands it's strictly heating oil delivery, and that you want him back handling leadership responsibilities plus delivery.

"Danny, there's one thing that doesn't square with me," interrupted Al. "It's not that we want him back as leader, but that we agreed to take him back as leader."

Danny was disturbed by Al's clarification. "Is it that important for you to be so picky with the words?"

"Yeah, Danny, it feels important to me."

"Okay, I'll make it work your way," said Danny.

Danny explained the remainder of his plan. "In the meantime, Suzy and Kate will invite the whole family for Easter Sunday like it used to be on Beach Avenue, the five brothers, our families, everyone together again, like before we lost Daniel."

It was still difficult to speak of his namesake and favorite nephew. He fought back the lump in his throat and continued, "Remembering the good times should put everyone in a good mood. After the meal, the five of us will go to my apartment, and based on what you've said today, I expect Ciarletta and Sons will be complete once again. We can then walk up to Pete's apartment in agreement. Suzy and Kate will make sure the table is cleared and the cards and gallon of wine are set up for our Boss and Underboss card game."

"Danny, you're the only one who can pull this off," said Al. "Pete respects you more than anyone else in this world; only you can make it work for the family."

The men warmly embraced, and Danny returned to Clason Point by bus.

Danny spent the following weeks talking with Pete about meeting with his three younger brothers, and how they all agreed that he could be an asset to the business in these good times. Danny stressed the need for Pete's guidance and leadership. Danny understood his younger brother better than anyone and appealing to Pete's old swagger would be very productive.

"Your brothers need your leadership. The business needs you."

"For you, Danny, I'm willing to listen to what they have to say, but I'm not sure that our history will allow us to be as we were in the past," said Pete.

"Ah, Pete, forget history," Danny pleaded. "Your brothers want you back. That's all the damn history you need to know."

Danny stopped with that statement. His strategy was not to push too hard now, but rather to let the three brothers express themselves as they had in Al's apartment. Danny felt that once Pete was welcomed back as leader, the issue of pride and honor, which were important elements of Pete's makeup, would allow him to return with his dignity intact.

* * * * * *

Danny, Pete, and their families went to early Mass on Easter Sunday at Holy Cross Church. When they returned, Suzy and Kate began to prepare for the arrival of the family. There was a feeling of excitement as the preparations proceeded. Danny and Pete put extra leaves on the dining room table, which now extended from wall to wall in the apartment. Danny assured Suzy there would be enough room for everybody. The wives had been praying that today would be the day the families would be reunited. Suzy and Kate were determined to make their preparations have the same feel as the old days on Beach Avenue: antipasti, a pasta dish covered with Ciarletta gravy, and roasted chicken with sausage stuffing, vegetables, nuts, and fruit, topped off with espresso and Kate's cream puffs.

Suzy knew Daniel had been missing for a year and two months; she kept a calendar hidden in a clothes drawer of her bedroom dresser. If Daniel could not be with her, perhaps her husband might return to her today. This was an intention Suzy felt she could pray for.

Danny, on the other hand, was banking on this festive occasion to get Pete in the proper mood for their after-dinner meeting with the brothers. Their approaches might have been different, but their objective was the same, return Pete to the family through the business.

Everyone arrived, the greetings were festive, and the food placed on the extended table. The adults were in the dining room, the children in the kitchen. Danny observed Pete closely. Pete greeted his brothers politely, almost shyly, and his brothers, not sure what to expect, were subdued but smiling broadly. Pete had not spoken to them since the breakup of the business thirteen months ago. Danny was overjoyed at the low key, but cordial reception Pete gave his brothers. He had every expectation that Pete would become more engaged and cheerful as the dinner progressed.

The meal was savory, the company joyful, and everyone was recalling the good days of the past on Beach Avenue. They had been cautioned, prior to the visit, not to mention Daniel's name. Danny continued to observe the demeanor of his brother. Although Pete was a gaunt shell of the man he once was, he seemed to be enjoying himself, not talking much but seemingly in an acceptable mood. For Pete, considering his physical and mental deterioration over this past year, his manner was a victory. Danny could not have been more pleased. Pete was seated at one end of the table with Suzy on his left, followed by her sisters and their husbands. Danny was seated next to Pete on his right, followed by Kate and the other brothers and their wives. This was how it used to be on Beach Avenue. The dinner concluded, the plates were removed, and nuts and fruit were brought to the table. As in the past, Kate and Suzy were in the kitchen preparing espresso and placing fresh cream in the cream puff baked form. The happy guests were at the table engaged in conversation and genial banter as they enjoyed the nuts and fruit, anticipating their espresso. The children had gone outside to play.

Grace, Suzy's sister, with her back to the open kitchen door, turned her head and with a broad smile and in a jovial tone, yelled out to the kitchen, "Hey, Suzy, don't eat all the cream puffs, okay? Remember to save some for us!"

Pete suddenly stood up from his place at the head of the table. Glaring at Grace, he shouted, "I've had enough of your uppity, better than anyone else manner. If you're so worried about the cream puffs, why aren't you in the kitchen helping your two sisters? You have always thought yourself better than anyone else, with your important job, fancy clothes, fancy apartment, always too good for this family. Well, that ends as of now! You have eaten my food for the last time. Emile, take your wife out of my home, and, Grace, know that you're not welcome back in my house."

Suzy and Kate stood frozen at the counter as they heard the outburst coming from the dining room. Grace, after an initial moment of disbelief, ran from the living room in tears to the bedroom to get her jacket from the pile of coats on Suzy and Pete's bed. The others at the table sat in silence not sure what to do. Emile, choosing not to confront Pete, slowly rose from his seat to attend to his wife. Suzy was now in the living room, trying not to show anger as she attempted to convince her husband that the playful comment was a harmless joke. She begged him to go to Grace and apologize.

Pete sat in silence; his rigid body told his wife he was refusing her appeal. Suzy, knowing Pete better than anyone, accepted that the damage was beyond repair. Although she was furious, she did not allow her anger to become apparent. Instead, she calmly looked at Pete, making sure he was looking directly at her, and rather sympathetically said, "My husband is lost. His life no longer holds any meaning. He has destroyed himself and now his family. Pete, I hope you can hear what I am saying. You left me and entered a different place. God have mercy on your tormented soul." With that, Suzy turned and slowly walked into the kitchen.

Danny moved to the hallway and begged Grace to stay until he had a chance to speak with Pete. "Grace, this has been a terrible misunderstanding.

Let me speak with Pete. Once he understands you were just teasing, I'm sure he'll apologize."

"Danny, you know I would do anything for you. I love you like you were my own family, but I'm afraid Pete is in no mood to listen to reason. I know he's suffering because of Daniel, but it's clear he will not listen to reason, not even from you. Besides, I'm too embarrassed and hurt by what he said to go back to his dining room. I'm afraid Pete will never be the same now that Daniel is gone forever."

Danny heard the words spoken out loud for the first time, Daniel is gone forever the words he had been denying for over a year. He put his arms around Grace and Emile and began to cry. Grace's tears soon followed.

After a moment, Danny composed himself. He knew it was time to get Pete ready for the meeting with his brothers. When he returned to the silent dining room, Suzy's sisters were in the kitchen trying to console her and Kate. Pete's body was taut and wooden, as he sat sipping his wine and glaring straight ahead. Al, Bob, and Phil were making small talk with their wives as they waited for Danny to return, unsure what to do or say.

As Danny moved toward Pete, he stood up and said, "My brothers, maybe it's best you and your wives also leave."

Danny counted his brother's request. "No, they can't leave. We're still going to have our business meeting."

Pete spoke directly to Danny. "No, Danny, I am not interested — it can never be the same." Then turning to his younger brothers Pete said, "Whatever you wanted to say to me today won't change our past. You made your decision a year ago; your actions at that time will forever keep us apart. You'll now have to live with that decision and get along without me."

"No, Pete, you're upset. You don't mean what you're saying," said Danny.

"Danny, I know you mean well, but my mind is made up. There can be no going back to the past. This matter is closed forever," said Pete.

The three brothers, followed by their wives, rose from the table without speaking and walked to the kitchen to say goodbye to the Gallo sisters. Then they went to Danny and gave him a warm embrace. Al turned away without looking at Pete, and Bob and Phil said goodbye to Pete without shaking hands. Pete nodded his head in their direction. The three brothers and their families left the apartment without another word.

CHAPTER 31

One evening, after approximately a year at his night job in Manhattan, Pete fainted. He was taken by ambulance to the nearest hospital, where he was diagnosed with low blood pressure. The doctors informed Pete's family that a new medical procedure, the implantation of a pacemaker, could correct Pete's problem and give him many more productive years. The fact that the doctors proposed placing a metal device in his body was more than enough reason for Pete to decline treatment and demand immediate release from the hospital. He refused to listen to the pleas of his wife and children.

Then, very gradually, something began happening to Pete's speech. He developed a stutter, which grew steadily worse. Talking was becoming more difficult, and he was having trouble forming words.

His mind seemed clear; he was able to function normally in all his daily tasks; and he continued to read his paperback detective novels. But by 1951, Pete was unable to form words in any understandable context. Barbara, his daughter, was puzzled by this development and took him to several specialists, including neurological, eye, ear, nose, throat, and lungs. The specialists were unable to find a reason for his inability to speak. One specialist thought it unlikely but did speculate that Pete's speech problem could be caused by his chronically poor blood circulation. The doctor suspected that with less blood going to his brain, Pete's brain cells might be dying from lack of oxygen.

Barbara decided to make an appointment with Dr. Gorman at New York's Cornell Medical Center, based on a recommendation by a neurological specialist. After a series of further tests, some of which Pete had not previously received, Dr. Gorman, like the other specialists, could find no physical cause for Pete's inability to speak.

He told Barbara, "Mrs. Rives, your father's voice mechanism is perfectly normal. I have found nothing to suggest why he is unable to speak. From everything I can see, and from the reports of the other specialists, there is no reason why your father should not be able to speak. To make your father's condition even more baffling, I'm absolutely convinced his poor blood circulation has no bearing on this problem. He has responded favorably to tests that would have shown the loss of brain cells. Can you recall any injury or accident that might have occurred around the time you first noticed his stuttering?"

Barbara thought for a moment, and said, "He did work very hard physically for about three years in construction. But no, he didn't have an accident or injury during that time."

The doctor, still puzzled, said, "No, hard physical labor in and of itself wouldn't be the cause for speech loss. Tell me, has your parents been experiencing any problems in their marriage" Barbara responded, "They have grown apart but they both seem to have accepted this."

Barbara thought for a few moments and then told the doctor, "This strained relationship began in 1947, but they are not divorced and still live together."

"And you believe this strained relationship coincides with your father's speech problem?" said the doctor.

"No, when their relationship became strained my father did not begin to stutter or show signs of any speech problems." Then Barbara thought for a moment. "Well, there is one thing I haven't mentioned. In 1947, on a trip to Italy with my father, my youngest brother disappeared and has never been found. We believe he is probably dead by now.

Doctor Gorman said, "There is nothing in his files indicating he received psychological. treatment after the disappearance of your younger son."

"No, he never wanted to speak to a doctor or anyone else, for that matter, about the disappearance of my brother Daniel."

Doctor Gorman rose from behind his desk and sat in a chair next to Barbara. "You say that your brother disappeared in 1947, which means he has been missing for approximately three years."

"Yes, that's correct, Doctor," said Barbara.

"Can you tell me the circumstances of your brother's disappearance?"

Barbara told the doctor everything she knew about Daniel's disappearance.

"After your brother was given up for dead, was there any noticeable behavior change in your father?"

"When you say behavior, do you mean did he start drinking or other things like that?"

"Well, yes, that's the type of behavior change I am referring to, any change that you would consider out of character for your father."

What immediately came to Barbara's mind was how her father had broken off ties with his brothers, and then over the next few years alienated almost everyone else in his family. She explained the unfortunate details of her father's irrational behavior directed toward his brothers, then the incident with Aunt Grace, and described other incidents that occurred between her father and his children and former friends.

Doctor Gorman leaned forward at his desk with a serious look on his face. "Mrs. Rives, I have a theory about what might be causing your father's inability to speak."

"You do?" said Barbara.

"It's very possible that the cause is psychological in nature."

"What do you mean by psychological?"

"Your father may be suffering from what we call 'mutism.' There are two types of mutism. 'Akinetic mutism' is a condition caused by a lesion in the third ventricle, which makes people unable to utter a vocal sound. This is also known as abulia. My tests show conclusively that abulia is not a factor in your father's case. The second type of mutism is called 'selective mutism,' and I believe this could be the cause of your father's inability to speak. This is a neuropsychological disorder that is often confused with depression. But I don't think that is the case with your father, and I know from my tests that he is capable of speech and understands language.

"There is a widespread theory that selectively mute people often unconsciously choose to be silent. People with selective mutism often experience severe emotional trauma, which causes them to remain silent. Despite their physical ability to speak, they seem unable to form sounds. There have been reported cases of selective mutism in people who have experienced untreated, intense, emotional trauma and pain. From your description of the circumstances surrounding your brother's disappearance, and your father's subsequent irrational behavior toward family and friends, it's my opinion that your father may have unconsciously stopped speaking so he would do no further damage in his relationships with family and others."

Barbara was surprised by such an unusual diagnosis. "But, doctor, how can a trauma cause a person who knows how to speak suddenly be unable to speak?"

"The human body often unconsciously compensates for the experience of long-standing emotional trauma," said Dr. Gorman. "I believe there are two factors at play with your father. First, after the misery and anguish he felt from cutting family and friends out of his life, his subconscious might have protected him from further pain by not speaking. If he could no longer speak, he could no longer destroy further relationships. Or it's very possible that his untreated feelings, after so many years, have now turned to a rage that is so internally strong that subconsciously your father dreads or may actually fear any verbal expression.

"Second, you must realize that feelings of guilt and anger are very harmful emotions. If unexpressed emotions are allowed to build and accumulate, it is common for the body to compensate in some way as a means of self survival. These mental compensations, when left untreated and unresolved for many years could have contributed to your father's mutism."

Fortunately, Doctor Gorman suggested a solution. "Mrs. Rives, don't think of selective mutism as merely a reaction to the 'sorrows of life' or feeling sad or depressed. This is a very precise medical problem that can be cured with proper treatment. I would urge you to have your father immediately start long-term psychological treatment with a competent therapist."

Barbara was pleased that someone had suggested a possible diagnosis with a solution. She thanked the doctor, but she did not mention how difficult she knew it would be to convince her father of the benefits of psychiatric treatment.

Barbara was correct. Pete refused to see a psychiatrist. After badgering him for six months, the three children gave up on their efforts to have their father seek treatment. Pete's mutism did not improve, and with each passing day, he continued to physically deteriorate.

CHAPTER 32

The seven boys had arrived in Opi as young adolescents although still young the boys had matured quickly over the past three years. Going through their formative years with only each other and dealing with the many physical and emotional changes during this period had been a difficult process.

In April 1950, the seven "angels" were back in the valley to begin their third year of forced farming. With the recent warmer weather, the hostages had been spending their Sundays outside, strolling around the small town and sitting together in the empty lot that had been bombed during the war. Klein was especially pleased to be outdoors on Sundays, referring to the air of Opi as "delicious Italian mountain air."

May and June brought pleasant sunny weather in the mountains, but it was still brisk, July brought much warmer days. One mild, sunny July Sunday, as they sat in the empty, bombed-out lot, Daniel turned the conversation to the subject of his virginity. "I often wonder if I was free and back home, would I be going steady with a girl from the Bronx? I was always a little shy around girls, and given my strict Catholic schooling with the priest and nuns always saying how sinful it is to have sex until you are married, I'll bet I would be just as I am now, never knowing what it is like to have sex with a woman."

Jem said, "The mistake you're making is if you were home and had the chance to be around American girls, talking to them, going to dances, or whatever you American blokes do to meet girls, you might not be as shy as you think."

Daniel was uncertain about Jem's analysis. "Oh, I don't know…knowing the way I am, well, I just don't know."

This subject had been on George's mind, and he asked Daniel, "What happens when you see a girl and you get excited? It seems as though all I think about is being with a girl, and when Paul tells us about his time with Theresa, I get, uh… now don't laugh, okay? But you know what I mean….it starts getting a little hard just by listening to him talk about her."

George, who was now blushing, continued, "I'll tell you, Dan, I don't know how I'm going to make it if we are here a coupl'a more years. You say if you were home, you probably wouldn't be having sex. What would you do? You know what I mean, how would you control yourself?"

The question had been asked, and Daniel wished he had never brought up the subject. He too was embarrassed, but he had to say something. With a self-conscious grin on his face, Daniel said, "Ah hell, George, why did you have to ask me that?"

"Sorry, Dan, I didn't mean to put you on the spot. It was just…well…I guess I'm glad someone finally talked about it. Forget it; just forget I said anything. I probably said more than I should have."

Jacob entered the two-way conversation. "Look, Dan, what makes you think you're the only one with these feelings? Jacob looked at Paul and with a wide grin said, "Except for you know who."

David continued, "It would be good for all of us if someone had the guts to talk about it. How about it, Dan? Maybe you could help the rest of us."

Paul jumped into the conversation. "Hey, Dan, I'm not embarrassed to talk about Theresa and me. It's okay. C'mon, if you can't talk with us after all this time together, who the hell can you talk to?"

Daniel felt much more comfortable, now that his friends seemed so supportive and encouraging, so he decided to continue. "Well, as a Catholic, it's…oh, it's…well, you know, doing it with yourself is a real bad sin. So, I go to confession to Father Mascia. He tells me not to do it again, but in my gut, I know that in a week or so, some night in bed when I'm feeling miserable and lonely, the urge gets so strong that I can't help myself. All I know is the relief is unbelievable. Just before it happens, a tingle starts in my ankles and travels up through my whole body, and when it happens, I shake all over. I can't believe Father Mascia really expects me never to do it. I don't know about him, but it's something I don't feel I have any control over."

"You're being too tough on yourself, Dan. I do it, too. It is part of human nature," said Omar.

Daniel was pleased that Omar had entered the conversation. He had been interested in asking Omar a question for a long time. "I hope you don't get mad if I ask you this, Omar, but does your holy man say it's a sin to do it?"

Omar responded simply without any emotion. "No, Dan, he doesn't."

Dan replied to Omar, "God, you're so lucky."

"Good show, Dan," said George. "It was first-rate that you were able to talk about it. I feel a whole lot better. I didn't know what to say or how to say it, so I didn't wanna bring up the subject, but thanks to you I'm not feeling so, so, what's the word?"

"Reassured?" "Comforted?" interjected Jacob.

The boys, who were now clearly men, were forced to sort out their manhood with no adult guidance, no experience to fall back on, and no one who had been through the difficult process of leaving one stage of life to enter the next. Although Paul was enjoying sex with a much older woman, even he was often confused. Perhaps, at some level, he was even more confused than his celibate companions. They had no way of halting the process, nor did they have any access to adult counseling. They had only each other to question and learn from. Their physical and psychological growth presented them with manhood, and the only way they were able to confront this natural process was through trial and error and talking with each other about their successes and frequent failures.

On this Sunday, after their first week in the fields, the conversation turned to one of their favorite subjects, America. After three years, Daniel was accustomed to the many questions about his homeland, an experience which had begun with his Italian cousins in Castellammare di Stabia. He was happy to talk about his American life to his fellow captives, who seemed so interested, because it made him, for that moment, less homesick. Daniel noticed that his friends were disappointed when he attempted to clarify the many misconceptions about his country. Daniel came to understand how important American culture and practices were for non-American youngsters.

As the "angels" strolled toward the church to sit in the sun, George asked Daniel, "You often talk about the business your father owns. Is he an American Capitalist?"

Daniel's lack of knowledge about world events became evident once again when he had to ask, "What's a Capitalist?"

Paul said, "C'mon, Dan, stop bullshitting us. Everybody knows about American capitalism and the wealth they have accumulated. You don't have to feel bad because your father is a capitalist, hell; you had nothing to do with it."

Daniel felt embarrassed that here was yet another unfamiliar word. "Honest, guys, I never heard that word. In America, we refer to people who own a business simply as businessmen. My family isn't wealthy. We own a house in a regular neighborhood, not a mansion somewhere."

Omar tried to clarify the word for Daniel. "I believe the word capitalist, at least in Europe and my part of the world, is used to describe American businessmen who abuse their workers by paying them very small wages and treating them like slaves. Tell us is this a correct description of an American businessman?"

"From what I know, that's not right. America doesn't have slaves. We had a civil war to end that," replied Daniel.

Omar immediately interrupted him. "Your people may no longer own slaves in America, but is it not true that in some parts of your land, the American Negro is not allowed to go to school, cannot drink from the same waterspouts as his white brothers, and cannot gather with whites? The thing that most angers people in my part of the world is that Americans boast about their democracy but try to hide the fact that not all their people are truly equal."

Daniel, feeling defensive, responded, "In the southern part of America, yeah, some of the things you said are true. Maybe there are some people in America who don't like Negroes, but there are plenty of others who are okay with Negroes and work with them. But one thing you said is wrong. Negro kids are allowed to go to school, even in what we call the South. They just go to their own schools."

Daniel thought for a moment and had to retreat a bit in his argument. "You know, Omar, I guess I have to agree in part with what you're saying. I once had a teacher who told us that Negro schools in some southern states of America aren't as good as the white schools in those same states." Daniel felt his face grow red with embarrassment. "Look, Omar, I love America, but I don't know why Negroes are treated badly. I just don't know why."

"Could that be part of the problem?" said Omar. "You don't know why the American Negro is not equal to the American white citizen."

Daniel gave Omar a confused look but didn't directly respond to his question. Daniel, who was now feeling more embarrassed than defensive, said, "Well, I guess I should know, but I don't. I lived in a neighborhood with all white kids. I don't know any Negro kids. For all I know, maybe the whites did keep them out of my neighborhood. I just never thought about why no black kids lived there. Maybe white people made it happen that way, I don't know. Omar, if what you say is true, then I guess I really don't know why negro people are treated the way they are."

Omar then said, "I've come to know you have a good heart, Dan, so I am not blaming you. I feel that many people in countries with a white population have been conditioned by the wealthy class to keep their eyes closed so they can continue with their greed to gather more wealth, which gives them more power. The British came to my country, inhabited our land, and told us how to live. They justified their crime of plundering by saying that Egyptian people needed to be civilized and they wanted to help us by teaching us their ways. Yet in British history books it is written that Egypt was the beginning of civilization for all mankind. So how could we be uncivilized? They sent well-meaning holy men to our country to give us their God and his teachings. They did the same thing in Africa and in the Middle East. The British entered countries they believed were inhabited by people who they believed were inferior to them, thinking that if they gave these people their God, and their ways of living the people they believed to be substandard, those people would fit their picture of civilized people. The Egyptian people tried to explain that we want the God we have and that our different ways do not make us uncivilized; they just make us different. They chose not to listen, and because of this many innocent people died, both the British and my countrymen."

Omar then turned the discussion back to American history. "Dan, did not the founding fathers of your country proclaim that all men are created equal with inalienable rights? At the same time that they were writing this down in their Constitution documents, they owned black slaves from Africa. Is this not proof that your country's founders chose to accept black men and women as creatures who were not equal to them, creatures who they did not see as human beings? Why was this?"

Without hesitating, Omar answered his own question. "It happened because if black men and women were less than human, then it would be acceptable to use them to make their owners wealthy. Even among us here in Opi, is it not true that there are no Italian boys as captives, only foreigners who speak English? It's my belief that when we were captured if they had dragged a boy into a car and he spoke Italian, they would have stopped and let him out. The people of Opi, like the British and Americans, feel justified in enslaving others who in their minds are different, I believe people who think in this fashion interpret being different as inferior and not human, similar to animals."

It was clear that Omar was well schooled on the topic of black versus white, as well as the topic of slavery. He finished by saying, "In Modern Arabic, the word 'abd' refers to the designation of a person as a slave, and it's often used when referring to dark-skinned people. It's disruptive to all cultures that people in many countries decide that a person who has dark skin can easily be considered the property of another person and can be sold and traded like cattle or tools."

The boys were quiet when Omar finished. His intensity had made Daniel and the others uncomfortable. They had learned to respect Omar's mind and his worldliness, and none of them wanted to, or knew how to challenge his views.

Paul had been waiting to enter the conversation, and he broke the momentary silence by explaining how America is perceived in Australia. "I don't know history like Omar, so I don't know much about black people in America. When my family talks about America, they get angry because Americans brag about how great their government is and how they think every country in the world should be a democracy like theirs. Then the next day you read about how America is supporting a dictator because he promises to help them. My father would always say, once a dictator helps America, he then automatically is called a 'good dictator.' Most citizens of Australia think Americans have a great land, but they think the American government is phony because of how they treat Negroes in their country!"

Klein, who was a quiet boy, having more to do with his personality than his inability to think or express himself, became animated, which was quite unusual for him, and said, "Paul, I am a little surprised that your father would say that. I have read the history of the white people of Australia being brought there by England so they could empty their prisons. Then, in time, the white people formed together and excluded the original natives, who were black people. I'm not sure what the name of their race is."

Paul reluctantly answered Klein's question without looking up and responding in a low tone. "They are called Aborigines."

"Yes, that's the name I couldn't remember," continued Klein. If I remember correctly from my studies, the Aborigines were black people who had lived in Australia for centuries and were often denied their rights when the white prisoners from England took over the political structure of Australia. "Klein's studies are correct," said Omar with a look of disdain on his face. Daniel, not wanting to believe what he had heard from Klein and then confirmed by Omar, asked Paul, "Is that true Australian history?"

Paul, now not as brash as he had been moments ago, but also not defensive, responded with a nervous smile, "Well, mates, you got me on that one, yeah it true."

The discussion of slavery always had a special meaning for the seven hostages. They were living examples of the subject. They had a personal understanding of the emotional side of slavery, minus the physical abuse or disfigurement that is so often a part of the master-slave relationship.

Jacob talked about slavery and how it might apply to the seven of them. "Y 'know, Omar has reminded me of something I've often wondered. Why do some people find it so easy to beat and mutilate a slave, but at the same time they're kind and generous to friends and even strangers? People who act like that must not see dark-skinned people as human. Is it possible that people that do such horrible things to other humans do not see them as human? I can't think of any other reason why people would so easily mutilate a dark-skinned person and then be kind to others who have white skin. Think of the way animals are treated. Aren't they often made to behave by causing them pain? I wonder if the people of Opi see us as animals. Do you think they expect us to one day become trained like their other animals? They don't always hit us, but we're all in pain just by being held here. I think they know that. Are we being slowly trained? We oughta think about this and remember to keep telling each other we're good people we're not animals, and no matter how long they hold us, we can't let them make us feel like we're not people; we're human beings and we must remember that we will always be human beings no matter how long we are held in this place."

There was silence once again after Jacob had spoken, as though all seven boys had finally understood an important, critical fact. Jacob often had the effect of clarity when he added ideas and concepts to their conversations.

Daniel was the first boy to break the silence by saying in a thoughtful manner, "I know one thing…. when I get back home, I'm gonna try better to understand how black people in America feel. Since I've been in Opi, the one thing I've learned is what it feels like not to have any control."

Jacob interrupted. "Dan, that's the word, control! We have no control over things. You're right, that's what bugs me, I have no choices."

Omar, after an unusual silence, entered the conversation once again by introducing a concept he had been pondering. "Let me ask each of you if you have noticed something that I find strange, or if you believe I am imagining a fact that is incorrect. Have you noticed whenever we talk about our Opi families, we refer to them as you're Vincenzo or my Nicoangelo. The way we use the word 'your' or 'my' before our Opi family's name is how you might expect a pet animal to speak about his owner if that animal could speak. Jacob's last comment made me remember this thought that I had put out of my mind, perhaps thinking it was foolish."

The boys discussed many topics during their free Sundays together. Daniel had never experienced the effects of war, except for some rationing, and he was most interested in learning about living conditions during wartime. He would often ask Jem and George to tell stories of their experiences during World War II. Jem was a good storyteller, but his World War II stories always seemed to end with the same theme: The British people were pleased to have American help in fighting Hitler, but if America hadn't entered the war, the British people would have eventually beaten Germany without American assistance. Daniel, who lacked an understanding of the historical specifics of the war in Europe, never disputed Jem's conclusion, but the other European boys were usually quick to challenge him.

Paul would often say, "Jem, you're crazy. Without the Americans, the Germans would've kicked your asses!"

George would then come to Jem's defense, "Jem and I may have been kids during the war, but we were there. I'm not saying we didn't appreciate the help we received from the Americans, but for sure we would've eventually beaten the Germans on our own."

Jacob now entered the conversation by supporting Paul's point of view. "In Switzerland we heard that because of the constant bombing and the buzz bombs, the poor British people were close to the breaking point."

"Poor British people, my ass," Jem replied sarcastically. "That may be what you heard, but George and I lived in the war. Let me tell you, the bombing only made us more stubborn and determined to eventually kill that bastard, Hitler." Jem continued, explaining how he and his friends had responded to the German bombing. "The morning after an air raid alert, we would leave early for school so we could explore the buildings and houses that had been destroyed the night before by a direct hit from a bomb. I remember how the rubble would be all wet from the fire hoses that had put out the flames from the exploding bombs the night before. The real fun was to grab a piece of broken wood or a piece of destroyed pipe and walk through the broken walls, piles of bricks, with broken glass all around, looking for things that weren't broken. One time I remember seeing a white sink that had been knocked loose from its base but had not been broken. It was just lying on the floor. Using a piece of broken pipe, I began smashing that sink until it was in small pieces like everything else around it. We had a lot of fun breaking up everything before and after school."

"Why was that fun?" asked Omar.

Jem hesitated, shrugged his shoulders, and said, "Gee I dunno. I guess it was just fun." Jem recalled his behavior and was able to tell the others about it, but he also was unable to answer Omar's penetrating question. Why was it fun?

George then asked Jem, "Hey, did you and your blokes go looking for odd pieces of shrapnel after the bombings? I once found a piece of shrapnel that looked just like a bird. One time when my dad was home on leave, he told me that he heard about a lad in London who found a piece of shrapnel that looked just like one of the German bombers.

Klein was rather fascinated and equally confused by the dialogue that was going on between Jem and George as well as the other boys about their actions during wartime. "I lived in Austria during the war, and thankfully we did not experience the bombing that England had. Maybe I would understand the word "fun" if Austria had been destroyed by bombing. I am confused when you talk about breaking up an old broken sink as fun, and why you two and you friends valued bomb fragments, part of the metal that was causing the destruction of your country?"

George had no idea about the discussion that ensued after his story of breaking the sink in the bombed-out buildings. After a lively discussion on this topic the common consent for the action was based on human perception of an individual's surroundings and conditions. Perhaps it is quite normal when the mind and eye become accustomed to so much destruction that wreckage, devastation and havoc can quickly become normal and in the case that George described the white porcelain undamaged sink that George smashed was in his eyes and mind not normal.

Jem and George had never once thought of the bombing of England as anything other than "fun," but now after Klein's comments they were silent, unable to respond. They too were suddenly confused by Klein's pointed question. Klein was correct; how could they have ever considered the results of the bombing of their country as fun? Klein introduced a topic that the boys had not yet discussed, the treatment of Jews during World War II. He was curious about the stories he had heard regarding the treatment of Jews by Hitler during the war. "Is it true that Germany had camps where they killed Jewish people?"

Daniel was not familiar with the events surrounding the word Holocaust, so he encouraged Jacob to explain what he understood this word meant to Jewish people. When Jacob was finished, almost an hour later, telling stories that had been told to him by his parents, the boys were both intrigued and horrified. They had come to know Jacob as someone who did not exaggerate or lie, and for this reason the boys accepted Jacob's explanation, even though the atrocities sounded unbelievable.

Jacob had a confused look on his face when he finished, and he asked the other boys a question. "Hey, guys, can I talk to you about something that has been bothering me?"

"Sure, why not?" said Jem. The others nodded in agreement.

"We've been in Opi for a little over three years, for me three years and three months. After my first year or so here in Opi, I began to wonder if the history of my people had anything to do with how I think and feel here in Opi, especially at night. When I am lying in bed unable to sleep, I often think of the long history of my people, who were in and out of captivity for generations. I wondered if this history has made me more accepting of my time on this mountain. I listen to you guys talk about how angry you are at being held prisoner, yet I'm not sure I feel the same. I am not sure that I would have tried the escape that Daniel almost got away with, and the suffering he went through because of his daring. There are so many questions that have bothered me since I was brought here: Is it because I'm Jewish that I feel differently than you? Do I easily accept my time in Opi because of my ancestors? Was I chosen to join you in Opi because I am a Jew? Is it possible that some Jew must always be held a prisoner somewhere in this world? I don't believe these things are true, yet that's all I seem to think about."

The others were surprised at the confusion of their friend. They were unable to understand the dilemma Jacob had expressed, because the idea of accepting their life in Opi was contradictory to everything they knew and felt. Yet it seemed that Jacob perceived his incarceration differently. They all used different words, but their responses were similar, clear, and definite. Jacob's captivity was an egregious evil act, and for him to consider his imprisonment as preordained was not only offensive, but also beyond their understanding.

Klein was especially disturbed that Jacob would even consider such questions; unfortunately, he did not have the legal, philosophical, or religious comprehension to respond more effectively, so he answered Jacob the only way he knew how. "We were all in the wrong place at the wrong time, Jacob. It's as simple as that. If you think because you're Jewish that makes it okay for these Italians to hold you prisoner, that's nuts."

Still Jacob wondered, and the limited knowledge and preparation for such a complicated question did not allow the other captives to be of much help to him.

One Sunday in the spring of 1948, soon after they had started their second year of farming, the boys had built their usual fire on a brisk day in the empty, bombed-out lot. Klein was making palatschinken pancakes on his improvised grill with ingredients contributed by the other boys. These pancakes are regarded as the national dish of Austria, and Klein was proud of the fact that they were invented in his home city of Linz.

As they were enjoying their pancake snack, Daniel brought up a topic that had been troubling him. "Guys, is it just me, or do you also think the people in Opi act as though we are lepers?" George was the first to respond to Daniel's observation. "I think I know what you mean. I've noticed how people don't wanna look at me. They act like I'm some sort of invisible ghost."

Omar added, "I think the people of Opi are uncomfortable when they see me. It might be the color of my skin and my different heritage that makes them so uneasy, but I believe what makes then act this way may not be the color of my skin, but the fact that somewhere inside they are uncomfortable with themselves for what they have done to us. And perhaps the best way for them to live among us, and at the same time live with their discomfort, is to pretend that we do not exist."

The others assured Omar they all experienced similar treatment. The captives concluded this behavior was the result of the heavy guilt that stirred within the people each time they saw one of their "angels."

Over their five and a half years of isolation, the boys discussed many topics, not quite understanding that their combined backgrounds, interests and intellect were enabling them to gain knowledge, but to also educate each other. Unknowingly they were giving each other the education they would have been receiving in their schools if they were home. They learned many facts and concepts as they ate their delicious Austrian Palatschinken pancakes.

* * * * * *

During the summer of 1950, the boys had formed an unexpressed bond of friendship that was unbreakable. It was nothing that had been discussed, agreed to, or consented via oath; it was more of a stressful three-year plus experience that they, and only they, had truly accomplished and were still sound of mind because of the influence of each other. Although there was great sadness associated with their plight, there was also an allegiance, a union that was based on instinctive intimacy. George and Jem were able to understand the Egyptian's dislike for their countryman, and Omar felt no personal bitterness toward Jem and George because of where they had been born. Jacob and Omar talked frequently about their cultural and religious differences without the animosity that might be expected. Daniel was not detested because he was born in America, a country viewed by the others as the world's "bully." The six boys were not jealous of Paul's emotional release due to his unusual but desirable liaison; rather, they were pleased for him. Klein was supported by the others, growing at his own pace, and eventually becoming confident and selfassured. Was it the nature of the "angels" that made them so tolerant and understanding, or was it the circumstances of their captivity that shaped their authentic brotherhood?

Jem had a saying that always sounded comical in Italian because of his strong Welsh accent. "Siamo compagni per la vita. (We are mates for life.)" They promised they would always be there for each other, always and forever.

The summer of 1951 passed uneventfully and in late October the mountain air was clear and brisk. The captives and a group of four girls were strolling and talking about customs in their various countries, when one of the girls, Giovanna Fincantieri, slipped a piece of folded paper in Klein's jacket pocket. Klein felt a hand going into his pocket, startled, he looked at Giovanna. She simply blinked her eyes and separated herself from Klein before he could speak; quickly moving forward, so she could join two other girls just ahead of her. Dusk soon arrived, and the young men returned to their individual rooms. Once he was alone, the first thing Klein did was unfold the paper Giovanna had passed to him earlier in the afternoon. Written in pencil on lined paper, was her personal message to him:

Klein, I would like to know you better. I hope you don't think me foolish, but I would be willing to come to your stable area. I am able to leave my house on Wednesdays and Fridays after dinner, and I would like to visit you on those evenings. My parents will not know I will be with you, and I can stay for only an hour and fifteen minutes. If you also would like to know me, then I will come to your gated animal shelter, so we can talk together. I will pass your meeting place next Sunday at four in the afternoon. If you prefer, I will not come by your shelter, do not look up as I pass. If you would like my company, wave your hand when you see me pass. Make sure you do not go to the road to speak with me. I prefer to draw no attention of the men who follow you on Sundays.

Klein read the note one more time, making sure he was reading the Italian correctly. Giovanna Fincantieri was a petite young woman of eighteen years of age, but she could easily pass for a much younger adolescent. She combed her hair back and tied it together just above her shoulders. In Opi, a woman's hair was either straight or curly, and tied in the back, made into a bun, or hung casually over her shoulders. A coiffed hairdo was unknown in this rural mountain town. Giovanna was a rather average young attractive Opi teenager, in both appearance and intelligence. She had delicate round hips and shoulders, smooth olive skin, and round facial features. She was a pleasant but undistinguished young girl, that is, until she spoke. Her light, tender voice was able to turn the pleasing Italian language into lyrical song. When Giovanna spoke, everyone was delighted, not so much for what she said, but for how the sounds of her words made listeners feel as though they were hearing beautiful romantic music.

Giovanna had become infatuated with the handsome, blond-haired Austrian boy, who possessed a kind of shyness that made her feel comfortable. The assertiveness of initiating a personal relationship with a young man was out of character and troubling to her but she nevertheless was willing to risk the embarrassment of rejection. Were her actions a rescue fantasy, a need to mature, a grandiose scheme to defy her papa, or simply an unrecognized desire to defy the cultural laws of Opi? In the end, none of these questions seemed to matter. She felt only the sensual excitement of being with the beautiful blond stranger, an infatuation with a young man trapped behind an iron gate.

Klein did not feel comfortable mentioning the note and the fact that Giovanna would be passing the empty lot at four this Sunday. The other captives decided to walk to the piatesa behind the church that afternoon, and Klein said he would meet them there later.

Paul, unwilling to allow any change of routine in their togetherness to pass without saying a friendly torment toward the "angel" in question. "Klein is going to secretly meet a girl, and he doesn't want us to steal her." Paul had no way of knowing how accurate his wisecrack was.

"Aha, c'mon, you guys, you know there's no girl. I had a hard week, and I just want to sit for a while in the sun and relax. I'll meet you at the piazza later."

"Oh, poor Klein, he had such a hard week he needs a nap." Paul walked away laughing while deliberately messing Klein's hair.

The six boys went off, enjoying their laugh at Klein's expense. The first emotion that Klein and the other six "angels" conceptually understood almost immediately upon arriving in Opi, would be the scarcity of joyfulness in their lives. And although Klein's response did reinforce his trusting, unassuming personality, at some level he was pleased to be able to give Paul this second opportunity for a friendly pester, simply because it gave his brothers and himself an opportunity to laugh, even at his expense and if only for a moment.

On schedule, Giovanna passed by the empty lot. Klein smiled and briskly waved. Giovanna smiled but did not wave back, continuing to walk without breaking her stride.

Wednesday arrived, and Klein finished his dinner quickly and waited by the gate. Giovanna arrived at seven o'clock, as promised. She immediately told Klein, "It is not in my nature to be the one to speak first, but in this situation with you being held here in Opi, I decided to write the note to you. I don't want you to think of my conduct as being overly bold, because that is not my nature."

Klein, now standing close to Giovanna but still separated by the locked gate, said, "I'm pleased you gave me the note. I'm very happy that you're here," he said. The nervousness of their first meeting soon passed, and they became more comfortable as they talked quietly. Two weeks passed with four wonderful, satisfying seventy-five minutes for the young boy and girl.

On the fifth night, Klein accidentally brushed against Giovanna's arm as she passed him a few cookies wrapped in paper. Klein held on to her hand and then reached for the other. They both slowly moved their faces close to the opening between the bars.

Klein whispered, "I long for the touch of your lips on mine."

Their faces came closer as they looked into each other's eyes. Finally, with cheeks pressed hard against the cold metal bars, their lips gently met. Klein was the first to speak. "I am so excited that you have entered my life. I hope I will be able to continue seeing you, even if only for two nights and with bars between us. My life has been without happiness for so long that I still think I'm dreaming that you want to be here with me."

Before leaving for the evening, Giovanna asked, "Do you believe all events have a purpose, Klein?"

"I don't understand what you mean," responded Klein.

"Is it possible that the purpose you were brought to Opi was for us to meet?"

"No," he replied in a firm, assured manner. "I cannot believe I was made to live this life so I could find someone as beautiful as you. How could the result of my miserable existence become you? No, our relationship has nothing to do with the people of this town." Klein gently kissed Giovanna good night and reminded her that he would be waiting for her visit on Friday. A blushing Giovanna hurried away.

Klein and Giovanna had been meeting twice weekly for more than three months. Despite their restricted, unusual circumstances, the young couple found themselves falling in love with each other.

One evening during their twice a week masquerade, Klein asked Giovanna a probing question. "What did you and your friends think when the seven of us were brought to Opi?"

Giovanna had often thought about the inevitability of this question. Her response was a mixture of confusion and disillusionment. "I love and admire my papa, and I am greatly influenced by him. I was fourteen years old when you and the others were brought to our town. Papa said you were foreigners who were going to keep us from starving so we could stay in our house in Opi. He also told me that you foreigners could not be trusted and might even be dangerous. But he assured me the men assigned to guard you on Sundays were armed to protect the people of Opi. In the beginning, we were frightened by your presence in our town. But as the years passed and we were able to see your friendly nature, we became more at ease. When we began talking with you, we were confused by our parents' warnings. I'm very sad to say that my papa's story of your presence in Opi was the first time that I have had any reason to question his judgment. My friends and I are disappointed with our parents, but you must understand, Italian girls are taught not to disagree with their papas."

Klein a young man in love with a lovely girl, unconsciously accepted Giovanna's pragmatic response rather than challenging the obedient Italian young woman; he calmly tried to reason with her. "I understand your devotion to your parents, but what has been done to us is not only unjust, but evil."

"Klein, I know you are unhappy about being held in Opi, but evil is such a harsh, damning word, to be saved only for men like Hitler and Mussolini."

He was still cautious and unwilling to be confrontational for fear of damaging the recent joy that had entered his life, so he tried to be diplomatic while attempting to convince Giovanna of the tragic harm that was being done to him and his brothers. "Do you believe that evil only looks like a man with a little square mustache, or a man known as Il Duce? Evil can look like anyone and be anyone. Before I was brought to Opi, I believed that evil only came from deranged, unbalanced people. But now I understand that evil can also come from people who are so terrified and confused by the unknown, which causes them to lose the sound judgment they once had and soon find reasons to justify their deeds."

Giovanna had lived a sheltered life, and his words forced her to consider a reality about her parents that she had been avoiding. The parents she admired so deeply, the two people she had put her trust in, the papa and mamma who until recently she considered infallible, were part of a deliberate conspiracy that had devastated the lives of seven innocent young men. Giovanna, although flustered, was also deeply in love. Was this unlikely young man becoming more important to her than her parents and the values she had inherited from them?

After a long pause — during which Klein became concerned that he had inadvertently demonized Giovanna's father, she finally responded. "Klein, you are the one suffering, so how can I dispute what you say? Please try to understand that my love is very deep for my parents, yet I'm saddened by the iron bars between us.

You have become more important in my life than my parents or my town. I don't know what will become of us, but I want you to know I visit you not only to try to undo what has been done, but also because you make my heart joyful."

* * * * * *

One day in January 1950, Jem and Orsolo had been chopping wood for most of the day. In the late afternoon, Orsolo ordered the work to stop and told Jem, "Go to your room and clean yourself properly. Then rest and I will bring your dinner at the regular time. Sometime after dinner I will take you upstairs to the dining room to meet with Mr. Pelaccio and Marisa.

Pleased at any opportunity for a break in the routine, Jem asked, "What's the occasion?"

"Mr. Pelaccio wants to speak with you."

The inquisitive young Jem asked, "What about?"

"He didn't say" Orsolo replied. "He simply asked permission to visit my house for the purpose of speaking directly to you. For your sake, I hope you have not taken advantage of that poor girl."

Jem said, "Stop worrying; I have never touched her."

After dinner, Leardo Pelaccio and his daughter Marisa were warmly welcomed by Orsolo, who opened a special bottle of wine. Caterina served strufoli, which is a pea-sized sweet pastry piled in the form of a pyramid and covered with honey and sweet red and white sprinkles. After a few friendly toasts, Leardo graciously thanked Orsolo and his wife Caterina for their hospitality, and especially for chaperoning his daughter Marisa during her visits with Jem.

"I hope that your daughter has not been violated in any way," said Orsolo.

"Oh no, no, my friend, I come here tonight to discuss with the young man his intentions toward my daughter."

Orsolo, now relieved, said, "Let me go to his room and bring him to you."

A confident Leardo said, "I would be most grateful,"

A few minutes later, Orsolo escorted Jem into the living room. Orsolo did not offer Jem any wine, but Caterina had a plate of strufoli waiting for him.

Leardo wasted no time in addressing Jem directly. "We are here, young man, to find out your intentions toward my daughter. You have been allowed to court her for a very long time, much longer than I would have agreed to, but out of respect for my daughter's wishes I have waited. Now I refuse to wait any longer."

Relieved that the question had finally been put to him, but also knowing his answer would surely mean the end of their pleasant time together, Jem responded directly to Mr. Pelaccio rather than Marisa, knowing this was culturally correct. Considering his very weak Italian language he tried to use formal words that he hoped would ease his rejection for Marisa, while making his point about being a captive. "As a father, you have every right to be proud of your daughter, Marisa. She's a wonderful, faithful, and beautiful woman, and she has been a comfort to me during her visits while I have been held here in Opi against my will. If I had been able to court Marisa in a normal way, I think my feelings might be different, but under these conditions I cannot offer marriage to Marisa."

Mr. Pelaccio's torso stiffened, and resentment seemed to overcome his entire body posture. He asked Jem to clarify his statement. "Young man, what are you referring to when you say, 'in a normal way' and 'under these conditions?' Has my daughter not made the effort to come to this house? Have not my dear friends Mr. and Mrs. Monteverdi been capable chaperones? You will have to explain what you mean because I do not understand."

After four and a half years being held prisoner, Jem should have been prepared for Mr. Pelaccio's irritable demand for clarification. In that moment, Jem thought, For God's sake, these people will never understand.

Jem quickly came back to the question. "Mr. Pelaccio, I'm referring to the fact that my six friends and I are being held in this town against our will. We are prisoners. If I was a free man, I believe things would have been much different between Marisa and me."

Mr. Pelaccio, who was now red-faced and defensive, said, "Young man, I can only understand from your comments that you have taken advantage of my daughter's good nature by not informing her sooner that you had no intention of staying in Opi and marrying her."

Jem lost what little calm he possessed. "Take advantage of your daughter? You arranged for Marisa to meet me." He quickly reconsidered his angry statement because of Marisa and softened his tone. "Mr. Pelaccio, I truly appreciated the opportunity to spend time with Marisa. She's such a wonderful woman, and I have enjoyed her company. Marisa is a daughter you should be very proud of."

Now back on the attack, Jem continued, "The people of Opi kidnapped me, brought me to Opi, and have been holding me prisoner. Why would I want to stay in a place where I am not free to make choices? Now, all of a sudden, you expect me to choose your beautiful daughter in marriage. Can't you see how impossible that would be for me, considering that I live in a prison?"

Mr. Pelaccio was visibly shaken by what he considered brash and rude comments from the young foreigner. He stood up and spoke directly to Orsolo and Caterina. "My dear friends, I feel sorry for you because you must take responsibility for this ungrateful and disrespectful foreigner. If I'd known of this man's vulgarity, I would never have allowed Marisa to be introduced to him."

With these words, Leardo took Marisa, who was now crying, by the arm and left the house. Marisa was the only source of comfort Jem had to depend on, but now she was gone. For all the independence, humor, and flippancy Jem displayed in public, he desperately needed Marisa, using her as his crutch to sustain his swagger, and now his support was lost forever.

Rosa immediately went into the kitchen. Orsolo was furious. He escorted Jem roughly to his room. After opening the door, he pushed Jem into the room and began shouting, "You have damaged my relationship with my friend and neighbor. How am I to greet Leardo when I see him next? What can I say to him except to apologize for the rude behavior of a foreigner, a foreigner I welcomed into my home?" His reality was so deluded that Orsolo actually believed he was the injured one.

Jem was furious at Orsolo's comments, and he no longer cared how Orsolo might respond. "You bastard; you finally spoke the truth. All this bullshit about how I will come to love Opi and live at peace in your wonderful town was one big bucket of horse crap. You finally said what you and the other people in Opi have always believed: the seven of us are foreigners to be used simply for your own benefit."

Orsolo, now red-faced with indignation, could no longer contain his resentment. He slapped Jem who fell against the rear wall, and again, this time with a closed fist struck Jem on the side of his head, which caused his body to slump against the wall and down to the floor.

Jem cupped his hands around his pounding temples and with sarcasm in his voice said, "Good night," as Orsolo stormed out of the room.

* * * * *

By the fall of 1950, back in New York, Danny was the only person Pete had not alienated. Danny regularly visited his other brothers and always encouraged Pete to come with him. Pete refused, remaining moody and inflexible, especially when it came to his three brothers. However, Pete's rejection had now extended beyond his three younger brothers. Pete no longer socialized with anyone, leaving his apartment only to go to his work in Manhattan. Pete was now a gaunt, devastated figure of a man, who no longer spoke.

Danny was unable to watch the continuing self-destruction of his dearest brother, so he decided he had to leave New York, the only home he had ever known. He told his wife, "Kate, there is nothing left for us in the Bronx but misery. I can no longer stay here and watch my brother slowly killing himself. Leaving Suzy will be difficult, but watching the hatred and bitterness that comes from my brother is making me ill."

On a Saturday afternoon in mid-December, Danny trudged up the stairs to Pete's apartment. Suzy and Kate had traveled to New Jersey to see their sister, Anna, and brother, Frank, for the Christmas season. Danny did not want to tell Pete of his plans with Suzy present; he felt it would have been too painful to see the disappointment on her face. Danny quickly came to the point.

"Pete, since the disappearance of Daniel, you've become a stranger to me. The brother I came to America with was a happy, wonderful man, a helpful brother, and once a great leader. The brother I now see is a man who finds fault with everyone and is destroying himself in the process. I fear you won't accept this, but the people you have wronged are only waiting for you to go to them and say you're sorry. They understand your torment. All you have to do is ask them to let you back into their lives, but I can see you are still not ready, and, for now, I can no longer stand by and watch the slow destruction of my dearest brother. Pete, it's too painful for me to stay in the Bronx with you. If some day God allows you to heal, I promise I will come back. But until then, understand that Kate and I must leave, not out of anger toward you, but because I can no longer live with a brother who has let so much anger and sadness consume his life. Kate and I have decided to move to Miami, Florida. The husband of our niece, Rita, has a job waiting for me at the A&P grocery store in Coral Gables, Florida. My job starts the day after the New Year's holiday. I will miss you and Suzy, but Kate and I must make this move."

Pete listened attentively to his dearest brother. He stood and walked a few paces to the nearest window. With his back toward Danny, he was silent as he gazed at the street in front of his apartment. Waiting patiently for a reaction, Danny remained seated and lit a cigarette. Pete continued to stand in silence, glaring at the street below. Danny flicked the ash from his cigarette.

Pete slowly turned and finally spoke. "You're the one I grew up with in Italy, the one I went to school with, in America. We helped our father build a business; we ran that business; and we trained our younger brothers. You're the one person I thought understood the harm that has been done to me. I never expected you to abandon me. You say you can't stay and be with me. Then do what you feel is right for you, but before you go, know that I have injured no one. I am the one who has been injured!"

Danny squashed the lit end of his cigarette in the ashtray and approached Pete with tears streaming down his face. He hugged Pete, knowing in his heart that this was his final private goodbye. Pete's arms remained at his sides. Danny turned and left the apartment, tears still rolling down his cheeks.

Immediately after a shattered Christmas holiday for the families of the two brothers, Danny and Kate left New York for Miami, Florida.

CHAPTER 33

The one constant thought that occupied the mind of each captive was how to escape. After being brought to Opi, each boy, except for Klein, attempted to escape to the forest without success. Daniel had been the only one to make it to the forest and paid a stiff price for his efforts. During those early days when the six hostages attempted their bungling escape efforts, when each believed he was alone and trapped in Opi, despair set into their psyches they began to believe that their mountain prison was escape proof.

During that first year, each boy agreed that whoever managed to get free would expose the evil conspiracy taking place in Opi. During their free Sundays, the boys were always looking for new faces or people they thought might be strangers. But this never happened, and it proved to be no accident, or a matter of bad luck; the people of Opi had planned well. Eventually, the boys presumed that any work needing an outsider was completed on weekdays while they were in the fields. After two years of never seeing any newcomers on Sundays, they concluded that the people had somehow planned for this detail as well, and they were correct in their assessment. Another factor was that in this rural area, there were very few strangers or visitors who might be "passing by," even during the pleasant summer months.

On a June Sunday in 1951, just prior to the beginning of their fifth year in captivity, the boys once again found themselves discussing the topic of escaping. In frustration, Jacob stopped the conversation. "I'm tired of listening to how we almost made it. Let's stop rehashing all our failures. We only wind up feeling sorry for ourselves. Aren't you guys tired of listening to the same old depressing stories?"

Paul was irritated. "Why are you being so bitchy? Hell, we've done our best."

"I'm bitchy because all I hear is moaning and complaining about how unlucky we've been," Jacob cried out.

Paul angrily responded, "Okay, if you don't want to hear me complaining then tell me what you do wanna hear."

"Well, rather than complaining, we could start by trying to figure out why these Italians keep stopping us from getting outta here. They've made their plans to stop us, so where's our plan? Why don't we do something together instead of each of us trying to run alone when we think we see an opening?"

George was annoyed with Jacob's comments. "Damn it, Jacob, we've been talking about escape since 1947. What the hell makes you think we can suddenly come up with a plan that's gonna get us out of this blasted place? My hopes have been raised so many times I don't know if I'm ready for another let-down."

Jacob, sympathizing with George, agreed that another disappointment would be painful. "George, I feel lousy, too, and I get angry when I think about how these peasant farmers have been able to stop us from escaping. But does that mean we shouldn't try?"

Daniel added, "You know, Jacob, I understand what George is saying. I too feel like one more disappointment is gonna break me, but you did mention something we've never talked about — planning an escape together. Maybe we should at least talk about it. Whaddya think, George? Who knows; maybe we can figure out what we could've done differently."

Omar added, "We could each describe our escape attempts, and how we have been stopped. Through this discussion we might be able to find a weakness in each plan, or the strength of each plan, and in that way develop something that might work. This might tell us how we need to attack a weakness. There is always a weakness; it just has to be found. Is it possible, as Jacob has suggested that maybe our mistake has been trying our attempts to leave only when we think we can, rather than carefully locating their weak link? At least Jacob's idea of involving all of us is something we haven't tried. If nothing else, it might give us new hope."

George was still not convinced. "Yeah, that's just what I mean. I get full of hope, and then the next day, guess what, I'm still here."

The six young men looked sympathetically at George. He frowned and squirmed with his head down and remained silent. The others understood exactly what George was feeling. The anguish and disillusionment that would follow another failed attempt could easily ravage their minds and bodies beyond what they have so far experienced. It had never been said, but lurking behind their hesitation to try escaping was the constant fear that the next serious letdown might be the one to extinguish their desire to go on living.

Finally, George broke the silence. "As Dan and Omar were talking, I was thinking of what I said. Have I given up on ever leaving this place? Is it possible that I'm ready to accept this miserable life as permanent? Are the people of Opi right when they tell me that I should be happy about staying here the rest of my life?"

Omar tried to give clarity to George's dilemma. "Repeated failure, over time, can destroy the soul. When this happens, people accept what is safe rather than risk the results of more torment. You're not wrong to feel this way, George. It's not unusual for a prisoner to feel this way. It can even happen to people who are living a normal life. I believe if we never find our way out of our prison existence, some of us might give up our spirit. We must never feel ashamed if that should happen."

George was about to continue, but he hesitated and inhaled deeply. He sat silently for what seemed like an eternity. None of the others spoke. It was as though they didn't want to interrupt George's thought process. Then, with a robust, animated surge of energy, as though he had suddenly found a hidden treasure of courage, George said with a great force, "Blimy, let's go for it. What the blooming hell; whatever it takes; let's be a team and beat these Italian farmers! Omar is right. If nothing else, at least we will have something to live for during our planning!"

Jem jumped up and yelled, not in Italian, but in his guttural Welsh English, "Hip hip hurray! Hip hip hurray! Hip hip hurray!"

The young men smiled at his enthusiasm, but Daniel was laughing and wide-eyed with astonishment as he repeated Jem's phrase, "Hip hip hurray! You guys actually say that? I thought they only said those things in English war movies."

Jem's pride was dented by Daniel's lack of understanding of British culture, and he said with firm certainty, "Ah, you Yanks will never understand. How many times do I have to tell ya, I'm Welsh? I come from Wales, not England! Wales and England are two different places."

Jem was feeling much better for having had the opportunity to demonstrate the fierce loyalty he felt toward his homeland. He looked at Jacob and said in a buoyant, confident manner, "Okay, Jacob, you're now the leader of our group escape attempt."

"Hold on," said Jacob. "I only suggested an idea. Before we decide on a leader or anything else, let's first decide what we're gonna do and how we're gonna do it."

Their energetic discussions went on for the next three Sundays. Even the passing girls couldn't distract the captives from their focus. The first and unanimous decision was the elimination of the forest as an escape destination. They often saw large bears, boars, and wolves roaming the fringe of the forest, and Daniel's experience proved the forest was not a good option.

They decided the next step was for each of them to describe, in as much detail as possible, the events of their escape attempts. Each attempt was then analyzed to determine why it failed. George volunteered to take detailed notes, which, when they were finished, amounted to twenty-four individual escape attempts over five years. Looking at the results, the overwhelming reason for failure at each attempt was that they were either outnumbered or were unable to locate implements that they could use as weapons to counter the guns of their jailers.

As the discussions progressed, Jacob, who initially had been reluctant to take charge, was now becoming the de facto leader because of his piercing, precise questioning. As the planning went forward, the group looked more and more to Jacob.

They finally decided their best chance would be to rush the protectors at the entrance of town, they further decided that if a plan could be successful, they somehow had to have to take escorts out of the equation if any plan was to succeed.

"C'mon Jacob, how about some good ideas?" said George.

"How about you guys come up with some ideas?" responded Jacob.

After a brief silence, Klein spoke up. "If we target the protectors in our plan then we've gotta find a way to get close to the protectors. How can we make them trust us?"

Daniel had a flash of inspiration and quickly responded, "Wait a second; why would they have to trust all of us? I think one or two would not make them as worried; seven of us might to too much for them to handle. If only one or two of us were able to gain their trust that could serve the same purpose; and would keep five of the escorts away from the front entrance when we go for it."

"Continue, Dan said Jacob, it sounds like you have something in mind." Omar also encouraged Daniel to explain, "Let's hear what you're thinking Dan."

"Well, let's say two of us try to get the two protectors to trust us, and really, that's what we're talking about, gaining their trust. That isn't gonna happen in a few days or even a few weeks. Somehow, we must get them to see a few of us as their friends, not as their hostages.

For that to happen, they'll have to get used to seeing a few of us hanging around the entrance of town. Then we'll have to figure a way to get them to start talking with us."

"That's going to be a tough one," said Jem. "Does anyone have any ideas?" Jacob was pleased with the progress of the conversation and added, "You may have hit on something. Whaddya think of this?" Jacob turned his head and looked directly at Daniel and Paul. "I think you two would be perfect for the job. Paul knows horses, and what's the most important animal to the men in Opi, their horses. Remember horses are important to the men in Opi, so it's a natural starting point. And Dan, like the rest of us, the people of Opi are interested in hearing stories about America. I bet they're dying to ask you questions about America; you could talk about your home and your father's business for hours."

Jem interrupted Jacob. "Remember Dan, your 'old man' is a Capitalist."

The boys enjoyed a good laugh at Daniel's expense, once again never missing a chance to make each other laugh, or at least smile. But the laughter at Jem's teasing seemed different today. There seemed to be more joy in their laughter, which was a good indication they were feeling more spirited.

Jacob continued his brainstorming. "Then there are cowboys, New York City, American movies…. There's is plenty of stuff to keep them interested."

Klein was also pleased with what he was hearing but decided to ask Daniel and Paul a pointed question. "How do you guys feel about this idea? Won't it be more dangerous for you than for the rest of us?"

Paul, the adventurous one, spoke first. "Sounds good to me, I'm ready." Daniel followed, perhaps more out of loyalty than bravery. "Well, Jacob, I can't argue with what you say, so it sounds okay to me. I'm in."

"Are we all in agreement?" asked Jacob. They all nodded. Jacob, still asserting his quasi-leadership, added, "Does anyone have anything else they wanna say?"

They looked at each other with a new sense of excitement. No one had anything to add at this point. "Then it's settled. We rush them at the entrance of town. Now we need to come up with a plan and then most important, practice every detail."

The young men were all smiles. Omar was right when he said they would at least have something to live for, a task to revive their spirits.

Paul stood and said, "Well, Dan, what the hell are we waiting for? Let's go to the front of the town and get started."

"Get started with what?" asked Daniel. "I don't know, probably nothing, but didn't you say they need to get used to seeing us? Well, let's go down there and have them start getting used to seeing us."

Daniel looked at the other boys, and then looked back at Paul; he jumped up and said, "Yeah, okay uh…yeah, I guess you're right, let's start." With smiles on their faces, placing their arms around each other, Paul said to the other five "angels," "See you guys in an hour or so." And now with a hint of humor in his voice he added. "And while we're gone, get to work on a plan, no goofing off just because we're not around."

Jacob's calm, encouraging command of the situation filled the boys with confidence. There was a new sense of hope as the planning process began and with it the belief that they would be able to execute their escape from Opi.

Daniel and Paul decided not to be too assertive during the first two Sunday afternoons. When they arrived at the entrance of town, they kept their distance, only waving and saying, "Buon giorno." They sat against a stone wall simply having a conversation and not paying any attention to the protectors. They soon left, waving to the men, saying, "Buona Sera." They followed a similar procedure for six Sunday afternoons at different times, each Sunday finding a different place to sit, or examining some stones or other things that made them look busy and interested in only what they were doing.

One Sunday, they were close enough for Paul to initiate verbal contact. "That's a nice looking horse you have. How old is that beauty?"

Surprisingly, one protector answered.

They instinctively knew that was enough for that day, and they pretended to continue their leisurely conversation. When they left, they waved and again said, "Buono Sera." The phrases 'good afternoon' and 'good night' were now a permanent part of their act.

Two months passed. Although Daniel and Paul were eager to speed up the process, they had to remind each other to go slowly. Spending so many years in Opi had taught the captives that familiarity, patience, natural flow, and tranquility were all an important part of the people's existence. The citizens of Opi were distrustful of anyone who didn't have similar qualities. They were also proud people. Pride seemed to be stronger than their history of hardship and calamity. Perhaps for this reason they acted as though "outsiders" would only disturb the perception of their established order.

Daniel and Paul continued the little charade on their cobblestone stage, although closer than they had been on the first Sunday. They had decided to continue moving slowly, maintaining their distance, only now they were able to shout in Italian, "Hi, fellas, how are you feeling today?"

The men in the wagon responded with a nod of the head, but no other reaction. By now Paul and Daniel needed to do more than just pretend to talk. They devised games to play. With little pieces of wood, they pretended they were playing "pitching pennies" against a stone wall in site of the two protectors, a game Daniel had played back in the Bronx, and box ball, a modified game of handball in which participants remain in a designated area. They acted as though they were having a good time and making gestures as each won or lost. After an hour or so, they would cheerfully say, "Buona Sera," and be on their way.

The following month, they invented different play activities that incorporated a part of the landscape at the entrance of town. From this position, they were able to hold a conversation with the men without having to shout. The men seemed to enjoy conversing. Perhaps it made their boring time on duty more pleasant. Daniel and Paul had to fight the urge to move closer, but their plan was working so well they decided to continue their protracted but casual sham.

They knew they had made progress when one afternoon the protectors seemed disappointed when the boys went to play a game rather than continue their conversation.

After the two boys said, "Buono Sera," and began walking up the street, Paul whispered to Daniel, "Let them come to us. I think we got them hooked." The two boys continued to be visible, but they made an effort to be disinterested in the two men. They would act surprised and be very apologetic when they got too close and were cautioned to stay back. This little "cat-and-mouse" game was being played out well by the two captives. Time was necessary, and the seven young men had become disciplined in the matter of time and understood its importance to the people of Opi. Being a part of Opi had taught the boys the value of remaining patient.

When living intimately with captivity, the simple passage of time takes on special meaning in terms of learning and then appreciating how to wait. Captives have an abundant amount time, it passes slowly as people change, the young men grew physically and, to a more limited extent, emotionally; but the location and physical circumstances remained a constant, and so the captives were forced to learn the meaning of patience. With such an ample amount of time in a slowly changing environment, agitation can become very chaotic.

In late May, the air was brisk in the mountainous region, and the top of the Apennine Mountains was still pure white with a heavy coat of snow. Paul and Daniel had made significant progress in establishing a trusting relationship with the men in the wagon. They knew the various men by name, and when Paul was permitted to stroke and talk to their horse, they knew they had the full confidence of the protectors. One sunny but windy May Sunday, Daniel and Paul said, "Buona Sera," for the last time. The two captives proceeded to join their friends in the empty lot on Via San Giovanni de Battista.

When they arrived, Paul enthusiastically told his brothers, "Our job is done, guys." Paul held his hands straight out in a cupped fashion, and said, "We've got them right here in the palms of our hands. They're no longer worried when I stroke and talk to their horses."

Daniel and Paul felt the following Sunday was the best time to escape via the road to the valley. Daniel made one final cautious statement. "I'm still worried about our escorts. They seem to be as relaxed as the protectors but the minute you five appear I know they're going to fall back into their 'on-guard' role. I hate to bring this up, but even if everything goes as planned, there's gonna be shooting. Is everybody ready for that?"

Paul disagreed with Daniel. "C'mon, Dan, I think you're wrong. Remember, if one of us gets killed or even wounded, they've lost a worker. Sure, they'll do everything to stop us, but killing us, nah, that'll be their last option, and that's why we have the advantage. Like we said, their hesitation is gonna work to our benefit."

George made a request. "Jacob, let's go over the plan one more time to make sure we all know our places."

Purely out of habit, the seven young men huddled closer and checked the street before they reviewed their escape plan. Jacob began giving instructions. "Dan and Paul will go to the entrance of town about a half hour after the church bell rings at five o'clock hour and do whatever it is they do down there. Once the church bell rings at six o'clock, announcing dinner, the bar will clear out. When the five of us see that the street is clear, we'll start to move. We can't wait too long, or our families will get suspicious. So, the minute the street is clear, we gotta move.

"Paul and Dan, remember how important your timing is gonna be. After the six o'clock bell rings, you have to remain with the protectors for approximately four minutes, that's how long it takes to clear the street at the bar area. Dan has been practicing his story and timing it, so he needs a few more minutes to come to the end. Let me remind you how these people react to anything unusual. I know the extra four minutes is going to be tricky, but you two gotta remember this is not the moment you want to spook them. We can't start our move down the street till the front of town is cleared."

Jacob looked directly at Dan and Paul, and said "This is important, I know you two will not let us down."

Jacob now focused his attention on the entire group. "Once we see the front of town is clear the five of us will start walking down the center of the street toward the town entrance and the protectors. During Dan's story Paul will have moved to the right side of the horse, pretending he is more interested in the horse than Dan's story. As we approach the exit of town, we know our escorts will be about twenty yards behind us as we'll be walking down the center of the main cobblestone road, shoulder to shoulder. Omar will be in the center, and Klein and I will be on his right, with George and Jem on his left. Now, this is the moment we gotta be ready for. Omar will give the signal to move. He will be scanning the area looking for Dan and Paul's escorts. The second he sees them, Omar will shout, 'Hey Paul.' When Paul hears Omar shout his name, he will jam the fork into the horse's' neck; we will all move at the same time. Klein and I on the right will start running toward the wagon, remembering to separate ourselves and weave. We don't wanna be running together or in a straight line if shooting starts. George and Jem will do the same on the left, and Omar will streak down the center."

Jacob hesitated as a women came out of a house across the road. She emptied a bucket containing water and closed the door. Jacob continued. "Ok, now remember Omar's shout to Paul is the clue for everything to break out so we can not hesitate. The fork in the horse's neck should cause him to rear up, causing the wagon to jerk, hopefully throwing the protectors out of the wagon, or at least be distracted long enough for Daniel and Paul to wrestle with their rifles so they can't fire at the five of us as we're running toward them. Dan, being next to his protector when the horse rears up, should have no problem wrestling with the rifle, so Dan's protector should not be a problem. Paul's protector will be our biggest worry. After Paul jabs the fork in the horse's neck, he will have to dash a few feet and try to wrestle with the rifle of his man in the wagon. Hopefully, Paul's man will be startled long enough for Paul to reach him before he can shoot anyone."

Jacob then brought up their unsettling concern. "We probably don't have to worry about our escorts. They're usually twenty yards behind us and we'll be at the entrance before they can do anything. It's Paul and Dan's escorts that'll be our biggest problem. When the horse rears up, hopefully Paul and Dan's escorts will run toward the wagon rather than shooting at us; if they don't shoot, we are in good shape, because we'll be down the dirt road, and as we know from Daniel's escape two years ago they only post men at the bottom of the road when we are working on the farms. If they start shooting, we've separated and we're weaving, so they can't hit all five of us. Let's hope we all make it past the wagon, but if not, at least one of us should. So, if any firing starts, some of us may get hit. Does everyone understand?"

Jacob decided to mention a point he had been harping on throughout the planning stage. "Again, if anyone feels it's too risky and chooses not to be part of this, remember what we decided. No one will be judged, and whoever gets free will bring back the authorities for all of us who don't make it out and for anyone who decides to 'sit this one out.' So, think about it this week, and if some of you are not comfortable, that's okay. Dan and Paul have already said they're not backing out, but that's their decision, and that should have no influence on your decision. If any one of us decides he wishes to stay out of this attempt, remember everyone understands and will respect that decision. We all agreed to this, and it remains a strong promise, we are brothers and we do not judge each other." Jacob hesitated and repeated, "Does everybody understand and agree to this? Does anyone want to comment or have a question?"

They all nodded in agreement and quietly dispersed to their homes for the evening. The excited young men went about their daily chores, and Monday, Tuesday passed quickly. Monday and Wednesday evenings, Paul and Theresa comforted each other. Paul said nothing about the plan to Theresa.

Giovanna visited with Klein at the usual seven o'clock hour. She placed her hands through the black metal bars and grasped Klein's hands, and they tenderly kissed their unusual kiss with cheeks pressed hard against the cold metal bars. Klein deliberately had not mentioned the escape attempt to Giovanna for fear of causing unnecessary concern, but he had to inform her this evening. If all went as planned on Sunday the injustice that had been going on might finally come to an end, and if so, he would soon come back for her. "Giovanna, I have something important I need to say."

"What is it Klein?" Klein had no fear of Giovanna divulging the plan to escape on Sunday, because they had agreed a year ago that if Klein ever escaped or was released, he vowed to return to Opi, marry Giovanna, and together they would return to Austria to live.

"Giovanna, we have been working on an escape plan for many months. There is some danger involved. It is not likely, but there is always the possibility that one or more of us might be wounded or even killed."

Giovanna frowned, making her dimples more pronounced. She was about to interrupt when Klein said, "No, Giovanna, let me finish. I'm gonna tell the other guys about us next Sunday before the escape attempt."

Giovanna was surprised that Klein was about to reveal their secret. "Klein, we said we would keep our relationship secret, so my parents won't know."

"Please let me finish, this is important to me." Giovanna lowered her head. "If by some freak chance I happen to get killed, I plan to ask my brothers to return to Opi and take you to my parents. I believe they would be happy to know we loved each other and planned to marry, and I know they would want very much to meet you."

Giovanna began to cry. She turned her head and looked down at the ground — she was unable to look at Klein.

"No, no, Giovanna. It's very unlikely someone will get killed."

Through her tears, Giovanna said, "Oh, Klein, I cannot think of life without you. Do you have to be part of this?"

Klein at first did not explain, but simply answered, "Yes, I must."

"But why must you involve yourself in something this dangerous? If you are gonna tell them we plan to marry when this nightmare is over, certainly they would understand if you chose not to be part of the escape!"

"Giovanna, it's not that simple. I have a bond with these men. I can't abandon them now. It's the same with us. I love you and would never abandon you. I also love these men, so I can't abandon them. Please don't ask me to turn my back on them now."

"Well, I don't agree, but I do understand. I should've known better than to ask you to do such a thing. I guess this is why I love you so deeply. If you are…oh, I can't even say the word. If something happens, I will do as you ask."

The remainder of the hour was grim for both lovers. Giovanna asked about the escape plan, but Klein felt it better that she did not know any details so that after their escape she could not be implicated in any way.

Sunday arrived and the young men met as usual. Paul had his fork and was anxious to start.

"Is there anyone who chooses not to go?" asked Jacob. "If so, now is the time to speak up." There was silence as the boys looked at each other. Jacob hesitated a moment longer and then said, "Okay, then today is the day." They clasped their hands together.

"Let's go to my room," said Daniel. "I have a good fire going in the stove."

Once the seven young men were comfortable, Klein interrupted the enthusiastic nervous energy floating throughout the room by saying, "I have something important to discuss with you before we attempt our escape."

Klein explained the relationship he had been having with Giovanna. The others congratulated him, and they were quite surprised that he and Giovanna could have kept such a secret for so long in this small town. Klein then told them he needed a favor. He explained his wish to have Giovanna brought to Austria to meet his parents if he were killed. The boys were excited for Klein, and as each told him not to worry because no one would die today, nevertheless they also promised if the unthinkable did happen they would carry out his wishes.

Jacob told Klein that since he planned to marry and since he was concerned about being killed and perhaps, he should not take part in the escape attempt. "Each of us I am sure would certainly understand if you choose not to participate" The other boys all agreed with Jacob.

Klein refused the offer to not be part of the attempt. He told the others that Giovana had made the same request and Klein repeated to the other captives exactly what he had told Giovanna why he had to be with his brothers in this escape.

Paul interrupted. "Wow, wait a second, are you telling me you told Giovana we were planning to escape today!"

Klein looked at Paul inquisitively and said, "Well, yes, of course. I had to tell her what to do in case I was killed."

There was a dreaded moment of silence. The others went numb from the impact of Klein's statement, and then they burst into sudden rage.

Jem jumped up and shouted, "Have you lost your mind, telling her? She's one of them!"

"Stop shouting, they can hear you upstairs," said Jacob. Then Jacob turned to Klein and said, "Do you realize what you have done? We can't go now. You've really screwed this up."

George, in an unusual display of anger, said, "Okay, so you fell for a girl, but what in bloody hell made you tell her we were planning on escaping? She's from Opi. Did you think you'd come before her family? Klein, I can't believe you did this!" Disgusted, George turned away from Klein and sat down.

"You should have discussed this with us before you spoke to Giovanna. I am afraid Jacob is right. We can't chance this now. It's too risky," said Daniel.

Red-faced, veins bulging, and with rage in his eyes, Paul stood face to face with Klein and said, "You ass! You dumb ass! I should stick this fork in your stupid neck. That dumb horse has more brains than you. God, you're an idiot." Paul hurled the fork against the stone wall nearest the stove. "Shit, all the weeks and months of kissing their sorry asses, and for what? Nothing! It's over. God damn you, Klein!"

Klein had never taken such verbal abuse in his life; he was completely unprepared for the antagonistic outburst from his friends. In Klein's mind, telling Giovanna was perfectly safe. He knew she would not tell. He never for one moment considered this to be a problem. He now began to doubt himself. What have I done? Was I wrong? He no longer knew what was right or wrong, all he knew was that the people he depended on most, the people he trusted most, had lost faith in him.

Omar, who had been silent throughout the past few chaotic minutes, spoke quietly, "Klein, are you sure in your heart that Giovanna is not just an infatuation that has consumed you because of your many years in this mountain prison? If that's the case, there's no cause for shame. It would be quite normal. I am sure any of us in the same situation would have acted as you did. So, please, answer this question only if you are positive, sure of your response. It's most important when answering that you have no doubt. Klein, do you understand my meaning?"

Klein was sitting against the stone wall of Daniel's room with his knees up and his arms folded tightly over his knees with his hands clasped together. He was frightened and devastated that he had disappointed his brothers. His mind was a whirling confused blur when Omar posed the question.

"Yes, yes, Omar…ask whatever you want, and I'll do whatever you say."

Omar was annoyed that Klein was unable to focus on his question, so he spoke more firmly. "Doing what I say is not what I asked. Klein, get hold of yourself. I need you to listen and understand me. There can be absolutely no doubt on your part. You need to be honest and absolutely sure of your answer. Now once again is Giovanna the woman you love, the woman you would sacrifice your life for?"

Klein was about to answer, but Omar continued. "Or is Giovanna the woman who has made these years tolerable for you?"

"Omar, I feel so badly that I upset everyone. I…."

"No, no, no," said a frustrated and now angry Omar.

The others, although still enraged, noticed the anger pouring from Omar. In the five years they have been together they never saw Omar so irritated and disturbed.

"Once again, Klein, that is not what I asked. You must stop being worried about how we feel and listen to me carefully. I am going to say this one more time, but before I do I want you to take a deep breath and exhale, then sit up straight, look into my eyes, and focus all your attention on my question."

The other "angels," although still infuriated with Klein, couldn't help but notice the change in Omar's demeanor, as well as Klein's reaction, forcing him back to the reality of his situation. Omar had frightened Klein, and he now did what Omar ordered, he sat up strait, his eyes open wide, and totally focused on Omar. The other five men were now silent and watching Omar also. They could not believe that Omar was capable of so much intensity and vehemence.

Klein then said, "Yes, Omar, I'm okay now. Just tell me what you want to know."

"I will ask you once again," Omar said. "Disregard how you are now feeling and focus only on answering my question with complete and sure honesty; if that is impossible or if you are unsure, I must know that also. Now do you feel you are able to answer my question with complete and certain honesty?"

"Yes, Omar I am ready." said Klein.

Omar responded by saying. "Continue your focus on me and keep looking into my eyes as I ask this question one more time. Is Giovanna an infatuation that any man might desire, or is she the woman you want to live with the rest of your life? You must think clearly and answer honestly because this is very important."

Klein responded without hesitation, "Giovanna is the love of my life. I want to spend the rest of my life with her."

Omar calmly asked Klein one last question. "Now, Klein, this next question is also very important, so listen carefully, remain focused and answer honestly with clear thought. Our lives may depend on your answer. And once again, if you are not one hundred percent positive, beyond any doubt, we must know that also. Do you understand one hundred percent positive?"

Omar waited for a response. Klein was still too intimidated to be annoyed, and he responded simply, "Yes, Omar, I understand."

Omar continued, "Is Giovanna simply infatuated with her handsome friend, please listen carefully or are you positive she also wishes to spend the rest of her life with you as your wife in Austria?"

Klein responded with confident assurance, "Yes, I know this with every bone and muscle in my body. We've made our plans. She has agreed to marry me in the church in Opi, and then she will come with me to Austria, where we expect to live our lives. I know this to be true beyond any other truth. Omar, we have talked about our love and how our relationship affects her parents, so I know she's loyal to me and our plan for life in Austria."

Omar turned to the other five men. "My brothers, I believe we have nothing to worry about. True love cannot be manipulated. We know the kind of man Klein is. If he believes in Giovanna, then she will not forsake him for her family or for Opi. I believe love to be the strongest bond between humans. If it exists and I can see in Klein's eyes that it does, then I am confident we have nothing to fear."

There was a long period of silence, as Klein nervously scanned the faces of his friends and waited for a response.

Paul squatted in front of Klein, grabbed his shoulders, and said, "Klein, I was out of line when I called you an idiot and said I should have jammed the fork in your neck. I was just so angry; I didn't mean what I said. I was wrong about everything. Buddy, do you forgive me?"

Klein nodded his head without looking up.

Jem, George, Daniel, and Jacob approached Klein one at a time, shook his hand, and apologized.

Omar looked around and said, "Can we agree that we will still have our 'meeting' with the men at the entrance to Opi later today?"

"This new twist makes me a little nervous, but I guess I'm in," said George.

"Wait," said Jacob. "You guess you're in? That's not good enough for me. If you have any doubt, don't go. No one will think badly of you."

George spoke without any hesitation. "No, no, I'm going, Omar's right about Klein. You guys know me by now; it's just me, always being so worried about things. I want more than anything to be with the six of you all the way."

The men were now re-energized and smiling. Jacob approached Klein. "If something happens to you and we get free, we will make sure Giovanna meets your parents. Now stop worrying; you're not going to die."

This statement released the pent-up negative feelings that Klein had been holding back, and he broke down and sobbed as he sat on the floor near the warm stove. His friends gathered around and comforted him. The seven, once again, were as one.

The five o'clock church bell finally rang. Paul and Daniel waited about a half hour and left the group to prepare for their role in the escape. The other five sat and waited for the six o'clock church bell to announce dinner. The bell rang on schedule, the men were leaving the bar, and could be seen walking up Via San Giovanni de Battista to return to their homes as they did every Sunday. The street finally cleared. The captives took their places and moved quickly and silently down the street shoulder to shoulder.

The moment Omar caught a glimpse of Daniel and Paul's escorts, he cried out in a loud voice, "Hi, Paul."

The five captives immediately broke their formation and began to run. The horse bucked and whinnied, the wagon bounced, and the protectors were thrown back but remained in their seats.

Daniel, who had been next to his protector on the right, was wrestling with him for the rifle. Paul, who was at the head of the horse, took a moment to get to the second protector. In that moment, the protector fired his rifle three times in the air. When the captives started running, Paul and Daniel's escorts ran toward the running hostages and started firing their pistols. George was hit on the shoulder and fell in front of the horse. Jacob was hit in the upper thigh; as he grabbed for his injured leg, he stumbled to the ground. Omar stopped to help Paul, who had lost control of his protector. Klein and Jem dashed past the wagon and made a sharp right to the dirt road and freedom, but they were suddenly faced with two men in a wagon who had moved halfway up the dirt road. Their rifles were cocked and aimed, as they issued a command to stop or die.

The three shots fired in the air, just prior to Paul trying to wrestle the rifle away from his assigned protector, signaled trouble on the cobblestone road to the two men who were stationed at the bottom of the dirt road. The escape plan had worked as designed; except for a fact the prisoners had no reason to plan for. When Daniel was able to escape, almost four years ago, the people put into place a backup team of rotating men in a wagon at the bottom of the road where it meets the valley during the evening hours and also when there was no farming activity on Sunday.

Klein and Jem once again chose to live as prisoners rather than die. They obeyed the command to stop and slowly walked back to the cobblestone road.

George and Jacob were treated by Dottore Tatti (Doctor Tatti). George was sedated with chloroform, and the bullet removed from the muscle directly under his shoulder bone. Fortunately for Jacob, the bullet had passed through the fleshy part of his upper right thigh. David was returned to his room from the Dottore's office after three days, George after six.

The seven young men were quarantined in their rooms for the next six Sundays. In late June, they were allowed to be together as usual on Sundays. Time had healed George's shoulder and David's leg faster than it healed the disappointment of their aborted escape attempt.

Daniel was now eighteen years old, a muscular strong young man going through the worst depression of his long confinement. He felt as though his entire life had been taken from him. He no longer envisioned a life outside of the town that held him prisoner. The memories of his Bronx home were distant and badly faded, and he no longer had any hope of going home again. Resignation dominated his state of mind, and he lay in bed at night questioning God and trying to accept Opi as the only life he would ever know as an adult. Daniel was convinced that the people of Opi never had any intention of freeing their captives. They couldn't risk their crime becoming public. He reasoned that when the captives were no longer of any use to the people they would be killed. He chose not to share these thoughts with his six Opi brothers. Why burden the guys with death? He thought. However, he often wondered if like himself, they had come to the same conclusion, and, chosen not to share their belief with the other "angels."

* * * * * *

In November 1952, the young men were completing their fifth year in the valley. None of them chose to discuss what had now become the obvious resolution to their predicament. Daniel's earlier assumption was correct. The others had also arrived at a similar conclusion: The people of Opi could not afford to ever release their seven captives. This Sunday morning after their farming families had been to church, the boys were sitting in their empty lot, as Jem was preparing a fire to ward off the winter chill.

Omar began to talk about an important decision he had made. "My brothers, what I am about to say affects me directly, but since we have become linked in so many ways over these past five years, I know my decision will also affect you. My brothers, I have decided that today I will walk past the guards on the lone road leading out of town. I understand this will most likely result in my death. I know the men in the wagon will do everything in their power to stop me. I am determined to either leave Opi or be killed. However, if a decision by Allah causes me to be successful in leaving, the first thing I will do is expose the people of Opi and have you freed."

No one spoke at first. Jem, who was about to ignite the fire, suddenly turned and faced Omar, with surprise and fear in his eyes, as he heard the words of Omar.

George was the first to respond to Omar's startling statements. "Omar, how can you calmly sit there and tell us you are going to commit suicide? Do you realize that's what you're saying?"

Omar responded in a half angry, half clarifying tone, "Yes, George, I fully understand the possible results of my intended actions."

A startled and irritated Daniel said, "Why did you wait until today to tell us? How long have you been thinking of this? Don't you think we should have been told before today?"

"My dear friends, I have made a personal decision, which I will not change, so why should I burden you when there is nothing you can say or do to change my mind? Telling you earlier would only have led to unnecessary and useless debate and concern."

The magnitude of such an important decision finally registered with Jacob. "How long have you been thinking about such a crazy idea? What did you do, wake up this morning and decide you wanted to die? Don't you think you should have said something before now? I just don't understand why after five years you have now decided to take this drastic step!"

Jem got everyone's attention by raising his voice. "Okay, everyone, stop for a minute and take a deep breath. I want to hear more from Omar."

Omar did not speak immediately; he was staring ahead at the mountain range. Finally, he said, "This has been on my mind for about a year. The reason I chose to wait was I knew this act would also affect each of you. Please don't think badly of me, but I cannot face more years of isolation."

Jacob asked a follow-up question. "What made you decide to leave by the road leading out of town?"

"I thought about trying to escape to the forest, and as Dan proved the odds of that succeeding was not promising. And also, we have all tried the forest numerous times without success, and when Dan did eventually make it to the forest years ago, he was lucky not to die. I have decided to force their hand on the town road. I would rather die from a bullet than experience the agony of hunger or being mangled by a bear or a pack of wolves, and then having my remains eaten by boars. I know the protectors will do everything in their power to stop me from leaving. They can't take the chance of having their history exposed to the world. They will try to stop me, and when they do, I will resist with all my energy. And this is where I will force their determination. Are they prepared to commit murder, or will they accept their long deceitful act as finished, and allow me to proceed out of town? I assure you; I fully understand that my actions likely will end in my death, and I know my death will affect all of you. The comfort you provided on our Sundays together will remain within my soul. Brothers, please try to understand, I simply can no longer continue living this life. As each of you can appreciate, it is a great misfortune to have your heart, mind, and soul in one place and your body in another. So, I ask you to please accept my decision with understanding and without any suffering on your part."

With a good amount of sarcasm, Paul quickly responded. "Oh, I see, sure that's a snap, without any suffering on our part? Well, it's awfully nice of you to tell us we don't have to feel anything."

Jacob felt Paul was being unfairly harsh, so he picked up the conversation as soon as Paul had finished.

"Omar don't be upset with us. It's just that we never expected this."

Jem once again jumped in before Omar could speak. "I probably know the answer to this, but I want to hear it from you. Are you certain this is what you want to do? Do you have any doubt, any doubt at all?"

The swift barrage of questions directed at Omar was greeted in his usual calm, dogmatic fashion. Omar chose to respond to Jem's caustic statement in a muted tone and involving each of his brothers. "My friends, I'm not angry that you have spoken so forcefully. I know it is selfish of me to tell you this without any warning." Then looking at Jem, he continued, "I have thought about this often and carefully, and I am positive this is right for me."

Paul, perhaps feeling a little guilty about his earlier scornful response, said, "Wait. Let's talk about this for a minute. Why can't we try to distract the protectors? That might improve your chances of success. There must be something we can do."

Before any of the others could add to Jem's suggestion, Omar interrupted, "Paul, I appreciate your expression of help, but under no circumstances do I wish for any of you to assist me in this. I could not find peace if I thought my actions might endanger any of you. This is my decision, and I must fulfill it alone."

George, the one "angel" who a year ago had been willing to accept the permanency of his mountain prison, and one of the two wounded in the summer of 1951's group escape attempt, was now unwilling to accept Omar's rejection of assistance. "There you go, being pig-headed as usual, turning down our offer of help because of danger to us. It's very hard for us to just sit here knowing you're about to die."

Omar looked at George with loving affection and responded to his plea. "George, please don't be angry with me, not now. I love you and my other brothers as I love my family in Egypt. Perhaps, if I explain what the prophet Mohammed has taught, you will be better able to accept why I need to do this alone. If I am killed during my attempt to leave, I will enter a state in conformity with my faith and the actions in my life. Before being kidnapped, I lived a life according to the teachings of the Prophet Mohammed. The Prophet teaches that Allah is a just God, and he will account for my sufferings these past years in Italy and understands that I was unable to fully practice the rituals of my Islamic faith. If I die, I am confident that Allah will be pleased with how I have lived my life. Therefore, the place in the earth where I will ask you to place my body will become comfortable, and in that there will be a sense of brightness. For those who have not pleased Allah through their deeds on earth, their place under the earth will be cramped, and they will feel as though they are being crushed, and they will experience darkness."

Omar then asked for their help. "Therefore, I am humbly asking my true brothers to bury me if I die today, according to my religious beliefs? Take my body back to my room; clean it as best you can with soap and water; and be especially attentive to the parts of my body where the bullets enter. Then wrap my body in clean strips of seamless cloth. If I were back in Egypt, the cloth would be linen, but I know here in Opi this will be impossible. Please do not be concerned. Allah knows how I have been living and will understand. I would ask you to go to your Opi families and request clean strips of seamless cloth so you will be able to cover all the skin on my body. Tie the cloth at the top of my head and the bottom of my feet."

Jacob reached for Omar's hand and held it gently. "Omar, I promise we will find a way to wrap your body as you have said — leave that part to us."

"Thank you, my brothers. I know you will be successful."

Omar continued explaining how his burial plot should be constructed. "Bury my body before twenty-four hours have passed. The hole in the earth should be long and wide enough to place my body flat on my back, making sure no part of my body is bent. You can lay my body directly on the dirt or on any kind of platform if that is easier. It is very important that I not be placed in any type of box. Finally place me in the hole so that I am facing Mecca. If you bury me in a hole by the cemetery, my head should be closest to the town. This will ensure that my head is looking toward Mecca. At the end of the world, I will be called from where I live, and I will be together with Allah in heaven. At that time, Allah will give everyone an accounting of how they lived their lives on earth. There will be no need for a judge. Allah and everyone will be able to see both the good and the bad deeds each person has done while on this earth."

Omar described heaven to his six Christian brothers. "There are different levels in heaven, with Allah at the top. The level directly below Allah is saved for the prophets and messengers. This place of honor, close to Allah, assures the holy ones of contentment for eternity. The next level is for those people who were given great wisdom and knowledge, and used this gift to help their brothers and sisters while they were on earth. If Allah gives a person the gift of great wisdom but they do not use that gift to help others, that person will be banished, never to have contact with Allah. The next level in heaven is for the poor and the sickly, those who have suffered here on earth, yet still lived their lives trying to be kind and helpful to others. Allah will reward them for their suffering. Others, whether they were rich or healthy or only average, will be assigned a level in heaven depending on the good deeds they performed while on this earth. Merciful Allah even provides a level in heaven for those who have done an equal number of good and bad deeds. However, they must first serve a period of purification, during which they are unable to see Allah. After this period of time, which is decided by Allah, they will join Allah in heaven, but at a lower level. Finally, Allah in his justice will send those who were unjust, greedy, or chose not to do good deeds for others to hell. These poor souls will never be allowed to be with Allah, their creator. So, dear friends, I hope you can understand the contentment I desire and the reason I have decided to leave you this day."

After Omar's explanation, his six brothers had a much clearer understanding of why Omar had come to such a fatal decision. They also knew Omar did not use words carelessly just to endear himself to others. Only now was it slowly registering with them, the extent of Omar's sacrifice over the past year in delaying his decision until today. Paul sat quietly with his head down, embarrassed at his earlier outburst. Omar made a point of reaching across to

Paul and touching him gently on the wrist, but Paul was unable to raise his head.

Daniel placed his arm lovingly on Omar's shoulder and looked directly into his deep, dark eyes. "You were more worried about how we would feel than you were about your own happiness. I now understand how much you love us."

The men huddled closer together, sitting on their stones in the empty lot. The sun was beginning its descent in the west. George had learned to express his emotions in a way he could not have if he had remained within his British culture, and he told Omar what they were all feeling. "You have been a good and wise friend. We're going to miss you terribly. If you are killed, I hope Allah will allow you to give us some of the peace you are going to find in death. If that can happen, the rest of our years will be much easier."

"I hope that your Allah allows you to stay spiritually connected to us," added Jacob. "Just think how nice it will be if we can feel you with us every Sunday."

Omar made one final request, speaking without any doubt that someday they would be free men. "If I am killed, and when you are finally freed, I wish for you to tell my family where my remains are located. I believe they would want to bring me back to Egypt."

The six men agreed, each silently doubting the possibility of freedom. Omar stood up and each brother gave him a warm embrace. Without a further word being spoken, he walked toward the cobblestone road, made a left, and slowly walked down the street leading out of town. The others sat in silence, which was soon broken by three sounds: first, the voice of an Italian yelling three separate times, "Arresto" (Stop), and then scuffling, more shouting, and finally the sound of a single rifle shot, followed by deadly silence. The six men ran to the entrance of the town. Some people rushed from their houses or stood in front of their open front doors. Others moved excitedly toward the sound of the rifle shot. When the six brothers arrived, Omar was lying motionless on the ground a few yards down the dirt road. Four men and two wagons were on the road. The two men stationed at the bottom of the road in the valley shot Omar as he began to move toward them. Omar's shirt was spattered with blood and both of his eyes were tightly closed as if he had died with all his outrage resolved. It was obvious that Omar had run blindly into the face of death with defiance.

The four protectors were standing around Omar when the captives arrived. People who had been in the bar were now standing by the carts. There was total silence, as the four protectors looked at the six other hostages with confusion and bewilderment.

Paul, immediately followed by Jem, rushed the four men, and started punching; knocking two of them down before they were restrained. At that point, the other captives instinctively rushed forward to protect Paul and Jem from the townspeople who had now gathered. The brief melee was quickly brought to order. The angry captives glared at the crowd as they circled Omar's body. The protectors assured the crowd they were fine and did not want anyone to take further action. Without a word, the six men gently lifted their dead friend and carried him back to his room.

As the six brothers slowly walked up Via San Giovanni de Battista, many people were on the street watching as Omar's body was being carried up the middle of the cobblestone road. They seemed as flustered as the protectors had been.

The six "angels" placed Omar's lifeless body on his bed. George and Daniel fashioned a platform out of scrap wood and then washed the platform thoroughly. Jacob washed Omar's body. Paul, George, and Klein went to the various families requesting clean cotton material for wrapping Omar's body, and the families were generous with their offerings. After covering Omar's body as he had directed, the six hostages proceeded to the valley and explained to the men in the wagons that they intended to dig a grave. The protectors from the top and lower roads led the six men to the valley with the seven escorts following behind.

A large hole was carefully dug outside the iron fence of the cemetery. This vigorous digging enabled them to deflect some of the anger caused by the needless death of a close friend and their feelings about the selfish attitude of their captors, who were unable to understand the complexity of what they had done. The following day, the captive prisoners told their captors they were going to bury Omar and would not work on the farms that day. Each family agreed. After breakfast, the families let them out of their rooms to bury Omar.

Omar's clean, wrapped body was carried to the grave on the wooden platform. No one else was on the road or the narrow sidewalk as the men proceeded down the main cobblestone road carrying their dead friend. The people of Opi chose to watch this solemn parade from behind their window curtains. Omar's farming family followed, along with members of the governing council. At the gravesite, the captives lowered the wooden platform holding Omar's body into the grave using ropes Daniel had borrowed from Vincenzo. As they covered Omar with dirt, the townspeople left without saying a word. The only people remaining were four protectors with rifles in two wagons, the seven escorts, Vincenzo, the head of the governing council, and Nicoangelo, the husband of Omar's Opi family. The escorts had handguns at their waists, clear for all to see. They maintained a distance from the gravesite, where the six brothers stood. It was curiously evident that Father Mascia was a missing participant in the burial procedure. The six brothers noticed his absence, and although they knew Omar would never have considered his presence as meaningful, they considered his absence as disrespectful.

The captives spent some time softly talking about Omar, and how they felt about him, and what he meant to them. The hostages had learned a behavioral pattern of the people of Opi never speaking directly to the hostages whenever there was a serious problem or crisis involving all, or one of the "angels." The hostages were never able to determine if this trait was the way the people of Opi normally responded or if their silence came from their profound guilt. In this particular case, their silence was probably wise. The six hostages were in no mood to listen to anything the people of Opi might have wanted to say. Even their sympathy would have been disingenuous and probably only serve to further anger the hostages.

During the following week, Klein convinced his Opi farming partner to allow him to bring to his room an unusually shaped stone that had been on their farm for many years. Under the supervision of his Opi family, Klein crudely chiseled the letters Omar on one side of the stone. The following Sunday the six captives were permitted to place the stone at the head of Omar's grave.

The six remaining captives, mindful of their time in Opi, had calculated in the early winter of 1953 they were soon to begin their sixth year of captivity. Jem had become a handsome, blond-haired, slim, and muscular nineteen-year-old, soon to reach his twentieth birthday. His positive attitude was not quite as forceful as it had been when he was first brought to Opi, but his frame of mind was still far from total resignation. Jem had learned to look at his life with a new perspective. He was not a beaten man, although he now possessed a similar level of conflict as the others because of his forced stay in Opi.

Daniel had recently turned nineteen years of age and had grown mentally as well as physically. Although his personal and mental growth occurred in a limited and distorted context of time and environment, he had been able to change unmistakably during this period, even though he had little choice or control over how he lived his life. Without schooling, travel, tutors, or the advantage of a wise mentor, the boy from the Bronx who was overly quiet when he first arrived in Opi, because he was concerned that what he had to say might bore others, was now confident in his ability to contribute. This change was due in large part to his six special friends and the luxury of uncluttered time. Daniel's self-confidence was an unexpected gift from his forced stay in Opi.

Paul, a twenty-one-year-old healthy-looking, muscular man, remained involved with Theresa. Their mutually satisfying sexual relationship had become the scandal of Opi. Theresa was now forty-three years of age and still physically vital. She expected her life with Paul would continue as it was for as long as he remained in Opi. Theresa understood that someday he would leave, and she would be left with only his memory and her lonely life. She might survive without his touch, but she would not permit herself to fall in love with him for fear of a broken heart.

The relationship between Theresa and the foreigner had become common knowledge. Tiziano was powerless to intercede. He would have to live with the disgrace and shame of being a father who was too weak to control his only daughter. For an Italian father, this was a particularly devastating stigma. Because of this Theresa never had to use a knife to gain her revenge; Paul's continued presence was a much more effective act of revenge in this small Italian town.

George had been a tall and slender thirteen-year-old boy when he arrived in Opi in 1947, and he had changed very little physically over the past five years. The farming tasks that had made the other boys muscular and firm did not have the same effect on George. However, during his years in Opi, his internal change was radical. He had gradually learned to shed his "stiff" British demeanor and was surprised to find that he had a natural, intuitive skill to console or intervene successfully when the other captives found themselves in an emotional crisis. However, George could not entirely shed his British cultural behaviors. He was going through his own personal, internal emotional crisis which he was unwilling to share with his brothers.

Klein, at twenty-one years of age, was still strikingly attractive and deeply in love with Giovanna. Although Giovanna no longer had to sneak out at night to meet him, she had accepted the severe restrictions on their time together. Many years ago, they had vowed to live an unmarried celibate life, satisfied, for now, to be with each other on Saturdays under the close chaperoning eye of Klein's Opi family, and on Sundays with the other captives and the few other women who had remained unmarried, all under the watchful eye of the escorts. Giovanna opted to accept the dual role of unmarried companion and loving daughter until the day Klein was free.

Throughout their five years in Opi, and soon to begin their sixth lonely year, Jacob had become a pillar of strength for the five other brothers, who credited him with making the stress of their personal conflict more controllable. He was somehow able to convince the others that their survival depended on keeping alive a belief that freedom was a possibility that lurked just around the corner. Jacob, for all his positive, courageous influence on his brothers, also needed encouragement from the other "angels" to help him deal with his Jewish heritage and his life of captivity.

The six brothers had been living with tension for some five years. Separation from family, friends, and society for such a long period caused a great deal of internal stress. They had no name for their feelings; they just knew that at times things became so difficult that they felt threatened by everybody and everything.

* * * * * *

During a peaceful conversation one Sunday in the winter of 1953, Paul was feeling particularly defensive about his relationship with Theresa, and he responded inappropriately to a simple statement by Daniel. "So, you think I don't have anxious thoughts? You talk as though I'm able to think straight. Let me tell you, my teeth clench the same as yours. I pace, I bite my nails, and my mouth is always dry like yours. Do you think you're the only ones with butterflies in your stomach? Sometimes my heart beats so fast it scares me."

Tension between the young men was as high as it had ever been. Each of the five boys was pleased when Jacob entered the heated conversation between Daniel and Paul. "You guys mentioned everything except how we tend to rub our hands together nervously. How could you two have forgotten our favorite habit?"

This mild bit of "inside" humor forced Paul and Daniel to smile at each other, and Paul gave Daniel a gentle, affectionate slap on the shoulder.

Four other "angels," were also laughing at this comment. Laughter was a behavior that was frequently missing in their lives in Opi. However, George did not find the comment comical in any way. He unexpectedly jumped up and shouted, "Stop it, stop it, stop it. How can you jerks laugh at the fact that we've all gone crazy? Are you so afraid to admit to yourself the fact that we've lost our minds? Jacob, you sit there making fun of us for rubbing our hands together, you of all people. I thought you, more than any of us, understood, but I see that even you're afraid to admit you're nuts like the rest of us."

Daniel, who was seated next to George, turned, and said, "George, tell me what's happened. What's wrong?"

George slid away from Daniel and shouted, "Stay away from me." George's back hit a stone wall. He vigorously moved his head right and left, and his glassy eyes were wide and full of fear. George's posture became that of a trapped animal, with slouched shoulders and head forward. He shouted again at Daniel, who was moving very cautiously toward him, "I warn you, stay away from me. I want nothing to do with you or your friends. You are all stupid and don't even know you've gone crazy. So just stay away! I'm warning you."

The other men remained seated, feeling that their active involvement might make things worse. Meanwhile, Daniel continued his calm, slow advance toward George. He tried to be tranquil and reassuring. Speaking in a whisper, he said, "George, everything is going to be okay, George, it's me, Dan. I'm your friend, your very special friend. "No, you're not my friend. You're as crazy as I am. Now get away from me, do you hear, get away from me."

Daniel continued his calm, soft, encouraging dialogue, making sure his movements toward George were slow and deliberate. He now lightly touched George's arm. George immediately pulled his arm away and started to run toward the door. Daniel dove at him and tackled him. Daniel's full body was on top of George as he grasped George's arms and held them close to his body so that George was unable to swing.

Daniel quietly whispered in George's ear, "You're safe now, George. I won't let anything happen to you. No one can hurt you. You're with your brothers. We love you. We are your friends; we'll never leave you. You're safe with us."

George slowly stopped struggling and eventually became still. Daniel remained on top of him, continuing to whisper comforting words. George began to sob. Daniel slowly moved off George, sat him up, and the two men embraced as George continued his crying.

The other four men slowly circled George and Daniel, each man making some type of physical contact with George. After a period, the enormous, overwhelming tension gradually seeped from George's body, and his eyes lost their frenzied stare. Daniel slowly released his hug. George reached out to touch each of his brothers, although he kept his head down, unwilling to make eye contact.

The six men sat silently in physical contact with George until he was able to fully return to his brothers. The six hostages spent the rest of the afternoon talking frankly about their feelings. George was silent and embarrassed but listening intently. They agreed to be more open with each other regarding their day-to-day feelings and emotions, especially their loneliness and sadness. They also agreed to be more alert to each other's moods. As dusk arrived, they volunteered to escort George back to his room.

George refused their offer, saying, "My outburst is over, and I would prefer that each of you understand and accept me as though I am now, stable and well. I have been enough of a burden for today."

The following Sunday, the six men continued their discussion of the previous week. They concluded that they had a better understanding of their distress and apprehension, which was caused by so many things they were unable to control. They knew that for now it was important that they accept their situation as a temporary part of their lives, and that somehow, someday, their terrible nightmare would end.

Jacob continued to expand on his discussion from last week. "We'll probably never get used to it, but we need to remind each other that these feelings are never going away. We're still gonna fidget and feel tight, have sleep problems, wake up sweating, and, of course, Dan's crazy dream will still be part of his nights. The point I'm trying to make is we need to remember that any one of us could at any time have the same experience as George had last week. It's a miracle that it took this long to happen. Let's remember we are all in this until the day our misery ends. George did us a favor by reminding us of that."

The way Daniel reacted to George's emotional outburst was purely intuitive, he had no knowledge or experience responding to such an occurrence. The six boys, including George, had no way of understanding the psychology behind George's temporary episode. The human brain reshapes itself to fit its new reality, and over time when an individual is constantly experiencing fear of isolation, fear of immanent death, fear of mental chaos and loss of control; the reshaped mind will easily be threatened once it accepts these fears as genuine. If the reshaped mind finds itself living in such precarious surroundings, with no clarity about what the future holds, or experiences a familiar symbol of its paranoia, or is attacked and ridiculed; it will feel the abnormality of bodily stress, and that the habit of rubbing hands together due to the prolonged stress, is bound to remain a part of their existence. The mind can easily trigger the final attack, causing the brain to mentally reshaped existence and become unbalanced and deranged.

CHAPTER 34

The weather in Opi was ideal from late spring to September. The air was especially clean and always seemed to have a mild, sweet scent. The days were clear and bright. Daniel found the weather in the valley from spring to autumn to be an unexpected source of pleasure, almost captivating. However, the winter months, which were brutally cold, windy, and shrouded by thick snow that fell two to three times a week. Daniel and the other captives always felt weary from their farming tasks, no matter what the season, but never totally exhausted. The wood-burning stove kept his room warm, and their outward physical needs were well met. Their emotional needs were a different matter, this became an ongoing problem throughout their time in Opi.

Daniel's winter weekends were spent helping with rotating the cheese, making wine; working with the small animals, chopping wood, cleaning the stable, and doing other tasks that helped pass the time. He was much happier when he was busy. If he sat alone in his room on Saturdays, his thoughts would always be of his home in America, and soon an overwhelming feeling of total loneliness would take over and absorb him for the remainder of the day.

When Daniel first arrived in the Sgammotta household he was made to help Gelsomina with her weekly bread making. Saturday afternoons after his bath was devoted to helping Gelsomina prepare the starter (biga) for her bread.

Mixing a saved piece of last week's bread batch (prior to baking), they added flour and water to the starter and beat it to make a soft batter; the biga was then covered, and the starter was allowed to ferment until the following day.

Sunday mornings, after Mass and a light breakfast, Daniel found himself alone with Gelsomina making bread for the coming week. She seemed to enjoy taking the lead in conversation during this time, which was the direct opposite when Vincenzo was in her presence. She would easily smile and encouraged Daniel to talk, seemingly enjoying his conversation, even though Daniel knew she didn't understand much of what he was saying. Gelsomina told Daniel that her fingers, which now were oddly shaped and swollen, could no longer properly mix and knead her bread dough and that his assistance was needed for this purpose. During the first months in Opi, Daniel often wondered why Gelsomina didn't have her daughters make bread daily during the week to maintain its freshness. Italian women always prepare their food daily; this concept of freshly made food was the basis of their meal preparation, but for Gelsomina bread making was the exception. Toward the end of the week her bread was always sprinkled with water and placed in the heating compartment of the wood burning stove which after a few minutes re-developed the bread's crust and softened the inside strands of previously cooked bread.

What Daniel failed to grasp during that first year of helping Gelsomina make her bread was that this task was Gelsomina's excuse to have private time with him. And as each month passed, he began to form a bond with his captive's wife. This time with Gelsomina was becoming his only pleasant experience in an otherwise unpleasant week. Initially this extraordinary reaction made no sense to Daniel, but quickly he learned to be grateful for the pleasure of any positive relationship he found in Opi. Although the dynamics of his feelings were confusing, they were not strong enough to destroy the positive relationship he had mysteriously found in the Sgammotta home. He eventually came to realize that he needed her as much as she needed him.

Gelsomina refused to tell Daniel her age, but she looked to be in her midsixties. Her eyes were sad and heavy, but deeply sensitive, and they immediately gave away her mood. She had a round face that could not hide her once youthful, beautiful features, which now showed the wear of many years of hard labor and grave tragedy. She wore her straight hair pulled back and tied in an intricate bun. She always wore long, black dresses with black, low-heeled shoes.

Working alone with her briefly on Saturday and then on Sunday morning, Daniel was able to observe Gelsomina's dual personality. In the company of Vincenzo, she completely deferred to him in all matters. She tended to be quiet and displayed a seriousness that bordered on sadness. But during her time alone with Daniel, her eyes, face, posture, and language would become lighter and refreshed with smiles. With Daniel, she felt free to express imaginative thoughts and creative ideas. Daniel found Gelsomina to be a friendly listener, interested in his feelings, his family, and his life in America.

One Sunday morning in late 1949, Daniel now sixteen years of age and able to make himself understood in Italian, was making bread with her, when he said, "Gelsomina, can I speak with you about my feelings of being a hostage in Opi?"

"Well, of course, I want you to think of me as your Mamma. I think of you as a son, so yes, speak with me about anything."

Daniel began. "It makes me angry to know you won't accept the fact that being held in Opi against my will is the cause of terrible loneliness and sadness in my life."

Gelsomina smiled, as though Daniel had made an immature, child-like statement. "Oh, my Donato, you must realize you came to us as a young boy. All young children growing into adults have such feelings, no matter where they are. You will see; soon your sadness will pass."

"See, that's exactly what makes me angry," responded Daniel. "You won't admit the cause of my sadness is that I'm a prisoner in your home."

"Donato, please don't say such things! You are here with me, and we are having such a good time together. We do everything in our power to make you happy. We are your loving family now. Let us love you."

"No, you don't do everything in your power. You won't let me go home to America!"

"Trust me when I say that the time will come when you will see how foolish these feelings are. Someday, you will choose to become one of us, find a nice Opi girl, marry, have children, and live out your years with us in happiness."

"If I'm becoming so happy, tell me why I have the same stupid, upsetting dream almost every night," said Daniel, who felt frustrated and defiant.

"Tell me of this thing you call an upsetting dream."

"What difference will it make? You won't understand."

Daniel was now vigorously kneading the ciabatta bread while Gelsomina watched him. "Donato, why are you harsh with me? I am only trying to be kind."

Now, Daniel feeling guilty, thought, why does she always do this to me? He continued, "Okay, here's my dumb dream. About three or four times a week, I wake up startled by the same scary dream. In the dream, Vincenzo lets me go home for the weekend, but all the time I'm with my family in America, I'm worried about not getting back in time for work on Monday morning. Then I wake up sweating. It makes no sense. I told you it was a dumb dream. Are you happy now?"

Gelsomina, raising both hands, tilted her head to the right, and with a slight grin, responded immediately to Daniel's riddle, "See, Donato, my prayers are already being answered! Your dream is telling you that your home is now with us in Opi. Listen to Gelsomina when I say you will soon find much pleasure with us."

Daniel rolled his eyes and mumbled to himself, "What's the use?" He continued to knead the dough, punishing every strand of gluten.

While a person sleeps, their brain does not shut down. In fact, the brain may go through a number of cycles, including Rapid Eye Movement known as REM. During a REM period the sleeping person is dreaming. Stressful things that happen during the day can often cause a shocking dream that may even wake the dreamer. When a person finds themselves in continuous stressful situations an identical nightmare may be a way for the person's brain to relieve the pressure of their daily stressful existence; and if the subject matter is disturbing and confusing the dreamer may often wake up.

Being able to share his feelings with Gelsomina, although often frustrating, eventually helped relieve some of his tension. Gelsomina, for all her stubbornness and apparent unwillingness to accept his feelings, she still remained a motherly comfort. But Daniel was not surprised that he was unable to penetrate her wall of denial. Gelsomina had the gift of being able to block Daniel's true emotions out of her reality.

She also possessed the uncanny skill of being able to deflect his feelings. Knowing his interest in her war experiences, she would often cleverly change the topic of Daniel's unhappiness by recounting her experiences during World War II. Daniel had come to understand her clever tactics but decided it was fruitless to dissuade her.

Gelsomina often talked about her time in the caves, when she and her girls sought refuge from the expected bombing by the Americans. With newfound anger in her voice, she told Daniel, "When the Germans made their headquarters in our little town, all the women and children packed whatever warm clothes and blankets they were allowed to take and went to the caves to protect themselves from the bombing. There was little money available at that time, and Vincenzo gave me everything of value to trade for food. My two daughters and my mother came with me."

Daniel knew this had been the most difficult time in his life, but he was more interested in the details.

"We were miserable. I had no money to buy food for my children, so what could I do? I sold, the little gold I had, and my wedding band, but through it all I was strong, and I kept my wedding vows."

Daniel then asked her, "Where'd you get food when you had nothing else to trade?"

"We went to the mountains in the fall. The farmers in the area had already harvested their crops. So, with sticks we would move the earth where the farmers grew their potatoes, looking for small potatoes left in the soil. Using these potatoes mixed with greens and herbs that grew wild in the mountains, we made a daily soup for our evening meal. We also went to farms in the area that had harvested their wheat crop. We would look for wheat berries that had fallen to the ground during their harvest. Using two stones, we would crush the berries into coarse flour, add water, and make flat bread in a skillet. Each day was spent looking for food for that evening. We lived like animals."

Daniel had no knowledge of caves, nor did he understand the cruel conditions of living without shelter in the mountains during wintertime. "Why did the caves cause the death of so many people?"

Gelsomina took a small cloth from her sleeve and blew her nose, wiped her moist eyes, and sat down, as though the question had suddenly caused great fatigue. "Donato, my words can never make you truly understand. There was little food; no medicine, not enough warm clothes, and the caves were always damp and cold. If a child or adult started to cough, there was no way to make the sickness go away. When sickness came, you waited and prayed that the dreaded typhus fever would not follow; it was the typhus that killed so many of our children and even some adults."

"What's typhus fever?" asked Daniel. "And why did it happen in the caves?"

"Water was hard to find, and it had to be saved for drinking and cooking. Typhus fever spreads easily when people who eat, sleep, and live together are unable to wash and clean themselves. A person would see the reddish spots caused by lice and fleas on their skin and wait for the dreaded fever. If the fever came, death always followed. Mothers wailed for their children. Adults with the fever went to a corner of the cave, away from others, and waited for their death. When you are constantly freezing, the body stops working even as the mind keeps going."

"Why didn't you and your family get the typhus fever?"

"When typhus fever started to spread, we moved to another mountain that also had caves. This mountain was close to an aqueduct that supplied water to the towns at the base of the mountain. There, we had all the water we needed for cleaning and drinking, but food was harder to find. We were very hungry during that time of our hiding."

Gelsomina described the solid rock caves. "Besides the dampness, hunger and sickness, there was also the darkness. Never have I known such darkness. There were no candles, so just before sunset, we'd get our family together and gather everything we owned, because we were afraid of the other people also living in the caves. We'd get under our few blankets because once the darkness came you couldn't see your own hand in front of your face. We slept next to each other for warmth. We put our girls in the middle between myself and my mother and tried to sleep."

"How long did you have to live in the caves?"

"Five months in that damp hell. When the battle of the Sangro Line was over, the women were told to return to their homes. Vincenzo was happy we'd survived. Even my old mother had lived. The only thing we could do that winter was pray and stay warm. Even those who had never prayed before became devout and started praying."

Daniel's feelings for Gelsomina would always remain a mystery. He found himself becoming closer to her, in spite of the part she played in the hell that was his life in Opi. He would often think how is it possible to feel so close to this woman? How can I feel toward her as I do my own mother? Daniel would never forget a saying Gelsomina frequently used: "La ironia é il modo Dio del per a rimanere anonimo (Irony is God's way of remaining anonymous)." He wondered if there was some truth to this saying.

Vincenzo, the person Daniel understood the least, was the one with whom he spent the most time. Vincenzo looked to be in his late forties when Daniel was first brought to Opi. His skin was a leathery olive brown. His full, thick head of black hair had become spotted with grey streaks during the years Daniel was in Opi, but his black, bushy mustache never changed color. His long, thin nose changed very little, and the geometry of his jaw softened, but his intense eyes did not; they remained glaring and challenging. Vincenzo was not a tall man; he had thick broad shoulders and arms that demonstrating both power and delicacy. His hips were as wide as his shoulders; his stomach was flat and muscular; and his thighs and legs were equally large and wide. Even as he aged, he was a powerful man with unusual stamina. Vincenzo had a raspy voice and a frequent cough.

As talkative and pleasant as Gelsomina was, Vincenzo was the exact opposite. Like so many others in Opi, he had gone to school for only a few years, enough to learn to read and write. Once that was accomplished, he was made to work to support his family. Daniel noticed that Vincenzo read papers and documents, but he never saw him reading a book. He saw him write his name and other common words but never a document or lengthy letter. He rarely spoke to Daniel in a social context. When he did speak, it was usually for instruction, direction, or clarification of a work task. They worked together farming the fertile valley land five and a half days a week for five and a half years, yet Daniel knew very little about his jailor. Daniel often wondered if Vincenzo would have made the decision to kidnap other human beings to save his people if he had lived in a more urban area and had the advantage of an education.

Vincenzo was never harsh or vindictive without reason, except at the very end of his life, nor did he seem shy in any way. He was demanding, but never once did he expect Daniel to work while he rested. Vincenzo managed to work alongside Daniel without slowing his tempo.

Once Daniel was able to speak the language, he frequently questioned Vincenzo about why he was being held hostage and when he would be released. During Daniel's first two years in Opi, Vincenzo chose not to answer Daniel's constant questions. He would take a puff on his cigar and simply not respond. Daniel was persistent in his questioning, and eventually Vincenzo would irritably reply, "Young man, I am not here to answer questions. I am here to provide for my neighbors, and you are here to assist me in that duty."

Then one day in 1950, Vincenzo became frustrated and relented, and very much in character, he told Daniel in short, quick sentences, "You think we are bad people, but we are not. After the war, the people of Opi were unable to survive. Our existence had been stolen from us by the Germans. I watched my neighbors and friends slowly dying. We took the only option available to us. I received no pleasure by bringing you to Opi, but I had no choice."

In time, Vincenzo became frustrated by Daniel's frequently repeated question and eventually answered the most often asked question. When do you intend to release me so I can return to my family in America?

"I will answer your question once, then no more of your pestering. Yes, I have disturbed your life, but only until our children and grandchildren can once again become responsible for the next generation, as I am now being responsible for my generation."

Daniel had been in Opi for two years when Vincenzo arranged a marriage between his daughter Angelina and the son of a man, he met selling produce at the market in Pescasseroli. Vincenzo was in favor of such an arrangement only if Angelina and her husband lived in Opi. The main objective of the Opi social order was to replace, through marriage and children, the males that had been lost during World War II. Angelina's husband agreed to live in Opi and be trained by and assist Patrizio in caring for the sheep as the flock began to grow.

When the price structure of wool drastically changed in the early 1950s, due to the importing of New Zealand wool and the introduction of synthetic fabrics, Opi and many other European towns turned from their dependence on sheep to farming for their existence. Vincenzo expected Angelina's husband to shift his work to farming. He refused, no longer feeling bound by the marriage agreement because of the change in his work status. Vincenzo felt betrayed when Angelina moved with her husband to Pescasseroli so he could work in a small machine factory. For Vincenzo, the line of succession of the Opi communal structure had been broken by a member of his own family. This was a shameful, shattering blow to Vincenzo and his great pride.

Daniel had expected Maria Antonia to marry and also move out of the house, but she never did. Daniel and Maria Antonia's relationship became an evolving story. She was an attractive, personable woman. Her appearance was very much like her father's; she had smooth, appealing olive skin, a thin nose that made her look stately, and long, light brown hair, which was always tied back. Her build was like her mother's, short and thin.

Although Daniel was never permitted to be alone with Maria Antonia, there was something about her manner that told him she had empathy for his situation. Their nonverbal relationship, which started after Daniel had been in Opi for a few months, was one he came to value and from which he gained a great deal of satisfaction. Daniel was sure these feelings were hormonally driven. He could think of no other explanation.

He was pleased that Maria Antonia had never moved away from the Sgammotta house. The cloudy sensual feeling for her — which he experienced only from a distance, was just another mystery. By 1950, Daniel had become sexually mature, and he assumed his attraction for Maria Antonia was part of that process. Unable to have any personal interaction with her, Daniel was unable to verify whether these feelings were something more than his maturing sexual urges.

The fleeting, frequent touching of his face and temples by Maria Antonia when she trimmed his beard and hair became more frequent by the mid-1950s. Her warm hand holding his chin as she slowly trimmed his beard aroused a strong sexual urge in him. Daniel would stare at her lovely, olive face; unable to tell her what was happening inside his body. Maria Antonia would shyly grin when she noticed Daniel staring at her face with his desperate, yearning eyes.

One day, as Maria Antonia was trimming his beard, he could stand it no longer. He reached up and touched her hand. Maria Antonia stopped breathing for a moment and turned to see if her parents had noticed. When Maria Antonia saw Vincenzo's eyes covered by his newspaper, she once again began to breathe and returned her gaze to Daniel, looking at him with equally passionate eyes. These few moments of shared passion ended abruptly when Maria Antonia removed her hand from Daniel's touch, glancing once again toward the dining room where her parents were seated.

This brief sensual touching without words continued throughout Daniel's time in Opi. He would lie in his bed at night recreating the feeling of Maria Antonia's hands on his face. He fantasized these same hands stroking his entire body. The time between haircuts became abbreviated, using the excuse that he wanted a shorter beard. Daniel waited anxiously for his beard and hair to grow.

With a comb in her left hand and scissors in her right, Maria Antonia would glance in the direction of the dining room before moving her left-hand past Daniel's lips and holding it there momentarily, pretending to be using the scissors. Daniel would feel the rush of energy to his loins. Maria Antonia would glance toward the dining room as her hand remained against his lips, and Daniel's hand gently touched hers as he pressed it against his lips. If her hand remained in place, Daniel knew Vincenzo and Gelsomina were unaware of what was transpiring between the pair of sensually thrilled young adults. If she removed her hand quickly, Daniel understood that one of her parents had moved to a position where they might notice.

* * * * * *

In the summer of 1951, Danny, the oldest Ciarletta brother at fifty-six years of age, was admitted to a Miami hospital with congestive heart failure. He survived for two days and then died on the third. His wife Kate had his body shipped to New York for burial services. Years earlier, they had purchased a double burial plot in St. Raymond's cemetery in the Bronx. The one-day wake was held in a funeral home on Soundview Avenue.

The receiving line at the wake included Kate and her sisters Suzy, Anna and the twins Margaret and Grace, and their brother Frank, along with Danny's four brothers, Pete, Al, Bob, and Phil. The three brothers, who had not seen or spoken to Pete since his outburst at Suzy's sister Grace, greeted him politely and respectfully, shaking hands, inquiring about his obviously deteriorating health, and asking about his children and grandchildren. They had heard that Pete was having problems talking, but they did not know he was no longer speaking. They interpreted the nodding of his head and his silence as continuing hard feelings, causing the atmosphere among them to remain cold.

The next morning, the immediate family gathered at the funeral parlor for the final viewing before the casket was closed, and then drove a short distance to Holy Cross church for the Funeral Mass.

Phil, the youngest Ciarletta brother, had always felt indebted to Pete for the way he had supported him when he first arrived in America. He approached Pete as the family was chatting while waiting for the casket to be moved.

Phil shook Pete's hand warmly, and said, "I wanted to let you know we're going to retire in three years and turn the business over to Bob's oldest boy, Leopoldo, and my two sons, Carl, and Leopoldo. I think Påtete is in heaven smiling, knowing two of his grandchildren named Leopoldo will be running the business."

Pete nodded and managed to put on a brief smile.

Pleased and encouraged by even this brief but positive response from his oldest living brother, Phil said with anguish in his voice, "Pete, what happened to us? I still don't understand how things went so wrong when we were so close."

Pete looked at Phil with older, sadder eyes and simply shrugged his shoulders. Phil interpreted Pete's response as indifferent and decided to leave the subject and move to less emotional topics. He told Pete about his brothers. "Bob and Gerasina are living on Long Island. Diana and I live in Yonkers in a nice little house off McClain Avenue. Al got divorced from his second wife about eight years ago, and with no children to keep him here, he's decided that when we turn the business over to the kids he is going to return to Castellammare di Stabia and live in Påtete's empty apartment." Phil shook Pete's hand warmly, as the family began moving out to the cars for their travel to the church services.

After the funeral Mass, the motor procession arrived at Saint Raymond's Cemetery for the burial. There was a final brief prayer service at the cemetery chapel after the burial. The family members were standing on the steps of the chapel saying goodbye to each other when Kate suddenly and publicly confronted Pete with fire in her eyes. "Pete, the night before Danny died, he asked me to tell you he understood your deep pain. His words to me that evening was, 'Tell Pete I love him.' Now that I've told you what I promised my dying husband, you must also hear from me. Danny and I loved your son Daniel as though he was our own child. When he disappeared, our hearts were also broken. We finally accepted his death and mourned his loss. We went on with our lives. But not you, no you decided to hate everyone who loved you. Danny was not able to live with your anger, so we moved and were forced to separate from our family. Because of you, Danny was denied his four brothers and my sister Suzy by his bedside so he could say goodbye, and for those years in Miami, I was deprived of the companionship of my sisters and brother. Pete, Danny may have forgiven you, but I am unable to find it in my heart to forgive you. I know the Almighty will punish me for this failure. I will say to God, 'Lord, I honestly tried to forgive Pete, but I failed.' Pete, I will ask you one question. What are you prepared to say to your Lord?"

Without waiting for a response, Kate quickly turned, walked down the chapel steps, and proceeded to Emile's car. The other family members were stunned at Kate's defiant outburst in such an inopportune, questionable setting. After a moment of hesitation, the rest of the family slowly followed Kate's lead and moved to their individual cars. Pete remained immobile, nostrils flaring, face red, eyes glaring. Frances went to her father, took him by the arm, and helped him down the stairs and into her husband's car to take him home with Suzy.

CHAPTER 35

In the fall of 1952, the captives were well into their fifth year of farming. The unhappiness and loneliness of their life was a burden they had learned to balance over their five and half years of captivity. Each "angel" had accepted the fact that a time would come when they were no longer needed, and that would mean death by some manner. They no longer enjoyed any zest for life. Attempting to escape was an activity that had become a distant memory. Their listless, quiet Sundays together, and the bitterness they felt toward the people of Opi, now extended to the few Opi females who were their age. Interestingly, all that remained for the six hostages was the curious, quirky satisfaction that came from the skill and competence they had attained in their routine farming chores.

The six captives believed they would never be freed by the people of Opi. They had concluded years earlier that when their usefulness to the people was over, they would be killed. This conclusion was no longer a fear kept secret by each captive. Their inescapable anxiety had been shared over a year ago.

Klein was the only captive to hold out some hope. He remained somewhat positive only because he did not want to destroy the continued belief held by Giovanna that the Opi "angels" would be freed. However, in the privacy of his room or when with his brothers, Klein expected that he and Giovanna would never experience married life in Austria. Giovanna's belief in their freedom came primarily from her father, who continued to assure her that marriage to the Austrian boy would someday become a reality.

Daniel was confronted with a new problem. Vincenzo had significantly changed. He was moody and short-tempered, and incidents of him losing his temper were increasing. Simple chores that had been acceptable in the past were now unsatisfactory. One day, as Daniel and Vencenzo were carefully storing the seed potatoes for the next year's crop Vincenzo accused Daniel of not properly arranging the seed potatoes in the huge straw baskets used for storage. He scolded Daniel and made him empty the third basket he had stored and insisted that he start over again. Daniel didn't have the energy to challenge Vincenzo for another unfounded criticism. He simply started storing the potatoes exactly as he had done previously, which was eventually acceptable to Vincenzo.

The following day, after their midday rest period, Daniel and Vincenzo were preparing an old planting area by removing the dead plant vegetation. After placing the vegetation on the large mucchio di spazzatura (waste or mulch pile), Vincenzo surprised Daniel by telling him to stop work because they were leaving the valley early. It was rare for Vincenzo to leave work early. This occurred only if there was an important town meeting or a special family event.

Daniel asked Vincenzo, "Why are we going in early. Is there an occasion today?"

"No occasion," said a raspy-voiced Vincenzo.

Their wagon began to move on the dirt road parallel to the hill town. Vincenzo's usual cough seemed harder and more frequent. Halfway up the road, Daniel noticed he was having difficulty holding onto the reins.

"Would it help if I took the reins?" said Daniel.

"No, I'm capable of controlling my wagon," Vincenzo said in a surly manner.

Daniel had made the effort to help, but after all these years he was not surprised at the brusque response from his stubborn farming partner.

As they approached the two men in the wagon at the bottom of the dirt road, Daniel could see that Vincenzo was in a great deal of discomfort. He noticed what looked like blood coming from the side of Vincenzo's mouth. Daniel pressed Vincenzo one more time. "Stop being stubborn, Vincenzo. Let me take the reins! Don't worry; the protectors won't let me get away."

"Controlling this wagon is not your responsibility."

By now, Vincenzo was barely able to hold the reins, and the horse — which was no longer a slave to the bit in their mouth — began to veer off the road. Daniel pulled on the reins and raised his voice. "Vincenzo, the horse is moving off the road! Give me the reins until we reach the protectors."

With the last ounce of strength left in his body, Vincenzo pulled the reins out of Daniel's hands. Daniel stood and waved to the men in the wagon about twenty yards away and shouted, "Puo venire qua? (Can you come here?)" In the time it took the men to get to the wagon, Vincenzo had lost his grip on the reins. The protectors stopped the horses. One of the men grasped Daniel by the arm and brought him to his wagon. The other protector took the reins of Vincenzo's wagon and struck the backs of the horses, which galloped toward town.

When they arrived at 25 Via San Giovanni de Battista, Vincenzo was helped to his apartment and Daniel was placed in his room and the door locked.

About three hours later, Maria Antonia entered Daniel's room with his evening meal. "Maria Antonia, why are you here? Why are you alone?" A wave of excitement rushed through his body. For the first time in over five years, the unspoken rule had been broken. Daniel found it difficult to concentrate on anything but the image of holding Maria Antonia in his arms. Once the sensual image had passed, Daniel noticed she was distraught and shaken, with no intent of falling into his arms; she seemed to be in terrible turmoil.

"I'm afraid Papa's condition is very serious. He's been taken to a hospital in Pescasseroli." Maria Antonia placed his meal on the table.

"Do you have to leave?" asked Daniel.

"Oh, Daniel, please understand. I cannot remain here alone. Mamma is expecting me to return." She hurried to the rear door, looked back at Daniel for a moment, and left, closing the door behind her.

As Daniel was eating his bread and bean soup, he became quite angry. He wondered, as he always did after disappointments, what caused him to feel such intense rage, a fury so intense that it sometimes actually frightened him.

The following morning, Gelsomina's hands were shaking as she handed Daniel his breakfast. "Vincenzo is in the hospital in Pescasseroli," she said. "There will be no work at the farm today."

Two days passed without any work. On the third day, Daniel was invited to spend time with Gelsomina and her daughters. They spent part of the morning in the new small piatas that had recently replaced the empty bombed out lot where the captives gathered on Sundays.

Angelina, who now lived with her husband in Pescasseroli, had traveled to Opi to spend the morning with her mother and sister. Around eleven o'clock, Maria Antonia went into the house to begin preparations for the afternoon main meal.

Gelsomina began to reminisce about Vincenzo. "Angelina, how am I to continue without my husband? He has been my strength and the strength of Opi. If God takes Vincenzo, I will only have my two girls."

Angelina, in her usual curt manner said, "Mamma, you always let Papa make the decisions, but now it must be your turn. You are a very smart woman. Papa held you back. You don't need to rely on others."

"Oh, Angelina, if that was only true," said Gelsomina, her mind filled with doubt.

At pranzo (main meal) they talked about the arrangements being made for Gelsomina and her daughters to visit Vincenzo in the hospital. Immediately after the meal, the three women cleaned the dishes, placing the extra food in their small outside pantry. Nicoangelo Leone arrived with a small car to take the women to the hospital. When he entered the dining room, he spoke directly to Daniel.

"Stand, I'm taking you to your room. When I return from Pescasseroli, I'll explain what will be expected of you." Nicoangelo escorted Daniel down the steps and placed him in his room, locking the door behind him. Daniel had been in his room for approximately ten minutes, when he heard the front door being unlocked. It was Nicoangelo once again, this time carrying two plates covered by a cloth. "Gelsomina will be returning late this evening from the hospital, and she wanted you to have food for your evening meal."

The following day his usual breakfast was not delivered. In the late afternoon he heard the front door being opened; it was Nicoangelo again. "I have been placed in charge of you while Vincenzo is in the hospital. I will be responsible for your meals."

"What's wrong with Vincenzo?" inquired Daniel.

"He has cancro della gola (cancer of the throat)."

Daniel was surprised to hear the news, but he was determined not to express any words of sympathy. On a trivial level Daniel had come to admire Vincenzo for his work ethic, and dedication to his immediate family and the people of Opi. However, Daniel's overpowering grievance toward Vincenzo, his long, extended captivity, would not permit him to accept the words he used in prayer offered to his God in the "Our Father," as we forgive those who trespass against us.

Although Daniel may not have had compassionate feelings toward Vincenzo, he was nonetheless curious and asked Nicoangelo, "How could this have happened so suddenly?"

Nicoangelo, very much out of character considering the way the people of Opi consistently interacted with their "angels," explained to Daniel what the doctors had told the Sgammotta family, "The doctors said Vincenzo had his sickness in a part of his throat, which I'm not able to say correctly, 'nasofax.' The doctor told us he had this sickness for a long time; and that he was surprised when he learned that Vincenzo was able to work with this disease." Nicoangelo added nothing further and left Daniel's room.

Daniel was surprised, but also captivated by the simple recognition Nicoangelo showed in this brief personal interaction, explaining Vincenzo's cancer. Daniel for the first time in five some years had felt as though he was being respected as another human being, and not, as the captives always felt, treated as just other animals on the farm.

Vincenzo's cancer was located behind his nose in the upper part of his throat. There are two openings on the side of the nasopharynx that lead into the ears. Vincenzo's cancer was found in the cells that lined his oropharynx.

The days passed slowly as Daniel remained isolated in his room. One afternoon, Daniel heard his name being called from the back of his room. It was the other captives. Today must be Sunday, he thought.

"Dan, have you heard? Vincenzo is dead," said Paul.

"He's dead? nobody told me" said a resentful Daniel. "It's not surprising that you would be the last to know," said George. The captives had become accustomed to the confusing relationships the people of Opi had with their hostages.

The following morning, Daniel heard his front door being unlocked. He was surprised once again to see Maria Antonia back in his room. He had not seen her, Angelina, or Gelsomina since the morning he had been invited to the small piazza. She brought his breakfast and midday meal. Maria Antonia was visibly distracted. Daniel's first inclination was to attribute her unusual nervous behavior to the fact that her father had recently died. "Maria Antonia, I have never seen you so nervous. Are you okay?"

"Yes, Donato, I'm fine. It's just that I must leave town, and I don't want to be late. I have come to tell you that papa died eight days ago, the evening after mamma and I went to the hospital. I'm very sad, but it was for the best. He was suffering. We knew he had chest pains and a sore throat for the past year, but he kept saying it was only his age, and he refused to go to the hospital."

Daniel, angry that no one in the family had informed him of Vincenzo's death, confronted Maria Antonia. "I'm upset that nobody thought to tell me your papa died. I worked with the man for more than five years, and no one told me...."

Maria Antonia interrupted Daniel. "Donato, we wanted to say something to you, but Nicoangelo told us not to speak of papa's death or allow you out of your room until the governing council had met and made their decisions about the future. That is all I am allowed to say."

"Well, I guess I shouldn't have expected much else, but I thought by now Gelsomina or you..., well, never mind, I should've known better."

"Donato, please don't be angry. All I ask is that you wait a few more hours."

"Wait a few more hours? I've been waiting for over five years," Daniel said angrily. "And now you tell me to wait a few more hours! Nothing's gonna happen in a few more hours? Nothing but me in this room, that's all."

"Donato, please, I'm sorry. I can't talk further." Maria Antonia hesitated and then said, "I will say this to you, but you must promise not to tell anyone that I told you. Do you promise?"

Daniel was still irritated, and not knowing what he was promising not to tell, said smugly, "Yeah, I promise."

"Donato, I know you are upset, but please try to understand there are many things I have no control over."

Looking at the shaken woman before him, Daniel suddenly realized that perhaps he had been unfair in taking out his frustration on her for being locked in his dour, windowless room for almost two weeks; Daniel softened his facial expression and his words. "You're right. I'm sorry. You're not the one I should be angry with. I know it's not your fault. What were you going to say?"

"There will be a meeting of the governing council tonight, and all six "angels" will be brought to the meeting. Please, Donato, no more questions. I've already said too much. I am leaving town now. Remember your promise not to say to anyone what I told you." With that Maria Antonia rushed for the front door. Before leaving, she turned to Daniel and said, "Mamma is in mourning and will not be coming out of the house or seeing anyone for at least a few weeks." She left and locked the door behind her.

Considering Vincenzo's death, Daniel didn't think it particularly strange that the entire town would gather to elect a new head of the council. What was curious, however, was the fact that the captives were going to be taken to a town meeting. This had never happened before. Daniel kept thinking about Maria Antonia's behavior. He had never seen her in such a shaken state. She seemed more anxious than sad. Then he thought, ah, this is it. Going to the council meeting might be the first step in getting rid of us.

Even with this fatal thought, he found it difficult to get Maria Antonia out of his mind. Daniel thought it strange that she would be leaving town, especially today, when the entire town was to meet with the governing council, but he was also curious about where she was going and how she would get there. Was she going to ride a horse or a wagon? Was someone taking her in a car? He suddenly stopped asking himself questions when an alarming thought entered his mind. They're gonna kill us tonight. Maria Antonia left town because she didn't want to be here when it happened. That's why she was acting so strangely.

A sense of calm came over Daniel. He was not frightened, and he gave no thought as to how he would be killed. He simply spent the next few hours recalling his youth in the Bronx and his time in Opi. He took to his knees and said some special prayers to the Blessed Mother, then had a brief conversation with his God, explaining his sorrow for the sins he had committed in his life. He felt prepared to die, but he was also content. Daniel was not angry, only sad about the past five and a half years. He was ready for his Opi life to be over. He thought about Omar's words just before he was killed and hoped he, too, would be welcomed by his God.

Later that afternoon, Daniel began thinking about his years with Vincenzo and the ambivalent feelings he had toward him. He had been working with Vincenzo for more than five years, yet he knew very little about the man. He knew most of his characteristics and how he worked, but beyond that Daniel had no clear picture of Vincenzo's personality or emotional make-up. He wondered how a person was able to keep himself so private, so insulated for such a long period of time. As the afternoon drifted into early evening, Daniel's thoughts of Vincenzo were replaced with the expectation of leaving his room and what awaited him and his brothers.

Daniel heard his door being unlocked. A familiar-looking, large man entered the room and ordered him to move outside and follow him. Daniel was pleased with the chance to leave his room, yet he saw an opportunity to exert just a little speck of control. Daniel and the others had learned many years ago to grab any opportunity that might give them even fleeting moments of power or control. This concept was so important, that even though Daniel's mind had been focused on his death for most of the day, he couldn't let this opportunity pass. He decided to be obstinate and experience one final moment of mastery. "Follow you? Why should I follow you? I don't even know who you are. How do I know what you are planning? I won't leave my room until you tell me where I'm going!"

The big man was annoyed and surprised at Daniel's response. "Come peacefully, or I'll drag you by the hair of your head. Now get moving."

Having had his moment of satisfaction, Daniel abandoned his "tough guy" role, shrugged his shoulders, and proudly walked with the man to the church.

As they entered the crowded building, he saw people sitting in pews, in the choir loft, and standing in the back and along the side walls. Daniel was escorted to the front pew. Jem, George, and Paul were already seated. Eight men were seated in chairs on the chancel at one side of the altar. Daniel recognized four of the men as being from the families of the other captives; but he did not know the other four older men. Father Mascia was also seated on the altar.

Klein and Jacob arrived soon after Daniel and were seated with the others in the front pew. The room was buzzing with muted talking. The six men asked each other if they knew why they had been brought to the church. Daniel whispered to his friends, "Maria Antonia told me this morning we were going to be brought to the meeting and had me promise not to say that she told me, but that was all she said." When Nicoangelo, the father of Omar's Opi family, stood and approached the front of the chancel, the talking quickly subsided into silence. Nicoangelo addressed the people. "Welcome to this important meeting. Father Mascia will open tonight's meeting with a prayer."

Father Mascia moved to the lectern and announced that he would open the meeting by reading from Luke, Chapter 6, verses 27 to 29 and verses 35 and 36:

"But I say to you who are listening: love your enemies, do good to those who hate you.

Bless those who curse you, pray for those who mistreat you. To him who strikes thee on the one cheek, offer the other also. But love your enemies and do good, and lend not hoping for any return, and your reward shall be great, and you shall be children of the Highest, for he is kind toward the ungrateful and evil. Be merciful, therefore, even as your father is merciful."

When Father Mascia finished, Nicoangelo rose again and spoke to the people. He mentioned Vincenzo's recent death and how important he had been to the town over the years. He paused, looked toward the ceiling, and then continued. "Now that Vincenzo is gone, I've been elected by the council members to take over the leadership position."

Daniel was surprised the people didn't have a chance to vote for their leader. He was seeing firsthand how communism functioned.

"First, let me review the events that have brought us to this evening." Nicoangelo proceeded to give a verbal summary of the events leading to the seven young boys being brought to Opi. Nicoangelo then switched topics by talking about Opi. "With our country now able to pay a meager pension to its older citizens, we no longer have to worry about our existence here in the Sangro Valley. Many of our citizens who survived our unwanted war have grown older and find it difficult to provide the proper security at the entrance to our town, which has been our custom." The six hostages exchanged glances. Daniel was convinced that his eerie assumption about the six hostages being killed was correct. The other five captives, after hearing the last comment, began to have similar thoughts.

Nicoangelo continued, "That brings me to the topic of tonight's meeting. As many of you know, the governing council has been debating the fate of our six "angels" over the past few months. Vincenzo, God rest his soul, and the others on the council were unsure as to the best time to implement our plan for returning the "angels" to their homelands. However, the governing council is united in its decision that now is the time."

Daniel was sure he had heard the last statement correctly, yet he was unwilling to change his belief that he was going to die tonight. The six captives had been listening very carefully to every word, but to a man they were convinced that Nicoangelo's remark about returning the "angels" to their homelands was an attempt to mislead the people into believing they would not be killed.

There was some hushed grumbling among the large crowd in the church regarding Nicoangelo's comment about returning the "angels" to their homeland. He raised his voice and requested the assemblage to first listen to the arrangements that had been made by the governing council before deciding on the merit of their plan. The people were now quiet and giving Nicoangelo their full attention.

Nicoangelo continued with his talk to the people, "Furthermore, we will end this chapter in the history of Opi with my full guarantee that everyone will be able to move forward with confidence that our people and our town will remain peaceful. No one will be disturbed in any way by outsiders." A low chatter began once again. This time an annoyed Nicoangelo raised his voice and said, "Please, my brothers and sisters, listen and I am sure you will feel confident in my message to you this evening."

Meanwhile the six suspicious hostages sat wide-eyed, gaping at each other. George began to mentally speculate. "He's giving the people a load of crap." Return to our homeland, not gonna happen! They must know the first thing we will do is report them to the authorities. How are they going to explain Omar's death? They're gonna hide what they plan on doing with us from the people. And he wants us to feel safe, and not get scared. They're going to kill us; they have no other choice.

Jacob was also sure they would never be released, and his thoughts were similar to the thoughts of the other hostages. I'm not surprised they're keepin' the truth from the people. They'll take us out of town after telling the people they are letting us leave for home. Then to the forest, shoot us, and bury us right there.

Regaining the attention of the people for a second time, Nicoangelo continued. "We've planned every detail of this matter and have taken the steps necessary to ensure its complete success. So please allow me to explain.

Then Nicoangelo did the unexpected. He moved his position on the altar and stood in front of the six captives, talking directly to them. "Opi "angels," we owe you a great deal. We want you to know that over the years we have made every effort to make your stay here in Opi as comfortable and peaceful as possible. Our plan was always to make you feel like part of our family. We understood this would not be a perfect situation for you, but I want you to know that we did everything in our power to make you, as boys and now as men — feel that Opi was your home. Please know that we were heartbroken at the death of our Omar. This was a tragedy for my family. As you know, the protectors pleaded with him…."

At this point Jacob stood and spoke directly to Nicoangelo in a firm but respectful manner. "Sir, may I interrupt you and speak?"

"Yes, of course," said Nicoangelo.

"You have complete control of us, and we have learned to accept this. However, I must, with all respect to your position as leader, ask you not to speak of Omar in any way. I believe I speak for my brothers when I say we feel that speaking of him by a representative of the town of Opi is not acceptable to us or to Omar's memory." Without any cue or look of recognition, the five seated men rose from their pew and stood with Jacob. There was still tension and absolute silence in the church.

Nicoangelo hesitated a moment and then quietly responded, "As you wish."

The six men sat down, proud of Jacob. At that moment, Jacob's successful confrontation suddenly empowered the six men with their first sense of meaningful potency since being brought to Opi. They were invigorated by Jacob's assertiveness and pleased that he was able to avert Nicoangelo's attempt at manipulating Omar's memory.

Jem thought to himself, what a great way to go out, telling Nicoangelo to shut up!

Nicoangelo continued speaking to the people. "Allow me to explain the plan that will give these six men their freedom." The enormity of the word freedom was unable to penetrate the years of fear, doubt, and confusion of the six hostages.

Freedom, he said freedom. Maybe we won't die, thought George.

Oh, this guy is smooth, they're planning something; they're not gonna let us go; they can't let us go, thought Paul.

For a moment, Daniel felt a glimmer of hope when he heard the word freedom. Then he returned to his expected reality. Freedom — he only said that to fool the people into thinking we are not going to be killed.

Nicoangelo finally began his review of the plan to free the six hostages. "The governing council has carefully taken the steps that will enable our friends to leave Opi and allow us to continue our lives undisturbed."

The people began a low chatter of conversation. Nicoangelo, who was now standing in the center of the chancel, raised his voice in an attempt to reassure the people. The audience soon fell silent, and Nicoangelo confidently began to elaborate. "We have had false Italian passports made for our six "angels." We used the individual pictures we took of them at last June's San Giovanni de Battista festival. The members of the governing council, along with Alberto, Paolo, Emilio, and Loreto, will take the six men by car tomorrow to the port city of Mazara del Vallo in Sicily. There, we have hired a boat to transport all of us to Carthage, in Tunisia. We have arranged for cars to meet our boat in Carthage and drive us to the Tunisian airport."

The six hostages had similar thoughts. So that's their plan. They don't intend telling the people we are to be killed. They will tell the others in town that we were sent home.

There's no way they are going to take us to an airport, the first cop I see I will run over to him and tell him I've been a captive for over five years. Thought Daniel

Nicoangelo walked over to a pile of papers lying on his seat, held them up to the audience, and said, "I have here in my hand airplane tickets for each of our 'angels,' which will enable them to return to their home countries."

Once again, there was uneasy stirring and quiet talking among the people in the church. Nicoangelo regained their attention by raising his voice for the second time. "At the Tunisian airport, we will give each 'angel' his plane ticket, his false Italian passport, and forged entry documents. If any of the 'angels' are foolish enough to tell the authorities about their stay in Opi, Tunisian authorities will naturally investigate and immediately determine that the six men entered Tunisia with false documents. Having no proof of personal identity other than the forged documents, they will immediately be placed in prison. So, as you can see, at the Tunisia airport when they receive their entry documents and plane tickets and are allowed to go free, they will have no choice but to use these documents to board their planes and return to their home countries."

Nicoangelo then looked at the six men. "I can assure you; you don't want to spend any time in the Tunisian prison system. If you do, you most likely will be lost forever."

Hearing this last statement, the six hostages wondered if perhaps they didn't plan to kill them after all. The plan Nicoangelo had just described would insulate the people of Opi from prosecution for kidnapping and false imprisonment. The six men began to listen with a different mindset. Yet, they were still a bit hesitant to accept the idea that their lives might be spared.

Turning his attention back to the citizens of Opi, Nicoangelo continued. "Once they are home, it is highly unlikely they will be able to convince their local authorities of such a tale. However, if by chance the authorities in their countries inquire about the accuracy of their charge, there will be no trace that they were ever in our town. Therefore, it will be impossible for any of them to prove they have ever been in Opi. Our united fellowship regarding this matter would surely be in opposition to the claims of six foreigners. So, my neighbors,

I can assure you there is nothing to fear. The governing council has made plans to thoroughly scrub each man's room and prepare it as living quarters for family members once the 'angels' are on their way. We also plan to dig up Omar's grave and respectfully bury his bones in the cemetery with a fictitious Italian headstone and dispose of the rock with his name carved on it."

This statement caused each hostage to remember the promise they had made to Omar about returning his body to his family once they were freed. How would they be able to keep their promise to Omar if his grave were moved? Damn! They've thought of everything, thought Jacob.

Nicoangelo asked if anyone wanted to speak before the meeting ended. From the rear of the church came a familiar voice. "Yes, I have something I wish to say." Walking up the center aisle was Maria Antonia. The people again began to buzz in low tones. When she reached the chancel, she climbed the two stairs, turned, and faced the people, waiting for them to be quiet. She began by talking about her father. "Vincenzo, my father, worked for years to protect the people of our humble town. He devoted his life to continuing Opi's rich history after the Germans stole our men. Those of us here tonight lived through that terrible time. We cried, but my papa, with great pain in his heart from the loss of his two sons, my brothers, acted to save our town. Like many of you, I also loved and respected my papa. If I am to be honest, as I stand before you tonight, I have to say my beloved papa was wrong to imprison seven strangers to save Opi."

The people stirred uncomfortably. Nicoangelo arose from his chair and moved toward Maria Antonia. He gently took her arm, trying to move her back toward the altar. She broke away from his grasp and moved back to the front of the chancel platform.

The low whispering of the people, when blended together, caused Maria Antonia to have to raise her voice in order to be heard. "Please, my sisters and brothers, listen to what I have to say!"

The attention of the people once more focused on Maria Antonia. "Father Mascia, who is a good and holy man, told us that history and our personal experience were justice enough for what we did, and he honestly believed he was right. We listened to his counsel. My sisters and brothers, please think carefully about what we have done. Can we honestly continue to live in silence while each day we are forced to remember what we did to our 'angels?' Who will take away the guilt we feel from knowing we have stolen another mamma's son? People of Opi, we stole seven lives so our lives could go on. Yes, we said we would be kind and generous to our 'angels,' and we told ourselves they would someday come to thank us. If we truly believed this, why did we continue to post guards at the entrance to our town? Why did we have our people watch them on their Sunday holiday from work?"

The eight men seated next to the altar moved toward Maria Antonia and surrounded her. She struggled as they began to move her toward the rear of the church.

Suddenly, a booming voice from the rear of the church shouted, "Gentlemen, leave that woman alone!"

Moving swiftly down the center aisle, a large man dressed in a dark suit, white shirt, and necktie continued his verbal order. "Remove your hands from that woman!"

The council members, seemingly caught off-guard by such an unexpected and booming challenge, stopped and turned. By the time they had recovered from the surprise, the man was standing on the chancel next to the altar. The people were dumbfounded at the sight of such a formally dressed stranger at the front of their church. He then brought Maria Antonia to the front of chancel. During the brief melodrama being played out in front of them, few people noticed that another welldressed stranger had moved inside the church through the front entrance with two uniformed officers, who positioned themselves beside the jacketed man at the door. The stranger on the chancel called for and received the full attention of the people.

He calmly addressed the audience. "People of Opi, I am detective Ricardo Fontana of the Roma Police Department." There was immediate silence. Detective Fontana continued, "There are detectives and uniformed police officers positioned at each door of the church and two police officers outside the church in a police van, which is blocking the road."

Detective Fontana could sense movement and murmuring at his back. He quickly turned, and in a firm manner ordered the governing council to return to their chairs.

Nicoangelo protested, "Detective Fontana, I demand that you and your men leave this peaceful meeting and our town. You have no jurisdiction in our community. Your presence here is illegal."

Father Mascia supported Nicoangelo. "Detective, you have desecrated this consecrated house of the Lord. As pastor of this church, I demand that you and your men leave this holy building immediately. You have no authority past the doors of this church. In God's name, I demand that you leave immediately."

Detective Fontana handed Father Mascia a form that had been officially stamped. He stated loudly for all in the church to hear, "Padre, may I remind you that police officers in Italy are permitted to enter religious consecrated areas in the execution of their duty with the properly stamped approval of a judge. My judicial notification allows me to enter and investigate this property; I am limited only in that I am not permitted to physically disturb religious property within this holy building."

Detective Fontana then removed other papers, folded in thirds, from the inside pocket of his jacket and asked Nicoangelo, "Sir, are you the elected leader of Opi?"

Nicoangelo replied, "Detective, I have been legally installed as the chairman of our governing council, which has authority over the operations of our town."

"Then you, Sir, are the person to receive this judicial authorization, which governs the L'Aguila province of the region of Abruzzo, of which the town of Opi is located. As you can see, this stamped document not only authorizes our presence in Opi, but it also requires us to investigate this matter. Therefore, as of this moment, I have judicial authority over whatever occurs in this community, and may I remind you, Sir, I have been listening with interest to the detailed description of the plans you had for these six men."

Nicoangelo returned to his seat, and he and two other members of the governing council reviewed the papers given to Nicoangelo.

Detective Fontana returned his attention to the noisy crowd and called for silence. After a few moments, the people became quiet. "Thank you, citizens of Opi. Your cooperation is most appreciated," said the detective. "I will ask you to remain calm and allow Ms. Sgammotta to finish her comments." Detective Fontana, reaching out toward Maria Antonia, took her hand and moved her back to the center of the Altar. "When Ms. Sgammotta has finished her remarks, I will instruct everyone as to our next procedure."

The six hostages only now allowed themselves to be receptive to the word freedom that had been spoken just five minutes ago. However, even though this official looking man seemed to be from the police, they were still not sure he would be able to make them free men. The people of Opi would surely, somehow, find a way to block their freedom.

The people in the church were absolutely silent and focused on Maria Antonia as she continued to speak. She started slowly, a bit shaken by what had just occurred, but in a matter of seconds she had regained her composure. "I made arrangements early this morning to be taken to the train station. I boarded the train for Roma, and there I explained to the capital city police what had occurred in Opi over these many years."

The assembled crowd began to protest, but she raised her voice to be heard. "My sisters and brothers, please hear me before you judge me. I've not betrayed you. Rather, I've freed us all from the heavy burden that we've been carrying these many years. In 1947, my papa, Vincenzo Sgammotta, believed that the course of action taken by Opi was the only option we had available to save our people from starvation. We believed we needed to do this in order to preserve the history of our town and our culture. My papa is now with the Almighty, and I believe in my heart that God understands that my father, although he was wrong, believed with all his will that his actions on our behalf were morally correct, given our circumstances. For this reason, I'm sure our compassionate Lord has welcomed Vincenzo Sgammotta to his eternal reward.

"I, and I hope others in Opi, believe it's time for someone to speak the truth on this matter. I, like you, remained silent, and cooperated. I, like you, told myself we were doing this for Opi and that there was no other way. We who disagreed and chose to remain quiet are the true villains. We were the cowards, afraid to challenge our parents, our leaders, and our priest. We are the ones who will not be forgiven, unless we begin to take responsibility for what we have hidden for so long. It's not easy to tell the truth when we know family and friends will look at us as betrayers. It's time for us to stop thinking of only today and begin to accept that when we die and ask the Almighty for entrance into his kingdom, he'll first ask, 'Did you ever admit you were wrong in this matter with your 'angels?' Did you ever ask for forgiveness for what you did to those seven boys? Did you do everything in your power to heal, as best as you could, those you wronged? If we say, 'Dear God, we secretly sent the men we injured to Tunisia so we could protect our own selfish interests,' then, like wolves, we'll have to hide in our dens from the hunters and be sorry for all eternity."

As she was speaking, Maria Antonia had slowly moved down the two steps from the altar and was now standing in the center aisle with her right hand on the front pew across the aisle from the six hostages.

She continued, "But if we have the courage to shout, 'Yes, Lord! At the end, we tried to do all that was humanly possible to heal those we wronged!' If we can tell God we took responsibility for what we did; if we say we are sorry and ask His forgiveness, surely our merciful Father will welcome us to eternal happiness. I plead with you: Let us now, with good and open hearts, tell the truth, no matter how much pain and humiliation it will bring to us and our town. If we send these six men to Tunisia and then pride ourselves on our cunning, our souls will never heal, and I fear we'll soon come to regret what we have done and quickly begin to hate ourselves.

"It may be that many of you here tonight may be saying, 'I did no wrong! I was not the one who brought these young men to our land.' Yes, that may be true. But we were all quiet and accepted the benefits of their labors. For this reason, we must also accept equal responsibility if we are ever to heal ourselves and our town."

The six hostages looked at each other with a hint of joy in their eyes. At that moment, the captives were able to internalize what had been troubling them for the past five and a half years. Finally, we have heard the words spoken, the words that the people of Opi have been denying for all these years. Suddenly they felt confident that they were going to be freed, free after all these years!

Maria Antonia, with arms raised, perspiration building on her brow, and now speaking to a deadly silent audience, said, "There's one final thing I wish to say before Detective Fontana addresses you. Let us not forget that as painful as it might be to explain to our children that mamma and papa are not perfect and have made mistakes, explaining our complete history, the good and the bad, this will help our children to understand that it's human to be weak, and that only the truth can help us find eternal happiness."

Maria Antonia slowly moved back up the steps, onto the altar, and stood behind Detective Fontana. The governing council remained seated and silent. The people in the church were alarmed but remained silent. Detective Fontana stepped forward and spoke to them in an authoritative tone. "My countrymen, I want to assure you there will be a fair investigation into this matter."

He looked at the eight members of the governing council and instructed them to stay seated so his assistant could obtain some personal information. Detective Fontana then spoke directly to the people with final instructions. "Officers from my squad will be taking the six men to the Roma police headquarters this evening. I encourage you all to go home and attend to your normal activities. An investigative unit will be formed tomorrow based on my report of this incident and I would expect them to appear in Opi the day after tomorrow. They will be responsible for a thorough and fair investigation, which may include interviews with some of you. Two officers will remain in Opi until the investigative unit arrives. Their duty will be to obtain a census of all residents. That will be all for this evening. You are now free to return to your homes, but do not leave this town until you have been interviewed by members of the investigative unit, who will complete their work within two to three days after they arrive."

Detective Fontana then instructed the six hostages to remain seated. He asked one of the uniformed officers to escort Maria Antonia to her home and wait there with her until given further orders.

As the people were quietly leaving the church, Detective Fontana gave instructions to the six hostages. "An officer will escort you to your houses to collect your personal effects. You'll then be taken immediately to Roma in the police van, and at that time you'll be given further instructions."

The police officer assigned to escort the six men to their rooms told the hostages to follow him. As he started to the door, he stopped, realizing the captives had remained in the pew and were not moving after his command. Time seemed to have stopped. They were not sure what to do. The police officer stepped back to the pew and grasped the arm of Klein, who was seated at the end of the pew, and stood him up. Then he gave a second, more forceful command for the hostages to stand and follow him. The five other men stood and followed Klein and the police officer toward the church door. They silently moved in single file, walking behind the officer who held Klein by the arm. They entered the police van, still incapable of communicating. The comprehension that their five and a half years imprisonment was about to end did not seem real.

Jem broke out of his trance-like state as the police officer was moving him into the van.

"No, no, my room is there." Pointing to the house next to the church, he yelled to the others, "I won't be long; I've a sack to pick up and want to say goodbye to Caterina."

The other five, jarred by Jem's directions, suddenly seemed able to return to reality, but they were still bewildered, silently staring at each other.

When Jem returned to the van, the officer drove to the next house. Paul gathered his few possessions and went to the first floor to say goodbye to Theresa. The front door was locked. He knocked loudly, but no one answered. He could see lights in the dining room, so he continued to bang on the door. He was about to strike the wooden door again when it opened. Standing in the doorway was Theresa's mother.

"I'd like to say goodbye to Theresa," said Paul, feeling impatient.

"Theresa has locked herself in her room and told me that she does not want to speak with you. She wants nothing further to do with you."

Paul was surprised. He turned, looked at the van, and then back at Theresa's mother. He hesitated and then simply said, "Goodbye, Mrs. Vecelli." He hurried down the stone stairs to the police van. The police van made brief stops at the Opi homes of Jacob and George where they picked up their few belongings, not bothering to say goodbye to their farming families.

Klein was the fifth man to stop at his room. He swiftly gathered his belongings in a cloth sack and went up the back stairs to speak with Giovanna. Klein knocked on the door, and it opened immediately. There stood Giovanna. She closed the door behind her and extended her arms to Klein. They said nothing, simply looking into each other's eyes. Then their bodies were tangled in a warm embrace. Giovanna was crying.

Klein whispered, "When the investigation is over, I'll come back to Opi. We'll be married in the church and start our happy life in Austria."

Giovanna pulled away from Klein, and while continuing to cry said, "Oh yes, yes, my love. I'll be waiting for your return." Giovanna, still crying, kissed Klein passionately and then pulled away, saying, "You must go. I'll wait for your return. Hurry back."

They kissed one more time, and Klein hurriedly descended the back steps. When he reached the bottom, he turned and shouted, "I'll be back soon!"

Daniel's room was the last stop. He gathered up a handful of personal items and hurried to his bed to retrieve one other item. He had decided after approximately a year of captivity, when the original winter jacket he had arrived with had to be replaced because of his growing body that he would one day walk out of Opi with his original winter coat under his arm as a symbol of his freedom. When Vincenzo gave him a replacement coat, he folded his original winter coat, tied the arms into a knot, and placed it in a compact bundle under his bed. Although he rarely moved his bed to check if his folded bundle was still there, he never forgot this promise to himself. As he moved toward his bed, he hoped it was still where he had left it. When he reached the bed he moved it away from the wall, knelt down, and was about to look to see if his coat was still there when he suddenly stopped, his body frozen by the charcoal words written on the lower part of the stone wall, smudged but still readable: Monte Cassino, Renault, black car, license plate CA 261, mountain road, Opi, and the number 25. There were the words he had written with burnt wood charcoal on that first night, thinking that somehow, they would be helpful in his rescue. The memory of those words, long forgotten, caused a sudden flood of emotion.

He whispered to himself, "So many stolen years. Damn these people." He slumped to the floor, sitting between the stone wall and the pulled-out bed, his knees bent up against his chest, his arms wrapped around his bent legs, and his hands clasped at the wrists. Tears began to flow, and soon he was sobbing. At some point, he felt a hand on his shoulder. Still crying, he quickly turned to see Gelsomina, dressed in black and looking weak and drawn, sitting on the bed next to him. Without thinking what he was doing, he placed his head in her lap and continued to cry.

Gelsomina gently stroked the back of his head. Finally, she spoke, "My Donato, often at night I'd wonder if you were here in your bed thinking of your mamma and crying. I'm sorry to see I was right. Allow me to say one thing: You, Donato, healed my heart when my two sons did not return from the Germans. I don't know if I would have been strong enough to survive the loss of my boys if God had not given you to me. After you came to our home, I was not strong enough to give you up. You became for me that I had lost. You not only helped put food on our table, but you also gave me back my life. You replaced the sons I had lost." Gelsomina then lifted Daniel's head, looked into his wet eyes, and said, "I know you must leave. I will continue to pray each day that you will someday lose the bitterness you must have in your heart toward the Sgammotta family."

Daniel stopped crying. His shoulders and head continued with a final shuddering movement as he suppressed his last sob, and then he said in a quiet tone, "No, Gelsomina, I never once cried, and I often wondered why, because there were so many nights of sadness. At night, in my bed, I often wondered why I became so fond of you. Gelsomina, I have no bitterness toward you. Somehow, I came to love you. I don't understand how or why, but instead of hating you for your part in my horror, I made you a replacement for my mother, as you made me a replacement for your lost sons. You were both my captor and my family. Saturday afternoons and Sunday mornings were happy times for me in my unhappy life."

Gelsomina, who was now crying, kissed the back of Daniel's hand and placed his open palms to her cheeks. She asked if he would do her one last favor. "Maria Antonia is upstairs and would like very much to say goodbye to you. Could you find it in your heart to grant her this wish?"

Daniel rose to his feet, looked into Gelsomina's sad eyes, and kissed her on the forehead. While her face was in his hands, he simply said, "Goodbye, Gelsomina."

With his bundled coat under his arm and his cloth bag, Daniel quickly went out past the animal stall; the tall gate was closed but unlocked. He climbed the back stairs, and as he entered the upstairs room, Maria Antonia rose from her chair. She seemed very unsure of herself. As she spoke, she was looking down, unwilling to make eye contact with Daniel. In her soft voice she said, "Thank you for coming to see me. I will not keep you long. I wanted the opportunity to explain something to you." Hesitating and nervously playing with her hands, she continued, "My papa dedicated his entire life to his family and Opi. As I grew older, I understood that it was wrong to bring you and the other boys to Opi. My papa, I loved him so. I didn't have the strength to tell him how I truly felt, because I knew it would break his heart. So, I remained silent these many years. In that time, I fell in love with you, not as a brother but as a man. After what we have done to you, I know you can never love me as a woman. To never know your love will be my punishment for remaining silent. I don't expect you to fully understand how difficult it was to love both you and my papa, and then have to make a choice. I'm not asking for your forgiveness. I know that would be too much to ask. All I ask is that you try to understand."

Daniel was silent for a moment. The feeling of Maria Antonia's hand on his cheek and lips while she was trimming his hair and beard was all that passed through his mind.

Maria Antonia, misinterpreting his silence, said into the void, "Donato, it is better if you do not speak. I accept your silence."

Her words brought Daniel's mind back to the present. Daniel tried to reply. "Maria Antonia…." He was unable to speak the next word his tongue seemed too heavy to lift off the floor of his mouth.

Maria Antonia, once again misinterpreting Daniel's silence, said, "No need for you to speak, you owe me no words. You have been through too many years of forced labor at the hands of my family. I have no reason to expect anything from you but contempt."

Finally, Daniel gained enough composure to respond. He reached out and touched the smooth, olive colored skin of her hand and said, "Maria Antonia, I longed to hold you in my arms all these years, while only being allowed to feel this hand on my face and lips."

Maria Antonia interrupted, "Please, Donato, don't speak of us. It's too painful to hear your words."

Daniel, thinking of the van and what it represented, yet wanting desperately to express his feelings, said, "In these few minutes, how can I say what I've wanted to say to you for the past five and a half years? After I am back in America and have time to think about my time in Italy, I will write you a letter."

Maria Antonia, still unable to look into Daniel's eyes, responded, "That would be wonderful. I would be very pleased if you found it in your heart to write to me. Take as much time as you need. And, Donato, if you change your mind and choose not to write, I will understand and accept that decision as well. You owe nothing to me or the Sgammotta family."

Daniel, who was torn between the van parked in front of his prison room and his desire to share his feelings with Maria Antonia, said, "Over the years you have shown me great kindness and, more importantly, you gave me a great deal of comfort. No, I do owe you. I promise I'll write after I am back in America."

She offered her hand in a gesture to shake Daniel's hand. He was about to take her hand, but instead he continued his right hand past her outstretched arm and held her waist, his left arm gently placed on her right shoulder, their bodies finally touching. The thrill of holding Maria Antonia after so many years of desiring her was exhilarating. He rested his head on her shoulder, the warm, velvet skin of her cheek pressing against his beard, the gentle touch of her breasts and hips tantalizing his every nerve. They held each other for a few moments. She was crying, and she impulsively moved back, but now for the first time she was able to look lovingly into Daniel's eyes. He moved his face slowly toward her mouth and their lips met and remained locked for a thrilling moment. Maria Antonia abruptly separated from Daniel. "Donato, please, you must go."

Daniel, now composed, squeezed her hand, and turned to leave. Suddenly he stopped, looked back at her, and said, "You were the one who made it possible for us to be free. We all know the sacrifice you made today. We will never forget you for what you did for us today. Maybe the people of Opi will someday understand."

As he entered the van and closed the door behind him, Jem, who was sitting in front of Daniel, turned, and softly said, "It was surprisingly difficult for all of us." As Jem turned to face forward, the van began to move down Via San Giovanni de Battista on its way out of Opi. Tonight, there were no men in a wagon with rifles to block the police van from leaving.

CHAPTER 36

The van arrived at police headquarters around two in the morning. The police asked a few basic questions: their full names, the dates when they were kidnapped (as best they could remember), where they were kidnapped, and information they thought would be helpful in finding their missing person reports from 1947. Due to the late hour, the former captives were to sleep on cots at the police station. Before they went to their room, the police explained that there would be an inquiry and what the police referred to as a debriefing that would take at least five days. The six men were disappointed, but the police insisted that considerable time was needed to obtain the necessary information, to complete the paperwork, and — most importantly — the men needed to spend time with the police psychiatrist and generally get acclimated to their new environment.

After breakfast the following morning, the former hostages were presented with clean underwear, shirts, pants, socks, and sneakers. They requested scissors, shaving cream, and razors. They were determined to remove the last remaining visible reminder of Opi, their beards.

After a glorious warm shower, the cleanly shaven men, dressed in their new clothes and sneakers, then met with the police interviewer. He asked specific questions, which forced the former hostages to explain their captivity in a chronological format rather than by random facts. By noon they were exhausted. The police assured them they were making good progress in collecting the necessary missing person reports. The police expected to be able to contact their families during the day, and the men could begin making phone calls to their families the following day. They had lunch and were taken to another building, which would be their living quarters for the remainder of their time at police headquarters.

They were brought back to the main building at four in the afternoon. Their missing person files, including Omar's, had been located, and one officer was in the process of making initial contact with each family. The hostages had earlier explained in detail what had happened to Omar, and the police were able to pass that sad information along to his family.

It was decided that Jacob would ask permission to speak with Omar's family as soon as possible. The men knew Omar's sister spoke English, and they decided they would travel to Egypt to attend the burial service, which they were sure his family would be conducting. Jacob spoke to Omar's sister that evening. He explained her brother's relationship with the other hostages and emphasized how close they had become during their captivity. Jacob talked in detail about Omar's decision and his mood on that final Sunday afternoon. Omar's sister was unable to contain her emotions after hearing about the relationship her brother had with the other captives. She was especially surprised, but also intrigued, that Jacob, a Jewish boy, spoke so tenderly and seemed to be so clearly enamored by her Egyptian brother. Through her tears, she expressed relief at knowing the details of Omar's state of mind on the day he died. She told Jacob her parents would take great comfort in knowing Omar was with friends during his time in Opi. Omar's sister said they were planning to move Omar's body to Egypt and hold a burial service. Arrangements were made for Jacob to contact her when he arrived home. He would then contact the other five men to coordinate their trip to attend Omar's burial services. His sister once again thanked Jacob for his phone conversation and told him that she and her family were anxious to welcome Jacob and the others to their home.

That next morning, they were scheduled to report for individual physical examinations. Having blood drawn from the veins in their arms for the purpose of performing various medical tests was a new experience for each of them. When the individual physical examinations were completed, the doctors were quite surprised at their excellent health. Each man exceeded the health standards for his age group. The only problem was some tooth decay, which would be treated when they arrived home.

The two examining doctors were intrigued by the excellent health of the former hostages and requested to meet with the six men as a group. The doctors had many questions about their living environment, eating, sleeping, work, leisure activities, and the type of medical attention they received during their time in Opi.

Jacob, who had an interest in medicine, had been allowed time with Dattore Tatti to learn from him. During their early years of captivity, the people of Opi had hoped that Jacob would marry and remain in Opi so that one day he would be able to assume the functions of Dattore Tatti. Jacob explained that a man by the name of Beniamino Tatti was the doctor for all the people of Opi. "Everyone simply called him Dattore. The front room of his house was used as the town's ambulatorio (doctor's office). Jacob explained that Dattore Tatti told him that he had been schooled in Naples but was ambiguous in his responses as to whether he was a licensed Italian physician."

With a surprised smile, one of the doctors commented, "Considering the excellent state of your health, I'm very curious to know the methods he used when you or others became ill. In close to six years of living in Opi, some of you must have become seriously ill, broken a bone, had an accident, or come down with an infectious disease."

Jacob explained how Klein's broken ankle and Paul's broken arm had been treated. He described in some detail how Dattore treated Daniel's back wounds when he was returned from the forest half dead. He also described what had been done to heal George's bullet wounds. Primarily, Dottore Tatti used herbs to treat infections and other common illnesses and seemed skilled in his treatment of the more serious injuries Jacob had previously described.

"Herbs?" questioned one of the doctors. "What kind of herbs?"

Jacob had learned a great deal about the use of herbs by Dattore Tatti. "He used a book called De Materia Medica, written by a Greek person named Dioscorides. Dottore Tatti told me Dioscorides lived in the first century A.D. and traveled with the Roman Legions, identifying, illustrating, and using the medicinal plants of the Mediterranean area." Jacob was quite knowledgeable of and was able to talk at length about the various herbs Dottore Tatti used to treat a wide variety of ailments. When he was finished, the doctors expressed their gratitude, and the men were taken back to their rooms.

On the third day, Daniel asked if he could contact his relatives in Castellammare di Stabia. The police were able to obtain the phone numbers of his Aunt Pia and her husband Rodolfo. The police called, Rodolfo answered, the police informed him that Daniel had been found alive and arrangements would be made for him to call them the following morning. The officer made it clear to Rodolfo that he was not to inform local newspapers or mention to anyone that Daniel had been found. An official statement would be made by the police after the men were out of the country.

When Daniel called the following morning, his Aunt Pia answered the phone. When she heard Daniel's voice, she began to cry. After a few moments, he asked about his mother and father. Zia Pia told Daniel that her brother Pete had lost touch with his family in Italy after he last visited Italy. Daniel thought it strange that his father would have lost contact with his sister.

Zia Pia told Daniel that Nonno Leopoldo died in 1950, and that her mother, Nonna Francesca was still living. Her sisters, Alessandrina and Leonida, also remained in their homes in Castellammare de Stabia. She explained that almost all the children of his father's sisters were living in Italy, but that only two still remained in Castellammare di Stabia: Uncle Iseo's son, Emilio, who now operated the bakery, since an accident to his father; and her daughter, Angelina, who was married to a local man.

"Does Ruffino live in Italy?" asked Daniel.

"Ah, Ruffino has made everyone in Castellamare di Stabia very proud." She told Daniel that Ruffino had received free schooling at the University in Bologna to study science; he now worked in Vienna, Switzerland, for the International Atomic Energy Agency and his position required him to travel the entire world. Zia Pia mentioned that he sometimes went to America to report at the United Nations.

Daniel inquired if she knew his address and phone number. She did not but promised to get the information and send it to Daniel's parents. Daniel promised to write to Zia Pia when he got home, and he asked her not to forget to contact Ruffino.

When Daniel finished speaking with his aunt, the police informed him they had spoken with his older brother. They told him to stay by the phone while they dialed his brother in America.

Daniel was waiting excitedly to hear his brother's voice. The phone rang once, and Daniel immediately picked it up.

"Danny, Danny, is that you?"

"Lee, it's me, Danny." They talked briefly, and toward the end of the conversation, Leopoldo told Daniel that he and Barbara planned to be at Kennedy Airport when he landed. They would take him to see Frances and his mother and father. Daniel felt a spine-tingling rush of elation as he realized he was finally going home. "I can't wait to see you and the rest of the family!" he said to his brother.

Although the hostages were disappointed that they were not allowed to leave for home immediately after arriving in Roma, they understood the wisdom of spending what turned out to be seven days at the Roma police headquarters. There was a great deal of information and emotions to process, and these days gave them the needed time and space prior to returning to their home countries.

Daniel felt uneasy when he was told that he was scheduled to meet with Dr. Amabilia Luciani, a psychologist, the following morning.

Dr. Luciani welcomed Daniel into her office. She started the session by saying, "Studies have shown that victims of kidnapping display high levels of distress immediately after release and a high frequency of traumatic symptoms for an extended period of time after they are free." She explained the feelings associated with trauma and distress, and ended on a positive note by telling Daniel that in time these negative feelings would pass. She then asked Daniel to talk about his experience as it affected him physically and psychologically.

Daniel first discussed the physical nature of his time in Opi. "This is gonna sound funny or maybe the better word is strange. In the beginning I found the farm work tiring, but after a while the work got easier. I think I was becoming stronger. The weather was cool except for August, but Opi was a beautiful place and working never made me sweat very much. The winter months were a different story with all that snow, but winter work was in a house or barn most of the time. Then after two years my body became really firm. They fed me well and I really felt good physically."

Doctor Luciani then asked Daniel a question that he perceived as unusual and even foolish. "That's wonderful to hear. Were you happy working the farm in Opi?"

Daniel's answer was short and quick. "Was I happy? I may have felt good about becoming stronger and bigger, but happy? No, I was never happy being a captive, I was angry! Now that he had expressed his anger at the word happy, he felt better, and began to tell the doctor how difficult the entire experience was for him. "This was the worst thing that has ever happened to me. It was the opposite of happy. I walked around for over five years feeling, I guess the word is beat-up, no, defeated is a better word. I always felt lonely and sad, and these feelings were with me constantly. I felt better on Sunday's but during the week, the feelings of sadness never went away. Most of the time my chest and stomach felt so hollow that I often wondered if there was something wrong with my body. I felt relieved when the doctor examined me and said my chest and stomach were fine."

Doctor Luciani was pleased that Daniel was willing to share his intense feelings so quickly. "I'm glad you mentioned your feelings of loneliness and sadness. First, I'm not at all surprised to hear that you experienced these feelings, and second, your chest and stomach symptoms would be quite normal given the loneliness and sadness you felt being held captive for such an extended period."

Daniel was relieved to hear the doctor's assurance that his feelings were normal.

Doctor Luciani continued with more analysis. "It would have also been normal if you had experienced feelings of shame, helplessness, abandonment, guilt, depression, loss of confidence, and perhaps even the loss of self-control.

Daniel and the doctor then discussed his relationship with the Sgammotta family. Daniel was interested in Doctor Luciani's opinion about his feelings for Gelsomina and how illogical and troubling this relationship was for him, especially during the early years of his captivity. Doctor Luciani talked about a number of reasons for Daniel's feelings for Gelsomina, but soon the discussion moved smoothly from Gelsomina to his unconventional relationship and feelings for Maria Antonia. Dr. Luciani encouraged him to keep his promise to write to Maria Antonia. She explained how this correspondence could be very useful in helping him interpret and comprehend their emotional connection.

Daniel told the psychologist about his recurring, confusing dream. "The same dream used to wake me up many nights of the week. Why do you think I had such a crazy dream…over and over, the same dream?"

Dr. Luciani gave Daniel a warm grin of recognition. "Don't be alarmed at the content of your dream. Actually, it would be more accurate if I referred to it as a nightmare. I am sure that your nightmare will no longer be a problem now that you are out of your continual stressful situation." Dr. Luciani described a rather interesting theory, recently developed, that addressed many of Daniel's questions regarding his feelings toward Gelsomina.

The psychologist introduced Daniel to what she called the Stockholm Syndrome. "This syndrome is thought to be an unconscious emotional response to the traumatic experience of being kidnapped and held for a long period of time. The positive emotional bond that often develops between the victim and captor is a defensive mechanism of the captive's ego to cope with the stress of isolation. Feelings such as rage, blame, disgrace, castigation, and accusation can all be displaced in the mind of the kidnapped person, because it might be too risky to express these feelings directly against the kidnapper. The premise behind the Stockholm Syndrome is that it's a life-saving defense mechanism for the victim. It is also believed that this unconscious mental process helps the captive avoid violent reactions, and in some cases, foolish escape attempts that could lead to death. After an initial period of shock, disbelief, and denial, it is common for victims of kidnappings to gradually accept their situation and experience feelings of imminent release alternating with disillusion, discouragement, and despair."

The doctor explained that when victims experience traumatic shock, isolation from normal surroundings, hearing repeatedly only what the kidnappers want them to know, not being killed by their captors, and being treated with unexpected kindness, they can easily fall into a certain pattern of positive behavior and feelings toward their captor. She assured Daniel that when a person is held prisoner, it is quite normal for the individual to eventually think their captor is kind, simply because they have not killed them. Victims often display a series of feelings that range from outrage to fear to passivity and, finally, friendship. The person who is kidnapped may begin to believe that the kidnapper is a good person simply because of their kindness. Many hostages eventually feel they owe their lives to their captors.

"But why did I have these nightmares every week?" Daniel asked. "And why would I be so worried about getting back to Opi on Monday? If I was dreaming about being home, you would think I'd be happy with my family. Why was it that my family in America was not the most important part of my dream? They weren't, Opi and Vincenzo were a bigger part of my dream."

Dr. Luciani responded, "I suspect the content of your nightmare went back to the fact that you were replacing your deep, intense angry feelings against Vincenzo for kidnapping you, in an attempt to prevent you from confronting and fighting with him. You might have been unconsciously afraid that if you continually confronted Vincenzo, he would have eventually killed you."

Understanding the doctor's explanation of the Stockholm Syndrome and his constant dream helped Daniel understand some of the reactions that he found so confusing while he was a hostage in Opi.

Dr. Luciani also speculated, "You probably tried to take control of your emotions but were unable to think clearly for the first week or so. It would have been perfectly normal for you to experience hope of survival and freedom, when at the same time you were having overwhelming fear that you were about to die. It is not unusual for people who have been held in captivity to feel this way for long periods after being captured."

Dr. Luciani then changed the subject. "When I spoke with the other men, they described symptoms of a diagnosis we call stress. Dr. Hans Selye, a Czech Biochemist at the University of Montreal, recently introduced this term to describe the way trauma can cause over-activity of the adrenal gland and with it a disruption of bodily equilibrium. Doctor Selye's work was expanded and refined, at the turn of the century, by Doctor Walter Cannon, a professor at Harvard University in America. Adding to Doctor Selye's experiments on what he called the "flight or fight response. Doctor Cannon found that in stressful situations bodily functions change; muscles tense and tighten for action, hormone levels rise releasing stored sugars into the blood, heart rate and blood pressure increases forcing blood to parts of the body preparing for activity, sugar and fats pour into the blood providing quick energy, chemicals are released into the blood to assist in the clotting process, breathing rapidly increases supplying oxygen to muscles, and finally perspiration increases to cool down the body.

So, I feel confident that a diagnosis of stress will be applied to the six of you in the context of how you behaved. It's important to understand that some of your daily behaviors were quite normal for people who experience the stress caused by long isolation. These feelings usually bring on physical symptoms, such as teeth clenching, pacing back and forth, being anxious or having anxious thoughts, being unable to focus and concentrate, always feeling threatened even when the threat is nonexistent, nail biting, dry mouth, rapid heartbeat, nervously rubbing your hands together, and what we call a nervous stomach, but what I learned you men called 'butterflies' in your stomach."

Daniel smiled and nodded his head. He knew these feelings well.

Doctor Luciani made one last point. "There is one final symptomatic stress behavior that's important: believing you are the only one experiencing these symptoms." Dr. Luciani paused and asked Daniel if he had any questions.

Daniel had been listening intently with his mouth open and a look of amazement on his face, as though he had just seen the greatest magic trick in his life. "How can you possibly know all those things? What you have said is exactly what I felt while I was held in Opi. How is it possible that you can know how I felt?"

Dr. Luciani smiled. "I wish I could say I am that brilliant and could read your mind, but the truth is: After Dr. Selye's works on stress, these behaviors have been researched by talking with hundreds and hundreds of people to find out what symptoms they experienced when they were held captive. As a matter of fact, Daniel, by talking with you and the other five men, I believe I have learned something new, a trait that I can share with other psychologists and psychiatrists, my colleagues. It is rare for someone to be held captive for as long as you men were held and be able to talk about your experience. Other doctors have not had the opportunity to talk with victims of such long-term captivity. I have learned from the others, and now from you, that around your fifth year of captivity all of you lost interest in living, and during that time you were convinced that the people of Opi were going to kill you. Thanks to you and the other hostages I will be able to share this important information with my colleagues."

"So, you think even feeling that we were going to be killed was normal?"

Doctor Luciani was quick to respond. "Oh yes, Daniel. I now regard this as quite normal."

Daniel smiled and slid down in his chair. "Boy, you don't know how relieved that makes me feel!" he said.

"Do you remember having an unusual number of headaches, or if you had the need to urinate excessively during the first year?"

Daniel thought for a moment. "I recall many days with headaches, but I don't remember having the need to frequently urinate."

Doctor Luciani moved on to other subjects. "Since you were not tortured, you were probably able to adapt to your surroundings and your situation sooner than what is considered normal. Another aspect of your long captivity is that all six of you must have had a strong will to survive until about that fifth year. You probably made an internal decision to live, within weeks of being kidnapped."

Dr. Luciani then referred to Omar. "When Omar decided to walk out of town, I suspect he had made a conscious decision that he no longer wanted to live as a hostage." Dr. Luciani continued by asking about the effect Omar's loss had on the remaining hostages. "After his death, did you feel as though your group unity and bond had somehow been broken?"

"No, I don't think so," said Daniel. "After Omar's death, I felt like a part of me had been killed, but I didn't feel our group changed. We believed he was okay with his decision. We knew he was a smart, mature guy, and he convinced us he was ready. I think Omar was even happy to die so he could be with his Allah."

That afternoon, Daniel was more relaxed with the doctor's questions and analysis. He asked her a question, which the six captives had constantly discussed during their time in Opi. "Do you know how we were able to continue living our sad, lonely lives for so many years without losing our minds? We were always afraid that someday one of us would go crazy, especially after the incident with George. Did he tell you about what happened?"

"Yes, George and I spent a good deal of time discussing that incident." Doctor Luciani leaned back in her chair, put her pencil down on her notepad, and looked at Daniel for a moment. "This question has been on my mind since I was assigned this case. Daniel, you are the fifth hostage I have spoken with, and I have concluded that your free Saturday afternoons, and especially Sundays together with each other, was the reason you all remained as stable as you did for so many years. The little we do know about isolation for long periods of time is that it can cause insanity. It's my guess that the crucial support and communication you had with your fellow captives, and, perhaps, the faith and loyalty you had in each other, enabled the six of you to get through this ordeal with your mental processes intact. It's my belief that without your Sunday socializing, and for some of you, Saturday afternoons with your Opi families, the six of you probably would not have been able to survive your ordeal. Someone in Opi had a good understanding of human nature or an intuitive sense that socializing with other people was necessary for maintaining your sanity and survival. I can't come up with any other explanation."

Daniel enthusiastically agreed. "You know, I'll betcha you're right. We really enjoyed being together on Sundays."

The doctor returned to the subject of Daniel's relationship with the Sgammotta family. She explained to Daniel that it was not surprising that each captive was able to establish some type of a friendly, or in his case, loving relationship with a member of his captor's family. "I was not surprised to hear similar stories from the other hostages. In addition to the relationships which you established with each other; it was probably very important that each of you was able to develop some type of personal relationship with other individuals. I can't possibly imagine the six of you surviving for almost six years without establishing these relationships."

"Doctor Luciani then emphasized, a strong, important recommendation. "The first and most important thing you must do when you return to America is consult with someone in the mental health field for the purpose of continuing the healing process we have started today. Think of our talk today as puncturing a can to let some of the air out so it won't explode. You still need someone to help you go into the can to examine the contents and try to make sense of what you find there. I believe the doctor you speak with in America will be extremely helpful to you as you adjust to returning home to your family, friends, and a new life.

Doctor Luciani finished her session by saying, "The police are not going to release the facts of your case until the six of you are out of Italy. They are concerned the publicity might interfere with their debriefing and perhaps delay your departure." Dr. Luciani then added one last caution. "When you are with friends and other people, you might see a change in their behavior. For example, if you join a group of people who are conversing and perhaps laughing, don't be surprised if you see them stop laughing or change their mood when you join them. It is nothing you have done. You have to expect to be treated differently when you return to your family and friends."

Dr. Luciani told Daniel that unless he had anything further to add, she was satisfied that the session was complete.

Daniel looked at the floor for a moment, sighed and hesitantly said, "Uh… No, no, not really."

Dr. Luciani could easily tell there was something more on Daniel's mind. "If there is something still bothering you, I would like to hear what it is. Even if you think it's foolish, I promise to take it seriously."

"It's not that I think it's foolish," said Daniel. "It's just something I think I should talk to a priest about."

"Of course, Daniel, I completely understand especially if it is something more appropriate for the confessional."

"Oh no, it has nothing to do with sin, at least I don't consider it a sin." said Daniel, his frustration plainly evident. Then, more forcefully, he added, "I…, I can't understand why God allowed this to happen to me! Why did God allow this to go on for such a long time? My mother always said, 'God wouldn't give anyone a burden they couldn't carry.' Well, this burden was too difficult for me to carry, and I don't understand why God made it last so long." Doctor Luciani was sympathetic, but she agreed this was something that Daniel should discuss with a priest. Daniel stood, thanked Dr. Luciani, and left the room.

On the day before Daniel was scheduled to leave for America, he was resting in his room after the midday meal when he received a call to report to the main office immediately. Arriving at the main office, Daniel gave the policeman at the desk his name. The supervisor behind the desk seemed upset with the youngster, and with a clear tone of irritation in his voice he said, "The captain gave us standing orders that none of you were to speak to anyone from the outside, but he found it necessary to make an exception in your case. Go to room number two and pick up the phone. A caller is holding for you."

As Daniel walked down the corridor toward room two, his head was filled with fearful thoughts. Damn it! I knew something was going to go wrong! They're making an exception for this important call. It has to mean someone is going to stop me from going home tomorrow. I knew this was all too good to be true. He cautiously picked up the receiver and said meekly, "Hello?"

He was greeted by an excited voice. "Donato, this is Ruffino. Do you remember me, your cousin, Alessandrina's son?"

Almost yelling into the phone, Daniel said, "Ruffino, yeah, I remember! How are you doing? I'm so glad to hear your voice!"

"Donato, what a wonderful surprise to hear you are alive. Zia Pia called me yesterday. It's a miracle! The agency I work for was able to convince the police to let me speak with you. I just wanted to call and hear your voice, and let you know I have not forgotten you."

Daniel was thrilled that Ruffino had called him. "Ruffino, I'm so happy you called. I thought of you often over the years. Zia Pia told me you are an important scientist. How great, your dreams came true." Daniel told Ruffino he still remembered the day when they went to the calcio game, and how Ruffino was so despondent about his chances of going on to a university.

"Donato, you remembered that? I'm ashamed to say I haven't thought of it since we last saw each other."

"Tell me what happened since I last saw you, I guess it's been close to six years ago," said Daniel.

"No, no, not now. The police will only let me speak with you for a few minutes. My job often requires me to visit the United Nations. Do you remember, twenty years ago, you promised to show me around New York City? Well, I am going to hold you to that promise the next time I'm at the United Nations." Ruffino gave Daniel his address and phone number, and made Daniel promise to send his phone number and address to him. "I won't take any more of your time. I know you must be worn out by everything that has happened to you in the past week, and I can only imagine how excited you must be about going home. I just wanted to hear your voice and let you know I have not forgotten our wonderful few weeks together many years ago. Remember, send me your American address and phone number, and we'll get together next time I'm in New York. You must tell me everything then."

Daniel thanked Ruffino for calling and especially for remembering him.

The time had come for the six young men to return to their home countries; each boy was scheduled to leave Roma at different times the following day. Their final dinner took place at a round table at the police headquarters cafeteria. The men were relatively quiet during their meal. After the dishes were cleared, they remained at the table quietly, each waiting for one of the former captives to rise and encourage his friends to follow him back to their room. There was sorrowfulness even in their stillness.

Jacob finally jolted the cumbersome atmosphere. "Guys, I don't know about you, but on this night when I should be feeling nothing but happiness,

I only feel conflicted and unsettled about tomorrow. I feel that I'm discarding one family for another, and my insides seem to be all tangled. In the morning, we will all go in separate directions. Is this our end together? Will we forever just be a memory?

When Jacob finished the six young men were left looking at each other. Slowly they began to take turns saying how they felt about leaving, but they were unable to add any deeper feeling to what Jacob had said. They eventually talked about how important it was for them to maintain contact, not only in their reunions but also by writing frequently and talking by telephone. Each of the former captive's comments, that normally would have been meaningful, continued to feel stiff and formal. They would have to be satisfied with what they had. They were going home and soon life would eventually make more sense. Possibly when home they would be able to sort out how their relationships, then talking with each other might be more relaxed, and genuine.

George was able to summarize perfectly how their attitudes might evolve and, more important, how they may learn to depend on each other during their healing process. "I'll bet after we are home for a time, the strange feeling we are having tonight about leaving each other, will become not only more comfortable, but we will find that we need to lean on each other in letters and phone calls during the months and years ahead. I know I will never forget any of you or our experience for the remainder of my life.

The following morning Doctor Luciani visited briefly and wished them well. She made a point of telling them that no matter how loving, caring, and understanding their families were, it would be impossible for their family and friends to fully understand what the captives had experienced in Opi. "So, remember to be patient with others, they may find conversation and socializing as uncomfortable as you." Her last comment to the men was that they would need each other more often than they could imagine.

CHAPTER 37

Thrilled to be leaving Italy after so many lonely years, Daniel Ciarletta's feet barely touched the broad marble steps of the Roma police headquarters. His carabinieri (police) escort suddenly concerned that he was following rather than leading his charge, called out, "Signore, piano, piano! (slowly, slowly!)" Daniel stopped and waited impatiently at the bottom of the steps for his escort. As the two men proceeded toward the police car, Daniel tried to remain in stride with the police officer, but his emotions propelled his body forward, always one step ahead of the carabinieri.

Forced to stop at the door of the police car, and feeling awkward from his uncontrollable elation, Daniel entered the car, clasped his hands tightly, and reminded himself to relax. His firmly pressed hands seemed to temporarily suppress his rushing energy. As the car moved out onto the streets of Rome, Daniel began to think about his many failed attempts from his Italian prison town and the disappointment that followed each abortive attempt. Although he had been assured, he was scheduled to fly home to America later that afternoon, he wondered whether something unexpected might happen. Will today be just another cruel disappointment? With this thought, his excitement turned to anxiety. Something is gonna happen to stop me from returning to America, I can just feel it. His mood quickly changed to tentative caution. He whispered to himself, "Please, Lord, don't disappoint me again. I wanna go home."

The carabinieri startled Daniel from his reverie with a reminder to use his seatbelt. When Daniel and the five other men had been rescued seven days ago, the driver of the police van had to show them how to buckle up. Today he needed no assistance.

Daniel tried to distract himself by focusing on the streets of Roma. He saw massive old stone buildings beside contemporary contoured glass and brick structures. Buses, small cars, and scooters briskly wove through the narrow streets, and pedestrians quickly dashing pass each other on the sidewalks; so contrary to the people of Opi who mentally and physically moved at a slow, cautious, deliberate pace.

Having been isolated in a rural hill town and held captive for so many years, he was mesmerized by the many unusual street images he was observing. The hurried rush of people on the sidewalks, large groups of people in fancy clothing crossing the street at red lights, the food carts at the curb, the small groups of people deep in conversation against large stone buildings, men in uniform standing in the middle of an intersection waving people and cars to proceed forward or wait for his direction. It was as though Daniel had been transported to a different world.

After a half hour amid the frenetic rhythms of the city, the police car entered a highway, and the scenery changed to open fields, rolling hills, and farms. Daniel was all too familiar with these views, which seemed to have a calming effect, relieving some of his nervous tension. He found himself becoming more enthusiastic, allowing himself to anticipate his new life in America and being reunited with family and friends.

Daniel understood that his life and daily routine were about to change dramatically. He would be faced with new experiences, new adventures, and have to relearn simple things like the days of the week. During his years in the Italian mountain town, the days of the week were all the same, thoroughly homogenized to the point where there was no need-to-know what day it was, except for Saturday and then his favorite day Sunday. But now, each new day would be different. Daniel would need to change the mindset he had become so used to. He suddenly asked the carabiniero, "What day is today?"

"Today is Giovedi (Thursday), Signore," said the police officer. Although the days of the week had become routinely similar in his mountain prison, years were a different matter. Each spring, the new planting season meant another year had passed. At the time of his rescue, Daniel now knew for sure he was nineteen years old; he had been able to verify this fact during his days of debriefing at the Roma police headquarters.

As the police car entered the airport, Daniel marveled at the big sleek silver airplanes with names on their sides. This was as close as he had ever been to an actual plane. He had only seen the giant flying machines in newsreels when he was a young boy or in the sky flying over his Bronx neighborhood as they made their landing approach to LaGuardia Airport across the bay from his Bronx neighborhood. When the police officer parked the car and Daniel opened the door, the powerful noise of the planes leaving the ground became ear-piercing. The airport, the planes, and the noise had the effect of reassuring him that he was free, and that he was really going home to his mother and father, his sisters and brother, and, hopefully, his old friends. As the two men left the car, the police officer led Daniel to what he referred to as "the terminal."

Walking toward the building, Daniel began to think of his family. How will they look? How will they sound? Will they accept me after all this time?

Will I still feel like the son of my mother and father, and like a brother to my oldest sister Frances, brother Leopoldo, and younger sister Barbara? Or after all these years, I may feel like a stranger in my own house?

At the entrance of the terminal, Daniel was startled when the glass doors suddenly opened without anyone touching them. He cautiously moved past the open doors while examining them carefully, concerned they might close as unexpectedly as they had opened. Once inside the terminal, he momentarily stopped, wide-eyed and open-mouthed; he was overwhelmed by an amazing sight. He was standing inside the entrance of the largest room he had ever seen, with a metal ceiling so high it was unimaginable. Huge windows joined together, forming a part of one high wall. Understanding Daniel's surprised reaction, his police escort hesitated a moment, and then said, "Avanti." They moved quickly along the glazed, shiny tile floor. The people who rushed past them looked different than the people Daniel had remembered in his Bronx neighborhood. Men were wearing tight-fitting suits and colorful shirts, some without collars. The long scarves draped around their necks looked like flags billowing in the breeze as they ran to catch their flights. Women were wearing short, tight-fitting skirts, exposing their shapely legs and brazenly outlining their hips. Surprisingly, some of the women even wore pants. Walking alongside men in robes were dark-skinned women with covered heads and colorful flowing clothes draped to cover their entire body. The style of dress was drastically different from the clothing he had become used to seeing in his prison mountain town.

Daniel was intrigued by all the new sights, his eyes leaping from one amazing display to another, with no time to pause and appreciate what he was observing. He stayed close to his escort, his head bouncing from side to side, as he tried to absorb all the new thrilling scenes. Besides the huge room and interesting looking people, there were small colorful areas serving strange-looking food, a huge wall clock, large murals, bright banners, and wall signs that included words and pictures he did not understand. The room, the colors, the people everything was exhilarating! Continuing to move forward, Daniel became fascinated by the noise in the high ceiling room. The many private conversations seemed to mysteriously move upward, joining together and magically forming a continuous hum that returned to the ears of the harried travelers as a synchronized whisper.

Daniel and his escort arrived at a ticket counter. The carabiniero handed official looking papers to the woman behind the counter and they had a brief conversation. Daniel's escort turned to him, wished him well, and moved briskly into the throng of moving people.

Carrying a single canvas bag, Daniel was told to join the line of people who were descending a long flight of stairs. Once outside the terminal, the passengers walked toward a large airplane. Upon entering the airplane, Daniel expected to see the same silvery metal on the inside as he saw on the outside of the plane. Another surprise! He was greeted by modern upholstered seats, cream-colored walls and ceiling, light blue partitions separating sections of the plane, and a carpeted floor. An attractive, uniformed woman personally welcomed him. Another woman helped strap him into his seat. The uniformed woman cautioned him not to loosen the buckle until he was told to do so over the plane's intercom, a phrase Daniel to have explained. At some point, the noise of the plane's motors changed, and the plane began to slowly move backwards and suddenly stopped. It remained stationary for a few moments and then began to move forward, maneuvering and making turns. The aircraft came to a gentle stop in front of its runway. After a few minutes, Daniel felt the plane move forward slowly at first, then picking up speed, faster and faster, bumpier and bumpier, the wings flapping and vibrating, Daniel's back being forced into the back of his seat as the plane accelerated. Suddenly, the bumping stopped, and although the plane's motors were still making their unfamiliar powerful noise, there was a sudden calm. It took Daniel a few moments to release the hard grip of his hands on the arms of his chair. His eyes remained focused on the back of the seat in front of him. Eventually, he slowly turned his head and cautiously glanced out the small window beside him. As the plane continued to climb, the objects on the ground became smaller and smaller. Daniel was beginning his voyage to America.

Soon a uniformed women was walking down the center isle of the plane, with a rolling cart in front of her, she was handing cans and glasses filled with colored liquid to the passengers. When she arrived at Daniel's seat, she asked the man sitting in the aisle seat what he wanted to drink, after responding she looked to Daniel sitting next to the oblong window and asked him the same question. Daniel didn't know how to respond so he said, "Anything is ok for me." The women handed him a plastic cup with ice in it and a colorful cold can. He noticed the people in front of him were pouring the contents of the cold can into the cup with ice, which was resting on a tray in front of them. Daniel was holding the two items in each hand, looking at the can trying to figure out how to manipulate the contents of the can into the plastic cup as the others were doing. The stewardess noticed the confuse manner of her passenger, and reached over the young man in the aisle seat and made the back of the chair in front of Daniel swing down over his knees giving him his own personal table. He placed the plastic cup on the table and looked rather strangely at the top of the cold can. He looked up to ask the lady for a can opener, but she had her back to him by that time serving the people across the aisle from Daniel. Daniel once again examined the can thoroughly, noticing at one end a small aluminum circle, but having no idea how he could open the can. The young man next to Daniel poked him with his elbow and said to him in Italian with a wide grin, "You have no idea how to open your soda can, do you, where have you been hiding, did you just come down from Mars?"

Daniel looked at the man and shrugged his shoulders. The young man said. "Pull up that little round tab." Daniel followed the man's directions hearing a puffing sound as a hole suddenly appeared on the top of the can. Daniel looked at his seat partner with a sheepish grin, his seat partner was smiling.

Seven hours had passed since Daniel's plane left the Roma airport, and he was feeling restful, almost sleepy. His intense excitement, his inability to focus, his muscle twitching had subsided. Now all he could think of was his house on Beach Avenue. He could see himself in the various rooms, picturing the joyous Sunday afternoon meals with his big family, his aunts, uncles, and cousins. His racing imagination made the final two hours of the trip pass quickly.

His wandering mind was interrupted by a male voice speaking over the plane's intercom announcing the plane's descent to Kennedy International Airport in New York.

"All passengers please return to your seats and fasten your seat belts."

With this announcement, Daniel's excitement once again began to rise. He was no longer thinking about his future life, but now only that the plane was about to land and soon he would be able to see New York City from his small, oblong window. Looking out the window, Daniel could still only see clouds. Suddenly, the wing on the right side dipped downward for a short time and then leveled off, the same maneuver happened three more times. The clouds no longer seemed puffy and round. They became thinner and seemed to be passing by the window faster and faster. Daniel could now see water through the streaking clouds. It was evening, and he wondered when he would be able to see land from the sky at night. Within a few minutes, he noticed little dots of light. That must be land, he thought. Could that be New York City? No, it can't be. There would be many more lights. The ground seemed to be getting closer and closer as the plane wings continued their dipping and leveling movement. Daniel was becoming impatient. This is taking so long. Why haven't we landed? The plane was now completely over land; the water was still visible, but off in the distance. He could see actual houses, roads, and cars. He thought, those are American roads and American houses, but where is New York City?

Daniel was sure the plane would be landing any moment now. Looking out the window, he was fascinated by how everything on the ground looked from his window. Then, suddenly, the plane was very close to the ground and flying over big buildings. He could see black, flat roofs with box-like structures on their surfaces. These buildings quickly disappeared, and now all he could see was grass and concrete, which was almost close enough to touch. He felt a bump, a thump, a skid, and then an unusual loud noise like a great wind passing by. He was overjoyed. I'm on the ground in New York. I'm home! The plane continued to move for a few minutes, and each passing moment brought more and more excitement. His brain was whirling; his body wanted to move; he was ready to burst out of his chair.

Then, in an instant, all his emotions were frozen as though someone had pushed an "off" button. He heard an announcement over the intercom, "Will Mr. Daniel Ciarletta please report to one of the stewardesses before leaving the plane? Mr. Daniel Ciarletta, please see a stewardess before disembarking."

They said my name. Oh God, something's wrong. What does disembarking mean?

The plane eventually came to a stop, and everyone seemed to rise at the same time. They were busily collecting their bags and luggage from the enclosed shelves over their seats. Daniel had one bag under the seat in front of him. After a few minutes confusion surrounded him, the plane had stopped, but the people weren't moving; his name had been called and he was unable to pass through the people blocking the entire center isle of the plane. He waited nervously, standing like the other passengers. Soon the line began to slowly move toward the front of the plane. Daniel began also to move, fearful what awaited him when he would pass a women called a stewardess and had to say he was Daniel Ciarletta. As he moved down the crowded aisle, he thought, maybe this is not America. What if I got on the wrong plane and Barbara and Lee are in New York and I'm in another country? That's why I couldn't see New York City from my window. Oh no! How am I gonna get to New York? I should have known something bad was going to happen! What'll I do now? Daniel anxiously approached the uniformed woman standing opposite the exit door of the plane. "I'm Daniel Ciarletta," he said cautiously.

The woman smiled and asked him to follow her out of the plane. Now he was sure something was wrong. He immediately asked the woman, "Did I get on the wrong plane? Am I in trouble? Have I done something wrong?"

The stewardess seemed sympathetic and was quick to assure Daniel that nothing was wrong. "I'm taking you directly to an airline representative, and I'll give him your entry papers so he can walk you through customs. Everything is fine. You will be home soon."

Thank you, Lord, thought Daniel, and he once again smiled.

As they left the plane and entered a hallway, the stewardess brought Daniel to a man in a blue jumpsuit. She handed an envelope to the man and introduced Daniel. Then she turned to Daniel and said, "He'll escort you to the proper gate."

Daniel followed the man closely. Although he had been told there was no problem, Daniel immediately asked his escort, "Will I be allowed to go home tonight?"

The uniformed man grinned and promised that his papers were in order, and he would be on his way soon. "These documents are notification from the Italian government that will be used in place of your passport," explained the man. His escort made a point of telling Daniel everything was fine and not to be concerned. "I will make sure your entry into the United States goes smoothly."

Daniel was relieved when he heard "entry into the United States." They walked through various hallways, making right and left turns, and then entered a large room. There were seven or eight lines of people who appeared to be showing papers to uniformed people at counters. The man took Daniel past the various lines and directly to a side office. He showed Daniel's papers to a man in the office. After a brief discussion, they both smiled and said Daniel could pass through. The man in the blue jumpsuit pointed to an opening with the word Exit over it, and he told Daniel to follow the other people who were going through the opening and out of the terminal. The man shook Daniel's hand and said, "Good luck to you, Sir."

Daniel was caught off-guard for a few wistful moments. His escort had called him Sir. I've never been called Sir before, he said to himself. The man in the blue jumpsuit had turned away and blended into the crowd. Daniel strained to find his blue uniform, but it was nowhere to be seen. Daniel had expected the man was going to take him to his brother, but now he was gone. Daniel stood frozen, looking at the opening in the wall where he had been told to go. Many people were rushing toward it. That's probably where I should be going, but what if I'm wrong and get lost? I have no phone number. The police in Rome called my brother and I never asked them for my American phone number. How am I going to get to Clason Point if I can't find Lee or Barbara? He was now perspiring, and his shirt clung to his damp chest. He knew he had to do something, so he decided to return to the man in the side office. Daniel politely excused himself and said, "I'm sorry to bother you, but I don't know which way I should go to meet my brother."

The uniformed man behind the desk looked annoyed, which made Daniel even more uneasy. He pointed toward the opening Daniel had been looking at. "Like I told you before, go through that opening, down the hallway until you come to a big room, and then just follow the sign that says, 'luggage pickup.'" The man abruptly turned away to continue his conversation with another passenger.

Nervously, Daniel blurted out, "But I don't have luggage. I only have this bag."

"Well good for you mister. Now please just leave; I have other people to take care of."

Daniel, now perspiring heavily, would not be put off by the angry man at the desk, and said. "But I can't leave. I have to meet my brother."

The man behind the desk stopped talking to the person in front of him, turned slowly, looked up at Daniel, and said, "Look, fella, are you deliberately trying to be a pain in the ass, or are you having fun breaking my balls? This is the last time I'm gonna tell you 'To leave, go where I told you, meet your brother, meet whoever you want, but don't come back to me."

Confused and uncertain, Daniel slowly moved toward the opening. Halfway there, he stopped and wiped the perspiration from his forehead. His legs seemed to be locked. He mumbled to himself, "The man said go and leave, but leave for where? How am I going to find Lee and Barbara? They won't know me after all these years, and what if I don't recognize them?" Alone in the crowded, noisy room, frozen by terror, perspiring heavily, not knowing what to do, or where to go, he felt as isolated as when he was in Opi. His immobility only seemed to make his terror more intense. I must move. I must do something. I can't just stand here. He forced himself to move one foot forward, followed slowly by the other. He began to inch his way forward toward the large opening and the long hallway beyond. Fear and anxiety still consumed his every step, but he forced himself to continue, unsure of what waited for him at the end of the long hallway. Once in the hallway, he stayed close to the side wall, keeping his hand on the wall as he walked. People were rushing past him. Finally, he reached an opening at the end of the hallway. There were many people, and the noise was deafening. He stepped out into the room, but immediately moved a step to the left, his back against the wall. Should I walk forward into the crowd? No, there are too many people. What if my sister and brother weren't here? S 'pose I'm lost; then what'll I do?

There was so much noise and confusion, people greeting each other, hugging, and laughing; the bright lights seemed to be blinding him; everyone was moving so fast. Daniel's head was beginning to throb. He wished the blaring noise would stop, and the bright lights now seemed to be burning his eyes. He felt his arm being pulled. Startled, he quickly turned to see the smiling face of his brother Lee.

"Danny, didn't you hear us? We were calling you!" Fear and anxiety had invaded every cell in his body. His face was drawn, and he was unable to move or respond. "Dan, what's wrong? Said Lee, your shirt is soaked!" Lee put his arms around him and held him tightly.

The physical contact with his brother relaxed Daniel's muscles, and the fear and isolation flowed from his body. Finally able to speak, Daniel said, "Lee… Lee it's really you, it's really you." Daniel held on tight, refusing to separate his clammy body from his brother.

Lee murmured, "It's okay, Danny, I've got you now. Take your time, whenever you're ready."

Daniel finally pulled back from his brother, and stammered, "I'm okay now. Just don't leave me."

With his arm around Daniel, Lee led him toward the center of the passenger waiting area. He kept repeating softly, "Your home! You're home! We were calling you. I guess you couldn't hear us." With his arm still around his brother's shoulders, Lee led Daniel in the direction of their sister. Daniel recognized Barbara immediately. She was still very pretty, but her eyes looked tired.

Barbara was crying as she embraced her brother. She kept repeating through her tears, "We thought you were dead. I can't believe you're alive! Oh, you're alive. All this time and you're alive."

The end of the tears and disbelief brought smiles of joy to Daniel's sister and brother. Lee and Barbara both mentioned how well and healthy he looked.

There seemed to be people circling around the three of them. Their faces were smiling and watching Daniel. He was very uncomfortable due to their proximity. Barbara abruptly said, "Well, Danny, aren't you gonna say hello?"

Daniel asked, "Gonna say hello, whaddya you mean, 'say hello?'"

One of the smiling faces then spoke to Daniel. "I came to see you. I'll betcha you don't remember me; I'm Skelly."

That single name acted as a mental trip wire, bringing Daniel back six years in time. Immediately all the smiling faces were familiar — his friends from Clason Point. The tall man named Skelly embraced Daniel, and now Daniel was smiling with all of them: Francis (Skelly) Donahue, James (Tiny) Koehler, Jack (Dutch) Schultz, John (Jack) Jaeger, Pete (Mitz) Sicilian, Louie (Giggy) Ferintino, and Joseph (Sal) Salvato. They were patting his shoulders, messing up his hair, and laughing. All Daniel could do was laugh and cry at the same time. He knew they understood his tears were a display of happiness.

It was impossible to make them understand at this moment the important role they had played during his years in Italy. For now, he simply expressed how much he appreciated their coming to welcome him home. Perhaps at another time and under different circumstances he would be able to find the proper words to explain the important role they played in his thoughts during his captivity over the past five and a half years. They all walked together through the terminal to a place where many cars were parked. His friends told him they were going to arrange an evening later with a few more guys for a real celebration. Daniel simply stood and watched their smiling faces and waving hands as they scattered to their cars. He still felt so alone, incapable of expressing himself to men so important and close to him, but yet so remote. At that moment, Daniel understood how difficult returning to life in America was going to be.

"Danny if you're ready, let's go and see Frances," said his brother.

There were so many questions as Lee drove to the Bronx that the conversation became an overload of information. Suddenly Daniel noticed how his brother was dressed. "Are you allowed to dress like that? Aren't you supposed to wear a priest collar and black suit?"

"Oh, that's right, you don't know. I left the seminary last year," Lee said. "I had some doubts. I felt maybe I wanted a family of my own. I left to have time to think, and eventually I decided that I didn't want the priesthood as a vocation."

This was a total surprise to Daniel. "You mean you're not a priest? How did Mom take it when you left the Franciscans?"

A look of concern now covered Lee's face. "Not too good. We'll talk about that later."

Daniel asked, "Have you gotten married?"

Lee said, "No, I'm living in New Jersey working as a technical writer."

Barbara then added, "I'm married, living on Long Island and have two girls. Frances is also married and has two children; she lives on White Plains Road, very close to Clason Point."

"Wow, I've… let's see, how many… four nieces and nephews? Boy, that makes me feel old," said Daniel with a big grin. He then asked about his mother and father.

Barbara said they were fine and quickly changed the subject. "We're gonna stop at Frances's place and pick her up."

A long bridge led directly to Bruckner Boulevard, which was a maze of concrete roadways that eventually led to Frances's house. Lee parked in front of a row of brick houses on White Plains Road. Daniel entered his sister's home and began walking down a long hallway. At its end, standing in the open doorway, was his sister Frances. She had gained some weight over the past years, but there was no confusing that beautiful Ingrid Bergman face. Frances yelled out Daniel's name, and they embraced and smiled at each other. Daniel was out of tears at this point, but he was very happy to be with Frances, his big sister, who had pampered him as her baby brother. Daniel was introduced to France's husband and their two children while Frances served coffee and pie. Daniel sat at the kitchen table with his sisters and brother. How long he had waited for this moment. He was completely exhausted, but he felt warm, happy, and truly loved.

Frances began to speak cautiously. "Before we take you to see Mom and Dad, you need to know the past years have not been kind to them." Before Daniel could ask what was wrong, Frances said, "Your disappearance has had an impact on their health."

Daniel then put down his coffee cup and sat up, giving them his full attention. "What's wrong with Mon and Dad," said Daniel. "C'mon level with me. What's wrong with them?"

Barbara was the first to speak. "When you were taken, Dad stayed in Italy for a coupl'a months, filing police reports and hiring a detective agency from Naples to find you. He thought gypsies had kidnapped you for money, but that turned out to be a false lead. When he came home, he felt terrible. He couldn't concentrate, and he was moody and hard to live with. In the meantime, Mom was also a wreck. First, she blamed Dad for letting you get taken, and then she began to believe that your disappearance was God's way of punishing her for her sins."

Lee interjected, "Then I left the seminary, and she saw that as another sign that she was being punished by God."

Barbara added, "Father Lewis talked to both of them many times, but nothing helped. After about a year Dad sold the house on Beach Avenue."

"What? We don't own the house anymore. Why did Dad sell the house? Where do they live?" This was shocking news to Daniel.

Lee now joined the conversation. "Dad and Uncle Danny moved to a twostory apartment house on Bolton Avenue near the old Patterson baseball field."

"But I dreamed of living in the Beach Avenue house again," said Daniel. He was obviously disappointed.

Barbara reached over and placed her hand on his. "We're sorry, Danny. I know this is not gonna be easy, but we felt you needed to hear the truth."

Frances finished the explanation. "Dad sold the house. With this money, he went back to Italy, hired two detective agencies, and stayed in Castellammare di Stabia with Grandma and Grandpa for two or three months. He came home when the money was gone. When he returned from Italy, there was a misunderstanding over the conversion of the business from ice and coal delivery to oil delivery. The brothers had a fight and Dad left the business."

"He left the business. How could that happen when he was the leader?"

Lee responded to Daniel's questions. "Danny, we were here when the breakup happened, and we're still not sure how or what happened. Let it go, its ancient history."

Frances placed her hand on Daniel's shoulder. "Is this too much, are we going too fast? We can talk about all this some other day."

"No, no," replied Daniel. "Go on, what else has happened?"

Frances continued, "Well, Dad began to act very strangely. He was no longer talking to his brothers except for Uncle Danny. Then one Sunday, out of the blue, I remember it was Easter, he told Aunt Grace, he didn't want her in his house any longer. That ended the Sunday family dinners. Gradually Dad got worse, making enemies with everyone in the family, arguing with friends, and getting angry with us for foolish reasons. It was like he was pushing everyone he loved away from him. One doctor called it self-destruction. Then Dad fainted one night at work and went to the hospital. They found out he had low blood pressure, and they wanted him to get something called a pacemaker, but he refused and signed himself out."

Barbara picked up where Frances left off. "Daddy was always exhausted. It was his low blood pressure, but he refused no matter how much we hounded him about the pacemaker. Then he started to stutter, and eventually he couldn't talk at all. The doctors could find nothing wrong. One specialist eventually decided he had something they called selective mutism."

"Selective mutism, what's that?" asked Daniel. "Are you saying Dad can't talk?" Daniel was still unable to comprehend so many sudden revelations. "How could he just stop talking if nothing was wrong? Are you telling me he won't be able to speak to me?"

Lee tried to explain. "No, Danny, he is no longer able to speak. The doctors felt there were two reasons: one was that dad subconsciously stopped talking so he would stop hurting everyone. The other was that your disappearance caused him intense guilt and anger, and because he refused to get help, it built up. Over the years, it became something the doctor called trauma; but whatever the reason, Dad no longer talks.

Daniel was overwhelmed by the descriptions of his father's illnesses. "And this trauma thing that made him stop talking; how could that happen?"

Daniel was visibly shaken by the information about his father. Barbara put her arm around his shoulder, trying to provide some comfort. "Now don't go blaming yourself. The doctor told us he could've been cured if he had gone to a psychiatrist. We had been after him for months to get help, but he refused. He could've gotten better. It's his fault, not yours."

"Oh, don't worry. I'm not gonna start blaming myself. It's the people from Opi. That's whose fault this is, those Italians!"

Lee, seeing Daniel's anger, decided to change the subject. "Uncle Danny could no longer watch the conflict surrounding Dad, so he moved to Florida. He died a year later. The doctors said he died of heart failure, but we know he died of a broken heart."

Daniel stared at his brother. "Uncle Danny is dead! Who else is dead?"

"Aunt Kate died the next year, but everyone else is still living," said Lee.

Daniel placed his elbow on the table and moved his open palm to his temple. "Uncle Danny and Aunt Kate dead, no house on Beach Avenue, no business, no more Sunday dinners; those lousy Opi people have not only stolen my life they have also destroyed my family. I hope they burn in hell for what they've done." Barbara, Lee and Frances were quite surprised at their brother's harsh wording and all three noticed the severe look of anger that showed vividly on his face. His fury was evident in Daniel's eyes, and in his clenched fists, which were being held so tight his knuckles were white, his back pressed against the upper portion of his chair, his lips pressed firmly together. Not only did Daniel's siblings not know how to respond to their brother's anger, but they were also unable to fully understand how such intense feeling could completely consume a nineteen-year-old boy.

Barbara once again placed her hand on her brother's shoulder. Nothing was said for perhaps ten seconds or so, but it felt interminable. During this time Daniel's posture was no longer erect, his clenched fists were now damp open palms, his eyes fatigued, his demeanor now open to receive whatever new horrific news was waiting for him. "Go on, what else happened?" asked a subdued Daniel.

Lee continued, "After Uncle Danny's funeral, Aunt Kate…"

Frances, who was relatively quiet up to this point, but could no longer stay silent, interrupted Lee. "Daniel I can't imagine what my 'baby' brother has been through the past six years, but you're home now and it would seem to me that the most useful thing for you to do is to concentrate on building a new life for yourself, rather than becoming an angry young man due to your family being different than expected. Perhaps this is going to be the most important part of your recovery, and I hope soon you will be able to understand that."

Frances's words were comforting, and someday soon Daniel would be able to internalize her complex recommendation, but for now he needed to explain something to his oldest sister. "Frances, you're right when you say you must go through something like I did for six years to understand how it affects you as a human being. One of my seven brothers in Opi, an Egyptian boy named Omar, put it best when he said, 'How can a person's body be in one place and their heart in another place?'"

Frances's words were a true comfort, and because of her tender remarks Daniel wanted to try to make her understand what he was about to call "anger," but in an instant changed to "survival," which changed the meaning of his response. "Frances there were three things that enabled me and my six brothers to survive almost six years of living our life in Opi. I would lie in bed each night before falling off to sleep, thinking of coming home to my family as I had known them for eleven years; next was something we called the 'Angel Club of Opi,' being able to be with the six other hostages every Sunday afternoon; and finally thinking of my friends back home in Clason Point. Every day your 'baby brother' depended on these three things. Now that I am home, I suddenly have learned that the first and most important thing seems to be slipping away, so please for now let me know the full truth about my family."

Lee continued, "After Uncle Danny's funeral, Aunt Kate was mad at Dad and let him have it in front of the family. It was hard to watch, but that's what happened. Then Aunt Kate died a year later. Cousin Rita believes that without Uncle Danny, she no longer wanted to go on living."

"What about Mom?" asked Daniel, his voice lowering with anxiety?

"I'm sorry to tell you that Mom has also changed," said Frances. "She no longer looks or acts like the robust, take-charge woman you knew in 1947. The strange thing about your disappearance is that Mom was the only one who believed you were still alive. No matter how hard we tried to convince her that it would be best for her to accept the fact that you were dead, she just wouldn't listen. She would sit in her upholstered chair by the window next to the front door in the apartment on Bolton Avenue praying her rosary. She would always tell us, 'Someday I'm going to see my Daniel walking toward the house coming home to me.'" Frances finished by saying, "Things have become very strained between Mom and Dad. After your disappearance, their relationship slowly went downhill, and now, although they live in the same apartment, they might as well be apart. There is no longer any happiness or laughter in their lives, only silence, anger and guilt. It's a very depressing thing to watch."

"Take me to Mom and Dad now," said Daniel.

* * * * * *

Lee's car entered Bruckner Boulevard, which took them to Soundview Avenue. Traveling east on the main thoroughfare in Clason Point, Daniel was surprised at the changes that had taken place in his old neighborhood. There were no longer empty lots along Soundview Avenue where he used to play ball. These onceempty pieces of land now held stores and row houses. Holy Cross Church and School had been torn down, and a new contemporary church stood in its place with a separate school building. The car stopped at a red light on the corner of Randal and Soundview Avenue, across from the church. Daniel spontaneously asked his brother to make a right and take him to their old house on Beach Avenue. They passed the Beach Movie Theater, which was now an Evangelical church. Bain's candy store had become a walk-in health clinic.

His brother stopped in front of their former house. Daniel got out of the car and walked up to the front stairs and stopped. Now standing on the sidewalk, he thought, how funny, I never thought of a house as something you sell. I always thought a house was part of a family. I wonder how people decide how much a house is worth. How can other people move into another family's house?

Daniel moved a few feet to the left so he could see the window of the bedroom he used to sleep in with his brother. Daniel's distress grew more intense. He was confused and once again angry that others were living in what he still thought of as his house. It was not a longing for the past or even anger at all the lost years. His unease came from a feeling of betrayal. My house is still here, the trees are bigger, but the patch of grass in the front is exactly the same; the stoop is still made from brick; the color of the house and shutters are different, but it's the same house, the same shutters. Someone else is sleeping in my bed. All those nights alone in my room in Opi, imagining sleeping in my bed on Beach Avenue, believing that someday I would be back in my house at 533 Beach Avenue. What will happen to all those memories? Are they lost forever? Where will they go? Will they just disappear? Daniel felt a silent numbness, as if he was frozen for a moment, and then the same sadness and hollow feeling in his chest and stomach that he so often felt in Opi began to overtake him once again. Daniel immediately returned to the car and asked his brother to take him to his mother and father.

It was a short ride to the apartment on Bolton Avenue. Francis had a key and opened the front door, but she also rang the bell. Daniel was first to walk into the hallway. He was having mixed emotions based on what he had heard from his sisters and brother. He passed a door on the left, which was the entrance to one of the lower apartments. At the end of a short hallway, there was a steep stairway going to a second-floor apartment. He started to climb the stairs, behind him his brother and sisters. On his third step, Daniel heard the squeaky door open a few inches and then stop. He bolted up the stairs two steps at a time and threw open the door to see his mother. They stared at each other for just a moment, and then Suzy extended her arms to him and drew him close to her.

She said nothing as Daniel whispered in her ear, "Mom, it's me. I'm home." Suzy began to cry. Daniel sensed his mother's weak grasp was all she could possibly manage. Finally, they separated. She stared at her son, moving her eyes up and down, closely examining him from head to foot. Still holding his hands, Suzy stepped back once more, examining him a second time, again looking at Daniel from head to foot.

She raised her eyes to the hallway ceiling and cried out in a loud, anguished voice, "Almighty, forgiving Lord, you did not forsake me. You have answered the prayers offered for Daniel!" She looked deeply into her son's eyes once again. "Oh, Daniel, I was so afraid that when I saw you, you would be weak and worn from years of abuse and punishment. But look at you, strong and healthy. God has finally forgiven me!" She strained to kneel in front of Daniel. She made the sign of the cross and said, "Thank you, Lord. I will never again abandon you!" With assistance from Daniel, she rose to her feet. Daniel leaned forward and kissed his mother on the cheek and embraced her once again. As she was holding her son in her arms, she whispered, "I knew you were alive. I knew you were alive. No one would believe me, but I knew."

Holding onto her son, she seemed to gain more strength in her frail arms. They parted for a second time. As they looked at each other with tear-filled eyes, Daniel was able to see what his brother and sisters had described. His mother's deep, hollow, recessed eye sockets were worn smoothly like stones rounded from years of flowing tears. Her brown eyes, those eyes that used to twinkle when he was thirteen, now only expressed suffering.

Suzy took her son's hand and led him toward another room. As they entered what looked like the living room, with the kitchen beyond, Daniel saw his father seated on a sofa. His heart momentarily stopped at what he saw. His once big, strong, vibrant father had become a thin, gaunt shell of a man with sunken cheeks, thin neck, and vacant, expressionless eyes. His father's eyes were completely deserted; they showed no joy, pain, no sadness, no feelings, only emptiness. Pete was wearing a dark blue suit, pressed pants, white shirt, a tie, and highly shined shoes. His shirt collar, now much too large for his neck, was misshapen from his necktie knot pressing tightly against his throat. His father's suit and tie brought Daniel back many years in time to Castellammare di Stabia, when he first saw Nonno Leopoldo in bed dressed in his finest clothes and beret.

Daniel moved quickly toward his father. He knelt at his feet and tenderly clutched his father's thin, wrinkled cold hands. These now distorted hands were the same warm, round chunky hands that used to enclose Daniel's cheeks, as his father would often kiss his youngest son on the forehead and tell him how much he loved him. Daniel rested his head on his father's wrinkled, thin, awkwardly shaped fingers. Daniel did not speak, knowing his father would be unable to answer.

Pete tried to move, and Daniel leaned back as his father tried to struggle out of the sofa. Daniel tried to help by holding his father's arm, but Pete removed his arm from Daniel's grasp. Pete continued struggling, but eventually was able to stand on his own. Reaching out, he took Daniel's face in both his hands, those same fleshy, warm, powerful hands, now wrinkled and no longer able to radiate heat. Looking at Daniel with forsaken eyes, Pete quietly and with great hesitation stammered, "Fffor… gggggive… mmmee."

Daniel leaned forward, took his father's frail, thin body into his strong arms, and their bodies touched in a warm embrace.

Pete let out a slight sob finally, some sign of emotion. Daniel held his father tightly as their heads rested on each other's shoulders. Daniel said softly, "I'm home, Dad. It's all over. I love you, there is nothing to forgive. You did everything a father could do to protect his son. You must no longer blame yourself for the evil acts of others."

Daniel thought angrily about how the acts of the Sgammotta family had not only affected him but had reached across the Atlantic and devastated his parents. Daniel was beginning to understand that along with his own healing he would have to help his parents through their healing process. Daniel kissed the back of his father's hand and rested his head next to his father's hip. Soon, Daniel could tell by his father's slow, steady breathing that he was in a deep sleep. Daniel gently raised his head, slowly and carefully removed his hand, and quietly left the room.